JUDGMENT

Also by Carey Baldwin

Confession

2-20-17

9.94

JUDGMENT

A Cassidy & Spenser Thriller

CAREY BALDWIN

WITNESS
IMPULSE
An Imprint of HarperCollinsPublishers

Excerpt from *Confession* copyright © 2014 by Carey Baldwin.

EPub Edition OCTOBER 2014 ISBN: 9780062314123

Print Edition ISBN: 9780062314130

10 9 8 7 6 5 4 3

For Erik

~~*My little angel*~~

A mother couldn't hope for her son to grow into a finer man.

Prologue

Fifteen Years Ago
Arizona State Prison Complex
Florence, Arizona

TODAY WAS CAITLIN CASSIDY'S eighteenth birthday, and in twenty-seven minutes, Thomas Cassidy was to be put to death by lethal injection for the murder of Gail Falconer: a crime so brutal, so sadistic only a monster could've committed it. Unable to bear the ticking off of the remaining seconds of her father's life, Caitlin squeezed her eyes shut, willing the merciless clock on the wall of the death-chamber viewing room to stop. Inside her chest, her heart slackened into a useless, gelatinous blob, its beat barely perceptible. With such an anemic pulse, she had no idea how oxygen still flowed to her brain. Yet vague as her heartbeat was, her thoughts were sharp and rapid-firing around a closed circuit.

Is he afraid?
He couldn't have done it!
Is he afraid?

A one-way mirror served as a window into the death chamber—a stark white room, well prepared and patiently waiting for the prisoner. An intercom transmitted sound into the viewing area. From her front-row-center seat, she'd be able to see and hear all that transpired as her father's sentence was carried out. Gail's parents, she'd been told, would be watching from a separate location. Their daughter had been left naked and beaten, her body posed for the world in the most humiliating fashion. They would not be required to sit alongside Thomas Cassidy's daughter.

The room suddenly colder, she shivered.

He couldn't have done it.

When she was a little girl, her father would get low on one knee, allowing her to climb up his back and sit on his shoulders. Now she drew the memory around her like a warm cloak, and as the scent of his starched collar came back to her, she regained a temporary sense of well-being. Her body tilted forward, and she recalled bouncing rhythmically atop her perch while her father trotted her around the room faster and faster. She'd sway and squeal—delighted, but also queasy with fear. Then, sensing her terror, her father would grip her hands firmly.

I won't let you fall, Caity. Just hold on tight and trust me.

His low voice had soothed her. His word had been all she needed back then.

When her father had spoken, she'd believed him.

Absolutely.

But who was she to trust now?

Her eyelids flew open, and she saw that not quite a minute had passed. The sight of the long, padded table that awaited her father inside the chamber made her stomach roll and her teeth chatter. Clamping her jaw shut, she turned away from the terrible sight and found herself looking straight into the muted brown eyes of Mr. Harvey Baumgartner. Her father's attorney crumpled into the seat next to her and produced a wan smile. She hadn't seen him enter the room, and even if she had, she wouldn't have known how long he'd stood beside her with that pitying look on his face—time was too scrambled up in her mind. The clock on the wall was her only orienting anchor, and her eyes were both drawn to it and repelled by it. She kept her gaze on Baumgartner, refusing to look at that damn clock again.

Tick. Tick. Tick.

Her hands rose to cover her ears, but she quickly regained control and smoothed back her long, heavy hair instead.

"Caitlin, dear . . ." Baumgartner's voice was tighter and higher than usual. As his hand cruised up and down the length of his silk tie, light reflected off his fingernails, which had been buffed and coated in clear polish. His distress had apparently not affected his commitment to personal grooming. All of the Baumgartners liked to put on a good appearance, and Harvey was no exception. "I want you to understand I did all I could."

I know. She wanted to answer, to offer him the comfort he seemed to be seeking, but the words stuck in her throat. She didn't know. Not really. Oh, sure, he'd tried hard to get her father acquitted, but who knew if a more experienced attorney could've succeeded where he'd failed. Maybe a different lawyer could've gotten her father's coerced confession thrown out of court.

But Baumgartner and his firm weren't the only ones who'd failed her father. Maybe *she* could've done more. Both she and her mother had stood by her father, believed in him and loved him, but they'd left the matter of his defense to his legal team. A mistake she'd regret for the rest of her days. She should've *done* something. She should've *made* them see the truth—that her father didn't do it. He simply couldn't have.

"There's not going to be a reprieve, Caitlin, you know that, right?" Baumgartner's hand stopped cruising his tie and went to his sleek, coffee-colored hair.

The last-chance hearing had already been held, and clemency had been denied. Baumgartner had explained it to her twice already, but apparently he feared she was still praying for a last-minute miracle.

And he was right.

She nodded. Then her fists clenched, and pain cut through her, so sharp and real it seemed as though the shards of hope she clasped had suddenly been crushed into bits of broken glass.

There's not going to be a reprieve.

The days of holding executions in the dead of night to allow for last-minute maneuvering by the defense were gone. Arizona was one of a handful of states that had decided it wasn't practical for executions to be held at midnight. No phone was going to ring. No messenger was going to come crashing through the doors mere seconds before the clock struck the hour. That kind of thing only happened in the movies, and this wasn't a movie. This was real life.

Real death.

She should've *done* something to save her father, and now it was too late. Her hands twisted together in her lap. She'd never felt this helpless in her life. All she could do for her father now was to be present here today. Her mother, however, had chosen not to attend the execution. She'd begged Caitlin to stay home, too. *A child shouldn't have to watch her parent die,* she'd said.

But if death had come to her father while he lay in a hospital bed, wouldn't they both have been by his side?

Now Baumgartner leaned in close enough for his tobacco-stained breath to settle humidly on her cheek. "It's not too late for you to leave, dear. I'll take you home right now if you like."

Again, words failed her. Her throat clogged, and the desperate sob she refused to let out quaked down her body, rattling her knees and legs. Sucking in deep breaths, she jerked a glance around the room. It was a small space numbed by flat vanilla walls, rows of tan chairs, and gray floor tiles. It was a room purposely stripped of any sign of humanity, deliberately designed to quell emotion.

More people straggled in, claiming seats in the back row. One of the men was tall, with highlighted hair and eyes so blue she thought they must've been enhanced by tinted contacts. She recognized him as a local news anchor, but the others . . . she didn't know.

"The state requires a certain number of witnesses, and these were drawn from a pool of volunteers," Baumgartner whispered, seeming to read her mind.

Volunteers!

"Don't look at me like that, honey. The witnesses are here to make sure proper care is taken and that . . . this matter . . . is handled as humanely as possible."

Her mind tried to process that information. People who were in no way connected to the case had volunteered to come here today and watch her father be put to death. As yet another wave of nausea rolled through her, she heard the thunder of footsteps in the hallway and the sound of a door scraping open nearby. Its earlier vagueness obliterated, her heartbeat took up the ferocious rhythm of a fighter ready for battle. If her opponent were a man, she would punch him in the face—but her enemy was no mere mortal.

Injustice could not be defeated with a fist.

Through the mirror, she watched two men dressed in white medical garb enter the death chamber. Then, escorted by several prison guards, her father was led inside, his steps slowed by the short chain between his ankles. A thick belt cinched the waist of his baggy prison uniform, and his cuffed hands attached to it. But his chin was high, and his gaze active, as if he were looking to take in every last sight, no matter how ordinary—or maybe he was just showing her he would not be cowed. His face had thinned, and his hair had changed color—it was gray now, not blond, but he was still her father. Prison had not changed his essence. Thanks to the intercom, she heard his chains clanking, and like a clapped bell, her bones began to ring with fear. She wasn't as brave as he. Then a voice in her head shouted:

Do something!

She shot to her feet and took a step toward the window. Just as quickly, a guard who'd been leaning against the wall moved toward her, and Baumgartner threw a restraining arm across her quivering chest. Though she knew her father couldn't see her, she lifted her chin, not bothering to wipe away the tears that streamed down her cheeks. Her father's chin rose, too, and somehow, despite the one-way glass, their eyes met . . . and held.

The quivering in her body subsided.

Her father's low, soothing voice replaced the screaming in her head.

Hold on tight, Caity.

Trust me.

Chapter One

Present Day
Monday, August 26
Superior Court Building
Phoenix, Arizona

HARVEY BAUMGARTNER HAD certainly changed in the fifteen years since Caitlin had last seen him, but sitting across the conference-room table from him again in *this* courthouse made her feel as though *she* hadn't changed at all. She was just as nauseous now as she'd been the day her father's attorney had taken her aside and coached her on how to behave in the courtroom. *If a tear falls, make sure to wipe it slowly so the jury notices. Dress more like a little girl and less like a teenager . . . and try not to look bored.*

As if she could've been bored by her father's murder trial. Baumgartner had given her her first introduction to courtroom *spin*, and she'd done everything exactly as he'd instructed her to— but in the end, none of it had mattered. She hadn't been able to save her father, and neither had Baumgartner. The forlorn daughter had been disregarded. She'd sat in a courtroom just a few rooms down from this one, wearing a ponytail tied with a yellow ribbon, a simple, homemade shift and polished, patent leather shoes . . . and her father had been sentenced to death anyway. She'd actually believed if she wore the right clothes, if her expression held just the right blend of dejection and hope, her father would be spared.

Baumgartner had convinced her appearances would do even more to persuade a jury than facts. The thought was more than enough to raise the temperature of her blood and banish the ghost of her teenage self—a ghost that appeared to have been hovering inside the Superior Court Building just waiting for her return. But that version of herself, the naïve young girl, had died along with her father.

She willed her mind to focus on the present, and the churning in her stomach disappeared. Pushing her shoulders back, she sat up taller in the chair and made her heart stiffen along with her spine. Maybe she hadn't been able to control the outcome of her father's trial or his sentencing, but one thing she had learned to control was her own emotional response—to the sense of help-lessness this place brought back, to Harvey Baumgartner, to *any-thing* she put her mind to. The old Caitlin Cassidy had been a weak wreck of a girl. The new Caitlin Cassidy did not rattle. Haul-ing in a steadying breath, she studied the alterations in Harvey Baumgartner's appearance.

His once-luxuriant brown waves were now heavily threaded with gray and had grown brittle, but the substantial expanse of forehead revealed by his receding hairline only lent him a more distinguished air. Less flattering was a new, ruddy complexion that telegraphed *too much scotch*. Still, he'd been the only man who'd stood up for her father, and his personal habits were none of her business anyway.

She quirked her lips into a professional, apologetic smile. "I'm sorry, Mr. Baumgartner, but I'm afraid I won't be of any use to your client. I don't advise you calling me as an expert witness in the Kramer case."

The attorney had been doodling circles on his notes, but as soon as she'd started to speak, he'd stopped and waved his hand in protest. "No. No. No. Caitlin, you and I go too far back to stand on formalities. Please, call me Harvey."

Until a few weeks ago, she hadn't seen or heard from Harvey Baumgartner since her eighteenth birthday, and though they'd spoken by phone several times since she'd agreed to act as a case consultant for his client, Judd Kramer, this was their first face-to-face meeting. She figured formality was her friend in this situation. It was hardly easy to disappoint the man who'd taken on her father's case pro bono. But no matter how Harvey wanted to spin it, she wasn't here to do him a personal favor—nor did she owe him one. Her father had been put to death, and Baumgartner had no marker to call in. Her only purpose here was to act as a forensic psychiatrist, a consultant who'd provide a professional opinion— and her opinion regarding this defendant would be anything but useful to his attorney.

"Caitlin, dear, you must reconsider."

Considering Harvey Baumgartner had first met her when she was thirteen years old, she hardly expected him to address her as *doctor,* but the *dear* felt manipulative—as if he wanted her to feel like that young girl still under his influence, still looking to him to guide her. She dusted her hands together, then gathered up her notes and squared her gaze with his. "My decision is final. I don't presume to know all the facts of the case"—though she did know a good many of them—"and I don't presume to know whether or not Mr. Kramer is guilty or innocent."

Baumgartner's wiry eyebrows rose high in an unsubtle challenge. "I would hope *you* know better than that, dear."

Again with the *dear*. She didn't need him to remind her that innocent men and women were railroaded into prison and worse every day. In addition to what'd happened to her own father, she'd worked several cases in conjunction with the Innocence Project and acted as a private consultant to many other defendants who'd been falsely accused. She knew what was at stake, and he knew she knew.

Biting back a sarcastic reply, she kept her tone matter-of-fact and firm. "What I do have for you is an informed opinion."

"And?"

"In my expert opinion, Judd Kramer lacks what the jury would call a conscience . . . or what Freud would call a superego. Your client feels no remorse for wrongs done—in fact, he doesn't believe those acts he admits to were wrong at all."

Baumgartner leaned forward, and even from across the table, his breath revealed the fact that he'd not given up smoking cigars. "To what wrong acts did Kramer admit?"

Her hand went to her stomach. "He didn't confess to murdering Sally Cartwright and taking a piece of her skull for a trophy, if that's what you want to know." But Kramer's recounting of his sadistic fetishes had made her feel as though maggots were swarming over her flesh. As for his behavior toward his family— well he wasn't the first man to skip out on his child's birthday party or seduce the babysitter. But the way he'd admitted, with a smile on his face, without so much as breaking eye contact, that he'd fantasized about putting his wife through a meat grinder and serving her to the children for dinner left no doubt in Caitlin's mind. "If you call me to the stand, I'll say Kramer has exactly the type of psyche that would permit him to commit the horrific crime of which he's accused."

"The man's never been in trouble a day in his life. He's a *police officer*, for Chrissake. I know this isn't the type of case that typically interests you. There's no coerced confession . . . no confession at all in fact. Maybe, like others in this city, you think the department went easy on him because he's one of their own. But this *is* a capital case."

Like most people, Baumgartner seemed to believe her opinion could be bought, or at least heavily influenced. What he didn't understand was that there was really only one thing that mattered to her: the truth. She couldn't bear to think of innocent men and women being beaten or bullied or tricked by lies into giving false confessions, then being convicted of crimes without real proof. Never again would she stand by and do nothing in such cases. She hadn't been able to save her father, but she'd devoted every day of her adult life to understanding how the mind of a murderer worked. She'd pored over case files of sickening crimes, studying the most heinous criminals in history. She'd stayed cloistered long hours with admitted killers, engaging them in conversational chess, trying to discern their true motives. Some days, she'd soak in too much of their evil, and she wouldn't be able to return home without finding a church and stopping in.

Not that she went to church to pray.

She couldn't bring herself to speak to God these days, so she'd just sit quietly, listening, and waiting for . . . relief. Inside the chapel, she'd find a place in the sun and let the light, filtered through the beauty of stained glass, rain over her skin and wash away the darkness of the day. Then she'd get up the next morning and go right back to her grisly work—because she knew of no other way to recognize an innocent man than to scour the minds of killers. And the *innocent man* was the reason she got out of bed in the morning.

But there was no part of her that wanted to see a *guilty* man set free.

After all, *someone* had committed the murder her father had been accused of. And that someone was still out there. That someone was most likely still living his life, free to come and go as he pleased. Free to bring his wife flowers—Caitlin was certain he had a family. Free to carry on his charade of decency—she was equally certain he was an upstanding citizen, the last person anyone would suspect. Of course, he might've died an easy death by now, a heart attack in his sleep, for example. But she hoped not. That someone had taken her father's life just as surely as if he'd injected the lethal chemicals into her father's veins himself. She'd spent a great deal of her earnings on investigators, hoping to solve her father's case. She needed to find the man who'd killed Gail Falconer *alive* and expose him to the world for the monster he truly was.

A muscle in her back complained, and she shifted in her chair, looking up into Baumgartner's eyes.

He frowned, and she realized he was awaiting a response. "I do understand the death penalty's in play here. That's why I agreed to come to Phoenix." A place so filled with painful memories she'd stayed away fifteen years. When she wasn't traveling for business, she lived in the same town as her mother—Boulder, Colorado. They'd both been desperate to escape this place they'd once called home. "That's why I sat with your client for six hours over the past three weeks." Six hours of compulsive rambling about his sick fantasies. As the glint in Kramer's eyes came back to her, she scratched at her arms. "Don't. Call me. To the stand."

"You'd tell the jury you think Kramer is capable of kidnapping, raping, and murdering a Tempe University coed, knowing you might be sending him to his grave?"

"*I* wouldn't be sending him anywhere. If you put me on the stand, however, I *will* tell the truth."

"And just what is the truth? That Kramer lives in a dark world that most of us would rather not know about? That's a fantasy world, dear. It doesn't make him a murderer. You know perfectly well most individuals who harbor these twisted fantasies never act on them. A collection of sadistic pornography doesn't make a man a sexually sadistic killer."

"Maybe not. But if your defense is that Kramer's depraved ideation is nothing more than harmless fantasy, it's not a good one. As *you* well know, most violent sexual offenders begin by simply imagining claiming their prey. Later, they progress through a series of stages before finally acting out against others."

She slipped her papers into her briefcase. "Your client's neighbor told the police Kramer couldn't stop talking about his desire to abduct and murder women—a classic example of leakage—meaning he's unintentionally revealing clues to acts he plans to commit. Mrs. Kramer told me her husband coerced her into rough sex on several occasions—too rough, and that he frightens her. Kramer himself told me, in great detail, just exactly how he would act out a set of sadistic rituals, then denied, of course, that he had ever done so. Yet the police found a murder kit in the trunk of his car. Procuring the items he needs to carry out his fantasy means Judd Kramer has progressed from imagination to action. If he's *not* the man who murdered Sally Cartwright, it's only a matter of time until he does kill someone."

Baumgartner pulled his lower lip between his teeth as if chewing on her words. Then a sly smile crossed his face. "You heard Atticus Spenser is testifying for the prosecution? They're going to use the FBI's mumbo jumbo profiling to help get a conviction. Spenser hasn't even got a graduate degree. Where does he get off calling himself an expert on the human mind?"

Baumgartner had done his research. He obviously knew there was no love lost between Spense and her—they'd been on opposite sides of a contentious case more than once. And there was also that personal incident a few years back . . . but fortunately no one knew about *that* little gem of a disaster except Spense and her. Still, she felt a flush rise to her cheeks and quickly put her attention back to the matter at hand.

Maybe Baumgartner had asked her to come in on the Kramer case in part because he'd assumed she'd welcome the chance to take the arrogant special agent down a notch. And maybe she would—but Spense would have to be wrong in order for that to happen, and he wasn't wrong—not about Kramer, anyway. "Regardless, I simply cannot testify on Mr. Kramer's behalf." For emphasis, she swept her hand out in front, accidentally knocking her pen from the table to the floor in the process.

As she bent to retrieve the pen, the door opened, and from her vantage point she spied a man's feet plant in a wide stance. Her eyes focused on his shoes, and her throat tightened—expensive, unscuffed loafers peeked out from beneath the type of soiled janitor blue pants she associated with a maintenance worker.

Something wasn't right.

"You'll have to come back later. I've got this room reserved until—" A flash of light coincided with the sound of Baumgartner's angry voice, and a series of pops cut him off. Beneath the table, she saw his legs jerk in time to the short bursts of light.

Gunfire!

A burnt odor hanging in the air made her stomach clench, and she suddenly understood what was happening.

Heart jackhammering in her chest, she dove to the ground, scrambling for cover. Her head cracked against the side of the table, sending pain ripping through her skull.

Pop.

Her shoulder started to burn. The gunshots should've been louder, but still she knew they *were* gunshots. Curling her body into a tight ball, she covered her head with her hands. Heat rolled in scorching waves down the nerves in her arm, and her hand went slack, dropping from her head.

Open your eyes, Caity. Do something!

She jerked her head up in time to see the loafers padding, slowly, deliberately toward her. Her limbs were trembling uselessly. While her heart pounded hard, stealing her breath, her brain hummed with escape plans, each one evaluated, then discarded in a nanosecond—until the moment she saw that the shooter no longer blocked her path to the door. Since the table above her offered little protection, she knew she had to move or die. At close range, he wouldn't miss. Maybe, just maybe, she could make it through the open door and out into the hallway. Then she felt something sticky and wet and warm spreading out beneath her, a flowing red river of it.

Blood.

Oh, God.

She'd never make it out the door alive—she knew that now. But no way was she going to wait huddled under a table for a killer to amble over and finish her off. The nerves in her skin no longer burned. Her arms and legs had gone mostly numb, and they were heavy when she tried to lift them.

Do something!

She grunted. Summoned all her strength.

Warn the others!

Just as a shot of epinephrine can restart a heart, the thought of others in the building infused her dead muscles with life. Jamming her elbows onto the cold, hard floor, she dragged her body out from under the table and catapulted to her feet, then ran like hell, right past the shooter, catching the briefest glimpse of his face.

She made it to the doorway.

"Guuuun!" she screamed, using all the breath she could squeeze from her aching lungs.

Chapter Two

GUN! THERE ARE some words that echo in the mind, and some voices that echo in the heart. Right then, Special Agent Atticus Spenser's mind and heart were both reverberating. Something about that voice—not just its urgency, not just its ferocity—pierced his chest and shocked his pulse into overdrive. He *knew* that voice, despite the fact he'd heard only a single, distorted beat. But now was not the time to try to remember where he'd heard it before or why it made him want to leap tall buildings to keep its owner safe. After all, it was his job to keep others safe.

Gun! He focused his mind, stripping the word away from the disruptive emotions the voice had triggered.

A shooter was loose in the courthouse.

He was on the first floor, in the public area of the building near the snack bar. The cry had come from behind him, maybe from the judiciary wing. The lone syllable had been a breathless call to action that left no room for doubt. This was no prank. He hadn't misheard. His hand darted beneath his jacket, closing over the Glock 22 holstered at his hip. He was already moving toward the sound of the voice, stalking the UNSUB. Around him, a few confused civilians stopped in their tracks like kids playing a game of freeze tag, but then they quickly shook their heads and resumed milling down the hallway, either uncomprehending or, more likely, in a state of denial. Without the benefit of training and experience—without the benefit of preparedness—disbelief would guide their actions, putting them at even greater risk.

First order of business: make the civilians aware and offer them a plan of action. Make them understand this was really happening and that they needed to act quickly.

Flashing his creds, he called out, "FBI. FBI." An immediate, awed hush followed. Then he lowered his voice and pressed his palm down in a stay calm gesture. "Get out if you can. If you can't get out, hide."

A teenage boy raised his tattooed arm and reached for the fire alarm. "No! Don't pull that alarm." Grateful his command had gotten through to the kid in time to stop him, Spense drew his service weapon from his holster, keeping it low. At Westside Middle School in Jonesboro, Arkansas, it had been the fire alarm that'd sent students and teachers scurrying outside, where they'd become sitting ducks for the two young snipers lying in wait in the woods. But there was no time to explain that a shooter would anticipate and use predictable human responses, like pulling a fire alarm, to his advantage. So Spense simply repeated: "Get out. If you can't get out, hide. Stay *quiet*."

His drawn service weapon seemed an extension of his hand. The familiar weight confirmed what he already knew—he was fully loaded and ready to roll. Experience had taught him to recognize the eleven-ounce difference between his loaded and unloaded pistol. Keeping his finger adjacent to but not in contact with the trigger—another behavior that had been trained into him—he narrowed his eyes and concentrated, trying to localize the voice, the word, that was now a mere memory of a sound.

Gun.

Around him, people whispered excitedly, some addressing him, but his ears were tuned to one channel only. Like sonar, he homed in on the ghostlike wake the word *gun* had left behind. Soon, he could hear the plaintive voice clearly in his mind again, a solitary vibration echoing down the tunnel that had become his world. He could imagine sound waves floating in slow motion through the air, practically see the word drifting toward him.

Over there! It'd come from over there.

He backed close to the wall, but not too close, keeping a safe space behind him. He didn't want to risk taking a stray round, and stray rounds had a way of skipping off walls. As time expanded, he wasn't sure if it'd been seconds or minutes since that first alarming cry, but he was absolutely certain enough time had passed that he should've heard the cry repeated . . . or if not . . . His throat tightened. If not, then he should've heard gunfire. But he'd heard nothing more, only the white noise from civilians hurrying past him in the opposite direction. Hurrying away from the danger.

Good.

Then, up ahead, he saw it, rust red fluid slithering down the hall, snaking its way toward him. Its telltale coppery odor turned his stomach.

Blood.

He stuck his pistol out in front of him, sidestepping forward. Automatically leading with his eyes and his gun, clearing slices of the hallway like cutting slivers of a pie as he moved.

"Got your back." He heard someone speaking low and calm behind him.

Swiveling his head, he spotted a uniformed deputy on the opposite side of the hallway. The bulk beneath the man's clothing told Spense he was wearing Kevlar, but the look on the guy's face said it all. Uniform was stepping up because it was his duty and because he was a brave man, but he was clearly out of his depth. Spense was the one with the experience, the confidence, to take on a gunman, and even though he wasn't wearing a vest, Spense should be the one to take the lead.

A quick nod, and Uniform assumed a cover position while Spense cleared the corner. Always, always leading with gun and eyes.

Now, the blood had reached his shoes. With the doorway, a *fatal funnel*, mere feet ahead, his careful, quiet approach came to an end. There was no safe way to clear the entry. He'd have to barrel through the door that was swinging on its hinges. If a shooter was waiting inside that conference room, Spense could only hope for the element of surprise. His new best friend, his cover officer, would be close behind, so getting it right was critical. Did Uniform have a family?

Spense pushed the thought aside. He twisted his head a half-second, making eye contact with his cover and mouthing: *on one.* Then, Glock out in front, he charged into the room, and the door thundered against the wall.

His heartbeat counted down the seconds.

One.

He swung eyes and gun left.

Two.

Then right. Before he could get to three he'd cleared the small room. The sparse furnishings and lack of connecting doors and closets left no place for a shooter to hide.

"Clear!" he called out, and his cover officer flew in behind him.

Two victims: One female, prone on the floor, the source of the snaking blood. And a male slumped onto the conference table—facedown in a pool of dark liquid.

Uniform was on his radio. "SWAT's on-site."

Spense said a silent prayer of thanks. Without backup, he would've been unable to stop and render aid to the victims. Leaving them behind to bleed out while he prowled the building looking for the shooter was one response that although drilled into him, he wasn't sure he could carry out. Luckily, he didn't have to make that decision because SWAT was already here, and that meant it was their show now.

He got to his knees beside the woman.

Checked for a pulse in her neck. It was either absent or too weak to pick up. A sick sense of foreboding came over him as his fingers slid over her clammy skin. Despite the cool temperature in the air-conditioned building, drops of sweat stung the corners of his eyes and salted the corners of his mouth. He swiped his forehead with the back of his arm.

He pressed his face close to hers, hoping to feel her breath against his cheek.

Nothing.

She'd stopped breathing. Gently, his fingers wove into the mass of shiny black hair, to sweep it away from her face, and the color, the sheen, the scent of that hair, even though tangled and matted with blood, sent recognition jolting through him, making his heart first stop beating altogether, then rage against his chest.

Goddamnit!

Caity!

Swiftly, he rolled her over.

"Caity!"

Sealing his lips over her nose and mouth, he gave two fast breaths, then turned his head to the side, checking for the rise of her chest, watching to be sure his breath had reached her lungs. Then he placed the heel of his palm over her chest. He didn't count the compressions, just worked hard and fast to pump blood through her body, stopping only to give more breaths, before starting again . . . and then again.

"Come on, Caity! Breathe!"

Nothing.

He pumped harder, faster, hoping not to crack her ribs but willing to do whatever it took to get her breathing again.

Suddenly, her arm jerked, and he heard a faint grunt release from her lips. "That's it, Caity. Stay with me." Rocking back on his heels, he noticed the ache in his arms and realized he'd been giving compressions long enough for muscle fatigue to set in. Not good. Caity'd been down minutes, not seconds like it'd seemed. He checked her pulse again. Thready and weak, but hell, at least it was *present*. She was breathing on her own, too—but for how long? Now that he had her breathing, he had the luxury of checking her wounds. He could see blood seeping from beneath her left side. Easing her slightly off the floor, he used his jacket to apply pressure to her flank wound and shot a questioning glance at Uniform, who was talking into his radio again. Spense didn't need to ask him why he'd given up reviving the man at the table. In the bloody stream surrounding the male victim, pieces of skull were strewn like bone stepping-stones.

"More casualties?"

"Not *inside* the building . . . at least not that we know of so far."

"And outside the building?"

Uniform grimaced. "A deputy was hit while transporting a prisoner into the courthouse. Prisoner's down, too. SWAT's evacuating and clearing the building, but no sign of the shooter, or shooters, yet."

"Tell our guys to pay special attention to anyone in a maintenance uniform." Spense kept his eyes on Caity's chest to make sure she didn't miss a breath.

"Say again?"

"How'd the shooter get a gun past security?" He checked Caity's pulse, and his jaw clamped down hard when he realized it was growing fainter.

"My guess—he didn't. He probably took a weapon off a guard *after* he was inside."

"Doubt it. No one's found a guard down inside . . . yet. And this was a *quiet* operation. Even if the shooter didn't bring the gun itself through security, he would've had to get a silencer into the courthouse somehow—no guard would have one on him. Anyway, the guards' guns are designed *not* to take a silencer. I say he had a pistol hidden inside already."

"Fuck." Uniform was on the horn again. "Look for a janitor, or any other worker who might be able to get a gun or silencer through security, piece by piece."

That was Spense's theory exactly. Courthouse personnel weren't always subject to the same security procedures as visitors. They might or might not be spot-checked on any given day. If a maintenance worker dismantled a gun and brought it in piece by piece, or brought in a special silencer, like the kind made to look like a Maglite, the risk of being caught was low. At least low enough for a sociopath to risk it. His gaze froze on Caity. The rise and fall of her chest was barely perceptible now.

Dammit.

Wishing he could breathe for them both, his own respirations deepened. No telling how long before the building would be deemed safe enough to allow paramedics inside. One fist opened and closed in frustration.

If the paramedics couldn't get inside to Caity, he'd have to get her outside to them—before it was too late. With a tilt of his head, he said, "I'm taking her out."

Uniform spoke into the radio, then shook his head. "Too dangerous. We're to stay put and render aid as best we can. The shooter might still be in the building."

Spense focused on Caity's face, colorless and slack—expressionless. How he wished she'd open those piercing blue eyes and shoot him her killer smile. Even one of her drop-dead glares would lift his heart about now. No. This beautiful, lively woman was not going to die because he'd failed to take action. Carefully, he scooped Caity into his arms and pushed to a stand, his thighs burning from the effort. Her neck dropped back, and he used the crook of his elbow to support her head. Then she moaned, as if in pain, cracking his heart wide open. "I'm getting her out *now*. Let 'em know." The possibility of taking friendly fire was as real and as dangerous as encountering a gunman.

Uniform gave a quick shout over the radio, then a curt nod.

Spense heard a firm response crackle over the airwaves: *Negative. Maintain your position until clear.*

Uniform raised one conspiratorial eyebrow at him. "Want cover?"

They'd never met, but they were partners now.

Spense flashed him a grin. "Cover'd be nice."

Then, with his new buddy clearing the way, he gathered Caity closer and carried her from the building.

Chaos was the only word to describe the scene outside the courthouse. Although onlookers and the media were being kept back from the courthouse steps, television trucks crammed the streets, and reporters buzzed around the edges of the scene, shoving microphones in the faces of witnesses and elbowing their way through the crowd, hoping to somehow insert themselves into the secured area. Escorted by members of the SWAT team, tightly banded groups of civilians raced down the steps to safety.

Shouts, sirens and crying created a tornado of sound around Spense, and for a split second, he felt the full-body tension and tingling in his fingers that, since childhood, had warned him when his brain was about to go haywire. One doctor had called Spense's *problem* a sensory processing disorder. Another had labeled it ADD. His mother had said the diagnosis simply didn't matter—she loved him no matter how much trouble he got into. Soon the sounds around him took on a texture and seemed to swim before his eyes. His temples were throbbing. He could practically feel his brain cells shift into overdrive.

Focus.

He hauled in a breath, then imagined bundling the extraneous noise around him in a roll of cotton. As his brain came back to center, the tightness in his muscles eased. Caity shifted in his arms, and he pulled her against his chest. Now his world consisted of just the two of them . . . and that ambulance off to the right.

A moment later, he laid Caity on a gurney and let the paramedics take over. One slapped an oxygen mask on her face and fit her with a neck brace, while another used scissors to cut open her blouse. Electrodes were placed on her exposed chest, and Spense's eyes darted to the portable monitor. To his untrained eye, the heart rhythm looked erratic, making his own heart beat unsteadily and his mouth go dry. He wanted to ask about the tracing on the monitor, but instead he kept out of the way and let the paramedics do their work.

"Run the Ringers wide open!" One man barked as he hooked up an IV, then shouted, "Let's roll."

Jarred by a sudden sense of loss, Spense swept his gaze over Caity, lying on the gurney, bloodied and battered and helpless. A gunshot wound to her shoulder and flank . . . and that was just what he could see. Every fiber of his being strained forward, and without even realizing he'd moved, he found himself at her side, his hand reaching for hers.

His senses were clear and sharp now. So far, from what he knew, there was no sign of an active shooter still on-site. And the situation at the courthouse was all SWAT now. Operators, each one outfitted in fifty pounds' worth of special gear, swarmed the building, executing what they'd been trained to do with precision and grace. Spense was not part of that team, and in soft clothes, he was good for little else than giving chase if they had a rabbit.

Caity would no doubt be in capable hands, but if she regained consciousness, he wanted to be there for her, to mitigate her fear, to remind her she was not alone.

His decision was made: He was going with her. A paramedic tried to shoulder him aside, and he flashed his creds. The answering look on the man's face humbled him—and Spense was not an easily humbled man. But the deference, the admiration, of honest men was the one thing that never failed to take his ego down a notch. Especially when those honest men put their lives on the line for others on a daily basis. He didn't feel deserving of the awe that came with his special-agent status—certainly not from *these guys*. Still, he was glad that a mere flash of his ID could buy him a ride in the ambulance alongside Caity and a blow-by-blow account of her condition.

"Please, don't let me fall."

Caity was talking! He bent his head, his lips making gentle contact with her ear. "It's going to be okay, sweetheart, just hang in there. We're going to take a little ride to the hospital, now. But, I'll be right beside you all the way."

A harsh moan escaped Caity's lips, then she repeated, "I don't want to fall."

"Hold on tight, Caity." Carefully, he squeezed her hand. "Trust me."

Her eyes fluttered open, and when she gazed up at him, he thought, he *hoped* she recognized him. He tried to work his mouth into a reassuring smile, but she was no longer looking at him. Her eyes rolled up in her head. Then her back arched, and her body began to seize.

Chapter Three

Monday, September 9
Good Hope Medical Center
Phoenix, Arizona

WARMTH SPILLED OVER Caitlin's check, and light seeped in through the cracks of her eyelids, but she didn't want to wake up. It was so cozy here in her medicated cocoon. The round-the-clock pain pills her nurse had been feeding her made the hospital bedding feel like the finest Egyptian cotton. The thread count must be in the thousands, the hundreds of thousands even, the sheets felt so soft and sleek against her skin. Almost like a whisper of air. And they smelled so good, like a man.

She wrinkled her nose, testing the scent's reality, and confirmed a distinctly masculine spice in the air. Someone in her hospital room smelled like a refreshing hike on a cool day.

"Caity?"

And that voice was familiarly enticing. Her body tingled all over in response to its low timbre. Like a schoolgirl experiencing her first French kiss, she could feel herself slipping under its seductive spell. When she heard herself sigh aloud, however, she resolved right then and there to hide the next pain pill in her cheek and spit it out when Nurse turned her back. And because she had a visitor, and because her mother had brought her up well, she also resolved to open her eyes . . . in just a minute or two. The darkness was really too pleasant.

"I know you're awake, Caity."

Her lids popped open at the amused accusation.

And there, leaning over her bedside, hand hovering above her hair, yet not quite touching, was Special Agent Atticus Spenser. The warm cognac of his eyes deepened to a double shot of espresso as they locked with hers. Her heart started to thump like she'd recently downed such a drink, but she didn't look away.

"Well, well. If it isn't Atticus Spenser, my arch nemesis," she croaked.

Nurse reached out and brushed her fingers over Spense's shoulder. "Don't take it personally. She's just loopy from the morphine. Always takes her a minute or two to get her bearings after a nap."

Blinking hard, Caitlin rose up on one elbow. Could that be *her* nurse? This woman's voice had gone butter soft, and Caitlin could've sworn she saw her toss her hair. The nurse *she* knew was all business and would brook no disobedience: *You're going to take this pill whether you think you need it or not. I have more important things to do than coax you like a child. Doctors make the worst patients.*

"You should mind your manners, Dr. Cassidy. Have you forgotten Agent Spenser saved your life?" The seductive voice had been replaced by a no-nonsense one. Yes, that was Jenny all right. Nurse's name had come back to Caitlin along with an improving level of consciousness.

She pursed dry lips—no, make that *very* dry lips. "I'm pretty sure Spense can fight his own battles," she managed through her aching throat as she struggled to sit up.

The bed started to whir. Spense was adjusting the position to a more comfortable one. As he did so, she couldn't seem to look away from his big hand working the buttons. A lump welled in her throat. Then a memory flashed to the surface: Spense's hand clutching hers. Spense's voice whispering in her ear.

Hold on tight, Caity. Trust me.

She jolted fully awake. Ah yes. After more than a year with no contact, Spense had reappeared in her world when he'd been called in to testify for the prosecution in the Kramer case, and she'd been consulted by the defense. For weeks, now, she'd been bumping into him at the jail or the courthouse. She didn't actually remember seeing him the day she'd been shot, but she'd been told he'd resuscitated her and carried her to safety. In her lucid intervals over the past two weeks, the police had explained the basics of how she'd landed in the hospital, and the doctors had explained her injuries: one bullet had grazed her left shoulder, another bullet to her flank had thankfully missed her spinal cord, but not her spleen. Between internal and external blood loss, her organs had shut down, and she'd gone into cardiac arrest. Spense had not only revived her, he'd gotten her medical attention in time to stop her from bleeding to death. Her spleen had been removed, and her surgeon anticipated a complete recovery. More than a little ashamed of that *arch nemesis* wisecrack, she glanced up at Spense. "Thank you. I-I wouldn't be here if not for your bravery. I'm sorry not to have said so sooner."

"Oh, but you did. You thanked me yesterday and the day before that and the day before that too. Quite nicely, I might add." A rather wide grin spread over his face. "I'd say you've been effusive in your gratitude."

Something in his tone made her cheeks go from warm to hot. He'd put a little too much emphasis on *effusive,* and like any red-blooded woman in her wrong mind, she had to admit to finding him somewhat . . . *sexy.* Hopefully she hadn't told him so. But whatever she'd said or done, she'd had a perfectly good reason. She'd been under the influence of multiple mind-altering drugs. Drugs she no longer needed. She was feeling much better, and from here on out, ibuprofen would do just fine for the pain—as for the seizure meds, her neurologist had agreed to discontinue them. At least she thought she recalled such a conversation. After all, her seizure had been posttraumatic, not epilepsy-induced, so the Tegretol was just a temporary precaution.

"Shall I tell you how you wanted to show me your appreciation?" The self-satisfied gleam in Spense's eye was downright mortifying.

Apparently, he had no intention of allowing her to save face. And if he wasn't going to let up and planned on going straight back to his old habit of goading her, she could give as good as she got. She no longer felt guilty about her earlier remark. "No need, since I'm quite certain I wasn't lucid at the time."

"You began by beckoning me to your side, then sniffed me with great enjoyment." He forged ahead just as though she hadn't plainly asked him not to. The man was impossibly ill-mannered.

"I'm sure I did no such thing. That aftershave you wear is *so* outdated." Of course, she was no Emily Post herself when it came to Spense—though she was very well behaved around *most* people.

"It's Old Spice," Nurse Jenny put in. "And I, for one, think Spense smells terrific."

"How does she know what kind of aftershave you wear?" Caity heard an undeniable note of irritation come through in her voice. She didn't know the name of his aftershave, but why would she? It was none of her business at all. She only knew that his aroma or essence—or whatever that *thing* about Spense was—made her spend far too much time thinking of him when he wasn't around and threw her off-balance when he was. And *off-balance* was not a feeling she welcomed under the best of circumstances, much less circumstances like these.

"No need for jealousy. Jenny knows what aftershave I wear because she asked me, nothing more to it than that. It's hardly classified information." He threw a wink Jenny's way, and they both had a quick chuckle at her expense. Then Spense jerked his head toward the door.

Taking the hint, Jenny sent him a lingering smile and departed.

He moved in closer—too close. "I wear Old Spice because it reminds me of my father, Caity. Sorry you don't care for it, but outdated or not, I'm not going to change."

Because of his father. That was the most personal disclosure Spense had ever made to her, and it piqued her curiosity. She wouldn't mind hearing more on the subject, but Spense backed away and pulled a let's-get-down-to-brass-tacks face.

"It's been swell exchanging barbs with you—just like old times—but we need to talk. According to your medical team, you're well enough to be interviewed. Do you feel up to having a real conversation?"

"Getting there." That pleasant buzz she'd awakened with had disappeared altogether, her side throbbed, and her skin felt raw and sore. But worse than any physical discomfort was an ache that ran deeper than muscle, deeper than bone. As she recalled what the police had told her, pain seared through to her very soul. "Baumgartner didn't make it. Is that right?"

"I'm afraid not."

When Spense confirmed what she already knew but didn't wish to believe, the pit of her stomach went rock heavy. Her father's attorney, his old friend, Harvey Baumgartner, was dead. "Kramer was shot, too?"

"He survived, but the guard who was escorting him into the courthouse didn't. The bastard—Kramer I mean—is right down the hall."

"I guess the saying's true, then: Motherfuckers never die."

He arched a brow in surprise but didn't seem to disapprove. "That's a saying? Among whom?"

"Doctors. Mostly trauma surgeons. Not an *approved* saying, of course." She already regretted repeating the cynical mantra—she'd always thought it unkind. But it was hard not to resent the fact Kramer had survived while two good men had lost their lives.

"Speaking of bad guys, that's one reason I'm here. I could use your help with the case. You're aware the shooter or shooters are still at large."

The case.

Gunshots and blood and the spilling of human life had been reframed into something businesslike, something manageable. Spense was here on behalf of the FBI. He had questions for her. *Good.* Cases were something she knew how to deal with. She shifted in the bed, causing the throb in her left flank to worsen, and, unable to stop herself, she groaned in pain.

Spense was all but on top of her then. "Don't try to rearrange yourself. I can adjust the bed or help you if you need to move." And then he did. He pressed a button, and the head of her bed rose higher so she had more support for her back. Defiantly, she swung her legs over the side of the bed, completely undoing his good deed. "I can sit without support, thank you." *Super.* She'd reachieved the motor milestones of a six-month-old. "And I'm happy to answer your questions." To show she was perfectly comfortable and ready to roll, she grimaced her way into a smile. "I wish I could remember more about that day, and maybe I will with time, but at the moment, the last thing I remember is the janitor's shoes."

"What about the janitor's shoes?" he asked, interest flaring in his eyes.

"I bent down—I'd dropped my pen, you see." Her chest grew unbearably tight, stopping her words. She forced out a breath, and went on, "Then I saw someone's feet. Big feet, so they must've belonged to a man, I think. And he was wearing a grimy maintenance uniform with pristine loafers. The shoes were out of place, that's why I noticed them. Does that help?"

He grunted. "Maybe. Now then, tell me everything you know about Judd Kramer."

She narrowed her eyes at Spense, who knew perfectly well she couldn't violate doctor-patient privilege. But, perhaps he thought she was too doped up to remember her ethical and legal responsibilities toward Kramer. Or perhaps her ill-considered *motherfucker* remark had given him the impression she didn't care about the accused man's rights, which she certainly did, no matter how repulsive she found the guy.

"I'll answer your questions about what happened in the courthouse that day, but I can't talk to you about my interviews with Kramer. Besides, at least in this instance, he's a victim, not the perpetrator."

Like her, Kramer had been targeted by a killer, and *victimology*, analyzing the victims and what they had in common with each other, would likely be key to profiling and apprehending the shooter. She knew that, but she couldn't violate privilege, even if she wanted to. Not unless Kramer posed an imminent threat to others, and since he was currently in police custody, he did not. "Why is there a policeman outside my door?" she asked, changing the subject and suspecting she wasn't going to like the answer. It'd been bothering her for a while now, but she never seemed to stay awake long enough to ask the question.

"I was just about to get to that, Caity. You may still be in danger. These hits were organized . . . surgical. This wasn't the crazed act of some lunatic who decided to wreak havoc in the courthouse and go out in a blaze of glory."

In her sedated condition, she hadn't had time to process what little information she'd been given about the shootings. A gray, queasy feeling came over her. Talking as much to herself as to Spense, she recounted the facts as she understood them. "There were four victims. Kramer and his deputy escort were shot just outside the courthouse, Baumgartner and myself inside. But no one else was harmed. The shooter made a facile escape . . . suggesting the attacks were well planned."

Spense waited, giving her time to soak it all in and come to her own conclusions.

"The deputy who was shot was probably collateral damage. Not a true target. Kramer was the primary, in my opinion," she said.

"One hundred percent—I agree. Kramer was the primary target, and Baumgartner was probably hit because he was defending him.

The easy explanation is that a vigilante or vigilantes wanted to administer their own brand of justice," Spense responded.

"What does Kramer remember about the attack? Can he describe the shooter?"

"Claims he doesn't remember a damn thing. But I think he's holding out—hoping to exchange information for some kind of plea deal. A Maricopa County sheriff's deputy and a well-respected attorney were shot and killed. Kramer knows any information leading to the arrest of the UNSUB is valuable currency."

"Maybe. Maybe not. He was adamant with me he didn't want any deals. Nothing short of an acquittal was what he was after." She glanced through the window at the uniformed officer sitting just outside her door. No doubt one was posted outside Kramer's room, too. Her guard might have been assigned for her own protection, but she hated knowing her every move was being scrutinized. In a way, she felt like a prisoner herself. "I know your theory is that the shooter was a vigilante. But maybe, like the deputy who was killed, I was just in the wrong place at the wrong time. I happened to be in conference with Baumgartner, but I wasn't on Kramer's defense team. In fact, I was telling Baumgartner not to call me to the stand when . . ."

"It's possible you were collateral damage. I'll grant you that much. But public perception is that you're on Kramer's side. Not to mention the fact that you've testified on behalf of other men—"

"Innocent men who were later acquitted. I testified on behalf of *innocent men*. Isn't that what you mean to say?"

"I'm not here to get into a political debate with you. I'm only saying public perception is that you're a bleeding heart and that you're on Kramer's team."

"So now I'm a bleeding heart just because I believe in respecting the constitutional rights of individuals. I realize that's a tough concept for you to grasp, but—"

"What the hell, Caity? I have respect for the suspect's rights. You make me sound like I make a habit of running over people, and that's just not true."

"What about the Hanson case? Are you going to claim you didn't lie to Craig Hanson in order to get a confession out of him?"

"Craig Hanson was guilty, and as you know, it's legal to lie to a suspect."

"It may be legal, Spense, but it's not ethical. There is a difference."

Spense squeezed his eyes shut, as if gathering his control, and she scooted back, realizing she'd worked her way so close to the edge of the bed, she was about to fall off. He was right about one thing—this was not the time for a political debate. She counted to ten. "Anyway, my point is I was not in actuality part of Kramer's team, and I have no intention of testifying on his behalf."

He rubbed his forehead, then squared his gaze with hers. "Good to know you're on our side for a change."

"I'm not on anyone's side—unless truth is a side. In which case, I'm on that one." Her voice went up an octave. "I don't believe there's any ongoing danger to me. Kramer was the real target. If you want to keep a guard outside my door for now, fine. But once I'm home, I don't want a protective detail. I'm not going to live my life in fear." Breathless, she paused. The exertion of sitting up on her own and the strain of battling with Spense had tired her out. Hopefully, it was mostly the drugs that made her so weak. Once they were out of her system, she knew she'd feel stronger.

"About that. I'd rather you not go directly home once you're released."

"Excuse me?" He'd spoken as if he were a parent, telling a wayward child what was good for her. She didn't care if her resentment came through in her tone or not.

"Don't cop an attitude until you hear me out. The locals have invited me in on the courthouse shootings since it's a big case, and I'm already in town to testify at Kramer's trial—it was my profile that helped the police zero in on Kramer in the first place. The Bureau's placed me in a nice apartment for my stay in Phoenix. I've got an extra bedroom, and building security's tight. I think it'd be best for you to bunk with me until we can be sure the danger's passed. It'd be an informal arrangement, but you'd be safe, and it would give us a chance to—"

"Bunk with you? Are you suggesting I'd be under your protection after I'm released from the hospital?"

"I said I have an extra bedroom. You need protection. I need your expertise and your inside information on Kramer . . . and Baumgartner, too, for that matter."

"Sorry, but I don't want to *bunk* with you, and you can't force me to accept your protection, informal or otherwise."

"Sure I can. You're a material witness to a major crime, and as such you will remain under my personal supervision until we catch the bad guys. Unless of course, you prefer a jail cell, but my place is more comfortable, and those prison phones are teeming with germs."

The tension in her back and shoulders ratcheted up a notch. Spense's threat might be an empty one, but it brought back the feelings of helplessness she'd experienced when her father had been carted off to jail for something he didn't do. Only she wasn't helpless anymore. Pissed was more like it. And the resulting adrenaline surge not only amped up her energy, it cleared her brain. "You're bluffing. No way can you lock me up under the material-witness act. I'm cooperating fully, and I'm not a flight risk. I hereby formally wave the bullshit flag."

"You may not be a flight risk, but you could wind up dead without protection, then you wouldn't be able to testify just the same as if you'd fled. So you make the call. You wanna roll the dice that I can't persuade a judge to lock you up for your own safety, or make the sensible, voluntary decision to let me protect you? You're the best hope we have of finding this guy, Caity. You're an eye-witness, not to mention you've spent hours interviewing Kramer about his deep, dark secrets, and that could help lead us to the individual who is so determined to see Kramer dead, he doesn't mind taking innocent folks out with him in the process. Think what a great team we'll make. You've got the fancy education, and I've got the street smarts. You have to admit, you're sort of the yin to my yang."

She was pretty sure she didn't have to admit any such thing, and her blood, if not boiling, was at the very least simmering—his free-and-easy interpretation of the material-witness act was yet another example of his *whatever-it-takes* attitude. But she was interested to know how he'd arrived at the mystifying conclusion that they'd work well together. She had a compulsive curiosity about how people's minds worked in general, and as inconvenient as it might be, she was particularly interested in *Spense's* mind. The guy was a walking contradiction.

Impulsive, quick to act or speak, he often put people off by blurting out just exactly what he was thinking. Spense's behavior showed all the telltale signs of an attention deficit disorder. Half the time, the man had no filter and no focus.

But the other half of the time, she'd never seen anyone with a sharper intellect. Somehow, he managed to control his impulsivity and channel his energy in the right direction when it mattered most. Spense had a keen ability to home in on the salient facts within a disjointed jumble of information and whisk them together into a cohesive pattern. The man could work a puzzle of just about any sort. Like a visually impaired man who could find his way in the dark, Spense seemed to have developed some sort of sixth sense and a unique coping mechanism for the processing difficulties she suspected he'd been battling since childhood.

As if to prove her unspoken point, Spense pulled a miniature Rubik's cube, attached to a keychain, from his pocket, scrambled it, solved it, and shoved it back in his pants pocket, all in less than a minute. She'd seen him do that on several occasions. And though she might be persuaded that, with enough practice, most people could learn to quickly work the cube using rote muscle memory, that didn't explain how Spense was able to solve the daily crossword in the time it took to her to order coffee. His brain didn't work the same way hers did, and she found that fascinating.

Tamping down her anger, she took the bait.

"How do you figure I'm your yang?"

"Yin."

"Whatever. If you want to convince me, let's hear your reasoning. Why should we team up to solve this case? I presume that's what you're asking me to do, in addition to *bunking* with you."

"I said I have an extra bedroom. Three times now."

"But you also said I should *bunk* with you. Which implies you want to sleep with me. That term didn't pop out of your mouth for no reason. I thought we were past that. I thought we were clear about maintaining a strictly collegial relationship."

"Christ, Caity, of course I want to sleep with you—you're gorgeous when you don't have a fat lip and shiners under your eyes."

"Gee, thanks." Gingerly she touched her tender mouth. She hadn't looked in a mirror since the shooting, but she could well imagine the raccoon eyes and swollen facial features.

"Maybe you caught me in a Freudian slip, but that doesn't mean I'm going to try to get inside your knickers. You're injured, and I'm not an ass . . . Witness my polite use of the phrase *get inside your knickers* rather than the more direct phrase: *fuck you*."

Of course he wouldn't take advantage of her in this condition— he'd just saved her life for goodness sake. She owed it to him to cut him a little slack, but there was just something about Spense that always got her back up. "So long as you understand that, I'd like to know why you think we should team up."

"The reason is obvious."

Thank heavens they were moving on. Actually, she was glad they'd cleared the air. It was all settled, and there was no need to ever discuss the nature of their relationship again. "Not to me, it's not."

"We're both puzzle solvers."

"Wrong again. I couldn't work a Rubik's cube to save my soul." She shrugged one shoulder, conceding genuine admiration. "Where did you learn to do that anyway? Can you show me the trick?"

"Actually, it's not a trick. But I'll tell you the story of how I learned, someday . . . maybe," he said, not meeting her eyes.

She wouldn't mind hearing that story—but he seemed suddenly evasive, so she let it drop. "I'm a forensic psychiatrist, not a psychic. And I'm not a profiler, either, so I don't know how I'd be of use to you beyond telling you what I recall about the shooting."

"First, my official title is criminal investigative analyst. Second, you're as much a profiler as I am, with or without the BAU algorithms."

Her resistance softened a bit. Spense had never acknowledged before that what she did had value. Plus, as one of the victims, she had a very personal reason for wanting this shooter to be apprehended. Perhaps she should hear Spense out before dismissing the idea of working with him on this investigation as total nonsense.

"I profile killers and you profile . . ."

She realized she was holding her breath, waiting to see if he would actually admit the truth.

"You profile innocents."

Her breath released, and her jaw opened slightly. She snapped it shut. Spense had just validated her work. Quite a shift from calling her a bleeding heart.

That still didn't mean they'd make a good team, however. "Not exactly. You look at a crime scene and deduce what type of perpetrator you're looking for. Whereas I look at the accused and deduce whether he's capable of committing the crime. I don't have any criminal investigative skills. I don't know how to work backward from the evidence at the scene." As she said the words, she realized there might be a rather large side benefit to working with Spense.

"Not yet, you don't, but something tells me you're a quick study. Hasn't it occurred to you that with your ability to recognize an innocent man and my killer radar, together we'd be more accurate than either of us could be separately? I'll admit I may have been wrong a time or two . . . but so have you, Caity. If we teamed up, we'd be formidable—not that I'm not formidable all on my own."

If she could pick up enough investigative skills . . . "But we have totally different objectives." Her mind was already made up, but she decided to let him convince her. "I've dedicated my life to helping innocent men and women keep their freedom. Your goal is to put people behind bars."

"My goal is to put *guilty* people behind bars. I have no desire to lock up the innocent."

Except me, apparently. She swallowed the sarcastic retort. "And I have no desire to set the guilty free."

Like the man himself, she found Spense's *gotcha* smile both charming and annoying at the same time.

"Like I said, you're yin . . . I'm yang. We're flip sides of the same coin—*justice*. At least on this one case, I think we should set aside our differences. The Phoenix police are asking for all the help they can get to catch this asshole. The chief wants a profile, and I intend to give him one. Are you in or what?"

The throbbing in her flank magically transferred to her head. It was true she wanted the shooter apprehended as soon as possible, before he could hurt anyone else. And she wouldn't mind being able to keep an eye on the investigation to make sure it stayed on the straight and narrow. "I need time to think about it."

"And I need your help to catch a killer. You know Kramer inside out, and you have personal knowledge of Baumgartner, too. You're a brilliant forensic psychiatrist, which is why I hate seeing you on the opposing side of a courtroom. I never thought I'd say this, but I want you on *my* team. So go ahead and tell me everything you know about Judd Kramer."

Covering her face with her hands, she shook her head. "I can't do that, and you know it."

Spense pulled a paper from his jacket and laid it on her tray-table. "Yeah. You can. Kramer signed a release. Claims he's an open book, an innocent man with nothing to hide. He's released you from doctor-patient privilege."

That wasn't impossible to believe. Kramer thought he was smarter than everyone else, and he hadn't told her anything he hadn't wanted the world to know. After all, he'd hoped she'd function as his mouthpiece in the courtroom. But what he didn't realize was that his behavior and subtext had belied secrets he never intended to reveal. Before she said anything at all about the man, she had to be sure he hadn't been misled into signing that release. "Great, so you won't mind if I just confirm that with Kramer myself. Since he's right down the hall, it should only take a minute."

Spense's mouth twisted in consternation. "You don't trust me."

"It's not personal, but I need to make sure Kramer wasn't coerced into signing that release. Surely, you can't object to that."

He turned his palms up. "I know what you've been through with your father, Caity. And I get why you object to certain tactics on my part. I really do. But one of these days, you're going to realize *I'm* not the enemy. I only hope that day comes sooner rather than later." He buzzed the nurse. "When you get a chance, Dr. Cassidy would like to take a joyride in one of those jazzy hospital wheelchairs."

"I'll be right in. It's time for her Tegretol anyway," Jenny answered.

Caity leaned close to the speaker. "Just the chair please, Jenny. My neurologist said she was going to discontinue the Tegretol order. Can you check with her please?"

"Doctors make the worst patients," came her reply.

"Good one, Jenny. Never heard that before." She started to climb out of bed and bumped into Spense's rather magnificent, special-agent-man chest and the familiar scent of what she now knew to be Old Spice. Any other day, she would've shoved him aside, but no way could she manage that with her light head and weak limbs. "Let me by, please."

"Stay in bed until the chair gets here. And just so we're clear, I'm coming with you. As of right this minute, you're under my protection."

Now that she knew the sentimental reason behind Spense's aftershave, she found the scent was growing on her—his arrogance, on the other hand, was not. "Come along if you like, but you'll have to wait outside while I talk to Kramer. *And just so we're clear,* I haven't agreed to a damn thing yet."

Chapter Four

As she wheeled through the door of Judd Kramer's hospital room, Caitlin shot a firm, stay-back look at Spense. Spense returned a determined glare of his own, and she knew he'd be keeping a close eye on her through the hospital unit's wide window. If Kramer so much as sneered at her, both Spense and the sheriff's deputy standing watch would come to her aid in a heartbeat. Kramer was debilitated from his injuries, and his arms and legs were bound to the bed by soft restraints, ensuring her physical safety. So it wasn't fear that set her teeth on edge when she saw him sitting up in his hospital bed. It was that feeling of needing to scrub herself clean after being around him. She hated the fact that he'd shared his secret thoughts with her, and she hated knowing he'd *enjoyed* her discomfort.

But as much as she despised looking into those blank eyes of his, she was glad Kramer was in an upright position. The whole point of this little excursion was to make sure he hadn't been intimidated into signing that release, and an eye-level conversation would keep them on a more equal footing. A lanky young woman wearing paisley scrubs and a name tag that read, BELINDA, scurried around the hospital bed. Caitlin hung back in the corner, quietly observing as the nurse tended to his IV, then scanned a packet of pills and administered them to Kramer.

Caitlin's hands curled around the wheels of her chair, and the cool metallic spokes pressed into her fingertips. That creepy-crawly feeling she got whenever she was near Judd Kramer had already taken hold. The last time she'd spoken to him, she'd had to deliver the news that she would not be testifying in his defense. And he'd been none too happy, even called her a few choice names. The recollection made her stomach tighten unpleasantly. It was hard to believe that conversation had taken place just two short weeks ago, the same day her meeting with Harvey Baumgartner had been interrupted by gunshots.

Her chin jerked up, and she set her jaw. No, she didn't relish seeing Kramer again, but if she was lucky, this would be the last time she would ever have to deal with him. Bracing herself, she vowed to remain undaunted in the face of any obnoxious and manipulative comments he might make. Judd Kramer was the last person she wanted to be around, but she had to be sure he'd signed that consent form voluntarily—it was the right thing to do. And who knew, maybe she'd glean something useful from him today. Spense thought Kramer was holding out on the police about the shooter's description. If she could get new information out of Kramer, this visit, while distasteful, would be more than worth it.

"I'll be out of your hair in a minute." Belinda smiled at Caitlin.

Kramer said nothing, keeping his gaze openly focused on the nurse's trim bottom. Once she'd exited the room, Caitlin rolled a little closer, the wheels of her chair making a soft, rubbery sound and catching a little on the carpeted floor. Not wanting to be within sniffing distance of the man, she kept back a good distance from his bedside. Still, she was close enough to notice the pallor of his lips and a slight rapidity in his respirations. His blond hair was oil-darkened from lack of washing, and the fluorescent lighting in the room did nothing for his pocked complexion. Not surprisingly, he looked like hell.

"How are you feeling?" she asked.

"Like shit. How 'bout you, Doc?" His grin showed his once-perfect smile, the only attractive feature on the face of an otherwise homely man, had been ruined. Two front teeth were missing, no doubt from hitting the courthouse steps face-first after being shot.

Kramer was lucky to be alive, and so was she. She tried to focus on the fact he'd been badly hurt rather than that he was most likely a cold-blooded killer and most certainly a cruel and twisted man who got off on other people's pain. This was the hard part, putting herself in his place, empathizing with him in order to establish rapport. But there was no other way to get him to talk. At least none that she knew of.

"I feel like shit, too, I guess." She couldn't quite force herself to smile at him, but she mirrored his language, hoping to set him at ease. Besides, the phrase aptly described how she felt, with her legs aching and the muscles in her arms shaking merely from the effort of rolling the wheelchair a few feet into the room.

"Well, well. The pretty little lady shrink stoops to the criminal's level. Trying to loosen him up?"

"You're onto me." She happily acknowledged his perceptiveness. She wanted him to feel safe and superior because that would work in her favor. Kramer had an odd, distancing habit of referring to himself in the third person whenever he was ill at ease. It was one of those behavioral *tells* he didn't realize he had. She'd know he'd relaxed and let his guard down once that odd speech pattern stopped.

"You change your mind about testifying for old Kramer here, or is this a social call?" His voice was hoarse and weak, but he still managed to infuse it with a menacing tone.

Too bad for him, she didn't intimidate easily. Not after spending countless hours interviewing psychopaths. "Neither. I am terribly sorry for what's happened, but I'm afraid it doesn't change my decision. My testimony wouldn't be useful to your defense."

"Don't really have a defense now that Baumgartner's boxed and rested his case." The corners of Kramer's mouth twitched, lifting his doughy, orange skin into a saggy, broken smile, reminiscent of a jack-o'-lantern that had begun to rot.

The callousness in his voice, the maudlin joke made at his deceased attorney's expense reinforced her prior conclusions: Kramer had no empathy for others. Human kindness wasn't in his nature.

"You'll find another attorney." There were plenty looking to make a name for themselves with a high-profile case like this one.

"I expect I will."

Ah, good, he'd dropped that third person self-referencing already. And why not? She was no threat to him, and since she wasn't going to testify, he no longer needed to put on a show for her. Her gaze went to the window, where Spense raised his brows, his question obvious. She gave him an a-okay head tilt.

"So if this isn't a social call, and you haven't changed your mind about testifying, to what do I owe the *honor* of your presence, Dr. Cassidy?" Kramer's eyes fluttered open and shut rapidly, and she decided to get straight to the point.

Clearly, he wasn't up for a long chat today. In fact, his condition seemed to be worsening by the minute, right before her eyes. His facial muscles slackened, and a bit of drool escaped his mouth, running down his chin. "I understand you signed a release, giving me permission to speak with the authorities about our interviews."

Their gazes met, and she suppressed a shudder. His stare was cold and disconcerting. The opposite of penetrating, it just seemed to bounce off her unchanged. Never reacting to her words or expressions. Flat. His stare was empty and dead. A full minute passed with no response, and she wasn't sure if he'd lost concentration or was simply being oppositional. "Did you sign that release voluntarily, Mr. Kramer?"

His eyes dropped to her chest. "This is boring. I'm having a hard time paying attention. Maybe if you unbutton your blouse, I'd be more interested in what you have to say."

That seemed a rather pitiful attempt at shocking her. He'd said so many awful things to her during their interviews, this present request, crude though it might have been, barely registered. "I see. I'm boring you. I'll just let you get back to your busy life." She shrugged and started to wheel her chair around.

"Hold on. Don't leave. I promise to behave." The plaintive tone in his voice was one she'd never heard from him before. It might even have been genuine distress. His shoulders heaved, and he thumped his chest. "I . . . don't feel that well, Doc. And it's too quiet around here for my tastes. You're not exactly great company, but you're better than that bitch out there."

He meant his nurse, she assumed.

"As soon as you leave, she'll be back here poking me and prodding me, all the while giving me the stink eye and putting on gloves just to touch me, like I'm a rodent carrying plague or something. At least you treat me like a human being. You're the only one who does anymore."

"Mr. Kramer, did you sign that release voluntarily?" She tried to bring him back around to the point as quickly as possible.

"Sure. I'm an open book. I told the FBI already. Nothing . . . to . . . hide." Kramer started breathing faster. His skin was getting pinker, which usually indicated better oxygenation, but his expression told her he was tiring rapidly.

"Maybe you should call your nurse." She was too far away to reach his call button, and it'd be slow going for her to wheel up to the bed, or she'd have pressed it herself.

"No. Not that bitch. Just stay with me a while longer. You can talk to anyone you want about me, Doc. An innocent man's . . . got no secrets." He let out a wheeze and a cough. "I'm okay. Let's have our little chat. Whatever you want to know, all you gotta do is ask. I signed the consent, and I don't regret it."

He seemed so eager for her to stay, and he'd recovered his breath again. Perhaps he had something important to get off his chest. She'd let him say his peace and send Belinda right in after her. She gave Spense the reassuring nod she knew he was looking for, then said, "All right, but we can stop anytime you want. And as long as we're clear you haven't been pressured into anything, and that I may be sharing anything you say to me with the authorities. Is there anything at all you can tell me about the courthouse shootings? Did you get a look at the person who shot you? Was there more than one?"

His cold eyes stuttered from side to side, before coming back to center and landing on her. What the hell was wrong with him? "Call your nurse, Mr. Kramer. I don't like the way—"

"No!" His torso jerked forward like he was trying to bolt from his restraints.

Her instinct was to wheel away from him, but she followed her training instead and wheeled closer, her muscles jumping and jittery from the effort. She didn't like the way his chin was bobbing up and down, nor the way his eyes were shimmying from side to side. She wasn't going to try to reason with him any longer. She was close enough now to reach the side rail of the bed where the call button rested. At least she thought she was. But when she stretched her arm out, she couldn't quite reach the control. Her eyes sought the window to signal Spense for help, but his back was turned, and she saw him bring his phone to his ear. She couldn't see the deputy and guessed he'd used Spense's presence to take a break.

Gripping the guardrail on Kramer's bed, she dragged herself to a stand. Her legs were too weak to support her, though, and she fell forward, her body landing halfway onto the bed, her face now inches away from Kramer's. His body was shaking, and she could feel the trembling of the pillow beneath her cheek. She stretched her fingers, feeling around for the call button, and suddenly Kramer's hand clutched her wrist. His nails dug into her flesh. His putrid breath was in her ear, and her gut knotted in revolt, but her sense of duty was stronger than her disgust. She pressed the call button.

"Help's coming," she said. By now white foam had replaced the drool sliding out of Kramer's mouth. His cheeks had gone a bizarre shade of red. Like nothing she'd seen before, not even during her med-school years. "Don't try to talk." She yanked her hand away and tried to push herself off the bed into a standing position, but her legs had turned to water.

"I . . . got something for you, little lady. Just for *you* . . . Because I like you." He sputtered out the words. "Because you don't treat me like an animal." The effort of the speech took its toll. Vomit and foam spewed onto the front of his hospital gown and onto the sheets. The putrid smell filling the air was the least of her worries, but . . . Oh, Lord, his breath, his vomitus, smelled ever so faintly of almonds.

Oh, no no no.

Something clicked in her brain, and she realized what was happening . . . But that was impossible. Wasn't it? She hadn't taken her eyes off him for at least ten minutes. His arms were restrained. He hadn't put anything at all in his mouth except . . .

Twisting his neck, he fixed her with those blank eyes of his. Only they weren't totally blank anymore. There was real fear there. "Find the Man in the Maze," he wheezed the words into her ear just as Spense rushed through the door. The corners of Kramer's mouth twitched into a macabre smile. "Fuck me if I didn't do somebody right at the end." Then his body went limp.

Her legs lost all remaining strength, and she clutched the sheets, dragging them with her as she began a slow slide to the floor. "Help *him!*" she cried out, as Spense gathered her in his arms. "He's been poisoned!"

Chapter Five

WITH A HANDFUL of detectives from the Phoenix PD, a representative from the sheriff's office, and the NCAVC coordinator from the Bureau's Phoenix field office hanging off the walls, squatting on the floor, and sitting in the lone visitor chair, respectively, Caitlin's room looked more like a police command center than a hospital room. Spense leaned against the head of her bed, going for casual but probably coming across as hovering. But to hell with it. He'd saved her life, and the way he saw it, that gave him a right to hover—a right to care what happened to her, whether she liked it or not.

Fuck me if I didn't do somebody right in the end had turned out to be Judd Kramer's last words. After he uttered them, he'd gone into cardiac arrest. Valiant attempts to revive him had failed, and the State of Arizona would now be spared the expense of a trial and the execution that most likely would've followed. Kramer wouldn't be mourned by many, and probably no one would've much cared that he'd succumbed to his injuries had his skin not popped cherry red.

"Cyanide, you say? Now what exactly makes you think so, Dr. Cassidy?" Detective Riley Baskin wrinkled one side of his cheek and squeezed an eye shut, then pushed out his lower lip, clucked his tongue, raised his eyebrows, and proceeded to repeat the entire series of facial gymnastics. Spense figured he either had a tic disorder or he was skeptical.

Spense stuffed a pillow behind Caity's back, his hand lingering protectively near her shoulder. "I'm not sure Dr. Cassidy is up to this. She's already given a preliminary statement, so maybe we should let her rest and come back this evening."

"I'm okay, Spense. I'd like to do this now. If I get too tired"—she gave him a pointed look—"I can say so myself."

"I mean you're a psychiatrist, not an actual doctor, so how would you know what cyanide poisoning looks like?" Baskin went through more facial gyrations, transforming his appearance from baby-faced to wizened.

Spense's shoulders tensed. He didn't care for the detective's attitude. "What the hell, Baskin? Psychiatrists *are* actual doctors. They go to medical school. They go through internships, just like the rest of them. Dr. Cassidy went to fucking Stanford. Now, I'm asking you nicely to show a little more respect for the witness. She's been through hell, and she doesn't need attitude from a sorry little pissant like you."

"You got a funny way of asking nicely," Baskin fired back.

It'd been a stressful week, and Spense was running on little sleep and even less patience. He could feel his control slipping. One leg jittered, and he had that restless energy that always seemed to precede his saying or doing something he later regretted. From the corner of his eye, he saw Special Agent Gretchen Herrera, the NCAVC coordinator from the Phoenix field office, working her brow. Agent Herrera's job was to act as liaison between local law enforcement and the criminal investigative analysts on loan from the BAU. In other words, she was the go-between for Spense and the locals, and Spense's calling Baskin a pissant wasn't making Agent Herrera's job any easier. He'd make it a point to get some shut-eye at his next opportunity.

"I'm sure Detective Baskin didn't mean me any disrespect," Caity said. "It's a common misconception that psychiatrists don't have medical degrees, and I take absolutely no offense. Besides, in all my years of training, I never once saw a case of cyanide poisoning, so he makes a good point. The main reason I suspected cyanide is because I read detective novels. I'm a big fan of murder mysteries, you see." She shot Spense a look that wasn't as appreciative as he'd hoped it would've been. In retrospect, maybe he should have let her answer for herself, and he was already kicking himself for antagonizing Baskin.

Baskin made a throat-clearing noise and addressed Caity. "You like Harry Bosch?"

"He's one of my favorite detectives." She smiled sweetly at Baskin, and Spense felt the hair bristle on the back of his neck.

Baskin unfolded his arms and relaxed his stance. "Well, then, I'd like to get a quick account of what happened from you, Dr. Cassidy, and feel free to include any of your own conclusions." His glance slid sideways to Spense, then back to Caity. "If you feel up to it, I mean. We can bounce and come back later if you want."

"This is the perfect time, while everything's fresh in my mind. Let's see. Suppose I just start with my observations." Several of the little group that had assembled in the hospital room reached for notebooks and pens. Caity paused while everyone settled in. Spense took a seat on her bed and crooked his leg to form a makeshift table for his laptop. She looked surprisingly well, considering she'd collapsed only a few hours ago. Her body had to be sore from the fall, but she'd turned down any further pain medications. Caity was definitely a scrapper. He'd give her that, and with the narcotics starting to clear from her system, she seemed to be getting stronger by the minute.

"When I first entered the room, Kramer seemed tired . . . and this is important: His face and lips were pale. But he didn't seem to be in any immediate distress. He simply looked like a man who'd recently survived a bullet to the belly. Within moments, I noticed his respiratory rate pick up." She closed her eyes. "Then his skin began pinking up, which normally would be a good sign, only Kramer seemed to be feeling worse instead of better. We had a brief conversation, then his body started to tremble. That's when I buzzed his nurse." She placed a hand on her stomach, as if suddenly feeling ill. With effort, Spense refrained from shutting down the interview.

Baskin consulted his notepad. "As soon as he entered the room, you told Agent Spenser you believed Kramer had been poisoned."

"I did."

"Given all the other possible explanations for Kramer going into cardiac arrest, I'd say poisoning would be the last thing that would come to mind. Don't you agree?"

"Obviously not, or I wouldn't have suggested it. His emesis—"

"His what?"

"His *vomit* smelled faintly of almonds. Now, I'll admit I've never smelled cyanide before, but I know it's supposed to have an almond scent—I read that in my novels. And the redness of the skin, I know from my med-school days, is the result of increased venous oxygen content . . . when it's due to cyanide ingestion."

"English please—for us *pissants* if you don't mind."

But Baskin had said pissant with a smile, and his face had stopped that ridiculous twitching. There was a glimmer of humor in his eyes, contrasting a hard determination. Spense wondered if he might be an okay guy after all.

"With cyanide poisoning, the body can't extract the oxygen that's meant for the tissues. So the oxygen remains in the venous blood, lending it a vivid red color," Caity explained.

"Well, we know it wasn't cyanide *gas* that got him, or you'd be dead, too. Did you see him put anything in his mouth?"

"The nurse gave him several pills before leaving the room."

"Anybody talked to the nurse yet?" Baskin addressed the others.

"She's up next on the interview list," the deputy squatting on the floor responded.

Baskin turned back to Caity. "You didn't see Kramer take anything himself, later, after the nurse left?"

Agent Herrera was nodding her agreement. "Let's say this does turn out to be cyanide. Sometimes that's a preferred method of suicide for those cowards who can't face the consequences of their actions." Her glance found Baskin. "Remember that arsonist a few years back? When his verdict came down, he crammed a cyanide pill in his mouth right there in the courtroom. Died within minutes."

"Exactly. Why couldn't Kramer have had the pill hidden on him? Popped it into his mouth somehow when you weren't looking?" Baskin persisted.

Caity shook her head. "Not possible. Kramer's arms were restrained. Nothing went into his mouth except the meds the nurse administered. Besides, if this were a suicide attempt, I expect he would've deliberately bitten into rather than swallowed the pill."

"How do you know he didn't?"

She paused, as if winded.

Jumping to her aid, Spense filled in for her, "If he'd bitten into a cyanide pill, death would've occurred much more rapidly— almost immediately. Assuming the nurse gave him the poison, his death took between five and ten minutes. So he must've swallowed not chewed, and that argues against suicide and supports the idea of homicide—presuming of course the autopsy confirms the presence of cyanide."

"Let me get this straight, Spense. You're asking me to believe Kramer's nurse walked into his hospital room, and right in front of God and everybody, poisoned the dickhead with cyanide. That's hard to swallow." Baskin grinned, looking around the room as if waiting for someone to get the joke.

"I understand your cynicism, Detective. But yes, I believe that's the only logical explanation given these circumstances. Cyanide acts too quickly for it to have been given beforehand. Now if you're asking me if I believe the nurse had *knowledge* she was administering cyanide—I don't. We'll need to rule out that possibility though."

"You think someone switched Kramer's pills. I assume the hospital has certain safeguards in place. So how the hell could something like that happen and nobody know?"

"You got me. We're gonna need to know more about hospital procedure to figure that out. Can you shed any light, Dr. Cassidy?" He was deliberately formal with Caity in front of the officers, setting the tone for them to show her respect.

Her smile rewarded him for his consideration. "Every hospital has its own unique policies and safeguards, so I'd suggest you check with the charge nurse, and the pharmacy, too. But I did see Kramer's nurse scan the packet of pills and his wristband before she gave him his medication. I assume she was matching the code on the packet to Kramer's hospital ID. The nurse was clearly following a protocol. I'm certain she wasn't at fault."

"Who is or isn't doing her job is the hospital's concern, not mine. I just care about how the cyanide got into Kramer's mouth." Baskin said something else beneath his breath, but stopped midgrumble as the door swung open and Jenny entered the room, wheeling a portable computer in front of her.

Jenny's face flushed at the sudden silence. It was as though she'd interrupted a group of gossips and believed herself to be the hot topic. Maybe she'd overheard them and assumed they were discussing her instead of Kramer's attendant, Belinda. "Sorry to interrupt, but it's time for Dr. Cassidy's Tegretol. Past time. I would've waited for you . . . people . . . to clear out, but it's beyond overdue, and my tush is on the line if she doesn't get her medication."

Caity seemed to be considering. Jenny was sporting her don't-be-a-pain-in-my-ass look, and Spense knew the easiest thing for Caity to do would be to take the Tegretol. But he'd heard her tell Jenny earlier that she didn't want it. "I'm sorry, but I'm not going to take it. I discussed this with my neurologist—"

"I did what you asked already." Jenny interrupted. "I checked with the neuro on call, and your doctor left him no instructions about discontinuing the medication. So what Dr. Bentley would like you to do is go ahead and take your Tegretol now, then tomorrow we can clarify the situation when your doctor, Dr. Singer, is back." Jenny's hands went to her hips for emphasis.

"Hang on." Spense jumped up and stalked across the room, then removed a pair of green latex gloves from a box on the wall. Kramer had just been poisoned, possibly by his nurse, Belinda. Now Jenny was here with a medication for Caity—one that should have been discontinued. "May I see what you have, please?"

Jenny handed over a plastic packet containing a single pill.

"How do you know this is Tegretol?" Spense turned the bag in his gloved hands, inspecting it.

Her chin came up. "Because it says so, right there on the label. I'll scan it of course, but I don't see—"

"Scan it now please."

Jenny frowned, pulled a handheld scanning gun from her pocket, waved it over the package, then Caity's wristband. Next, she checked the computer screen. "It matches. This is Dr. Cassidy's Tegretol," she said, with a defensive rise in her voice.

"Where did you get it?"

"The pharmacy sent it up." Her eyes widened. "You think there's a problem with the medication. I haven't done anything wrong, and I don't like the implication that I might've made a mistake."

Spense tilted his head. "I don't think you made a mistake, Jenny." He lowered his voice persuasively. "You know I think highly of you. But this is important, and I need to understand how this process works. Okay?"

Jenny nodded, but her smile was gone and her hands shook a little as she put the scanner back in her scrubs pocket. "Sorry. It's just there's a lot of talk going around and I . . . well, never mind. Ask what you need. I'm here to help." She looked up through her lashes at Spense, and he held back his smile. He and Jenny had developed a friendship. He'd flirted openly with her in front of

Caity earlier today, but it had been a jackass move—one he didn't plan on repeating.

"Does someone bring the medications up to the floor?" Spense asked.

"Not usually. The normal way is that the pharmacy tubes the meds up to the unit, then . . ." Jenny looked around the room, blinking nervously.

"You're doing fine, Jenny. So *normally* the meds come up through the tube system. What about this packet right here? Was this delivered in the usual way?"

"N-no. The unit clerk said the tube system jammed, and a pharmacy tech brought this up."

"Do you know if any other medications were hand-delivered to the floor?"

"I'm not sure." Her throat worked in a long swallow. "People are saying Judd Kramer might've been . . . murdered. Is it true?"

Spense gave Jenny a particularly gentle look. "I'm not at liberty to discuss it. Now then, no one is suggesting you've done anything wrong. But let me be clear. Whatever pill is inside this packet, Tegretol or no Tegretol, Dr. Cassidy isn't taking it." He extended his hand toward the door. "Thanks, Jenny. You've been superhelpful."

She pulled her lower lip between her teeth. "Okay, well, I guess you want me to go now." When no one contradicted her, Jenny eased out the door, and Spense turned to Baskin.

"Get this to the crime lab, will you please?"

Baskin snapped on a pair of gloves. "On this particular matter, I gotta agree with you, Spense." He had one foot out the door when he turned back and grinned. "Don't get used to it."

As Spense watched Baskin exit the room, on his way to take *Caity's* medicine to the crime lab, his chest constricted. Just because the Tegretol hadn't arrived via the tube system was no reason to think someone was trying to poison Caity. The system probably jammed all the time, but . . . there were plenty of other reasons to worry. If Caity was right, and Kramer had been poisoned, they'd know soon enough—once the autopsy and lab reports were back. He pulled off his gloves and was about to offer to go for coffee when the door flew open and Baskin burst back in, face grim, cell in hand.

Caitlin swung her legs around, like she was ready to bound off the bed. "What's happened?"

Baskin put up his hand in a stop sign. "Stay put, Dr. Cassidy. You're safer here for now. Thompson, plant your ass outside this door, and don't let anyone in, and I mean *no one*. Not nurses, not doctors either. Miller and Jenkins, come with me. We got a DB in the hospital basement."

"DB? Is that . . ." Caity's voice trailed off.

"Dead body. Pharmacy tech got her throat slashed." Baskin fired a look at Spense. "It gets worse. After our killer nearly cut her head clean off, he posed her naked body and carved out a piece of skull for a souvenir."

For an instant, stunned silence paralyzed the room. Then Spense and Caity asked in unison, "Was it the temporal bone?"

Chapter Six

Thursday, September 12
Federal Bureau of Investigation Field Office
Phoenix, Arizona

"I'D LIKE TO see the thumbprint." Caity stood at a narrow window in an interview room on the fifth floor of the Phoenix FBI field office. "May I open the blinds?"

"Sorry." Spense rushed to her side. "Safety regulations say the blinds stay closed."

Disappointment flitted across her face. "What's the point in having an outdoor rock garden that looks like a thumbprint from above if no one is allowed to open the blinds and look down on it?"

He shrugged one shoulder. "The cool factor. Or sheer vanity, maybe. I hear the architect used his own thumbprint."

That made her smile, and Caity's smile was a far more impressive sight than the field-office rock garden. At least to him. Spense had spent a lot of time picturing that smile while Caity lay in her hospital bed, unconscious. He'd waited hours at a time, day after day, for her to open her eyes, look at him, and smile, then fall back into a drugged sleep. And here she was now, standing on her own two feet, like a big-eyed kid on a field trip asking to look out the window at the thumbprint—and all he could do was give her some lame reason why it wasn't allowed—if you could call national security a lame reason. "Hey, come over here." He gestured to his laptop on the long mahogany table in the center of the room. "I'll show you a satellite view of the garden. You can see the thumbprint that way."

"Can't we just peek though the blinds? Wouldn't that be okay?"

"I'm sorry, but tell you what. When we finish up here, I'll take you for a ground-level tour of the garden. We'll grab a lunch and picnic outside."

"Awesome." Here came that field-trip smile again.

He wished he'd taken more care to cultivate a friendship with her before she'd gotten shot. The truth was he'd always liked her—a lot. But he wasn't used to a woman shooting him down in private, then showing him up in court. Over the years, throwing barbs at each other had become a habit, and it had taken Caity nearly dying to make him realize she deserved better and how much he wanted to protect her. His gaze found hers and hung on. Her eyes reminded him of the water that pooled at the base of Havasu Falls. They were the same dramatic blue. He'd only been to Havasupai, the little Shangri-La at the bottom of the Grand Canyon, once, but he'd never forgotten that otherworldly hue. Caity's eyes took him back there—to a place that made him feel refreshed and connected to the universe. He was still staring into her eyes when Agent Herrera walked in and cleared her throat conspicuously.

"Let's all have a seat."

Herrera wasn't his boss, but she was in communication with

his boss, the ASAC back at the BAU in Virginia. Since Phoenix was Herrera's turf, her recommendations would carry a lot of weight. Spense gave a nod of cooperation, then noticed Caity moving gingerly as she made her way to the conference table. He slid a chair out for her and took the adjacent seat while Herrera took her place across from them both.

"Great to see you out of the hospital, Dr. Cassidy. Are you feeling well enough for a meeting?"

"Absolutely." Then she nodded. "Please, call me Caitlin."

"If you'll call me Gretchen. I wish I could open the blinds, Caitlin. You see, there's a rock garden below, and from above it looks like a—"

"A thumbprint. She knows. A thumbprint she's not allowed to see because opening the blinds is prohibited." It made sense to keep them closed. Spense knew his irritation was uncalled for, but he was feeling a bit like a kid himself, and he wanted to watch Caity's face when she saw the garden.

"Spense can give you a limited tour of the grounds in a bit. But for now, I have some news and a few things to discuss. First off, you should know that the lab tested the Tegretol with your name on it, Caitlin, and the pill did in fact turn out to be a cyanide tablet."

Spense's fists tightened at his side, but he kept his face expressionless. As did Caity. Herrera might as well have told them she'd had bologna for lunch. Nobody reacted. Caity was obviously practiced at playing it cool. A master of self-control, she would've made a killer Dalai Lama. She was unshakable . . . except he could still hear her plea, still feel her hand clinging to his.

Don't let me fall.

He'd asked her to trust him, and he'd sworn to himself he'd

not only keep her safe, he'd catch the bastard who'd hurt her, no matter how long it took.

"I expected it would prove to be cyanide." Caity's calm voice brought his attention back to the conversation. "What about Judd Kramer?"

Herrera nodded. "The M.E. listed his cause of death as cardiopulmonary arrest secondary to cyanide poisoning. Manner of death—homicide. If the UNSUB hadn't attempted to poison you, too, the M.E. might have ruled Kramer's death a suicide. But given that, along with the dead pharmacy tech found posed in the hospital basement, I'm afraid there's no question about it. We have a very dangerous and very determined criminal still at large, so I'm going to need you to stick like glue to Agent Spenser for the time being."

Caity didn't protest. She'd already agreed to stay at his place, accepting informal protection from him. As he'd anticipated, she'd come to her senses once the danger was clear. Caity might be stubborn, but she wasn't stupid. Leaning forward, she folded her hands on the table, her jumping little finger the only sign she was affected by the news that a stone-cold killer had her in his sights. "Will the rest of the task force be joining us soon?"

Pulling a gray knit sweater loosely over her white tailored blouse, Herrera smiled. She tucked a strand of sleek, naturally blond hair, cut in a clean, stylish bob, behind one ear. Gretchen Herrera was a striking Hispanic woman. Her skin was honey brown, her eyes a dark, polished onyx. She was almost as tall as Spense—over six feet—with a body made of pure, lean muscle and legs up to her eyeballs. She never wore makeup or tight clothing, but that did little to deter the male agents from ogling her. "No. It's just going to be us today."

From her question, Spense understood that Caity had expected the other members of the task force to attend the meeting today. She'd accepted his invitation to help develop a profile for the shooter-slasher-poisoner, just like he'd known she eventually would. Now the determined looked on her face and her eager questions, signaled to Spense, she was in this for the long haul. Not surprising. After all, her father's old friend had been murdered, and another man, criminal though he might have been, had died before her eyes. And Caity had been quick to note the killer's signature, *removing a piece of temporal bone,* was the same for both Sally Cartwright and Darlene Dillinger—the pharmacy tech. That had to have set the wheels in her head spinning. But the cherry on top, the bit that made Spense one hundred percent confident Caity's change of heart would last, was that Judd Kramer had given her a personal gift, a mysterious clue whispered directly in her ear. Of course she wanted in on the investigation. A smile tugged at his mouth, but he suppressed it. At this point, if he hadn't already invited her, Caity probably would've begged him to let her in on the case, and the prospect of working *with* her instead of against her pleased him more than a little.

"Why won't the others be joining us?" Her lips parted slightly, and he had to look away to keep his concentration on the topic at hand.

Herrera leveled an intent look at Caity. "Because at this stage of the game we don't want to contaminate the process. If you're going to be part of this, your first lesson is that a good profiler starts from the crime and works backward, not from the suspect forward. If I bring a bunch of detectives in here, and they start jawing about who they like for the murders, that could skew your profile. And a bad profile could throw the investigation way off course."

"I think I see. We don't want to come up with a profile to fit our suspect. We want to come up with a suspect who fits our profile."

"Exactly. However, once you've constructed a profile, we may throw the suspects at you and let you tell us who sticks, but first, we need that uncontaminated work product."

"I have to admit that in a warped kind of way I'm looking forward to this." Caity's voice contained a note of controlled enthusiasm.

Spense sent Herrera an I-told-you-so look. He enjoyed nothing more than solving a good puzzle, the tougher the better, and Caity—she was cut from the same cloth whether she knew it or not.

Herrera ignored his look, keeping her focus on Caity. "This isn't going to be easy, Caitlin. You understand what we're asking you to do?"

Spense chimed in, "We're asking you to put yourself inside the mind of a killer, and that can be a very dark place." He warned her, because he knew Herrera expected him to, but he also knew Caity had placed herself inside the minds of killers before. From what he'd heard, in her quest to differentiate the innocent from the guilty, she'd talked to almost as many murderers as the entire group of FBI investigators assigned to the Serial Murder Study. She was driven to understand the criminal mind, and the reason wasn't hard to figure—at least not for Spense. Caity wanted to be able to recognize a killer by his psyche because she needed to be one hundred percent certain her father hadn't been one. Unfortunately, Spense wasn't at all sure that was the case.

"I'm fully prepared to place myself in the killer's head, to see the world from his perspective. I'll eat breathe and sleep the UNSUB if it will help. In fact, I'm prepared to do *whatever* it takes to help catch this . . . bastard." Even her expletives were uttered in a soft, collected voice.

"Great. Then I just need to clear up one other matter before I give you two my blessing."

If Herrera hadn't had his full attention before, she did now. "What other matter?"

"Not to worry. Caitlin's got her security clearance, and we've got the thumbs-up to bring her in as an outside consultant. I can have the contracts ready to sign within the hour."

"Then what's the problem?" he asked, impatience coming through in his tone. This was his boss's call, not Herrera's.

"I hope there isn't one." Herrera spread her arms as if she were gathering them all together into a huddle. "The decision rests with your ASAC at the BAU, but *if* I'm going to recommend this partnership to him, I need to know the exact nature of your relationship."

"No relationship," he and Caity said in unison.

Herrera's eyebrows inched up, and she sent them a dubiously tilted gaze. "Okay, then I need to know the exact nature of your *nonrelationship*."

He glanced at Caity and tried to telegraph that the ball was in her court. However she wanted to spin it, he'd go along.

"Spense invited me to his bed, and I declined." No blush colored Caity's cheeks. No hesitation punctuated her words.

Apparently, she didn't want to spin it any way at all.

"Under what circumstance? Are there unresolved issues between you?" Herrera asked.

"It was four years ago. Spense and I happened to sit next to each other at a lecture at Johns Hopkins. The topic was spree killers versus mass murderers—romantic, don't you think? We introduced ourselves, exchanged a few polite comments, and learned we were both staying at the Belvedere, so we shared a cab back to the hotel."

Spense kicked back in his chair and stretched his legs, more than a little curious to hear Caity's version of what he'd come to think of as *the incident.*

"We had a drink in the bar—and I'm sure you can figure the rest."

Caity hadn't been drunk, but she had been sporting a buzz. She'd been relaxed and half-giddy, and if he'd only known what a departure that was for her, he would've tried to appreciate it more. As he recalled, she'd laughed at his jokes—all of them. Tugging at his collar, he forced himself not to stare at her hands, which were now folded on the tabletop, one little finger offering the occasional twitch. He doubted she was aware of that tiny tell of hers.

"Later, it turned out we were both in town consulting on the same case. Discussing the matter further would've put us in an awkward situation, and I certainly wasn't interested in pursuing a social relationship with Spense after that, so we simply agreed to put the matter behind us and proceed as if it never happened."

"*We* never agreed to anything. When I found out Caity and I were on the same case, I thought we should clear the air. But she wouldn't take my calls. And yes, it's affected our present relationship." He turned to Caity. "You can't hide from Herrera. She's like a human lie detector."

"I'm not hiding anything." Caity pushed to her feet, defiantly, if a little slowly. "I have the utmost respect for Agent Spenser. He saved my life, for goodness' sake, and I'd be pleased to be part of the investigation. I see no reason why a personal incident that happened four years ago should prevent us from partnering up professionally. *I* have no hard feelings."

It was on the tip of his tongue to make a snappy comeback about how hard his feelings were, but he bit it back. "No problem on my part either. I'm eager to take advantage of Dr. Cassidy's expertise."

"You're going to be staying in the same apartment. Please, make sure that's all you take advantage of. People talk, and I'd hate to find out after the fact that I made the stupid decision to recommend putting two people together who can't keep things professional. So don't make me look like an ass with the BAU, Spense. I've worked too hard to have you screw up my chances of making profiler because you can't keep it in your pants."

"Thank you, Gretchen, but I don't need you to admonish Spense on my behalf. I can look out for myself."

Herrera's eyebrows didn't inch up this time. They jumped to her hairline. "My mistake. I see that now. So, if you're both certain, let's get started." She shoved several large manila envelopes across the table. "I've put together a set of comprehensive case materials. You're going to need this to generate a profile for the task force. Inside, you'll find a synopsis of the crime and the environment at the time of the crime, autopsy and forensics reports . . ."

"What do you mean by a synopsis of the environment?" Caity's interest seemed to have shifted entirely to the case and away from him.

"Weather, the political and socioeconomic climate. There's also in-depth background information on all the victims, but we're hoping you'll fill in even more on Judd Kramer, based on your clinical interviews. And you'll also have access to the medical examiner's findings and conclusions. That should be enough to get you started. I'll expect a preliminary profile by tomorrow."

"Tomorrow. Sure, I don't see why we can't have everything analyzed by then." Hands at her side, he saw Caity's little finger jerk.

Spense leaned over and offered a handshake to his new partner. "Welcome to the world of criminal investigative analysis, Caity."

Herrera said her good-byes and was making her way toward the door, when she turned to send them a considered look. "And guys, try not to get too distracted by this Man in the Maze business. Just work the profile, the way you know how. Lives depend on you getting it right."

Chapter Seven

Thursday, September 12
Tuscan Meadows
Phoenix, Arizona

A PARTIALLY OPENED door and the strains of Taylor Swift welcomed Dizzy Leonard to the party. Filling her lungs with a deep breath of courage, she pushed her shoulder against the ornately carved wood and dared step foot inside Lila Busby's home.

She invited you.

That's what Mom'd said, and Mom wouldn't lie. Her mother's happy face had told her it was true. This wasn't some mean-girl gag. She'd really and truly been invited to Lila's sixteenth birthday. And now here she was with the ceramic kitten she'd bought with money she'd earned pooper-scooping Mrs. Grogan's yard, wrapped in shiny red paper and tied with blue ribbon. The blue ribbon would distract from the Christmas paper, and though Dizzy had worried the gift might be too juvenile, she'd heard from Andy Bower that Lila loved ceramic kittens. Lila had an entire collection of porcelain felines according to him. The thought that Andy would lie was as inconceivable to Dizzy as the thought of Mom lying. He just wouldn't, that's all.

She smoothed back her short hair, glad she'd taken the time to straighten it for once. Remembering how its usual mousy brown had gleamed in the mirror when she was done, she resolved to keep up her appearance better from now on. The nervous, fluttery feeling that had taken over her stomach when Mom let her out of the car was still there, but this was a case of mind over matter. Mom wanted her to have friends. She wanted to have friends. And now, for the first time since she'd taken those pills, the girls at school were giving her a chance. She bent the stiff corners of her mouth into a smile, raised her chin, and walked straight into the most beautiful living room she'd ever seen—except in a magazine, of course.

Columns had been painted onto the walls, creating the illusion they held up the high ceilings. The marble coffee table had fancy claw legs, and there were big, colored urns everywhere. Dizzy had never seen so many urns . . . and the window coverings . . . Dizzy put a hand on her heart.

Real drapes.

At home, the curtains were so thin you could see right through them, and Dizzy had to hide in the bathroom to change clothes. Lila Busby's family was rich. Lila was as pretty and popular as Dizzy was . . . not. Lila had fake columns and real drapes. But what really gave Dizzy that less-than feeling was the fact that Lila Busby had Andy Bower. Their names even sounded good together. Dizzy's smile tightened. That was okay. She just wanted to have friends, so Mom would stop worrying. And Andy wasn't exactly within her reach anyway.

As she psyched herself up to walk through the room toward the sounds of voices and music, she felt a hand on the small of her back and jumped, nearly dropping her gift.

"Is that the kitten?" Andy took the box from her hand and turned it around, examining it.

Breathless, Dizzy nodded. She tried not to, but she couldn't help staring at the long black lashes that framed Andy's ice blue eyes. His face was manly enough for the longest lashes. He could wear fake ones and still not look like a sissy. Andy gave the box a shake, and she reached out, not wanting him to break the kitten.

"Don't worry, Diz. She's gonna love it. C'mon. The party's this way." He tweaked her nose, set the gift on a table crowded with boxes and bows, and tugged on her hand.

She barely remembered the short walk to the kitchen. Andy had her by the hand, and she could feel her palm sweating, her arm trembling all the way to her shoulder. Taylor Swift was still on, and it was almost like she was singing to *them*.

Almost.

As soon as Andy caught sight of Lila, standing over by the chips and dip, he jerked his hand away from Dizzy and went to slip his arm around Lila's waist. The house was big, but it seemed the whole party had crowded into the kitchen, and the conversation buzzed loudly in her ears. Between that and the music, she couldn't make out what Andy said to Lila. Then her body went stiff, and her throat constricted. She *could* hear what Lila was saying, shouting really, just fine.

"What the fuck is she doing in my house?" Lila had a big piece of cake on a small paper plate in her hand. She stuck a plastic fork in the cake and headed straight over to Dizzy. "What the fuck are you doing here?" Lila repeated.

"I-I . . . Happy birthday, Lila." She pointed to the gift table in the living room. "I brought you a present."

For a moment, Lila looked like she might be glad to see Dizzy after all. "What is it?"

"A kitten. For your collection." Dizzy's shoulders lowered from where they'd risen around her ears. Lila liked kittens. And she'd *invited* her. There was nothing to worry about.

"O.M.G." Lila looked around the room. "A toy kitten. Guys, Dumb Dizzy got me a fucking toy kitten."

Dizzy heard more buzzing in her ears. Andy was bent at the waist laughing. A lot of the kids were laughing, but not Lila. Lila was scowling and pointing to the door with one hand, her paper plate wobbling in the other. "Get the fuck out, loser!"

Dizzy's chin dropped, and she felt tears welling in her eyes. She started to go, but then hesitated and turned back to Lila, suddenly filled with the need to speak up for herself. "You *invited* me," she whispered.

Lila showed her teeth, like some wild angry animal. "I wouldn't invite a loser who tags after my boyfriend . . . like a *kitten*. My mother sent that invitation because your mother told the principal you don't have any friends." Lila raised the hand that held her plate.

A sick premonition of what Lila was about to do came over Dizzy, but she didn't feel like standing up for herself anymore. So she didn't. She just stood there and waited for Lila to smash the plate into her face.

"Bye-bye, Dizzy. I hope you enjoyed your cake."

Chapter Eight

Thursday, September 12
Rutherford Towers
Phoenix, Arizona

SPENSE HAD SETTLED Caitlin on his couch with a knit throw his mother had given him over her legs and three pillows behind her back. She would've argued it wasn't necessary to make a fuss, but this was her first day out of the hospital, and she'd been on her feet most of the day. It really did feel good to take the weight off. The two-bedroom apartment the Bureau had found for Spense was small but well suited for their needs.

He hadn't been kidding about the extra security. They'd not only had to swipe a pass card to enter, they'd had to stop and sign in with a guard on the first floor, then use a different card to access the elevator. Cameras scanned every inch of the building's public areas. Were it not for the fact the killer had already proven his cunning at evading security, she would've felt quite at ease here. But as matters stood, until this UNSUB was in custody, she wouldn't feel truly safe anywhere.

Her eyes came to rest on her pistol, which she'd placed within reach on the coffee table. From the day her father had been designated as a person of interest in the Falconer murder, her family had started receiving death threats. Even before she was of legal age, her mother had given her a revolver. Caitlin had carried that revolver for a few years, then traded it in for a semiautomatic pistol—and she'd never looked back. Her current defensive weapon of choice was an easy-to-conceal Ruger LCP. With a barrel length under three inches and a loaded weight of under a pound, it fit her hand and was small enough to stash in her purse with room left over for a lipstick—or in her case, a Chapstick. She wasn't a crack shot, and her subcompact pistol wasn't going to drop a criminal from any distance, but up close and personal, she felt confident she could hit her mark. A heavy sigh lifted her chest, but she held on to it. Ironic that after all these years, her life was once again in danger over a crime she had no part in because yet another outraged citizen felt the need to take the law into his hands.

Except . . . something about the vigilante theory didn't feel right. *Don't get distracted by the Man in the Maze.* That's what Special Agent Gretchen Herrera had advised. But Caitlin's mind kept returning to Kramer's whispered words.

Since she had absolutely no idea who or what the Man in the Maze could be, it wasn't likely the profiling process would be contaminated merely by taking Kramer's words into account. She wasn't a criminal investigative analyst by trade, but she didn't agree with Gretchen on this particular point. Judd Kramer had given them a clue that was intriguing enough to be straight out of one of Harry Bosch's case files. Maybe Baskin and his crew hadn't been as interested in this nugget as she thought they might have been, and maybe Herrera had warned them off the topic altogether for now, but she and Spense were about to brainstorm, and to Caitlin that meant every clue, every detail of the case was up for discussion. One thing she knew for certain about the brain: censoring ideas was the surest way to thwart insight and understanding.

Spense wheeled a standing whiteboard into the living room, and it fit right in with the stark, businesslike tone of the apartment. Polished maple gleamed on the floors, bright light flooded the room from on high, and the furniture was modern industrial. Tucking the warm, mom-made throw tighter around her legs, she sent Spense an impatient smile and watched as he unpacked markers and notepads, then powered up his laptop.

In her hands, she held one of Gretchen's packets. Her pulse surged as she opened it and removed a synopsis of the crimes. Her palms were sweaty, her heart was beating fast, and her fingers tingled in anticipation of creating her first ever profile. The brain was a remarkable organ, and no subject interested her more. But understanding the derailment of human behavior into the realm of criminality wasn't just curiosity for her. It wasn't a hobby, or even a profession—it was a compulsion. A chill sank into her bones. She simply couldn't stop herself from shoveling down into the darkness, no matter how personally painful the dig. She had to know *why*. What would make a man go so terribly wrong? She needed to be able to differentiate an innocent man from a killer because if she couldn't tell the difference, she'd never be able to trust in anyone again. She shivered as a father's words to his young daughter came back to her:

Hold on tight, Caity. Trust me.

She needed to believe in her father.

And so she kept on digging, deeper and deeper into the darkness—a strange way of searching for the light, perhaps, but it was all she knew to do. For years, she'd immersed herself in the study of deviant behavior, but her tools were limited. She needed new perspectives, new methodologies. To date, she'd only seen the criminal process from the psychiatrist's side of a case. But working with Spense would give her a chance to observe how the other half lived.

A bloody shoeprint in the courthouse conference room had been identified as originating from a Ferragamo, and the task force now referred to the entire case by that name. Although the primary legwork for *Ferragamo* would be carried out by the police and the sheriff's office, Caitlin would have a chance to familiarize herself with police reports and watch a keen investigator in action. Spense might be a profiler now, but like most criminal analysts, he'd been a field agent prior to moving over to the BAU, and from what she'd heard, he'd been one of the best. He *knew* how to work a case, and she was suddenly itching to learn from him.

Germinating just below the surface of her mind was a tiny seed of hope; acquiring investigative skills meant she'd be in a better position to solve the Falconer case on her own. And one thing was certain: Absolutely no one else was interested in looking back on a crime that had been put to bed so definitively.

The detectives who'd worked Gail Falconer's murder were convinced they'd gotten their man—her father. The Innocence Project had to prioritize their cases, and a man on death row would always rank higher than a man who'd already been put in the ground. One after the other, the slew of private investigators she'd hired had come up empty. At this point, she had only two choices left. Find the real killer and bring him to justice herself, or let go of the past, knowing that proving her father's innocence would never bring him back to her. Now the sigh she'd been holding in finally released.

Letting go was no option at all.

Spense, apparently done with his preparations, interrupted her reverie. "Can I get you a drink? Something to eat before we get started? We may be in for a long night."

She realized he was trying to be polite, but if this was going to be her temporary home, she'd rather not be treated like a guest. And she didn't want Spense taking on the role of nursemaid in addition to bodyguard. "Thanks for offering, but if I need something, I'll get off this couch and get it myself. Last time I looked, I still had the two legs."

"Those two legs gave out on you less than seventy-two hours ago. I seem to remember scooping you off the floor of Judd Kramer's hospital room." He grinned sideways at her. "But hey, have it your way. You wanna keep falling down, I'll just keep picking you back up."

That settled, he widened his stance, and her gaze went to his bare feet. She'd never seen Spense in jeans and a T-shirt. He looked like a regular guy. A regular *ripped* guy. Her stomach dipped, and she hurriedly refocused on the whiteboard. Nothing says *good times* like dry-erase markers and a table covered with crime-scene photos. An electrifying tingle, entirely unrelated to the way Spense filled out a T-shirt, swept down her spine. There was a reason her home was piled high with detective stories. Above all else, just about, she loved a good mystery.

"The Man in the Maze." She pointed at the board. "Don't forget to put that up."

Spense pulled out a dry-erase marker and wrote *Man in the Maze* in small print on the bottom right corner of the board. What the deuce? Surely she couldn't be the only person on the case who thought Kramer's dying declaration was important. "I'd put that up top if I were you. That way we can branch off from Kramer's clue. Down there in the corner, there's no room for corollaries."

"I knew you'd turn out to be a micromanager." Spense did a face-palm. "Tell you what. I'll circle the *Man in the Maze* in red to signify its importance, and I promise we'll come back to it. But that's not where we need to begin."

Swallowing her eagerness, she resolved to listen first and speak later. She definitely had her own ideas about things, but she was also here to learn.

Spense scrawled the word *Profile* at the top of the board, where she had intended the Man in the Maze to go. "Once again, *it's not our job to come up with a suspect*. We've got less than twenty-four hours to create a profile of the UNSUB, so the police know what type of animal they're looking for."

"Right." She rubbed her fingers together, realizing she had little idea of where to start, despite the fact she had been reading up on profiling. "So we'll be interpreting the mind-set of the killer, whether he's organized or disorganized, and speculating as to his intelligence and educational background . . . any likely psychopathology."

Spense nodded. "I see you've done your homework. You're going to be a tremendous help, especially in the crazy department."

"Psychopathology department."

"You say potato . . ."

Her mood was upbeat. Solving a puzzle with Spense held a

certain appeal—*sex appeal,* a little voice whispered. She wet her lips. No harm in enjoying his company, as long as she kept her boundaries firm.

"Anyway, as I was about to say, we also need to determine things like estimated age, gender, and ethnicity. Even geographic location."

His words put her back on track but also gave her pause. How were they going to determine the killer's age, or geographic location? How many times had she scoffed when a prosecutor stood before a jury and made outlandish, unsupported claims: *The killer is a twenty-three-year-old white male who lives within a three-mile radius of Tenth and Vine. He drives a red Camaro and recently had his oil changed using a Groupon. He flosses his teeth in the mornings, but not at night.* Next would come the kicker: *And therefore, you must find the defendant guilty as charged.*

Spense made a fulcrum of his fingers and wobbled a marker between them. "I know what you're thinking, Caity. But the Bureau's amassed a lot of epidemiological data—statistics we can put to use to help construct the most accurate profile possible. Anytime you feel we don't have the goods to make a claim, just shout it out, and I'll fall in line. Not looking to railroad the wrong guy here."

Statistics sounded good to her. She was an empiricist to her very core. Whether it was because of what had happened to her father, or simply because of her scientific training, she *needed* facts to support her conclusions.

"Relax, Caity. I promise you. We're not going to sit around and pull a profile out our asses. This is too important. If we make a mistake, that could send the investigation off course, and the UNSUB could get away with murder. We'll have to make use of our experiences and instincts at some point in order to build a complete profile, but I'd suggest we begin with some cold hard facts. Then we can go off on a wild hair later if it's warranted."

If by wild hair he meant the Man in the Maze, she wasn't going to argue. "Okay. I'm guessing the killer's age would be something you could use epidemiologic data to estimate."

"Bull's-eye." He drew a target-shaped circle on the board. "Unfortunately, age is one of the hardest inputs for a profile, and in this case, it's even more difficult to determine than usual."

"In what way?"

"Epidemiology tells us an UNSUB usually chooses victims similar in age and ethnicity to himself. Unfortunately, in this case . . . the victimology is problematic. There's too much discrepancy among the targets to make their ages a useful predictor. How do we pigeonhole the UNSUB with victims ranging in age from their late twenties to their late fifties? Now ethnicity is easier. I think it's safe to assume the UNSUB is Caucasian, since all the victims were."

When he wrote *Caucasian Male* in the upper-left-hand corner, she nodded her agreement. She hadn't seen the shooter's face . . . or had she? She couldn't remember, and yet her gut was pinging, confirming they were on the right track. It was possible she had seen his face, and it would all eventually come back to her. Maybe her gut was telling her something her memory refused to reveal. Suddenly, she had an idea about how to estimate the killer's age.

"It's true, the victims varied in age, but we both agree Judd Kramer was the *primary* target." Labeling herself a victim left a bad taste in her mouth, but if they were going to do this, she couldn't let emotion get in the way. She didn't have to live her life like a victim, no matter what had happened in that courthouse, but for purposes of this profile, that's exactly what she was. Her vital statistics, her social history, her *secrets* might figure into this case, and they had to be taken into account the same as all the other victims'. To stop her little finger from twitching, she clasped her hands in front. "Wouldn't it make sense to assume the UNSUB is more similar to Kramer than to the other targets?" The admiring look Spense aimed her way made her chest puff. She was getting the hang of this.

"That's just exactly what I was going to propose. That we use Kramer as our primary prototype, with the understanding, of course, that we're making an assumption, and the profile may need to be adjusted. So there's our beginning—we already have the UNSUB's likely race, age, and gender. Gender is typically easy to figure. A crime like this one was almost certainly committed by a male. Besides, we have an eyewitness, who actually saw the shooter—you."

"I only saw shoes. It's possible the killer could've been a woman disguised as a man."

"But you told Baskin you thought you'd seen a man, and even though you don't remember seeing his face, your first instinct is the most likely to be correct. Besides which, the UNSUB used a gun and a knife on his victims. Statistically speaking, our UNSUB is likely to be a male."

Something was clicking in her brain. "Sticking with the shoes for a moment, I'd add upper-middle class, employed, and college-educated."

A grin spread across Spense's face.

She supposed he understood how she'd come to that conclusion, but to double-check her reasoning, she explained. "We know, from the bloody footprint, the shoes I saw were Ferragamos—expensive, but not so expensive they're out of reach of someone who cares about making an impression—the kind of shoes a professional wears. Someone like a banker, or a professor." Her breath caught. "Or an attorney."

"Or a *psychiatrist*," he teased.

A tickle started up in her throat. "Maybe we should amend the profile to say attended college and possibly graduate school. We're dealing with a highly educated, intelligent man. I mean these crimes were well planned. The killer ingeniously circumvented security at both the courthouse and the hospital, then got away without anyone noticing."

"And don't forget, other than the one bloody shoeprint, he left no trace evidence at either scene. Not that we've found so far. He's a hell of a planner, I'd say."

An ingenious determined killer . . . and he was after *her*. She wrapped her arms around her waist, staring at the profile they were building brick by brick. "Something's bothering me."

"Good." Spense took a seat beside her on the couch. "Something *should* be bothering you."

"A minute ago, when you said *UNSUBs* pick victims near their own age, you were speaking of serial killers, right?"

"That's where the data comes from, yes. The Bureau's amassed a lot of statistics on serial killers."

"If we're operating off the assumption our guy's a vigilante and not a serial killer . . . would the data even apply?"

"I'm glad you brought that up. Once we make the assumption he's a vigilante, it takes us down a limited path as far as our profile. So maybe we should put that issue to rest before we move on."

"You don't believe the shooter is a vigilante." It was written all over his face.

"The truth is our UNSUB defies classification, and that's something we don't run across often."

She thought about that lecture she and Spense had attended a few years back—the one about the difference between spree killers and mass murderers. "You're right. The courthouse shootings would put him in the category of a mass murderer—at least they would if Kramer and I had succumbed on the scene. But the hospital murders technically make the UNSUB a spree killer. And then, there's the matter of the temporal-bone trophy, which suggests something entirely different."

"Bull's-eye again." Spense retraced the target on the board in bold black marker.

A new idea bubbled to the surface. Kramer might have been the primary target, but the pharmacy tech was also key to the profile. Darlene Dillinger's throat had been slashed, and a piece of her temporal bone had been taken. Given the time it would take to carve out the bone, and the tools . . . and the skill . . . this UNSUB had to have fantasized and mentally rehearsed, or equally likely, actually performed the act beforehand. He'd known exactly what to do when the time came.

"Let's go back to the question of a vigilante. What argues *for* that theory, Caity?"

The more she thought about it, the less likely it seemed the vigilante theory would stand. And yet, if it hadn't been a vigilante's hatred for Kramer that motivated the murders, what had? She didn't know—yet. That would be their challenge. "Only one thing I can think of, but it's a humdinger."

"Exactly. The question of *motive* is best answered by the vigilante theory." He got up and began pacing in front of the board. "And you're right about that being a humdinger. No other motives that can connect the dots among *all* the victims spring to mind.

But I *know* this man is not a vigilante because even though I don't know *who* he is, I'm absolutely sure of *what* he is—a serial killer."

Her chin bobbed furiously. Spense was right. Of course he was right.

"Tell me how I know that, Caity."

Spense was mentoring her. Making sure she understood how they arrived at their conclusions, and that was good. "Because of Darlene Dillinger. Her murder has to be the work of a sexual sadist. Her body was posed in a shaming position, with her clothing removed and her ankles tied to her wrists to display her genitalia. The UNSUB used her undergarments to gag her, stuffing them down her throat before he cut it. The UNSUB is a misogynist with detailed fantasies, and he couldn't resist acting on those fantasies when he had the opportunity."

"And don't forget the temporal bone. It's the same signature as in the Cartwright murder. So if you're asking me if this is the work of a vigilante, the answer is *hell no*. Either we have a copycat on our hands, or Kramer really was innocent like he claimed, at least innocent of Sally Cartwright's murder. Either way, there's a sexually motivated serial killer loose in Phoenix." He stretched his arms behind his head. "You sure you're not hungry?"

Strangely enough, she was. All this profiling talk had somehow improved her appetite. The thought of tasting real food again made her mouth water. With the all the white rice and tapioca pudding the hospital had been feeding her, she could go for a nice big slice of a pepperoni pie about now. And there was no Nurse Jenny around to stop her. "Starved. Should we order pizza . . . ooh . . . or maybe Arizona Mexican?" A Navajo taco would hit the spot for sure.

He grinned. "I was thinking I might whip us up some kung pao tofu if you're game. I've got edamame, too."

Struggling not to make a face she said, "Perfect. That sounds very . . . nutritious. How can I help?"

Thirty minutes later, she found herself sitting across the kitchen table from Spense, facing down a bowl of gray curd dowsed in a spicy peanut sauce.

He stuffed a gob of tofu in his mouth and made an exaggerated noise of enjoyment. "Delicious, even if I do say so myself."

She looked at him, wondering if he really liked this stuff or if he was watching his diet for some reason. He certainly didn't need to mind his weight, but maybe he was in training or had some sort of issue with his cholesterol. It'd be a miracle if tofu could fill up this big man. Spense appeared to her to be well over six feet, and after seeing him in a T-shirt, she knew for sure he was all muscle.

A few mouthfuls later he slowed down and sent her a look that was even more surprising than the menu. It was the same look he'd had on his face that night he'd put the moves on her, and it gave her a fluttery feeling in her gut that made her uneasy. She suspected their earlier conversation about Baltimore might have stirred up old memories for him—like it had for her.

"Why did you reject me, Caity? It's obvious you're physically attracted to me."

"Is that so?" His arrogance was really insufferable, but there was a little bit of peanut sauce on his chin, and that was what saved him. It was hard to be too mad at a man wearing kung pao. Especially when he was right. "You want me to be brutally honest?"

He found his napkin and dabbed in the general direction of the sauce but failed to erase it from his chin. "If the truth is brutal, then, yes."

"I really can't recall." She did recall, but she thought it was better to shut this down before the nice working rapport they were developing went straight to hell in a handbasket.

"It's because I called you a mix of tangy and sweet, isn't it?"

If he knew what a lame line that was, then why had he used it? To her, it signaled he was a player and not to be taken seriously. And this was the worst possible time to bring it up again . . . but there was something in his coaxing tone that was hard to resist, and the set of his jaw told her he wasn't going to simply let this drop the way she'd hoped he would. "Was I supposed to enjoy being likened to the perfect curry?"

He turned his palms up and gave her an innocent grin. "I admit it wasn't my best line."

To this day it bothered her that he'd exerted so little effort in his so-called seduction. Now more than ever, since she knew he was perfectly capable of intelligent conversation. "I mean if you'd put a little elbow grease into it . . . paid me a genuine compliment instead of rambling on, comparing me to various dishes from around the globe."

"If I'd told you the truth, I don't think you'd have believed me, and anyway, I hadn't had dinner."

She smothered her laugh in her napkin. "I can't imagine how you ever get laid. Does the culinary excursion thing generally work for you?"

"Honestly, pretty much anything I say usually works for me."

He was so lucky he was still wearing that kung pao, but if he didn't get real with her soon, his luck was going to run out.

"In my experience, lines work because women *want* to believe them," he said. "It's reality they don't want to believe—that you remind them of the one that got away for example . . . which you certainly don't . . . remind me of anyone but your lovely sweet-yet-tangy self."

Damn his charm. Maybe she was being too hard on him. After all, they'd been bantering back and forth for years, and it wasn't as if she'd ever put her cards on the table for him either. "You said if you'd told me the truth . . ." Her voice trailed off, and her breath seemed to catch in her throat. She'd been battling her attraction to Spense for years, and suddenly, he was right here, sitting in the kitchen with her, talking over tofu. It felt so . . . real.

"Would you believe me if I said that when you smile at me, it's like I've never seen a woman's smile before?" He reached across the table and took her hand.

Her fork went clattering to the floor, but she didn't mind.

"That it's as if you invented the whole concept of smiling right there on the spot? And when you give me that *Caity* look, all earnest and eager, suddenly the noise in my head disappears. Would you believe me if I said you make me feel like I really *am* the man I want to be?"

She tried and failed to look away. "I'd *want* to believe you."

"Then trust me, Caity. It's not that hard."

She eased her hand from his grip. This wasn't the right time for them. Not now, not while they were trying to work as a team. "It's a conflict of interest."

With a sigh, he shoved his chair back and rose from the table. "Yeah, well, I don't really give two flips about that, but I can see you do, so I'll keep my hands to myself . . . for now."

A long, awkward silence passed. Then Spense took his plate to the sink, rinsed it, and slid it in the dishwasher. She did the same. Finally, she offered the only answer she could. "I'll think about it, Spense. But not tonight." Then, she sailed past him on her way to the living room. "Are you coming or not? We've got a profile to finish."

"SO, WHERE WERE we?" Willing to let personal matters drop for the moment, Spense resumed his place at the whiteboard. Pushing Caity would only make her put up higher walls, and they had other, urgent matters at hand. They'd promised Herrera a profile by morning, and that was what Herrera was going to get.

"We were saying maybe Kramer didn't kill Sally Cartwright after all," she chimed in, as though the kitchen conversation had never taken place.

If Kramer really was innocent, that meant both he and Caity had read him wrong. Spense had been certain Kramer fit the profile he'd created for the Cartwright case. Hell, Kramer *did* fit the profile. But a profile was only a starting point for an investigation, not the be-all and end-all, and he knew that well enough. Without hard evidence, a profile meant jack. That was a sticking point for Caity and him, too. She seemed to believe he'd jump to conclusions that weren't warranted, when in reality he was he was a stickler for hard, cold facts. But she was right about one thing, he didn't mind bending a rule now again to get a killer off the streets.

"Of course it's possible Kramer was *preparing* for his first kill but simply hadn't had a chance to carry out his plans yet." Caity got to her feet and wobbled to the board to add a note of her own. In big red letters she wrote the following:

Judd Kramer: Guilty or Innocent?

"Can we table that discussion for now?" Spense asked. "It's an important question, but it's not really ours to answer. We're not looking to prove our UNSUB is the man who killed Sally Cartwright. Though he may well be. That's a job for the Tempe Police

Department. Right now we need to focus on the Ferragamo murders."

Her face fell, but then she nodded her agreement.

"So our UNSUB is a white male in his late twenties to early thirties. Average enough looks not to be noticed. College-educated and intelligent. Given his expertise with guns and knives, I suspect he has past military or police training. He's also familiar with security at the courthouse and nursing procedure. So top of the list would be either a legal professional or a nurse though I wouldn't rule out other occupations. With Google around, it's easy to obtain expertise on just about anything. Anyone who was sufficiently motivated could find out courthouse and hospital security protocols." He took a breath. "Now that we've got that nailed down, let's move on to the psychological profile. That should be a cakewalk for you."

She seemed too intent on the profile to register his compliment. "Our killer is organized, intelligent, and makes very few mistakes—so that means he's not operating under any delusions and has a good grip on reality. In other words, he's evil, but not insane. He's also fearless. And that fearlessness is what really stands out to me in determining his psychopathology. He had the guts to walk into a county courthouse, teeming with law enforcement, and take out four people, then follow that up with the assassination of a hospital patient while said patient was under armed guard." She raised her dry-erase marker high in the air. "That kind of fearlessness, notice I didn't say *recklessness*—our guy is very careful—marks the UNSUB as a psychopath. It's not merely a matter of failing to avoid danger; he deliberately seeks it out. And that makes him unpredictable because he may engage in behavior so risky we would never expect it."

"Do you think the UNSUB was a stranger to the victims or someone within their same social circles?"

Her mouth twitched at the edges.

"Not a total stranger. At least not to Kramer."

He admired the way she tackled the issues head-on, despite the anxiety it must cause her. "You seem pretty certain of that."

"I am. Kramer told me to find the Man in the Maze, suggesting he suspected who might've targeted him. I'm not sure if that means he *knew* his assailant, or simply that he was in some kind of trouble with this Man in the Maze. I mean if he knew the guy's true identity, wouldn't he have told me his name?" Closing her eyes, she continued, "One thing I am sure of is that Harvey Baumgartner definitely did *not* recognize the killer. I remember something from that day. Something that happened just before my world went blank. Baumgartner spoke to the gunman."

Spense nodded. "That's good. Take your time and just relax into the memory."

"Baumgartner said . . ." She squeezed her eyes harder. "He said: *You'll have to come back later. I have this room reserved.*" Her eyes popped open. "Baumgartner thought he was talking to a maintenance worker who'd come to clean the conference room, so it couldn't have been anyone he recognized."

"Baumgartner didn't recognize him. But I find *this* to be the interesting point"—Spense wrote the words *Kramer knew who was after him* on the board—"*if* the Man in the Maze isn't just some bullshit Kramer threw out to get the last laugh on you. I wouldn't put it past him to have sent us to chase a monster who doesn't really exist."

Chapter Nine

Friday, September 13

From: Man in the Maze <395204@253.0.101.212>
To: Labyrinth <list.27040302@253.0.101.212>
Subject: Hangman

Greetings students and happy Friday the thirteenth! Thank
you for your postings this week. I take such pride in all of you.
In particular, I must commend the Hangman. Your description
of your sister, and the ways you intend to enjoy her suffering
are most titillating. Let me make you this offer, my friend:
I would love to participate in your games if that would be
something that would please you. From what you've reported,
your sister deserves what you intend to give her and more. If I
am by your side, you surely will not lose your nerve.

   To the rest of you: Keep planning and watching for
your opportunity. If you are prepared, your time will come.

Should you succeed in your mission, don't forget to post a photograph of the spoils of war. When you show me the precious labyrinth, it honors me. As I have promised, I will promote anyone in possession of a labyrinth to the rank of lieutenant. With that rank comes the privilege of acting as a mentor. As a trusted officer of the group, you will be authorized to bring in another member of your choosing. Only you and I will know his true identity. And please has anyone considered recruiting a *she*? Don't overlook the possibility, for that would be most delectable to have a whore to train up in our ways. Some of the greatest hunters have employed female helpers. Again, stay alert for the opportunity to fulfill your destiny. Your time will come. And we will all be here to delight in your achievement.

Chapter Ten

Friday, September 13
Federal Bureau of Investigation
Field office
Phoenix, Arizona

DETECTIVE BASKIN'S FACE was screwed on so tight, Caitlin was amazed he could open his mouth to speak. And in truth, his words had been a little difficult to understand when he'd read the profile she and Spense had penned last night.

Gretchen Herrera, looking impeccably smart in a crisp white blouse and gray blazer, drummed her fingers on the conference-room table. Caitlin and Spense had been summoned to the same fifth-floor field office location where they'd met with Gretchen yesterday. Only today, Detective Baskin had also been invited for the unveiling of the profile. "You don't seem satisfied," Gretchen addressed Baskin.

"With this profile?" His lips puckered, and his brows slanted into a deep V. "No. I can't say that I am."

"Give me some specifics. What exactly don't you find useful?" Gretchen replied, seemingly unfazed.

"None of it. I don't find any of it useful." Baskin's gaze flicked about the table, his tone conveying no small amount of aggravation. "We're looking for a *vigilante*. I thought that would've been perfectly clear."

Caitlin watched for Spense's reaction, but Spense didn't say a word, and Caitlin suspected he was giving Baskin plenty of rope.

"And because we're looking for a vigilante, we don't need a profile at all. We just need evidence, *real* evidence that will lead us to the shooter."

"You mean the shooter-slasher-poisoner," Caity corrected Baskin, then followed her words up with a soft, conciliatory smile. No reason for her to antagonize the detective. She'd leave it to Spense to play that role. "Rather a complex MO for a run-of-the-mill vigilante."

"Thanks for making my point for me. That's not a *complicated* MO; it's not an MO at all. The UNSUB is simply employing whatever means are most likely to succeed under each particular circumstance. That's why he used a pistol at the courthouse and switched to poison in the hospital."

"Don't forget the knife." Caitlin certainly couldn't forget what the killer had done to Darlene Dillinger. Heat crept up her neck. Baskin seemed to be disregarding the woman's murder altogether, having put her squarely in the category of collateral damage—as if she didn't figure into the equation at all. But to Caitlin, she not only figured . . . she *mattered*.

"I agree with Baskin . . . about the MO." Spense jumped in, saving Caitlin from losing her cool despite her best intentions. "The pistol and the poison are simply a means to an end, hardly something I'd consider an MO. The UNSUB used the most efficient method he could find at the courthouse, then later on Kramer at the hospital. So when your *chief*," Spense put special emphasis on the word to let Baskin know who was really calling the shots in the investigation, "first asked me to develop a profile for the Ferragamo case, I wasn't sure one would be useful."

Caitlin was surprised by Spense's composure, but she shouldn't have been. Today was important, and Spense was always at his best when the pressure was on.

"So then, this was just a perfunctory exercise for you. You don't think the profile is useful either," Baskin said in a voice infused with sarcasm. He snapped open the file and read aloud for the second time in ten minutes: "Caucasian male, approximate age late twenties to early thirties. No facial scars or deformities. Height five-nine to five-eleven, weight approximately 170 pounds. College degree or better. Professional occupation. Organized, highly intelligent, with a history of frequent job changes due to conflict with authority. Recent trigger such as job loss or divorce." He scowled. "Likely military or *police* background." Here he paused and rolled his eyes. "History of trouble with the law, probably voyeurism. Extensive online and other pornography collection of a sexually sadistic nature. Geographic location unknown. Consider recent relocation to the Phoenix metropolitan area." He snorted. "I must be missing a page or something. I don't see anywhere where it says if he wears boxers or briefs." Baskin slapped the papers on the table. "For fuck's sake, you call this police work?"

"I call it a criminal investigative analysis. Each characteristic listed is well supported either by epidemiology or by our experience with serial murderers. I can explain point by point how Dr. Cassidy and I arrived at our conclusions, but I think that's a waste of time. You're not here to learn profiling."

"Damn straight I'm not. I'm here to catch this goddamn vigilante—the asshole who took out one of our own." His clamped fist came down hard on the table as he glared at Spense. "And you sashay in here and hand me this load of crap. This is the profile of a *serial killer.* If I'm wrong, say so."

"I never sashay, I waltz." Spense gave a forced smile. "You're not wrong about the profile, though."

"So you agree it's a useless piece of shit." Baskin sent Caitlin an apologetic look. "No offense to you, Dr. Cassidy."

"None taken." She couldn't quite figure the guy. He was obstinate and close-minded, but something about him told her he'd lay down his life in the line of duty if called upon.

"You're right that this is the profile of a sexually motivated serial killer, not a vigilante. You're wrong that it's crap. If you're looking for a vigilante, you're looking for the wrong guy. Have you interviewed the likely suspects under your present theory? Victims' family members, members of the community who've been outspoken about Kramer's guilt? What about the staff at the courthouse, maybe one of them got tired of watching felons duck their punishment."

Baskin shifted in his seat and steepled his fingers. "All courthouse personnel have been questioned except one janitor—and he's in the clear—dead from a heroin overdose."

The hairs on the back of Caitlin's neck started to itch. "That seems suspicious to me."

"And yet it's not. The guy had a habit. He was clean at the time of his hire, but his friends confirmed he'd started using again with a vengeance. Since he was tucked away in a wood box *before* the hospital murders, I'd say we can safely rule him out. So far we got nothing. Family members and close associates all got rock-solid alibis. Local radicals want to take credit but can't come up with any facts not already made public via the media. Thompson even talked to the Baumgartners and crossed them off the list yesterday."

"Then hear me out. What I was going to say is that when your chief asked us to come up with a profile on Ferragamo, I wasn't sure it would be worthwhile to do so. But that was before Darlene Dillinger's body was found. After what the UNSUB did to Darlene, I knew we had a sexually motivated killer on our hands. And that's why this profile is worth the hard work Dr. Cassidy and I put into it. You're a smart man, Baskin. I know you'll see what I mean if you just set aside your personal beef with the chief for one minute."

"I got no personal beef with the chief."

"Didn't he recently deny your request for vacation and pass you over for promotion?"

Baskin pushed back his chair and got to his feet, then began pacing around the long mahogany table, eyeing first Gretchen, then Caitlin and finally Spense.

"Suppose, just suppose, your profile is right. If this isn't the work of a vigilante, we got no motive. You got any idea *why* a serial killer would want to kill Kramer *and* Baumgartner? You got a reason a serial killer would want to kill *Dr. Cassidy*? Because until you do, I'll circulate the profile, but the task force focus is going to remain on a vigilante killer."

"I'll admit we don't have the motive nailed down. But think about what Kramer said with his dying breath: *the Man in the Maze*." Caitlin reminded him of that rather pertinent fact.

Baskin halted near her chair, stooped down, and whispered in her ear: "He's fucking with you, Dr. Cassidy. A leopard doesn't change his spots just because he's gasping his last breath. Kramer used his to send you off on a path that leads nowhere. If he has his way, you're the one who's going to wind up in the center of a dead-end maze."

Chapter Eleven

Saturday, September 14
Paradise Valley, Arizona

"I SHOULD'VE BEEN a lawyer." Spense let out a long whistle, then turned his Bureau-issued Isuzu Rodeo off Lincoln Boulevard and onto Lost Dutchman, heading north. They began the winding ascent into the hills of Paradise Valley, and Caitlin imagined the *Bucar,* as Spense liked to call his Rodeo, blushing a deeper shade of red as it strained and surged up the twisting roads, past driveways crammed with luxury vehicles. Matching Range Rovers, his and hers Mercedes, BMWs, and the occasional Rolls were enough to give any Bucar an inferiority complex.

Caitlin couldn't deny the area was impressive. There was no more exclusive part of town than this Phoenix suburb. But it wasn't the multimillion-dollar homes or the fancy cars that made her envious of its residents. It was the vistas. Each home was set on an oversized lot with plenty of room for giant saguaros and verbena-covered yards. Cactus wrens sucked nectar from saguaro blossoms, and jackrabbits scampered in the yards. The jackrabbits were ubiquitous despite the resident coyotes that feasted on them. These coyotes were bold, often tromping right up onto the front porch like a gang of Girl Scouts, but the rabbits were quicker, and just as fearless.

The higher the Bucar climbed, the more nature abounded, and the views progressed from great to magnificent. But still, she thought . . . "I simply couldn't be an attorney. It wouldn't be worth the price."

"The price?" he asked.

"Of selling out your integrity."

"Is that what you think about lawyers? That they're only looking out for themselves."

"Maybe not all of them. But *these* guys who live up here in the hills are mostly corporate attorneys and ambulance chasers."

"The justice system doesn't work without attorneys, Caity."

"The justice system doesn't work with them, either."

One eyebrow climbed his forehead. "If I believed that, I wouldn't be able to do what I do: track down bad guys and turn them over to the courts. I know you think the system failed your father—"

Her spine went ramrod straight. "I *know* the system failed my father. It also failed my mom and me. Our entire family was destroyed by that failure, so don't expect me to show the lawyers any love."

"You feel that way about Baumgartner, too? I heard he took on your father's case pro bono. What's your opinion of him?"

Ah, now they were getting down to the nitty-gritty. He wanted to know what she thought of Baumgartner's character. And he wanted to know for a very specific reason. She could practically hear the victimology wheel spinning in Spense's head because the truth was neither one of them had a good answer to Baskin's question about why a serial killer would target Kramer, his attorney, and Caity. Spense was fishing for dirt on Baumgartner, looking for a reason a sexually motivated murderer would want a man like him dead. If he could find a crack in the respected lawyer's armor, he might find a reason someone would want him out of the picture. Spense would probably be fishing for dirt on *her* next.

"I didn't know him well enough to judge him fairly. I was just thirteen when I met the family. My parents knew the Baumgartners from church, but they weren't exactly in the same social circle. It was more like they viewed it as their Christian duty to socialize with less fortunate members of the congregation—like those lowly Cassidys. At least at first I thought so, but then Harvey Baumgartner and my dad seemed to develop a genuine friendship. Not long after that is when Gail Falconer's body was found, and my father was arrested for her murder. Harvey really stepped up to the plate by taking him on and believing in his innocence." She swallowed back the emotion that was welling in her throat. "Trust me; I'm grateful to him for that. And that's why I dragged you over here today. I need to pay my respects to the family. We may not be all that close, but we're connected by our histories."

"I expect you'd be more grateful had Baumgartner secured an acquittal for your father."

She didn't reply because that much was obvious and also because they were now chugging their way up the ridiculously steep driveway to the Baumgartner residence.

Louisa Baumgartner met them at the top of the drive, welcoming Caitlin with a brief hug. Caitlin introduced Spense, then Louisa admonished them to mind the step-up to the gate that led to the house. Spense let out another admiring whistle as he stood on the terrace of this hilltop home admiring the stunning view of Camelback Mountain. The front of the house was mostly glass, with no curtains obscuring the multimillion-dollar vista, but Caity could see evidence of sun shades that could be lowered for privacy, or if the occupants were away. The garage door was open, revealing three vehicles: a red Ferrari and a pair of BMW SUVs. "Is that Harvey's Ferrari?" she wondered aloud.

Louisa first nodded yes, but then changed her mind and shook her head. "No. I thought you were asking if the car belonged to our son, Harvey Junior. Harvey Senior drove the blue BMW. The gold one is mine, and the Ferrari belongs to Junior. Is that relevant to the case?"

Not that Caitlin knew of at the moment. There were three car covers in the garage, making her wonder if Harvey Junior lived at home, which seemed odd for an adult with enough money to drive a Ferrari. She didn't have to wonder long.

"Junior's back home temporarily. Just until his divorce is final, though. He hasn't decided if he wants to stay in Phoenix, so he didn't want to buy his own place or get into a long-term lease. The house, of course, goes to his soon-to-be ex." Louisa Baumgartner's tone sounded bitter, and Caitlin suspected she was none too sorry to be losing a daughter-in-law. "Of course, now that my husband's gone, I'm hoping more than ever that Junior will stay close."

Her dark eyes brimmed with tears that sparkled on exceedingly long lashes—probably extensions. Despite what she'd been through, Louisa's appearance was impeccable. She was dressed in a black silk pantsuit—probably a Dior. Her highlighted hair shone from conditioning and flowed in perfect layers that complemented her high cheekbones—probably filler. Her forehead was Botox smooth, her lipstick a tasteful shade of blushed nude. Her understated taste in makeup and clothing, however, didn't quite offset the impact of garishly large breasts—most definitely silicone—on an anorexic frame. Her age was impossible to discern without checking ID. Despite her Paradise Valley zip code, Louisa Baumgartner appeared to be the type known hereabouts as a *Scottsdale Blond*.

Louisa led them inside. Caitlin had never seen their home before—they hadn't been those kinds of friends. The interior of the Baumgartner home seemed as perfect as its mistress. Creamy walls met high ceilings above and marbled floors below. White lilies lent the place grace and a delightful fragrance. Mammoth Southwestern oil paintings hung on the walls, and the grand piano displayed family portraits—adding just enough warmth to keep the place from feeling like a museum. "I've begged Junior not to move away. I don't know what I'd do if I lost *both* my men." Like her tears, the distress in Louisa's voice seemed genuine.

Caitlin clasped her hands to stop herself from reaching out to comfort the woman. She *knew* what it felt like to lose the person you loved most in the world. "I'm so sorry for your loss," she offered the standard condolence, fighting a torrent of dammed-up emotion that threatened to sweep her away. Her life had become tragically entwined with a family who shared little in common with her own. Baumgartner had witnessed her father's death, and now she'd witnessed Baumgartner's. She had no words that would change Louisa's loss, any more than Baumgartner had had words to comfort her the day her father had been executed. "We came to pay our respects."

"Greatly appreciated. Dad thought very highly of you, Caitlin. And I hope you'll update us on the case while you're here." A man who appeared to be around Caitlin's age descended the main staircase, and her breath got trapped in her lungs. For a moment, she thought it was Baumgartner himself. Obviously, this must be Junior. He looked exactly like Harvey Senior had when she'd first met him, back in the day when he'd defended her father and coached her on how to behave for the media and the jury. The last time Caitlin had seen Junior, he was an awkward teen at an after-church pizza party. Now he exuded panache.

"We'll update you as best we can. Nothing new for now." Spense's answer signaled to Caitlin that loose lips sink ships. Spense would no doubt prefer to collect information rather than provide it, and that stuck in her craw. This family had lost a husband and a father. She'd wanted to come here today for exactly the reason she'd stated—to offer condolences, but Spense seemed to be on an intelligence-gathering mission rather than a sympathetic one. She regretted having to bring him along, but she could hardly ditch her bodyguard with the UNSUB still at large.

Harvey Junior extended his hand to Spense. "I'm certain you will. If there's anything you need from us, anything at all, just let us know."

"I will," Spense said matter-of-factly.

"Of course they'll keep us updated, sweetheart. Caitlin will make sure of it," Louisa said.

Caitlin hated not telling the truth about the case. She could understand not mentioning the Man in the Maze to the Baumgartners, but surely they could let the family in on a few of the details—such as the fact that Judd Kramer's death in the hospital had been ruled a homicide. She sent Spense a questioning look, and he gave her the *no-dice* eyes.

"Caitlin, you look so . . . grown-up. I can hardly believe my eyes." Junior gave her a brief but enthusiastic pat on the back.

"I could say the same to you."

Louisa slipped her hand through her son's elbow and steered him to an overstuffed couch. When Caitlin and Spense seated themselves on the opposite love seat, Caitlin had to hold her body rigidly to keep herself from being swallowed up by the cushions. Louisa tinkled a silver bell, and a young woman in a traditional black-and-white maid's uniform appeared.

"Will you bring refreshments, Elizabeth?"

"Right away, ma'am." Elizabeth was quite young, likely less than twenty, and exceptionally pretty, with a heart-shaped face and perfect features. Her eyes never left the ground, and her speaking voice was barely audible. Either Elizabeth was shy, or she'd been trained to be invisible.

Spense opened his mouth, and Catlin suspected he'd been about to decline the refreshments, but Elizabeth had already disappeared.

"I'm sorry for your loss," Caitlin repeated lamely to Junior. She'd come here out of duty, and the situation was an awkward one. After all, she'd survived the shootings while Baumgartner had not. It would only be natural for his wife and son to wish things had been the other way around. Caitlin's throat had gone painfully dry, and that made speaking difficult. She could really use some water and was anxious for those refreshments about now.

Leaning forward, Spense rested both hands on his knees and angled his body toward Louisa. "I wish we had more to report, but as of now, we don't have any solid leads on your husband's killer. Would it be all right if we asked you a few questions?"

"Of course it's all right." Junior said, then seemed to notice the worried look on his mother's face and edged closer to her. "And I hope you don't mind my asking for details. But surely you can understand, we'd be desperate for any news. Imagine how we felt having to learn from the papers that Caitlin was present and had been badly wounded," he said, his face as drawn and tight as his mother's now.

"No apologies necessary. Let me be clear that even though we don't have any viable suspects at this time, we want to nail this guy as much as you do. The police and sheriff's office have put together a twenty-man task force, and we're working around the clock on the case."

A look of relief spread over Junior's face. "A twenty-man task force. I guess Dad's murder will be getting the attention it deserves." The catch in his voice said it all. He must've been very attached to his father. "Thank you."

Caitlin took note that Spense had not referred to the case by its moniker—Ferragamo. That must mean for the time being at least, Spense didn't want the family to know about the bloody shoeprint. Caitlin understood what it was like to be an interested family member and have information withheld from you, but she understood his reasoning. Until the Baumgartners had been eliminated as suspects, he didn't want to disclose that shoeprint. But she also remembered that Thompson had interviewed them and wasn't interested in pursuing things further.

Noiselessly, Elizabeth reentered the room and set a tray laden with crustless tea sandwiches and cookies on one of two travertine coffee tables. Another young woman, also unusually pretty, and also dressed in a uniform, trailed behind Elizabeth with a china teapot, cups, glasses, and a pitcher of water. There was one martini, complete with olives, and one Fat Tire beer on the tray as well. Junior grabbed the Fat Tire, then sank onto the couch. His mother reached for the martini.

Louisa's outward politeness seemed incongruous with the fact she had apparently left standing refreshment orders that didn't include ascertaining her guests' preferences. Water was in fact all Caitlin required, but in her home, humble though it might have been, her mother would've never ordered herself a drink and not offered one to her guests. Caitlin felt a twinge of unease, vaguely recalling her mother saying: *Louisa Baumgartner is more interested in appearing to be nice than she is in actually being nice.* Caitlin set the observation aside as both unproductive and unkind. It didn't matter how phony Louisa was; she'd lost her husband and deserved their sympathy.

"Would you two like something with a little more kick than tea? I should have offered, but I assume one of you is driving, and you're both on duty, correct?" Maybe Louisa had read the look on Caitlin's face, or maybe Caitlin was overanalyzing, making a mountain out of a martini. She snagged a glass of water and gulped half, then came up for air. "Thanks for offering, but no. Water's great. And just FYI, I'm not on duty because I'm not law enforcement."

"Oh. I didn't know. I suppose I just assumed since you were going to testify in court for Judd Kramer, and because you're here with an FBI agent, that you were official."

Caitlin was surprised by Louisa's lack of understanding of her late husband's work, but she shouldn't have been. He likely didn't discuss his cases at home, and there was no reason his wife would know exactly what Caitlin's role was. "I'm a psychiatrist—a private consultant." Louisa and Junior exchanged baffled looks. "But I am offering my services to help develop a profile on the killer."

"That's nice." Louisa sipped her martini with her little finger crooked, and Caitlin had to struggle to keep from smiling at the affected gesture. Another sip, then she turned toward Spense. "Well, Agent Spenser is it? You said you want to nail the man who murdered my husband. If you know the killer is a man, then you must have *some* sense of who he might be."

Spense shook his head. "I'm afraid not. I can only say we have strong reason to believe, based on our profile, that the killer is a man." He'd left off the part about Caitlin believing she'd *seen* a man wielding a gun in the conference room that day. She was about to pipe up and say so, when Spense sent her a warning look.

Louisa picked up a cookie and delicately nibbled off the frosting. She dabbed at her lips with a linen napkin and slid her gaze to Caitlin. "But didn't you see the shooter, dear? Surely you must know his sex. Couldn't you try to identify him in a lineup?"

She gulped more water and answered truthfully, which was her preferred course of action whenever possible. "I don't remember much from that day. I do know . . ." she hesitated. "I do know that your husband, Harvey, didn't suffer. It all happened too fast." The crime-scene photos of Harvey Baumgartner facedown in a pool of blood flashed before her eyes, and she blinked them away.

Louisa's hand jerked, and what remained of her martini splashed onto her black silk suit, leaving a small wet stain. She looked around the room as if dazed, then back at Caitlin. "Thank you so much for telling me, dear."

Junior set his beer on a stained-glass coaster and pressed his hands to his face. A sigh rumbled out of him, and at last he pulled his hands away to reveal red eyes rimmed with tears. "You said you wanted to ask us some questions about Dad."

"Did your father have any enemies that you know of?" Apparently, Spense had waited long enough. He jumped at the opening.

Junior fixed Spense with a surprised look. "Of course my father had enemies. He defended men no one else would take on." He tilted his head toward Caitlin, but she didn't need to be reminded that no one but Baumgartner had believed in her father. "But if you ask me, it's pretty obvious what happened in that courtroom had little to do with my father's enemies. This is all about Judd Kramer. This has to be someone in Sally Cartwright's circle looking to avenge her death. Her father or her boyfriend, either one . . . or maybe *both*."

"Sally Cartwright's boyfriend and father both have airtight alibis," Caitlin supplied. The way Spense narrowed his eyes at her made her decide to let him dole out the information as he saw fit. Obviously, she'd said too much for his comfort, and he was the veteran investigator, not her.

"Maybe they hired someone else to do it for them. Like a hit man." Junior was full of helpful ideas they'd already thought of.

"That's always a possibility. We're looking into that, too. Did your father receive any specific threats after he took the Kramer case?"

"Oh, yes." Louisa set down her empty martini glass and rang the little bell for Elizabeth. "But Harvey turned those notes over to the Paradise Valley Police one by one as they came in. There were so many of them." Oddly, she didn't seem upset about the threats or angry that nothing had been done about them. She just stated it flatly as a point of information. Still, her earlier tears had seemed genuine, and anyway, everyone handled grief differently. Caitlin herself preferred not to put on a show of emotion for others.

"I wonder if it might be a good idea to try to lift some prints off those notes," Junior said.

Spense's brow dipped at the suggestion, but he didn't rebuff Junior. Nor should he have done so in her opinion since Junior was doing his best to be helpful. "The notes have been finger-printed already. But we've not been able to match them to any prints in our criminal databases."

"What about Sally Cartwright's family? Did you compare prints from those notes with *their* prints? Her family wouldn't be in a criminal database, so it could still be them," Louisa put in.

"Done. And not a match." Spense pushed to a stand. "I think we've intruded enough for one day," he said, seemingly ready to get out of there before he was pressed for more information or offered more suggestions as to how the police ought to proceed.

"If I think of anything important, I'll give you a call," Junior offered, without waiting to be asked. "And just for the record, like I told Detective Thompson, I was out of town that week. Work-related. I was in New York when I got the call from Mother."

Spense pulled out a notebook and poised his pen in the air. "Who can verify that for me?"

To her right, Louisa Baumgartner gasped. "Are you joking?"

"No." Spense added no conciliation, no sympathy to his voice.

Maybe ruling out the family as suspects was the sensible thing to do, especially if Thompson hadn't bothered to verify the alibis, but it left a bitter taste in Caitlin's mouth. She reached for one of the little crustless sandwiches, choked it down, and chased it with water.

"Any number of people. I'll fax you a list. How about you, Mom?" Junior slung an arm around her. "You weren't playing shoot-'em-up at the courthouse the other day, were you?" He pecked the top of her head. "I'll have her check her calendar and get back to you."

"Great. The sooner we rule you two out, the better." Spense handed mother and son his cards, then Caitlin followed him wordlessly to the car. On the way back to his apartment, she kept silent. And not because of how he'd handled the family. He hadn't been unkind, just neutral, professional. But Spense had known about the threats to Baumgartner's life, and he'd never mentioned them to her. Her knuckles ached from holding her hands in tight fists, and her stomach had gone sour. If Spense hadn't told her about the threats, she didn't want to think about what other information he might be hiding from her. Watching how easy it was for him to lie to the Baumgartners set her nerves on edge. She understood his reasons for keeping secrets from this family very well, but what she didn't understand were his reasons for keeping secrets from her.

Chapter Twelve

Saturday, September 14

From: Dizzy <848852@253.0.101.212>
To: Labyrinth <list.27040302@253.0.101.212>
Subject: Hello

Greetings Labyrinth. Greetings Man in the Maze. My name is Dizzy. I'm fifteen years old, and I've been lurking for a little while after stumbling across your group. I'm coming out of lurkdom in response to the Man in the Maze/Hangman post. I want to become a member of the club. I don't know what I have to do to join, but whatever it is, I will do it.

You said you would like a whore to train up in your ways. Well, I can be her, that's what everyone calls me anyway. I just need a place I can go to talk to someone, even if it's only online. At school, things are really getting bad for me. I can't walk down the halls without kids throwing cups and trash at me. Last week, someone took a piss in my locker. My best friend won't talk to me anymore because she knows if she does, she'll be next.

My mom tried to fix things with the principal, and yeah, you can imagine what a shitstorm my life has been since then. Even worse than before, if that's even possible. I don't sleep at night. I cry all day. My head is filled with poison and pain. I have no one left in this world. I will be yours to punish if you will only be my.friend. I can't take my life anymore. Maybe one of you would like to kill me. I tried to do it myself, but I lost my nerve. If it would give you pleasure to off me, I give my consent. At least then I would be worth something to someone.

Dizzy

Chapter Thirteen

Sunday, September 15
Rutherford Towers
Phoenix, Arizona

CAITLIN TOOK ANOTHER sip of her Arnold Palmer and placed it on a coaster. She aimed a smile at her former nurse, Jenny, who sat kitty-corner from her in a leather armchair in Spense's living room. "Thanks for stopping by and thanks for the get-well gift." The handmade pottery mug Jenny had presented her had a Southwestern motif crafted by a local artist. It also had a special handle, and Jenny had called it a *hand-warming* mug. "It's truly lovely, but it really wasn't necessary."

Jenny waved in protest. "It's nothing. I just wanted you to know I'm thinking of you. I know I can be gruff at times, but it's just my way. I always had your best interest at heart."

Catlin laughed. "It was *for my own good,* I remember." They'd had their ups and downs, but she was grateful to Jenny, nonetheless. "I'm sure I was a big pain, but I appreciate all you did for me."

"How's the recovery going?" Jenny leaned in attentively.

"Very well. No seizures since that first day, even without the Tegretol."

Jenny's cheeks pinked up at the mention of the Tegretol, and Caitlin wished she hadn't mentioned it. "Good to know. I-I . . ."

A key turned in the latch, and both Caitlin and Jenny turned at the sound to find Spense filling the doorway. The entire room seemed to expand with his presence. He had on a dark, lightweight suit jacket, slacks, and a tan shirt that brought out the golden hue in his eyes. When his arm lifted to rake a hand through his thick brown hair, cut short in typical Bureau style, his jacket opened to reveal the Glock holstered at his hip. He looked every bit the special agent: tall, dark, and devastating . . . and packing heat.

Jenny sent him a sweet smile. "Oh, glad to see you, Spense. I had no idea you'd be home. I just dropped over to check on Dr. Cassidy, and it's good to see she's doing great. I guess you've been taking good care of her."

"I can't take credit. She doesn't let me do anything for her." He cocked an eyebrow at Caitlin. "Regular pain in the ass if you ask me."

Since she'd been released from the hospital, Spense had barely let Caitlin out of his sight except to shower. This morning, he'd been out of the apartment less than ten minutes, dropping off a gift for a neighbor's birthday. Jenny knew enough about their situation—that Spense was providing protection for Caitlin until the shooter was apprehended—to have realized he wouldn't be far from her side. It suddenly dawned on her that Jenny hadn't stopped by because she was concerned for Caitlin. Her shoulders stiffened at the obvious deception.

People lie all the time. It's no big deal.

But it was. She hated lies, even small, inconsequential ones. In fact, she hated the little lies the most because they were so unnecessary. At least the bigger lies generally had a purpose—to protect oneself, or maybe a loved one. But why had Jenny lied? Why pretend she hadn't expected Spense to be around when it was obvious she'd been hoping to see him?

Not that it was any of her affair if Jenny had a thing for Spense. She simply didn't care for disingenuous behavior on principle. "Are you sure I can't get you a coffee or soda or something?" Caitlin asked Jenny for the second time since she'd arrived, doing her best to make her former nurse feel welcome. If Jenny wanted to spend time with Spense, there was no reason for her to stand in the way. She'd be just fine hanging out in the kitchen giving them a chance to talk or . . . whatever.

"No thanks. I don't want to overstay my welcome." But Jenny didn't rise from her chair.

Ack. More deception. Why couldn't the woman just own her intentions? "Don't be silly. You've only been here a few minutes."

"Don't go," Spense put in. "Stay for lunch if you like."

Caitlin felt a devilish satisfaction knowing that should Jenny decide to accept Spense's invitation, she'd be in for a bland experience indeed, not the spicy one she suspected Jenny was hoping for. Mock meat loaf, made from some rubbery substance called seitan, was on the menu today.

"Oh, I couldn't possibly, but thanks."

Maybe she'd been forewarned Spense was a vegetarian. After all, she'd known what brand of aftershave he wore. Good. Although there was no reason, Caity would just as soon have Jenny be on her way. But despite her protest, Jenny *still* didn't make a move to leave. "Thanks again for coming," Caitlin offered hopefully.

Apparently there was Super Glue on Jenny's chair.

Spense shrugged. "No lunch? Your loss." Then he settled him-self on the couch next to Caitlin. He watched Jenny for a moment, and the tension among the three of them grew palpable. Some-thing was up. Finally, Spense broke the awkward silence. "What's going on, Jenny? Don't get me wrong, it really is great to see you, but for some reason I get the feeling this isn't a social call."

The flush on her cheeks deepened. "Well, now that you men-tion it, I've been curious about the investigation. Anything new?"

Caitlin didn't blame Jenny for wondering. After all, it was Jenny who'd brought her a pill that had been bagged and tagged in her presence. Naturally, she'd be interested to know the crime lab's findings.

"Did you confirm the pill was cyanide? The one I brought into the room? Because I would never do anything to hurt Dr. Cassidy, and I could lose my job if it looked like I'd made a mistake with the medications and nearly killed a patient."

Spense leaned forward, keeping eye contact with Jenny. "I'm afraid I'm not at liberty to discuss the matter."

Jenny's shoulders sagged, and a hurt look came over her face. "Oh, okay. Well, maybe you could at least tell me if it's true the police are calling this whole mess the Ferragamo case because of a bloody footprint found at the courthouse?"

Now *that* set off Caitlin's radar. The cyanide findings had not been made public, but because Kramer had been poisoned on the same hospital floor where Jenny worked, she could understand how Jenny and the rest of the staff might've put two and two to-gether. But the Ferragamo case? That moniker hadn't been made public, and there was really no way for Jenny to know . . . unless someone on the task force had leaked the information. "Where did you hear the case called Ferragamo?"

"Oh, I don't know, in the news I suppose." Casting a glance to the corners of the room, Jenny crossed, then uncrossed her ankles. Caitlin noticed Spense eyeing Jenny's pretty legs, but she didn't blame him. Jenny was wearing those short shorts that were so popular with the college coeds. Jenny was no coed, but she was off duty and had the legs for just about anything.

"No, you didn't. That information hasn't been released to the press," Spense challenged Jenny's assertion, but kept his voice nonconfrontational.

"Well, I must've just heard it around then."

Caitlin noticed perspiration beading on Jenny's forehead.

"Around where?" Spense asked.

"The hospital, of course. Cops in the ER are always talking, and word spreads like fire in a hospital. Or maybe I heard it somewhere else." By now, Jenny's entire throat and chest were covered in red blotches. She was holding something back, and that something was making her squirm in her seat. Spense looked at Caitlin sideways, as if he, too, had noticed Jenny's whole demeanor was off.

Caitlin drew a deep breath and smoothed her expression into her go-to look for this sort of situation: neutral but expectant. "What else have you heard?"

"I-I heard that pill I brought you turned out to be cyanide, and that Judd Kramer's death was ruled a homicide—due to cyanide poisoning. You don't think the police might come after *me*, do you? I swear I didn't know what was in that pill. I swear it." She buried her face in her hands, smothering a sudden sob. Caitlin couldn't tell if she was being sincere or just putting on a show.

Spense reached out and patted her hand. "No one thinks you did anything wrong. To my knowledge, the police aren't looking at you as a suspect. So please don't worry. But some of the questions you've asked lead me to believe there's a leak in the team somewhere. You said you might have heard all this somewhere outside the hospital. Whether you did or not, I don't need to know, but *hypothetically speaking*, if there were an information leak that needed to be plugged, where do you think it might be?"

"I do want to help, but . . ." Her eyes dropped to her hands, and she seemed to be reading her fingernails like tea leaves. "Hypothetically speaking?"

"Hypothetically speaking."

"Someone could have gotten inside information from a friend."

"Hypothetically speaking, would this friend be a police detective?"

Silence. Then finally, "I promised not to reveal my source."

Without warning, Caitlin's patience dissolved. "First, you're not a reporter, so *revealing your source* doesn't apply. Second, this is a murder investigation. Do I have to remind you four people are already dead? What if protecting your source costs other people their lives?" Caitlin raised her hand for the purpose of ticking off the dead one by one. "A deputy sheriff. A respected attorney. A man accused, but *not convicted* of a crime, and a pharmacy technician who worked beside you at Good Hope. That could've been *you*, Jenny. So don't give me any more bull about not revealing your source. Where the hell did you hear the term *Ferragamo*?"

"From Louisa Baumgartner." Her gaze was unfocused. Her voice shaky.

Harvey's wife. But Spense had been careful not to mention the bloody shoeprint to the Baumgartners. Which meant someone inside the investigation had leaked the information to the family. Likely one of the detectives had let it slip. Surely not Baskin. As lead investigator on the case, she'd hope he would be more discreet. Her entire body tensed. What little confidence she'd had in the task force was beginning to evaporate.

Spense worked his Rubik's cube, then put it away—just that fast. "How do you know Louisa Baumgartner, Jenny?"

"I guess I've known her forever. My aunt is her best friend—they're in the Woman's Club together, and Harvey Jr. was a friend of my brother's when they were in high school. After my mom died, Louisa took me under her wing. She's practically family."

"And you just now saw fit to mention this?" Caitlin could hardly believe her ears.

"I had no reason to. Why would I?"

Spense threw his arm across Caitlin's chest just in time to stop her from leaping from her seat. "Because Jenny. There's a killer on the loose. If you knew the family of one of the victims intimately, I'd say that's something you should have shared with the police from the get-go. And quite frankly, you don't seem too torn up about the recent death of a family friend."

Her head jerked up, and her eyes snapped. "I never said *he* was my friend. I don't like to speak ill of the dead, but Harvey Baumgartner was a creeper. You, know what I mean? I tried to tell Louisa, but she had a blind spot where Harvey was concerned. I'm not saying I'm glad he's gone, but . . . well, I'd say you had it right the first time. I'm just not all that torn up about it. In my opinion, Louisa and Junior are better off without him."

Chapter Fourteen

Sunday, September 15
Southwest Museum of Art
Phoenix, Arizona

"TELL ME AGAIN, why we're here," Spense said. "I'm all for culture," he added quickly, sounding not the least bit *for it* to Caitlin. "And, yes, we did finish our homework and turn it in to the teacher, but a field trip to the museum isn't at the top of my to-do list—not while we're trying to catch a killer. When we're not revising and evaluating the profile, I like to use the downtime to sleuth around and see what shakes loose. Guess it's the old field agent in me, rearing his good-looking head."

They traversed a green lawn, then passed an impressive bronze statue of Native American women in front of a massive, cornmeal white adobe building complex. Spense paused to crane his neck at the high arches that led into the main lobby of the Southwest Museum of Art. "Nope. Not how I'd choose to spend my afternoon . . . no matter how absolutely outstanding the architecture is. Is this a Frank Lloyd Wright?"

Delighted by Spense's sudden interest in Arizona architectural history, she smiled. "No. Not every building in Arizona was designed by him. This is the work of Bennie Gonzalez. But you're not too far off. The story goes that Bennie, as a school-aged boy, worked in his uncle's brick factory. One day, he caught a glimpse of Frank Lloyd Wright and decided on the spot he wanted to design buildings rather than make bricks. I don't know how true the story is, but I'd like to believe in the little boy who grew up to make his dreams come true."

"Very inspirational, I gotta say. But still, we're on the killer's clock here. What's the reason you dragged me down here?"

The beautiful clear sky, the warmth of the sun on her face, the image of a little boy who'd grown up to be an architect vanished in a heartbeat. They were here on urgent matters. She pressed her back against the door and stepped into the lobby with Spense on her heels. "You said if we got the profile hammered out, we could chase a wild hair. Well, this is the wild hair."

She checked her watch. Her friend Suzanne Kristoff was supposed to meet them in ten minutes, and Caitlin wanted to check out the pottery and textile exhibits beforehand. "You saw that lovely mug Jenny gave me—with that Southwestern motif. The more I stared at it, the more something was pinging in my brain. At first I couldn't put my finger on what, but eventually I realized I've seen that design many times." She paused for effect. "It's called the Man in the Maze motif."

His eyebrows lifted. "Whoa. That is interesting. So the Man in the Maze is your wild hair, and that motif is why we're visiting the museum?"

"You've never been here before?"

"I haven't. Museums aren't my thing." He turned his palms up. "Sorry to disappoint you, but I promise I'm teachable. And this place looks swell. Very Southwest, just like the name."

"That's because it *is* Southwest. The museum showcases Native American art and culture. And as it happens, I know the curator. Suzanne and I were at Stanford together. We weren't in the same classes or anything, but we both spent an inordinate amount of time at the library. It's really a cute story, if you'd like to hear it."

"Doll, I'd like to hear anything you want to tell me." He reached an arm around her shoulder, and she fought the urge to lean into him.

Moving forward, she managed to escape his arm and the dangerous sensations being near him brought on. "I'd bump into her often—she was usually chewing her pencil to shreds. Anyway, one day I smiled at her, and she smiled back. Then I sat down next to her, and lo and behold if she didn't turn out to be one of those rare individuals who *didn't* yap at you the whole time you were trying to study. So I sat next to her again. And after a while, we started saving a seat for each other. And there you have it, a friendship was born." She didn't add that Suzanne had turned out to be not only one of the few people who didn't yap at her, but one of the few real friends Caitlin had.

"Maybe you should try smiling more often. You never know what could come of it." He winked. Seriously, he winked at her like they were on a date instead of an investigatory excursion. And *he* was the one who was supposedly all *killer's clock*.

"Anyway, that's where we met. The library. At Stanford," she said, not cracking a smile at all.

"I see. Well, good for you." Then, he looked away, rather

abruptly, like she'd offended him somehow. Maybe she shouldn't have brought up Stanford. He'd referred to her education as fancy more than once, and though she'd never known a brighter man, she gathered school had been a real struggle for Spense.

"Anyway, take a look around you."

He swiveled on his feet, walked the perimeter of the room, and came back to her. "Amazing." He joked, but she knew he'd seen it, too. The Man in the Maze motif was ubiquitous in Native American pottery, textiles, and other art forms. An entire room of mazes, sometimes called Southwestern labyrinths, surrounded them.

Together, they walked down a long hallway and entered the pottery exhibit. Baskets and bowls, jugs, and plates, abounded. Many depicting the Southwestern labyrinth, and at its center, a man.

Find the Man in the Maze.

Well, she'd not only found the Man in the Maze, she'd found hundreds of them. What was she supposed to do next? Maybe Baskin had been right. Maybe Kramer really had been fucking with her.

"Caity." Spense's forehead furrowed. "You feeling okay? Because you look done in."

"I'm fine."

"You sure?"

"Spense, it's super annoying to have to repeat myself. I'll let you know if I need to take a break. It's not like I've overexerted myself."

"Fine by me, I'm just checking. But I have to give you credit—you found the Man in the Maze."

"The pieces are lovely, aren't they?" a voice behind them said. It was Suzanne, looking stunning as usual in stilettos and a designer suit, gallery lights shining off golden hair, swept into a French twist. Professional and yet so feminine. Suzanne had always had the polish Caitlin lacked, a result of growing up moneyed, no doubt. And yet the two women had more in common than they had differences, and they'd formed a lasting bond.

Caitlin gave Suzanne a quick, shy hug. Even with friends, she'd never felt comfortable expressing affection, or showing emotion, and though they'd kept in touch, she hadn't seen Suzanne since a Stanford class reunion a few years back. "Thanks so much for taking the time out of your day for us, Suzie."

"Believe me, I'm thrilled to be of use." Suzanne's gaze ran over Spense's chest, then darted back to Caitlin. The curator gestured to follow her, and then led them through the wing and outside into a breathtaking, stone courtyard.

"We'll have a good amount of privacy out here. It's slow this time of day." They pulled three lawn chairs around a small round table, near the wading pool. Reflected images from the palo verde trees above swayed in the blue water and the fragrance of honeysuckle saturated the air. Caitlin drew in a long, deep breath of Arizona.

Phoenix was her home, and she'd forgotten how much she'd once loved it. She'd forgotten the climbing trails, the birds, the yowl of the coyotes. Like she'd conjured it up with her memories, a coyote in the distance began to sing, and for one moment, she felt at peace. Here in this beautiful place, surrounded by the spiritual images the native artists had created, she felt at long last as if she were home.

Then Spense drummed his fingers on his wristwatch, as if to remind her they were in a hurry.

Time to get down to business, and she'd forgotten her manners. "Suzanne, this is Special Agent Atticus Spenser."

"Atticus? How wonderful." Of course Suzanne wouldn't bother with the special agent title. She always knew just how to talk to a man. Criminal investigative analyst or bartender, it didn't signify. Suzanne was equally at ease with both.

"Call me Spense. I'm sure you're busy, so we'll get straight to the point. What can you tell us about the Man in the Maze?"

Neatly crossing her legs at the ankles, Suzanne tugged at her skirt and shifted in her seat. "Caitlin gave me a heads-up, so I've printed out some information for you. And I have brochures." Suzanne passed them each a booklet and a sheaf of stapled papers. "This gives a detailed history of the Man in the Maze as Southwestern legend and art motif, but I'm happy to give you the Cliff Notes version."

"If you don't mind," Spense encouraged. He *was* in a rush. Though Caitlin had no idea where they were headed next. If they were supposed to be following up another lead, she wasn't aware of it. In fact, Gretchen had given her the opposite impression. That Spense and she were supposed to create a profile, then butt out until the locals needed them again.

"All right. Well, for starters, the Man in the Maze motif is what's known as a unicursal labyrinth."

Caity didn't follow, but Spense was nodding. Of course, the puzzle master would be familiar with unicursal mazes. She waited, figuring someone would define the term for her sooner or later.

Spense did the honors. "Unicursal means there's only one path leading to the center."

Suzanne uncrossed her ankles and leaned forward. "He's right. So you see, technically the Man in the Maze is a misnomer because these aren't mazes at all. Mazes have many branching and confusing paths, but here, we have only one." She traced an imagined Man in the Maze motif with her fingertips. "This is not a maze. This is a *labyrinth*. The motif originally sprang up as an illustration of an indigenous legend."

"If the Man in the Maze illustrates a legend, can you tell us the story?" Caitlin prompted.

"That's difficult, because interpretations vary widely. But in general, the Man in the Maze legend is an uplifting one. Many people believe the story is about finding a single path to harmony. When you get to the center of the maze, you are at one with either the creator, or in some versions, mankind. Like most art, I suppose the meaning is in the eye of the beholder."

Spense pushed his chair out, and the feet made a scratching noise on the cobblestones below. From above, a pygmy owl, perched in a mesquite tree, answered with a soft *whoo*.

"You look disappointed, *Spense*." Suzanne's voice dropped softly on his name. She had that way of making you feel as if you'd always known her.

"Not at all. It's a wonderful legend. It's just that I can't picture our UNSUB seeking spiritual harmony or oneness with the universe. Doesn't fit. Maybe *this* Man in the Maze has nothing to do with anything."

Suzanne shrugged. "Well, the other detective seemed to think it might."

That took Caitlin by surprise. To her knowledge, no one else was following up on this angle until other leads had been exhausted, and she wondered why Suzanne hadn't mentioned it before. Then again, there hadn't been much opportunity until now. "Who else has been asking?"

"A Detective Baskin from the Phoenix Police Department. I'm meeting with him in an hour."

Baskin? But he'd specifically said he thought the Man in the Maze was a dead end. She exchanged a glance with Spense. "Why would Baskin steer us away from the Man in the Maze, then turn around and contact Suzanne behind our backs?"

"The locals can be very protective of their turf. This is still their case, Caity, we're just advisors. And remember, Baskin doesn't report to us." Spense turned to Suzanne. "You mentioned there are other interpretations of the legend. Are any of them related to death?"

"Oh yes. Some people view the center of the maze as death rather than enlightenment, and some view death and enlightenment as one and the same thing. So one's journey to the center is all about learning to accept the ultimate destination."

Spense leaned forward. "Go on."

"Then there's yet another view that the man at the center of the maze is a teacher, a leader who instructed his pupils in the ways of his art, but he became evil, and ultimately his people killed him. Then, according to yet another riff, the Man in the Maze was so powerful, he came back to life."

Her cell rang. After a brief conversation, she hung up. "I'm so sorry, but we have some VIP guests up front, and I really ought to greet them. Is there anything else I can tell you before I go?"

"You've been a great help already. Thank you, but I think we'll let you get back to your work. And Ms. Kristoff . . ."

"Suzanne."

"Suzanne then," Spense smiled affably, but his tone carried a warning. "Anything we discussed is not for public disclosure. If word got out that we're looking into the Man in the Maze connection, it could compromise a criminal investigation. I assume we can count on your discretion."

"I'm not supposed to mention our meeting to the detective?"

"Sorry. I meant not to anyone outside of law enforcement. Detective Baskin is lead on this case. Naturally, we wouldn't ask you to keep information from him."

With a grace that seemed inherent in her every move, Suzanne rose. "Got it. And you can count on me." She placed a hand on Caitlin's shoulder and gave a gentle squeeze. "Lovely seeing you, Caitlin. If you're going to be in town awhile, you and Spense should come out with Jon and me some night."

It was clear from her tone Suzanne thought they were a couple. Caitlin didn't feel the need to correct her. It wouldn't be worthwhile to get into their personal affairs. "Sounds wonderful. We'll have to arrange that once things settle down with the case."

And then Suzanne was off, leaving them on their own. Caitlin wasn't sure what to make of the various story interpretations, and she was beginning to doubt this Man in the Maze was related to Kramer's Man in the Maze at all.

"I don't know what to do next." Leave it to the locals was one option, of course. But she'd made the mistake long ago of relying on the police and the courts to handle her father's case, and look how that had turned out. With lives—including hers—at stake, she couldn't stand by and wait for someone else to find the UNSUB.

"We could start by testing your profiler mettle," Spense said with a wink.

Chapter Fifteen

SPENSE THOUGHT HE detected a glimmer of excitement in Caity's eye when he suggested they put her profiler skills to the test. He recognized the effects of an adrenaline rush brought on by the prospect of a solving a puzzle whose solution—or lack thereof—could spell life or death. Her cheeks flushed, her pupils dilated, and her posture, even while sitting, had a certain spring to it.

"I'm game," she responded without hesitation and without knowing what he would suggest.

A bright twilight was descending on the little courtyard in the Southwest Museum of Art. Spense could see a squirrel nibbling in the flower garden, and with no one else in the area, this quiet, spiritual place provided an ambience conducive to the task. He folded his arms and leaned forward, resting them on the tabletop.

"Close your eyes."

She didn't ask why. At his request, she simply let her eyes flutter closed. He grinned to himself at how easily she complied with his commands. He couldn't deny the charge he got out of that, given the way she normally argued with him over the smallest point.

Then he took a good look at her face, full of trust, ready to do his bidding, and his chest grew tight.

She was so damn beautiful.

So damn good, and he was about to send her straight to hell and back. Right now, she was enjoying the game, anticipating the challenge, but there was dark work to be done. Profiling was an art as well as science, and what better time to introduce that subjective element than now, when they were pursuing a lead as ethereal as the Man in the Maze? Sometimes, the only way to break a case was to leave the constraints of your own mind behind and *become* the predator. Not like a medium, but simply by empathy—a quality that cold-blooded killers lacked, yet one that was absolutely necessary for a profiler. "This is the hard part, Caity. Before we go any further, I need you to understand that this is the moment where things get real—and not in a good way."

She frowned, but her eyes remained closed.

"We're about to leave the realm of cold hard facts, the stuff you and I both love, and enter . . ." His voice trailed off before he could finish his thought. If he told her the truth, that she was about to enter the twilight zone she might laugh, and the atmosphere would be ruined. "We're going to utilize a different part of your brain. I'm going to ask you to put yourself inside the killer's mind and see the world from his point of view. Are you ready for that?"

He watched as her throat worked in a hard swallow.

She nodded and placed her hands palms down on the table.

"Okay." He lowered his voice to a whisper. "The meaning of art is in the eye of the beholder. So imagine you're looking at a beautiful tapestry with the Man in the Maze motif. What do you see?"

She smiled. "Peace. A path to understanding."

"Good. Now let's do it again, only this time I want you to look at the maze from the inside. Only you're not Caity anymore. You're our UNSUB, a stone-cold killer at the heart of a labyrinth. *Now* what do you see? Describe it for me."

The evening breeze lifted her hair, and she breathed deeply. Spense inhaled along with her, taking in the scent of the Arizona outdoors—verbena, honeysuckle, and wildlife—and nearly reached out to stop her. He hated to send her down the rabbit hole of the UNSUB's mind. "Close your eyes. You're the Man in the Maze. Now . . . tell me what you see," he repeated.

She cleared her throat, as if resisting the descent into darkness. One more breath, then she began: "I'm the Man in the Maze."

"Where are you, what's happening in your world?"

"I'm in the museum wandering through the exhibits with my wife at my side. I love to come here on Sunday afternoons with my beautiful lady on my arm, especially when I've just found a new girl, and my mind's buzzing with planning and preparation. It relaxes me, and I like showering my mate with attention before I go on the hunt for fresh meat. She's been a good wife, and she deserves to feel appreciated. Her favorite room is the textile exhibit, and she likes to hold my hand and lean on me just a little as we walk." She smiled in a cunning way. "I'm sure we look very happy to everyone who sees us, and that's a good thing because as long as my wife can convince other people we have a perfect marriage, she doesn't interfere with my activities. She doesn't expect me to be a good husband anymore."

Caitlin paused a long time, so Spense prompted her. "Why not?"

"She knows me too well and gave up on that a long time ago. But appearances are very important to her, to both of us really. So I take her out on Sunday mornings, and in return she doesn't ask where I go on Saturday nights. The Southwest Museum of Art is her favorite place to pretend we are happy because it also lets her pretend she's smart. We both like to pretend—so many things. And anyway, I don't mind a bit of culture. It gives me something to talk about with the coeds other than the usual discussion of their boyfriends and how their boyfriends don't satisfy them, inside the bedroom or out. I know I can take them to a place where they've never been before."

Caity's body jerked, and he knew she didn't want to keep going. This time he didn't prompt her. It was her decision whether to continue. A long time passed, minutes maybe, then her shoulders relaxed, and she began again.

"As I think about the coeds, and what I will do to them, how I will make them grateful for the lessons I teach them, I give my wife's hand a comforting squeeze. She smiles at me in full performance mode. Sometimes she gives such a good performance, *I* even believe in the charade. I smooth a hand over my silk shirt. I'm dressed up, but not for the museum. It's because we've just come from church. The minister likes to talk, and I like to use that time to fantasize.

"His long sermons give me plenty of time to think of all the things I want to do to the coeds. I laugh to myself about how hard church makes me. I look at my bulging crotch, knowing my wife sees it, too. Then I check out my shoes. They've gotten dusty from the walk up the pathway to the museum. I'll have to polish them before class tomorrow and adjust the mirror. I have a tiny mirror in my loafers that looks like a penny. It lets me see up the skirts of the girls in my classes. I've been doing that for years. Long before I ever got bold enough to do what I really wanted to them." One of her hands balled into a fist. "I love giving them my attention, and I love letting them see how smart I am. They look up to me, as they should, and I inhale their worship like oxygen. I am their teacher. I am the Man in the Maze."

The wind picked up, and a plastic cup blew across the cobble-stones, making a clunking noise. He worried it would draw her out, but she continued, barely missing a beat.

"My wife leads me to a large bowl in a glass case at the museum. I see the decorative labyrinth, and I think how much I'd like to be the man at the center of that maze. In the dark, dead center of the labyrinth, I alone would hold the power. I would teach my ways to my little minions, and they would go out into the world and do the things I'd taught them. Afterward, I would make them prove their loyalty by producing a tribute.

"Isn't the Man in the Maze remarkable? my wife asks.

"*Yes*, I answer. I love this idea. It's taking hold of me. I can feel the fingers of it digging into my flesh like talons. The coeds aren't enough for me anymore. That look of fear in their eyes seems just an appetizer. Each time I relive the moment of their death, it loses its potency. I need something to hold me over between my con-quests, and that's when I decide. I *will* be the Man in the Maze. I'll find willing pupils, and we can share the excitement of our kills with one another. Then I will have the pleasure of their work, as well as my own."

Caitlin's hands clamped around the arms of her chair. Her body shook, as if she might cry, but the spasms passed without tears. She opened her eyes, and her gaze found Spense. "Let's get back to the apartment," she said in a tremulous voice. "I need to look at the autopsy photos and ME reports again. I think I just might be onto something."

Chapter Sixteen

Sunday, September 15
Blue Hawk Trails
Phoenix, Arizona

SPENSE POINTED OUT the house, and Caitlin pulled her Mustang to the curb. He'd insisted they had another errand to do before returning to Rutherford Towers. As anxious as she was to get back and study the Ferragamo reports, the exercise at the museum had taken its toll. She'd been stunned at the way her mind had opened, and she'd had an insight that might very well break the case wide open. But she was too excited and too fearful she might be mistaken to discuss it with Spense yet. This was one of those times where she'd seen too much. On her own, she would've stopped by a church. She needed time to clear her head before looking at the autopsy photos. This errand of Spense's gave her that chance.

It was good to be driving again. Her doctors had given her the thumbs-up for three weeks out, and tomorrow would be three weeks. Taking the liberty of shaving a day off that time empowered her and made her feel as if things were getting back to normal although, of course, they really weren't. But she'd take her normalcy in whatever small doses she could get it. For now, all she wanted was to feel like herself again and reclaim at least some of her independence. Driving her own car helped. It was a small thing, and yet it'd been important to her. Baskin had been by her apartment and brought her things to Spense's before she'd been released, so she hadn't even been home since the hospital.

She'd promised Spense if they took her car to the museum, in the future she wouldn't argue about riding in his unmarked vehicle, and after checking her car for tracking devices, he'd agreed. He must've understood how miserable it felt, going from the hospital, where her nurse did just about everything for her, straight to his apartment, where she was under his constant watchful eye. And taking the chance to literally be in the driver's seat, even for a day, had actually worked. She was practically giddy from the joy of punching the accelerator and honking the horn, and so now didn't protest when Spense announced they had one more stop to make—his mother's place.

He'd directed to her to a cul-de-sac in a well-kept gated community, Blue Hawk Trails. The homes were uniform, modest, and conveniently located. His mom's house had a little more personality than the others on the street, thanks to a striped awning that must've been hell to get past the homeowners' association. Maybe his mother was sleeping with someone on the board. Caitlin grinned at the thought. "I didn't realize your mom lived in Phoenix."

"After my father died, she relocated here to be near her sister. You also didn't know the name of my aftershave, and there's no reason you should. But, if you want to know something about me, Caity, all you have to do is ask."

Right. Which is why he'd gone all mystery man on her back in the hospital when she'd asked him something as innocuous as how he'd learned to solve a Rubik's cube.

"But we're here now, and this is my mother, so maybe we can pick this up later."

She found it rather charming that Spense had been so anxious to get over here to help his mom. She suspected all that *killer's clock* business earlier had really been him worrying that his mother would climb a stepladder and pull that box down from her closet herself if they didn't get to her place on time.

He opened his door. "Mom's probably looking out the blinds right this minute. She's probably already boiling the kettle to make us some hot cinnamon tea."

Caitlin looked up at the house. Two eyes and a nose *were* currently peeking out from behind the blinds. How adorable. "I'm looking forward to meeting your mother." She shoved out of the car, then allowed Spense to escort her up the sidewalk.

As soon as they stepped inside, she could hear the bright whistle of a kettle. Mrs. Spenser was indeed brewing something up . . . likely the cinnamon tea Spense had promised. Just the idea made her mouth water. Sure it was summer and hotter than blazes outside, but that's what air conditioners are for—so you can drink hot tea on a hundred-degree day.

Spense gave his mom a bear hug, made introductions, and bolted up the stairs. His mother wanted her memento box from the top shelf in the closet. Caitlin understood that Spense didn't want his sixty-eight-year-old mother to risk a fall, and she wondered what his mother normally did in these situations. After all, Spense's official residence was back in Quantico, Virginia. That had to be hard on her. Hopefully, she had a neighbor to help out.

Mrs. Spenser smiled after her son, then beamed at Caitlin like he'd just brought home his best girl. "Would you like some tea, dear? I can steep some in a matter of minutes. I've got this new licorice variety I've been wanting to try."

"Not cinnamon?"

"Oh yes, I've got that, too. Atticus enrolled me in a tea-of-the-month club years ago, and I got hooked. You might say it's my biggest vice, but I don't plan to quit it anytime soon."

Caitlin warmed inside, imagining what the world would be like if everyone's biggest vice were not being able to quit the tea-of-the-month club. "I'll try the licorice, if that's what you're having."

"Good. I'll brew up the cinnamon for Atticus. That way if you don't like your licorice, you can switch." A wrinkle in the space between her eyebrows deepened. "If you don't mind drinking after him, I mean."

Caitlin had a feeling this was her coy way of ascertaining if she and Spense had maybe swapped the occasional spit. "I don't mind."

Her eyes crinkled into a happy smile. "Be right back." And off she trotted into the kitchen. Soon Caitlin heard the sounds of cabinets opening and closing, and the rattling of spoons against dishes. She hoped Mrs. Spenser wasn't getting out the good china on her account. While she waited, she wandered about the living room, taking in colorful throw rugs that brightened up dark wood floors and breathing in the scent of potpourri. In the corner, an upright piano stood with sheet music opened and the keyboard cover up. As if someone had recently been playing. Her heart-strings tugged as she remembered her own—then happy—family, gathered around the fire, her father strumming his guitar, her mother singing her favorite song—"Molly Malone."

She glanced back at Mrs. Spenser, busy in the kitchen, then resumed her prowl. To the right of the piano, an open door led to a study, she presumed, given the big maple desk inside. And on the desk, center stage, she saw something that quite interested her— an oversized Rubik's cube. "Mrs. Spenser? If you don't mind, I'm just going to take a look . . ." Her voice drifted off as she entered the study, and curiosity overtook her manners.

The walls were covered in photos of Spense as a kid, most of them taken with a very handsome man whom she assumed was his father. There was one of the two of them fishing, and Spense had the teensiest fish dangling from his line and the biggest grin decorating his face. His dad was wearing one of those old fishing caps with the lures pinned to it.

In photo after photo, she saw father and son. Spense as a baby. Spense as a toddler. Spense as a grade-schooler. Always with Dad, and always smiling. And then . . . the photos changed to Spense alone, his smile one of those pasted-on-for-the-camera jobs. Her hand went to her heart. That made one more thing she hadn't known about Spense. His father must've died when Spense was still in grade school. She hadn't realized he'd lost his father so young. Suddenly, she wanted to know more about him—much more. Why hadn't she asked him more personal questions? They were sharing the same apartment, and he'd saved her life, for goodness' sake. Regret at her own standoffishness swelled in her chest. Why was it so hard for her to make a real friend? His words came back to her, making her cringe.

You should try smiling more often—you never know what might come of it.

She went to the desk and reached for the big Rubik's cube.

"That was his father's. But you can handle it if you like."

She drew her hand back. "Oh, no. I-I wouldn't want to scramble it up. I'm sure I couldn't put it right again."

"Wouldn't be any problem if you couldn't. Atticus can fix it in 26.3 seconds."

Caitlin arched one eyebrow. Spense's mother was a darling, but Caitlin didn't find such an *exact* number credible.

"I suppose that does sound like a fib, but it's the honest truth. We've clocked him, you know. As a kid, he made me get out the stopwatch and time him over and over while he tried for a personal best."

Laughing, Caitlin moved to the bookshelves, where a vintage copy of *To Kill a Mockingbird* had caught her eye. The binding was cracked with use, and it was obvious, for more reasons than one, the novel had been well loved. Caitlin loved it, too. She and Mrs. Spenser had that in common.

"I know what you're thinking. You're thinking I'm an awful mother to burden my son with a name like Atticus." Mrs. Spenser's tone said she'd been asked to explain herself on this count in the past.

"After Atticus Finch, the hero in *To Kill a Mockingbird*, right? I suspected that was where his name came from. I mean, it's not all that common."

"No. It certainly isn't. And yes, he's named after Mr. Atticus Finch. His dad had a conniption when I said I wanted to name our boy Atticus, and he fought me right up until the delivery. But when they put that baby boy in my arms, and I looked into my son's eyes, I knew he should have a name to live up to. I wanted him to grow up to be a man of integrity—like Atticus Finch. So I didn't back down. After weighing what I'd just been through to give him a son, Mr. Spenser relented."

"It's a fine name."

"Well, he doesn't go by it though, so I guess his daddy lost the battle but won the war. Atticus always took his father's side in everything. They were very close. Inseparable, really."

Caitlin nodded. That much was apparent from the photos. She could just picture the two of them. Spense tagging after his father everywhere. Maybe sitting on the counter and watching him shave. The Old Spice Spense wore suddenly seemed like the sweetest smell on earth: A man's tribute to his father. Goose bumps rose on her arms. She wished she could wear her father's aftershave. What a lovely thing that would be, to splash on the scent of happy memories every morning. And she had so *many* happy memories of her family, but somehow she'd let her life become all about the bad ones.

The murder.

The trial.

The execution.

Caitlin sighed and moved back to the desk, her gaze arrowing straight to the Rubik's cube. "So then, this cube. You said it belonged to your husband."

"That's right. My late husband, Jack, died of a heart attack at forty-five. Atticus was only eight years old at the time."

Her throat tightened with emotion, and not just sympathy, there was something else—a flash of fear. His father had had a heart attack at forty-five—only ten years older than Spense was now. A family history like that was a giant red flag. But . . . heredity wasn't everything. Lifestyle counted, and Spense took care of himself. That much she did know, and maybe now she understood why. She'd wondered, but again, never asked. Her breath released, and her shoulders relaxed. Her heart opened with the realization: Life is short. And sometimes it's cut even shorter. Reaching out, she took the cube in her hands. "Mrs. Spenser, I hope you don't mind my coming into the study on my own. It's just this cube caught my eye. You know Spense is such a whiz, and I don't know, I suppose I'm curious about all those puzzles of his."

"Oh, dear me. I don't mind a bit. I expect you would be curious about Atticus and his cube—the way he scrambles the one on his keychain every time his mind goes wandering."

"Yes. That's exactly what I've noticed. Every time he's tired or distracted, he pulls out his keychain and works the cube."

"There's a story behind that." Mrs. Spenser retrieved a Kleenex from her apron pocket and dabbed her eyes before they brimmed over.

Regret washed over Catlin. Spense hadn't wanted to talk about the subject, and obviously there was a reason—a painful one. "Please, you don't need to explain. I've already overstepped—"

"It was the day of Jack's funeral." Mrs. Spenser's eyes focused somewhere out the window. "Beautiful, clear day like today. And my Jack was a fine man. Deacon in the Baptist church. He had . . . so many friends. Seemed like every one of those friends packed our house after the service. Singing hymns at the piano. Loading the kitchen counters with casseroles and cakes." She shook her head. "It was standing room only all through the house for a long while. And when the guests were finally gone, Spense let out a yelp. I came running and found him in his father's study. I've tried to keep a study for Jack in every house we've had since . . . but I'm getting off track. The point is, someone had scrambled Jack's cube and Spense was fighting mad. Jack was so proud of solving the puzzle, and he'd kept it right on his desk, where everyone could admire it."

Rapt, Caitlin hardly noticed when Mrs. Spenser reached out and took the cube in her hands.

"So long story short . . ." She chuckled. "Folks always say that when there's plenty more to come. Have I bored you to the bone yet?"

She shook her head. "Please, go on."

"Where was I?" Mrs. Spenser glanced about the room, seeming a bit disoriented. "Oh, yes. Spense was fighting mad. And he dropped down in the middle of the floor and swore he wasn't going to get up until he'd put the cube right again." She dabbed her eye. "Now that may not seem like such a big thing to you, but the truth is my son has a learning problem. I don't like to call it a disability because Atticus is about as able as they come. Most of the doctors thought it was ADD, and we tried different medicines, but not one of them helped. He not only couldn't work a puzzle, he was already eight and could barely write his name, and he couldn't read a lick. But there he was, refusing to get up off the floor until he did what I knew would be impossible."

An image of a young Spense, struggling to put right his father's legacy, made her heart squeeze a little harder in her chest. "So what happened?"

"Well, I thought it best to let him be. I called him to dinner later on, but he'd have none of it. So I took a sedative and went to lie down, just for a bit. But I was worn down, and when I woke up it was already three in the morning, and I could see the light in the study was still on. I rushed in and found Spense, just about to click the last piece of the puzzle in place. He looked up at me with pride in his eyes. In spite of everything, in that moment he was happy. Caitlin, I hope you never know what's it's like to lose a husband, or to watch your child struggle with his self-confidence. But if you ever do, I'm here to tell you there's a way to get through." She blew her nose, making a delicate ladylike sound into the tissue.

Caitlin dug her nails into the palms of her hands and held her emotion in check.

"I will never know how Atticus managed to solve that Rubik's cube, but to me, it was an answered prayer. You see, whatever he did to work that cube, he figured out how to apply it to his school-work. He found a way to cope with his problem. He learned to read, and his math scores went way up. At night, he'd practice with the cube, working it over and over until finally it was no challenge for him at all. The school psychologist said she thought he might be forming new neural pathways. That's a fancy way of saying he retrained his brain, but I guess you know that."

Well, that certainly explained his contradictions. He'd apparently learned to cope intellectually, but some of his social impulsivity remained. "Incredible."

"A real miracle. Anyway, that's how the whole puzzle thing started. After that night, I brought him a new kind of puzzle every week: Tangrams, ciphers, logic puzzles—he especially loved peg solitaire. If I brought it, he solved it. And from then on, I never heard one word about that child being *disabled* again."

"Hey, where are you guys?" Spense poked his head around the corner, then joined them in the study. He looked from Caitlin to his mother and back again, a suspicious frown on his face.

Guilty heat crept up her neck. He must know they'd been talking about him.

"Is this the right box?" He twisted toward his mother.

"It is, son." She dusted her hands on her apron and shot an admiring glance at Spense. But her words were meant for Caitlin. "Not a day goes by I don't miss Jack Spenser, but one thing's for sure. After his dad died, Atticus stepped up." Her eyes never left Spense's face as she spoke. "He sees that I have everything I could possibly need, and a good deal of what I don't. If you ask me, he's more than lived up to the name I gave him."

His mouth lifted in a giant grin. "It's just a box, Mom."

"Sure it is, son. Just a tiny little box off a high shelf. Who wants tea? I expect it's black as berries by now."

Mrs. Spenser scurried into the kitchen, and Caity's heart lifted at the woman's joy over her son. Looking at Spense, she saw him differently. Not just as an agent who'd put his life in danger for her, not just as an exasperating man who made her feel things she didn't want to feel, but as a devoted son, a boy who'd lost his father too young and taken the weight meant for a man on his shoulders. More than anything, she wanted to believe in him and trust him with the things that mattered most to her. Could it really be so hard? She gritted her teeth and screwed up her nerve. "Spense . . ."

He was flipping through his phone, checking the missed calls. He'd turned his phone off when they'd stepped inside his mother's home—one more sign of the care he took with her. He slipped his cell in his pocket and glanced up. "Yep?"

She cleared her throat, nervously, deciding to start with an easy request and build up to the doozie. "If I asked you to get the evidentiary files from the police on the Sally Cartwright case, would you do it?"

He shrugged. "I know you think Sally's case is connected to the Ferragamo case. And as much as I doubt Kramer's innocence, it's a question that really ought to be asked, especially given the tie-in *signature* of the missing temporal bone."

"You'll do it, then?"

"I'll consider it. Technically, we should leave the investigation to Baskin and his crew, but since they're already overextended chasing down crime-scene evidence from both the courthouse and the hospital, I'm betting looking into the Cartwright case is a low priority."

"So you'll do it." Her mouth had gone dry. This was a good start. He'd agreed to her first request, so maybe she should just keep rolling.

He nodded, slowly. "It may come back to bite us in the ass, but yes, I'll have Herrera get hold of the Cartwright files."

She let out a long sigh and fought to keep her voice from shaking. "Fantastic. And I've got another request, since you owe me."

He shot her a huge grin. "How the hell do you figure I owe you? I saved your life, and the way I see it, if there are any favors to be handed out, I should be on the receiving end."

"You *owe* me precisely because you did save my life. My life is now connected to yours. I won't ever be rid of that . . . erm . . . connection."

That made him throw back his head and laugh, rather loudly. "Roger that. But since I'm doomed to be connected to you, too, you owe me right back. Stop dancing around your point, Caity, and just tell me what else you're after."

She took a deep breath.

"Spit it out for Chrissake."

"I need you to get me the evidentiary files on Gail Falconer."

His head was already shaking before she got out the *ner* in Falconer. "Sorry, Caity. No can do."

"You mean no *will* do." Why had she thought she could count on him? Just because of some tear-jerk story about his father? Well, she'd lost a father, too. She gulped back the anger that was boiling up from her gut and making her insides burn. Giving in to emotion never got a person anywhere. "If you wanted to get your hands on the Falconer files, you could do it. You don't even need an excuse, but if you think you should give one, you can simply say you think they might be connected because Baumgartner represented the defendants in both cases."

"By that reasoning, I'd have to ask for the files on every client Baumgartner represented over the past fifteen years. I doubt anyone would want to go through the hassle of finding them for me. Not to mention I'd look like an asshole."

"But my father's case and Kramer's were both capital murder cases, so that sets them apart from his others. Besides, the cases are connected through me." She pressed her lips and said a Hail Mary, knowing her next argument wouldn't fly, since Spense was convinced the shooter was a serial killer. "You could milk the vigilante angle."

He waved her off.

"You're just making excuses. If you don't want to help me, say so."

"Look. I'll admit I could get the Falconer files if I really wanted to. And I do understand what's going on here. I get it, Caity. And I do want to help you, but this isn't the way."

"I'm not sure what you think is *going on* here, but what I'm asking is for you to help me investigate the Falconer case."

"What I think is you want to use your shiny new skills and your not-so-shiny new amigo—assuming we *are* amigos now—to prove your father's innocence and clear his name."

"I want to know the truth. I *deserve* to know the truth."

"I'm tempted to quote Jack Nicholson from *A Few Good Men* here, but that's too easy, and I don't want to sound flippant. So let me ask you this. Is the truth really what you're after? What if the evidence points to your father's guilt?"

Her heart started tripping faster. He was seriously considering her request; she could tell. "It won't. Because he's not guilty. He *can't* be."

His face drained of color, and he looked past her, over her shoulder, like he'd just noticed the most interesting spot on the wall. "The Cartwright case is a good chance for you to learn some criminal investigative skills, and I'll help you with that because it's relevant to Ferragamo. But even that means there's going to be hell to pay for overstepping our bounds as consultants."

Her hope was sinking faster than a barometer in a hurricane.

"So if you want me to agree to the one, you have to promise to drop the other."

"The one being the Cartwright files and the other being the Falconer case."

"Right."

"You won't help me investigate Falconer even though you know my father might have been executed for a crime he didn't commit."

"That's the whole point, Caity. You say *might* to enlist my help, but the truth is you're absolutely convinced your father was an innocent man. I don't want to see you hurt again. If you find out you're wrong, how will you ever get over that? I'm not sure I could if our places were reversed. And if I'm being honest, I've read through the court transcripts already."

"When did you do that?"

One shoulder lifted. "While you were in the hospital."

"*Why* did you do that?"

"You think I didn't know you wanted to get the case reopened? Your investigators have been making themselves a pain in the ass with the authorities for years. It's no secret, Caity. I read through the transcripts because I care about you. But it's because I care that I won't get the evidentiary files for you now. If you want them, you'll have to figure a way to get them on your own."

"If you truly cared about me, you'd help me."

"I am *trying* to help you, Caity. So please drop this. Don't make me say something I'm going to regret."

She couldn't breathe. She couldn't talk. All she could do was stare at him in disbelief. She'd thought he was her friend, but that wasn't true. "Stop patronizing me and say what's on your mind," she ground out.

He rubbed his palms over both eyes, then half turned away. "From what I've seen, based only on the court transcripts mind you, I believe your father raped and murdered Gail Falconer."

First her lips went numb, then her whole face. That old, familiar stiffness came back to her heart, like it was too brittle to pump the blood through her veins. A voice in her head was screaming at her to yell at him, to fall on him and beat his chest with her fists. But that would only make things worse. Her chin came up. "Fine," she said, keeping her voice soft and controlled. "No worries, *amigo*. I'll ferret out the real killer myself."

Chapter Seventeen

Sunday, September 15
Rutherford Towers
Phoenix, Arizona

CAITLIN SAT CROSS-LEGGED on Spense's floor with crime-scene diagrams, autopsy photos, and ME reports organized into neat stacks in front of her. Next to those stacks, her e-reader was charging. Also on the floor, Spense leaned on his elbows, stretching his long legs out beside her.

From the sheepish look on his face, she thought he must regret the harsh words they'd had at his mother's house. And maybe she did, too, but one thing she didn't regret was knowing where he stood on Falconer. If Spense had no intention of helping her with her father's case, she preferred to know it now. That way she'd be better prepared when the time came to strike out on her own. Meanwhile, she had no intention of letting her personal disappointment get in the way of solving the Ferragamo case.

Watching Spense at the end of a long day, with a loosened collar, his hair tousled, and faint lines of fatigue building up around his eyes, made a lump well in her throat. There was no denying the fact she enjoyed his company and she cared about what happened to him. When he was happy, her own mood lifted. When he was weary, she wanted to offer him respite in her arms. Which is why she had to be more cautious than ever around him. A relationship of a romantic nature between Spense and her would spell professional disaster and was entirely out of the question. But over the past week, she'd begun to hope they could be real friends—and now that hope had been dashed. No matter what, she could never let someone into her heart who believed, without ever having known him, that her father had been a monster.

An hour ago, she'd wanted to lash out at Spense and raise her voice to him, tell him go to bloody fucking hell, but she'd refrained, and those urges had passed. She didn't feel those things anymore. In fact, she didn't feel much of anything except numb. Numb and ready to focus on the task at hand, which was not her disagreement with Spense but finding the Man in the Maze.

"So, are you going to let me in on this epiphany you had at the museum, or are you going to make me wait for it?" Spense interrupted her thoughts, bringing them back on track.

"I'm going to make you wait for it," she answered. "But not for long. I just don't want to get too excited until I verify a few things first. It's been a long time since med school and the anatomy lab." Flipping to the second page of the Ferragamo crime synopsis, she asked, "Okay if I use a highlighter on this?"

"Sure. These are just copies. Go for it."

Swish.

She did love the look and sound of a yellow marker on the page. Probably the perpetual student in her. She sniffed, and the familiar sharp scent got her neurons firing like she was back in school.

Swish. Swish.

"What are you highlighting?"

Everything. She'd always been an indiscriminate highlighter. But that wasn't what he really wanted to know. "I'm interested in the descriptions of the temporal bone. Did you know that what we commonly call the temporal bone actually has four distinct parts?"

"Nope."

She arched an eyebrow. "That was semirhetorical. I wasn't expecting you would."

"So I should just let you proceed. Tell you what, next time you ask a semirhetorical question, just say so, and I won't interrupt."

He was trying to be playful, but she wasn't in a playful mood. She knew that Spense used humor to diffuse anger, but she wasn't angry anymore, so the effort was wasted. "According to this autopsy report on the pharmacy tech, Darlene Dillinger's throat was slashed with a serrated hunting knife. Noted, too, is that *a piece* of the temporal bone was carved from her skull and presumed to have been taken for a trophy. But what I'm not finding is any specific notation as to exactly which of the four parts of the temporal bone the killer claimed for his prize."

"You think that's important." He eased closer to her, looking over her shoulder, and she shifted positions so he could see what she was doing.

In an effort to keep any unsteadiness out of her voice, she cleared her throat. It wasn't that easy to stay cool around Spense. "It's critical we find the answer. Sally Cartwright was strangled with a garrote. Darlene Dillinger had her throat slashed—the MOs are different."

"Which partly explains why Baskin doesn't seem to care both women had a piece of the temporal bone removed."

"But *you* taught me a killer's MO often changes with time, as he becomes more expert in his craft. And from all I've read, his *signature* will almost always stay the same. So what we need to determine is whether or not the Cartwright murder and the Dillinger murder actually share the same *signature*. Unless the same area of the temporal bone was removed, the signature isn't the same. I'm betting it was the same, and I believe it was the petrous part of the bone. But I want to be sure before I tell you the reason why."

"Baskin thinks removing Darlene Dillinger's temporal bone was simply a vigilante's attempt to replicate the signature in the Cartwright case. He thinks it's his way of saying *fuck you* to the police."

"That's a plausible idea if you assume the vigilante has been let down by the police in the past and wants to show the world they're incompetent. But it seems unlikely. A vigilante would never want the public to think Kramer might be innocent; besides, as you and I both know, based on the nature of the crime, whoever killed Darlene Dillinger took his time. Took *pleasure* from the act. The UNSUB unquestionably is a sexual sadist. Like you said before, Judd Kramer *may* be innocent, *or* he may be guilty and we have a copycat killer on our hands."

"You know what bugs me about the copycat theory?" Spense tugged his ear. "This"—he tugged harder—"is my semirhetorical-question signal. I don't really want you to answer."

In spite of herself, she smiled.

"What bugs me is a copycat wouldn't *only* imitate Kramer's

signature, especially such a difficult one. It's much more likely he would've also used the same MO as in the Cartwright case. With different MOs, either he's *not* a copycat, or he sucks at being one."

"But if the UNSUB is *not* copycatting the Cartwright murder, then we have to strongly consider the possibility that Kramer is innocent, despite what our guts and all the evidence tell us."

"Let's examine our choices," Spense said. "Choice number one: Someone is copycatting Kramer's murder of Sally Cartwright. Since he used a different MO and only copied the signature, that would mean we have a really stupid UNSUB on our hands—which contradicts all the evidence that the Ferragamo killer is highly organized and intelligent. The other huge problem with the copycat-killer theory is motivation. Even assuming our bad copycat viewed Kramer as competition and wanted to get rid of him for that reason, there's simply no obvious motive for a copycat to go after Baumgartner . . . or you. As a matter of fact we have the same problem if Kramer is innocent. The issue with motivation is the only reason I don't want to knock Baskin upside the head for focusing on the vigilante theory. I don't agree with him, but with no other motive tying the murders together, I do follow his reasoning."

"Which brings me to my epiphany at the museum. What if the UNSUB is *neither* copycat *nor* vigilante?"

"Then Kramer is innocent, and the UNSUB in the Ferragamo case killed both women—but the motivational dilemma remains."

"Maybe. Before I say any more, how long will it take you to get the evidence photos from the Cartwright case I asked for?"

A muscle flickered in his jaw. "They're in the other room."

"But how did you get them so quickly? I just asked you for them an hour ago."

"I've had them all along. I'm sorry. I should've told you right away. I've been thinking Cartwright and Dillinger are connected for a while now."

But he hadn't shared that with her. He went to retrieve the evidence files, and she wiped her damp palms on her jeans. That made one more thing he'd kept hidden from her. It seemed whenever Spense wanted information from her, they were a cozy one-for-all team. But when the shoe was on the other foot . . .

Dropping to the floor beside her, he handed her the files.

"Look, Spense, if we're going to be working together—"

He gently grasped her shoulders and turned her toward him. "If we're going to be working together, I have to stop holding back. Whatever information I have, whatever concerns, from now on, I promise I'll share them with you. It's not fair to expect you to trust me when I'm keeping things from you. When I say I'm sorry, I mean it, Caity. Won't you please give me a chance?"

He'd had a chance already—this would be a second or maybe third chance. She was losing track of how many times he'd held things back from her. "I *want* to trust you. But it's not really a matter of my giving you any more chances. It's a matter of whether you take them." She felt a quiver in her chin and took a deep breath, waiting for it to pass. She hadn't cried since the day her father died, and she wasn't going to start up now. "Frankly, I don't see a single logical reason for you to keep things from me."

His hands dropped. "It was stupid of me. But some part of me worried you'd cramp my style. I bend the rules sometimes, and I didn't want you trying to rein me in on the case."

It took a minute for what he was saying to sink in. And then she let out a long breath. He was probably right. There might indeed be times when she would *cramp his style*. But over the years, she'd come to understand that trying to force her views on others usually had undesirable results. If she had any hope of making a difference, she had to work within a flawed system. "I'll speak up when I think it's called for, but I'm not in charge of your morality, Spense. I'm only in charge of my own." She reached out her hand for a partners' shake. "But like you said before, if we're going to be a real team, you have to stop withholding information."

He took her hand, then traced the letters, *thanks* into her palm, and her heart seemed to flip in her chest. "So, Dr. Cassidy, what can I do to help my partner?"

Damn his charm. Keeping her expression neutral, she said, "I need to compare the section of Sally Cartwright's temporal bone found in Kramer's possession with the image of Darlene Dillinger's skull."

While Spense searched the Cartwright file, she located the Dillinger autopsy photos.

"Here's a good close-up of Kramer's trophy." Spense lined the evidence photo up with the autopsy shots she'd selected.

As she compared the photos her heart banged hard and fast against her ribs, and the *whoosh* of her pulse magnified in her ears. "There." Her voice edged up no matter how hard she tried to control it. "You see this. This piece of the temporal bone Kramer took corresponds exactly to the piece taken by our UNSUB."

"Doesn't seem the same to me. Kramer's bone is square and there's a triangular piece of Darlene's skull missing."

"I'm not referring to the shape or size of the incision. I'm talking about the *location* of the wound. See how this piece of bone found at Kramer's apartment looks porous? That's the *petrous* section of the temporal bone. It's called petrous after its rocklike appearance. Compare that to Darlene's autopsy photo. Our UNSUB removed a section of temporal bone just adjacent to the inner ear: the petrous part—the section containing the otic capsule has been removed. When Kramer was arrested, the papers reported a piece of Sally Cartwright's temporal bone was found in his possession. Nothing was ever mentioned about it being the petrous section. A copycat *couldn't* know about that. So maybe the UNSUB killed both Darlene Dillinger *and* Sally Cartwright *or . . .*"

"Or what? I don't follow."

"One possibility that *leaps* to mind is that the UNSUB really is the Man in the Maze."

"Still not following."

"From the legend, we know that the Man in the Maze was a teacher. According to Kramer, our UNSUB calls himself the Man in the Maze. We're in Arizona, so it makes sense the moniker might be related to the Southwestern legend."

Spense tilted his head and looked away, as if lost in thought. She waited for the idea to sink in. It didn't take long.

"Christ."

"Now you follow."

He nodded. "In the legend, the Man in the Maze teaches his ways to his students. That could explain why we have the same signature but different MOs. One killer is the student, the other the teacher. But maybe Kramer was the UNSUB's teacher, not the other way around." Spense's eyes lit up. "Either way, that *might* answer our question of motive. If the UNSUB and Kramer were student and teacher, then when Kramer was apprehended, the UNSUB might have worried Kramer would make a deal with the police and lead them back to him."

Her hands shook with excitement. "I believe the Man in the Maze, not Kramer, played the teacher's role. But I agree the

UNSUB might have gone after Kramer because he was afraid he'd make a deal and give him up to the police. That would also explain why he had to take Baumgartner and me out, too, because he was afraid of what Kramer might've revealed to us."

"I'm with you on most of this, Caity, but we should be careful. That exercise we did back at the museum was exactly that—an exercise—not evidence. It's just a way of getting in touch with possible scenarios by giving your brain permission to put yourself into the mind of a killer. And maybe you're right. But we need more than your instincts to go on. The truth is, we don't really know if the Man in the Maze exists. We need more to go on than Kramer's word."

"But we *do* have more to go on. We *do* have evidence." She pulled out the brochure from the museum and opened it to the pottery section. "Look at the Man in the Maze motif."

He scratched his chin. "The unicursal labyrinth with the man in the center, I remember. That's all well and good, but other than Kramer's word, there's nothing that connects the Man in the Maze to the crime."

"The maze in question is a unicursal labyrinth, right?"

"Sure, but there were no labyrinths drawn or carved onto the victims, no Man in the Maze jewelry or pottery left at the scene. If this guy's obsessed with the legend, it seems like there would be."

"Our UNSUB *is* the Man in the Maze, Spense. He didn't *leave* a labyrinth on the bodies. He *took* a labyrinth . . . as a souvenir." She pointed to the photo of Kramer's bone trophy. "It's hard to tell from this photo, but let me show you a dissected view of petrous bone." She powered up her e-reader.

His head snapped back in surprise. "You have a picture of dissected petrous bone on your e-reader?"

"I have *Netter's Human Anatomy Atlas* on my e-reader. My hardcover copy is too heavy to lug around, and besides, I swear, even after all these years, it still smells like formaldehyde." She navigated to an illustration of dissected bone. "What does this look like to you?"

"It looks a hell of a lot like the mazes we saw at the museum. *That's* what the UNUSB carved out of Darlene Dillinger's skull?"

"Yes. The petrous bone contains cavities and passages that accommodate the inner structures of the ear. That's why it's called the *bony labyrinth*."

Suddenly, Spense's cell vibrated, and Caitlin let out a startled yelp.

"Jumpy little thing, aren't you." Spense winked at her and looked down at his cell, the smile quickly vanishing from his face.

"What is it?" She held her breath, knowing from Spense's expression this had to be something big.

"It's Baskin. He's got a suspect at the station. They want us, and in particular you, to come down in the morning to observe his interrogation."

Chapter Eighteen

Monday, September 16
Phoenix Police Department
Mountainside Precinct

SPENSE SHIFTED IN a flimsy, aluminum-legged chair made of cheap red plastic. The seat he'd been offered in the precinct computer room was identical to the chairs in the interrogation room. This one must've been designated specifically for suspects because a screw had been loosened and raised and was currently poking him in the ass. The seat itself wobbled, and the girth was far too narrow for his frame. It was damned uncomfortable, which of course was the point. Detective Thompson had pulled up a similar chair for Caity, but Spense had put the kibosh on that fast and scavenged a comfortable spinner for her from another room.

Although she'd sworn off the good stuff, she was eating ibuprofen like candy, and he knew her flank hurt like hell. If you asked her, she'd deny it, but he could tell by the way she grimaced when she thought he wasn't looking. Caity hated being babied, and he didn't get that at all. Personally, he loved being on the receiving end of a little extra attention when he was sick. But maybe that was a guy thing. Stretching out his legs, he gave her shoe a gentle kick.

"Quiet." She flicked her hand at him.

"I didn't say anything."

"But I'm trying to concentrate, and you're bothering me."

"The interrogation is being recorded, obviously, since we're watching a computer feed. If you miss something, we can just rewind."

"Shh."

Temporarily giving up, Spense rested his forearms on the counter that ran the perimeter of the room. On top of the counter, computers were spaced every few feet to accommodate multiple officers engaged in various tasks. That's why they called the place *the computer room*. Cops were clever like that. Caity's eyes were fixed on the live feed coming from the interview room. The suspect interrogation was just getting started, but the warm-up was one of the most important parts of the process. The lights in the room and the multiple computer screens running at the same time were distracting him, but Baskin was interested, for once, in their observations. Shaking the cobwebs from his head, Spense made an effort to focus.

The interrogation room was set up to maximize the suspect's discomfort. The more dependent he felt on the officers for his basic comfort, the better. At the moment, Detective Thompson was trying to convince a Mr. Silas Graham, aka *the suspect*, that he was a Mets fan. Thompson was a diehard Yankees man, but to hear him tell it now, he had the Mets' starting lineup tattooed on his dick and jacked off to the "Star Spangled Banner" every morning. This was Thompson's idea of building rapport, and Spense had to give him credit, because he'd managed to get Graham talking and waving his hands around, arguing over who was the best relief pitcher. Thompson was even faking a Bronx accent. That was some serious police work going on in there because what Spense knew of Thompson, the guy had a low opinion of suspects, usually referring to them as assholes and motherfuckers. But right now, he had Graham eating out of his hand. "I had no idea Tommy was such a good actor."

"Quiet . . . *please.*"

He nudged Caity's foot again, and finally she turned around and sent him her drop-dead glare—which had been his goal all along. To irritate her further, he gave her a wink.

"Spense, can you just rein it in a little?"

He might've gone too far because she no longer seemed irritated. She seemed concerned, and that's when he realized his brain really had gone off track. Pulling in a deep breath, he yanked his focus back to center. Sometimes that was like trying to reel in a marlin when all you had for line was dental floss, but over time he'd developed the mental muscle to make it work. He knew how to shift gears when it really mattered, and he did so now. "Sorry."

"It's okay. But I'm trying to take notes and watch the interrogation at the same time."

"I'm a pretty good multitasker when I have to be. Why don't you tell me your observations, and I'll jot them down as we go. That way you can focus on the suspect and leave the note taking to me."

"Thanks." She passed him her pen and pad. "Okay, Thompson just asked Graham what he had for dinner last night, and his eyes moved to the right. They've done that every time he's had to access his short-term memory."

He scribbled it down. "Pretty standard."

"Sure, but you can't count on using the same template for everyone. Some people march to their own neurolinguistic drummer. So I'd rather we start from scratch and observe Graham rather than rely on what's typical."

"Agreed." Caity was right. Every individual had his own unique, nonverbal tells, which was why you couldn't just read a book and expect to know whether or not someone was lying.

"There, did you see that. He's looking up again."

Thompson had just asked how he thought the Mets were going to fare this season and what he thought they should do to improve their chances. That meant when the suspect looked up, he was using his imagination, not his memory. His nose twitched, too.

"Got it. Looks up and nose twitches when using his imagination." In other words, when lying like a son of a gun. Spense watched Baskin enter the interrogation room, turn a chair around, and straddle it, his back to the camera. "Bad cop enters stage left."

"Mr. Graham, I've got a few questions for you," Baskin said without preliminaries.

"Am I under arrest?"

"Should you be? What would we be charging you with, Mr. Graham?"

"I don't know."

"Then no. You're here voluntarily. Free to go anytime." Baskin scooted his chair to the right. Now he and Thompson had Graham completely boxed in. "But I thought you wanted to cooperate. Did I get that wrong?"

"No. I do want to cooperate, but I'm afraid no one told me what this is about. So how can I help if I don't know what you want?"

"Well, we'll get to that, eventually. Mr. Graham, where you were last Wednesday night?"

Graham's eyes moved right, using his recall. "I was at home."

"Alone?"

"Alone." Graham shrugged, seeming unconcerned.

"Where were you the afternoon of August 26."

"Uh. The twenty-sixth?" His eyes rolled up, and his knee began to jitter. "I went to the movies. I think. I mean I can't really remember for sure. I might've had a job interview. That's been nearly a month ago, you know. Where were *you* August 26?"

"Rounding up low-life felons like you."

"I'm not a felon. I'm an accountant. Maybe I need a lawyer after all."

"Nothing official's going on here, but if you want to lawyer up, it's going to look bad. Still, if you insist, we'll get someone down here for you. An accountant eh? But you can't account for your whereabouts." Baskin slapped his knee, let out a guffaw, and gave Thompson a friendly push.

"Like I said, I'm cooperating."

Graham had no alibi for the day of the courthouse shootings—judging from his body language, he'd been lying about the movie and the job interview, but that would be simple enough to track down. Baskin and Thompson continued to press him about his whereabouts the days of the murders, and after about twenty minutes, Baskin excused himself and entered the computer room.

He immediately crossed to Spense, leaned over, and muttered under his breath, "Next time you go off chasing your own tail, run it by me first."

He was referring to Spense and Caity's outing to the Southwest Museum of Art no doubt. "Sure, buddy, and you do the same. Funny you didn't mention you were going to follow up on the Man in the Maze—we could've carpooled, saved on gas, maybe had a sing-along on the way."

Baskin opened his mouth, but then cut his gaze to Caity, apparently reconsidering whatever snappy comeback he'd had planned. He smiled at her and dragged a hand through his hair. "You look damn good without those raccoon eyes, Dr. Cassidy. You're feeling better, I hope."

Spense didn't like the overly familiar way Baskin spoke to Caity, but if she minded, she didn't let it show.

"Much better. Thank you. And thanks for calling me down to the station. I've enjoyed seeing you in action today."

Baskin seemed to gain an inch in stature. "Anytime you want to see me in action, just say the word. I'm happy to have you. Maybe you'd like to tag along next time I—"

"Dr. Cassidy is not available for *tagalongs* until the UNSUB has been apprehended. Surely, you wouldn't want to put her in harm's way."

"I'd be fully prepared to offer her my protection, so I don't see how she'd be any more in harm's way than when she's tagging along with you, Spenser. But maybe we should get down to business."

He looked at Caity, apparently uninterested in Spense's opinion, but Spense wasn't going to cry over it or anything. Still, the way Baskin blew hot and cold toward Caity bothered him. One minute he was dismissing her and the next minute preening in front of her. Spense rubbed his neck to release the tension that had been building up.

"What do you think of our suspect, Dr. Cassidy?" Spense knew Baskin would supply more details on Graham only *after* he got their take on things. Better to let them draw their own conclusions before feeding them prejudicial information.

"So far, I like him. He's the right height and build for our UNSUB, and he's clearly lying about his whereabouts on the days of both the courthouse shootings and the hospital murders. And that's without him knowing why he's being interrogated. But it's not enough to be certain. Maybe he just happened to commit another crime on those particular days, or did something else he's ashamed of, like visiting a prostitute."

"If you think he's lying, we're going to lean on him hard. See if we can get a confession." Baskin dragged a hand through his hair, preening for Caity again . . . like a weasel.

"I do think he's lying. Who is he? How did you find him?" she asked.

"Combination of luck and good police work. The guys in the bullpen have been passing around the profile you guys came up with and have been told to be on the lookout. Mr. Silas Graham, here, bought himself a ticket downtown by driving under the influence last night. Then his arresting officer matched him up with your profile."

The profile had proved useful after all. Maybe that accounted for Baskin's sudden interest in their opinion.

"He had a brief, inglorious stint in the army. Twenty-nine years old, professional, recently lost his job at a big accounting firm in New York. Relocated to Phoenix two months ago, currently looking for employment. Busted two years ago for peeping on his neighbor's teenage daughter. Long history of substance abuse. And, while he was he was high as a kite, he got graphic with a female cop about what he'd like to do to her in the sack."

Spense nodded, this could definitely be their UNSUB, but you can't arrest a guy because he fits a profile. You need actual evidence for that. Still, he was grateful Baskin had circulated their profile despite his skepticism. Mark of a good cop.

"How long can you hold him?" Caitlin asked.

"We can't. This is his first DUI, so once he's sobered up, he's free to go, and he's been stone cold for hours now. He's answering questions voluntarily, so unless we can get a confession, we gotta let him go at his request."

"Will he take a polygraph?"

"He's declined. And he's getting antsy. I'm expecting him to dip any minute."

"What about a search of his home?" Caity pressed Baskin.

"We don't have enough for a warrant, but Thompson's got the touch. He'll offer to drive him home. Graham's car's impounded. Maybe Thompson can strike up enough of a rapport to wheedle an invitation to come inside and take a look around. All depends on how comfy Graham gets with Tommy."

Caity look worried. And she should be. They'd have eyes on Graham, of course, but he wouldn't be the first person of interest to give them the slip. But there was nothing to be done without more evidence. "I hate to agree with you, Baskin, but I don't think we've got enough for a warrant either. We'll have to keep digging." Spense exchanged a glance with Caity, then turned again to Baskin. "Before we head out, you got a second? We've got some information we think you'll be very interested in."

Chapter Nineteen

Tuesday, September 17

From: Man in the Maze <395204@253.0.101.212>
To: Labyrinth <list.27040302@253.0.101.212>
Subject: Warning

Greetings pupils. As always, thank you for your magnificent postings, but I'm afraid we must curtail them for a while. You see we are no longer safe. A brave lieutenant has eliminated one threat to our members, but more abound. And now I fear the lieutenant himself may present a danger to Labyrinth. The authorities may be close to identifying our group. Do not ask me how I know this. I have my sources. For this reason, I must ask you to refrain from posting until further notice. Though I always look forward to sharing your pleasures, we must be discreet.

I may have urgent communication for you in the near future. So please continue to watch for my messages. In the meantime, this site is to be used only by me for my instructions to the group. We have always protected one another, and I vow I will keep you all safe and find a way for us to resume our games. Until then, stay prepared and watch for your chance. Anyone who collects a labyrinth will be rewarded as soon as it is safe to do so.

Chapter Twenty

Tuesday, September 17
Rutherford Towers
Phoenix, Arizona

"I MADE COFFEE." Caitlin gave Spense the perkiest smile she could muster when he appeared in the kitchen. Her side had ached most of the night, and between that discomfort and her preoccupation with the case, she'd hardly slept.

Spense, on the other hand, had apparently slept rather well. They kept their doors open, and she'd heard him snoring from his room. Maybe something had triggered his allergies, or maybe he'd just slept in the wrong position, but snores or no snores, she'd found his presence reassuring.

"Thanks." He snagged the pot and poured himself a cup. "You're up early. D'ya sleep okay? Because I thought I heard you snoring."

"That was you."

He grinned. "Nope. I think it was you."

Pushing her hair out of her eyes, she arched one eyebrow. It certainly had not been her. And it was time to change the subject to the thoughts that had kept her up all night. After the interrogation of Silas Graham yesterday, they'd had a long conversation with both Baskin and Thompson, filling the men in on the Man in the Maze. One of many questions the detectives had posed to them was how, if the Man in the Maze truly existed, did he connect with Kramer?

"I mean there's not exactly a Match dot com for serial killers. So how did they find each other?" Caitlin began the conversation in the middle of her thoughts, as if Spense could read her mind.

But maybe he really had read her thoughts because he'd picked the thread right up. "My guess would be either personal contact or the Internet. You'd be surprised how many truly creepy sites are thriving out there. Which brings up another point. According to our profile, Kramer knew the Man in the Maze might be after him but he didn't seem to know his true identity. If he had, I believe he would've given you a name."

He took a sip of coffee, and she noticed he was using the cup Jenny had brought over—the one with the Man in the Maze motif. Her mind racing with possibilities, she pulled out a chair and sat down hard. Spense fixed her with an expectant stare. As if waiting for her to catch up . . . and suddenly she did. *Good Lord*. How had she missed it before? Of course they met online. That's why Kramer didn't know his real name—he only knew him by his *handle*.

"You think the Man in the Maze finds his students . . ." As soon as the word popped out of her mouth, her hand went to her chest. This was one of those little gems that comes as a gift. Apparently while she'd tossed and turned last night, her subconscious mind had been solving the riddle.

Students.

It was all so *obvious* now. Teachers didn't usually confine themselves to one student. And the Man in the Maze from the legend had *pupils,* not *a pupil.* Spense motioned for her to continue like he was one step ahead and waiting for her to catch up. Maybe he'd been doing more than just snoring last night. "So like a cyber kill club or something? You think there may be other students? Because if there are . . ." She realized there were troubling sites out there, and illegal ones, too, but she'd never understood how they operated without being caught.

"If there are more "trainees," our UNSUB could be the Man in the Maze or any one of his minions." Spense took a long slurp of coffee and gave her an appreciative look. "This is damn good, Caity."

She didn't see how Spense could remain calm. Her legs were bouncing up and down beneath the table. She wanted to jump up and *do something.* But what? "Okay. If there's a kill club, and if they have a Web site or loop or whatever, can't you just call up one of your cyber guys at the Bureau and have him track the club down?"

"I'm afraid it's not that simple. Yes, the Bureau has their eye on this kind of thing. There's an entire FBI division devoted to cybercrime, and dozens of specific cybercrime task forces, but it's not that easy to locate these subversive groups. They come across our radar on occasion, but other times, we're not that lucky. Have you ever heard of the deep web?"

He wasn't tugging his ear to signal *semirhetorical question,* so she answered, "No."

"Then let me explain it in terms a psychiatrist can relate to. You believe in the power of the subconscious mind, right?" This time he did tug his ear, so she kept quiet. "Well, these groups operate in the cyberspace equivalent of the subconscious mind."

Intent on this new information, her legs settled down, and her mind homed in on his words. "Go on."

"The brain contains all sorts of information that can't be easily accessed. Most of the information is below the surface, and we often need a specific trigger—like a smell or an old song—to access those memories or that bit of knowledge. And sometimes, we need special techniques, like hypnosis to get to them. The deep web is a lot like that."

Instantly, she got it. Because Spense really had found an analogy she could wrap her head around.

"There's an enormous underground network in cyberspace. Just because you can't see it doesn't mean it's not real. It's there, only hidden. You can't get into the deep web with a Google search, because the sites aren't registered anywhere. And they operate mainly through file sharing, so there's no static page."

"But, if the sites are not searchable, that means they're not accessible, doesn't it? So how do people get to them?" Maybe she hadn't gotten it after all.

"Oh, they're accessible all right. You just have to find the right trigger. By typing the right words into the address bar, it's possible to stumble upon a particular site, and there are other ways if you know what you're doing. But more likely a member who knows you, in person or from another site, recruits you. Most clubs require you to protect their privacy once they allow you in. There are programs that use layers of encryption, sometimes called onion routing, to direct traffic through a network of volunteer relays, making it extremely difficult to track a user's location. Anyway, that's my lesson for the day. Deep web for dummies." He spread his palms. "Not that you're . . ."

She laughed at his sudden sheepishness. "No offense taken. I appreciate you dumbing it down for me."

A deep-web kill club.

That sounded like fiction, but she recalled a recent case . . . that one too had involved a cop . . . like Kramer. The group had operated in the guise of a fantasy role-play site. From what she'd read, many of the members were indeed just engaged in role-playing. She touched her throat. If the Man in the Maze really had his own club, and Kramer had been a part of it, how many of the members were just creepy role-players, and how many were the real deal—psychopaths out hunting their prey? And even if they rounded up all the club members, would the authorities ever be able to tell the difference? "They can't all be real killers in the club. Surely some think it's just a game."

"Undoubtedly. And that makes it damn hard to go after them proactively. How can you convict anyone from the club for their part in things? Is it a conspiracy to commit murder or mere fantasy? I'm not sure anyone can really know . . . until somebody turns up dead."

Spense's phone buzzed again. He looked at it and held up one hand. Then he set his cup down too hard in its saucer, and it clattered, sloshing coffee on the tablecloth. Heaving a rough sigh, he said, "Saddle up, Caity. We gotta roll."

Chapter Twenty-One

Tuesday, September 17
Sun Valley Apartments
Phoenix, Arizona

SILAS GRAHAM WAS dead. Acidity from her morning coffee rose in Caitlin's throat, leaving a bitter taste in her mouth. An overripe, half-peeled banana on the outdated linoleum counter saturated the room with the smell of rotting fruit, and she had to work hard to suppress her gag reflex. As she studied Graham's slumped body, his cherry red cheek squashed against a glass breakfast table in his east valley home, her hands opened and closed at her sides in disbelief.

Another cyanide poisoning.

The room was crawling with uniforms, and Spense seemed to be climbing the walls. He'd worked his cube several times already and was currently up in Baskin's face, arguing—though she couldn't hear what they were saying. CSIs swarmed the one-bedroom apartment, and the air hummed with their voices. One was under the table now, swabbing suspicious spots and photographing Graham's face from beneath the glass tabletop. They'd been instructed not to move the body until the ME arrived. Baskin motioned her over, and she joined the huddle on the other side of the room.

"What the fuck happened here, Thompson?" Baskin's gloved hands were in the air, and the vein that bisected his forehead seemed to have doubled in size. Red crept up around his collar. "You were supposed to escort Graham home yesterday and parlay an invitation to search the place, and that's *all* you were supposed to do."

Thompson's lips flattened, and a stony look came over his face. "I saw an opportunity, and I took it."

"You had every *opportunity* to pursue your line of questioning *on camera* down at the precinct. But you didn't. You pull shit like this, it's gotta be done the right way. You lie to a suspect, tell him you've got the goods on him when you don't, you gotta do it *on camera*. Jesus H, Thompson, do you know how this looks?"

Resentment flared in Thompson's eyes. "It looks bad, I know. But we got the guy off the streets, didn't we?"

Caity had been watching silently, merely observing like Spense had instructed her to do, but she couldn't restrain herself when she heard Thompson's words. Silas Graham might be their UNSUB, the Ferragamo killer, but she doubted he was the Man in the Maze. Alive, Graham might have led them to a network of killers, but now . . . "This man is dead, Detective. Is that the way you've been trained to get criminals off the street?" Her face went hot, and she took a step toward Thompson. She was crowding him, and she knew it, but she took another step closer anyway. She could feel the nervous energy coming off him, smell his mint mouthwash.

"I'm not going to apologize for my actions, especially not to you. You got no business here at my scene. I did my job, and I got a confession."

He did his job, all right. The swagger in his voice, the proud jut of his chin told her he'd do it again. Anything was fair game, just as long as he got his man. It was men like Thompson with their bullying, rogue tactics that led to coerced confessions from innocent men—like her father. "You expect anyone to believe you followed procedure? Let me tell you what I think. I think you planned to question Graham off-site so you could go maverick. I think you wanted to be free of the cameras, so you could use illegal means to an end. I think the gash on Graham's cheek isn't from landing facedown on the table. I think it's from your fist!"

Thompson put a hand in the air, a wide cut clearly visible on his right knuckle, and leaking blood under his latex glove. "You gonna let this bitch talk to me like that?" He was eyeing Baskin.

Spense grabbed her by the shoulders and tugged her out of the way, then *he* was in Thompson's face. His fists came up, and for a minute she held her breath, thinking Spense's control might slip, and he might do something he'd regret. But he didn't. He simply froze Thompson with an icy stare. "Listen to me very carefully, Detective. I want you to apologize to Dr. Cassidy, and I want you to do it now."

"I won't. *She* came at me. She accused me of breaking the law."

"And you didn't?" Baskin's eyebrows seemed to be attacking his hairline.

"I swear on my mother's grave, no, I swear on my *pension*. I might've wanted to take the mofo out myself, but I wouldn't do something that stupid. I'm not gonna throw my career away, I'm not gonna throw my *life* away for a scumbag like this."

As he edged closer to Thompson, a muscle ticked in Spense's jaw. He looked like he was about to demand an apology for Caity again, and his fists were not only up but cocked this time. She caught Spense's eye and tugged her ear to signal *no response required*. She didn't want Spense fighting her battles for her. His whole body stiffened, and she saw his inner struggle on his face, but a few tense seconds later, he stuffed his hands in his pockets and backed away from Thompson.

Caitlin used the moment of quiet to press her back against the wall, breathe deeply, and regain her composure. Then she stepped forward, and this time she didn't crowd Thompson. "Suppose you tell us just exactly what happened."

"It's like I said the first three times. I drove Graham home yesterday, and I gave him my number. So this morning, he calls me up, asks can he get a ride to the grocery store because he's out of Jack, and I say sure, I'll swing by. So I take him to Safeway and after, I get my foot in the door on the pretext of needing to take a crap. When I get inside, I figure I really should take a crap, or else he'll know the whole thing's a setup. So I go to the can and do my business, and he has his pornos right there by the john. *Penthouse, Hustler*—he did have a stack of *True Detective* mags, but I figure that's no big deal. Though I did hear a lot of serial killers like the detective magazines. Anyway, I was thumbing through a *Hustler* when *this* fell out."

He pointed to a photograph on the table. It showed the bloodied remains of a woman—her torso battered and genitals slashed. Ropes of tendons and flesh dripped from her neck. It appeared as though someone had half sliced, half ripped the head from her body. The head itself was not in the photograph. Caitlin forced herself to look at the image. Flinching now would only reinforce Thompson's point that she really had no official business at the scene. Spense had allowed her in partly because she'd asked, but mostly, she suspected, he simply didn't want to let her out of his sight. She eyed the doorway. If she threw up, it'd better not be in the toilet. There was evidence in that bathroom.

"And that's when I knew for sure Graham was our guy. So I sat down at the table with him, and I showed him the photograph, and he said it was just role-playing. He said he downloaded it from an Internet site and didn't know anything about the woman. Said he just used it to beat off. I want it noted that I wanted to beat him myself when he said that, but I remained professional. I next explained to him I was going to pull him back down to the station. I told him he could come voluntarily, or I could arrest him."

"You didn't have any basis for arresting him," Caitlin interrupted. "You don't even know if this photograph is real, much less how he obtained it."

"I was *lying* to get his cooperation."

Her jaw clamped tight. Lies were par for the course in police work. Even Spense thought it was okay to tell a suspect you had proof that didn't exist. "How did you get him to confess?" Her voice came out as a thin, shaky thread as her father's face flashed in her memory.

"I told him we lifted his fingerprints from that plastic pouch at the hospital, the one with the cyanide pill we took off your nurse." Thompson's lips stretched into a snarl. "Then he said there was no way that was possible because he'd been wearing gloves. By the time he realized his mistake, it was too late. I *had* him."

"You recorded this conversation, I hope." Baskin was nodding now, as if he might approve of the good work after all.

"Yeah. Yeah. Of course. Only I had the recorder in my pocket, and there was some kind of mechanical failure. So no, I don't actually have it although I did record it as I should. It's just mechanical failure and nothing I can do about that. But I'm sure we'll find plenty to prove Graham is our UNSUB once we're done tossing the place."

Baskin inclined his head toward Graham's body. "And that's when he bit down on something and started foaming at the mouth?"

"It is, sir. That's correct, sir."

"Did you try to revive him?" Caitlin asked.

"He was dead. So no, I did not try to revive the motherfucker."

A uniform emerged from the bedroom holding an evidence bag and crossed the room to show them his discovery. "Jackpot," he said, and rattled the bag. "I think I found the cyanide, here, and in the bedroom, there's a computer and get this . . . the asshole's still logged on."

Chapter Twenty-Two

Tuesday, September 17
Phoenix Police Department
Mountainside Precinct

IT'D BEEN A long day. They'd spent hours at the crime scene, then grabbed a late lunch and headed to the precinct—where she'd been waiting even longer. Caitlin sat, throbbing head in her hands, in the break room. Spense had directed her to stay put while he attended to an important matter. An important matter he hadn't seen fit to explain. The ache in her head worsened, and she felt pressure building behind her eyes. A thought flitted across her consciousness—that maybe if she cried, the pressure would subside. Instantly, she shut the stray thought down because once she opened the floodgates, she knew she wouldn't be able to stop.

Control meant survival.

Control had been the *only* way to endure her life. She'd watched as a lethal cocktail had been injected into her father's veins. She'd *seen* his death, and that was all she could handle. She couldn't bear *feeling* it, too. No. Crying definitely would not help. And this morning, at Graham's apartment, the no-holds-barred tactics used by Thompson had dredged all her distrust of the police back to the surface.

Detective Thompson had lied to Silas Graham. And now Silas Graham was dead. The leeway he'd taken with the suspect made her sick to her stomach. She shot to her feet. She didn't want to keep sitting around in the police station waiting on Spense any longer. She had to get away from here.

She was just reaching for the door, when it swung open and Spense strode into the room, carrying a cardboard box with a lid that barely contained its contents. He placed the box on a table near the doorway and took her hand.

"You okay?"

She jerked her hand away. "Of course I'm okay. Why wouldn't I be?"

"You seemed angry . . . with Thompson, with everyone really. I'm not sure I've ever seen you get that close to losing it. Caity, I'm not condoning Thompson's actions, but we don't know what transpired in that apartment, so first, don't go assuming facts not in evidence. Second, not all LEOs are like him."

He really meant *he* wasn't like Thompson, and it made her chest hurt that he felt he had to say so. She knew Spense was a good man, a man of integrity—not someone who assumed every suspect was another species. But she also knew that in the past, he'd lied to get a confession. Her gut clenched. Did the fact that man had been guilty make it right? What if he'd taken the easy way out—like Graham apparently had. "I didn't lose it."

"I said you came close." His voice was low and soothing.

"Maybe, but so did you."

He turned his palms up. "True that. But for you, it's completely out of character. You wanna talk about what's got you so worked up?"

"Not now." Not ever. "And by the way, thanks for keeping me cooling my heels for hours."

His eyes shifted to a spot on the wall. "Look, I'm sorry I took so long in there, but I wanted to access ViCAP . . . and I had something else I needed to pick up."

"Sorry?"

"No, it's my bad. I shouldn't talk in Bureau speak. The Violent Criminal Apprehension Program provides a database of violent crimes, especially unusual ones or those that show any signs of being a serial—like a signature."

She felt her shoulders drop. She was tired and impatient, but she wanted to know more. "How does that work?"

"Say a detective enters a case with an unusual signature in New York, then another enters the same signature from a ten-year-old case in Arizona. ViCAP will match the cases and spit them out as possibly connected. I entered the information about the temporal-bone trophy into the system. We'll know soon if we get any hits. If there's a network of killers out there carving up skulls and stealing their victims' bony labyrinths, the database may tell us. But I'm not counting on it. This may be a relatively new group; besides which, ViCAP only works when you use it. If the case detectives didn't enter the data in the system, we won't know about the similar cases."

She sucked in a breath and closed her fists. If they were right about how the Man in the Maze found his pupils, and there really was a cyber kill club out there, she didn't want to think about how many more murderers might keep on getting away with it because they could no longer interrogate Graham. While he fit the UNSUB profile and had confessed to the Ferragamo murders, he simply did not fit her constructed image of the Man in the Maze. She was convinced the Man in the Maze was a teacher of some sort. In her exercise at the museum, she'd seen him so clearly as a professor. And Sally Cartwright had been a coed at Tempe University . . . like Gail Falconer. Her ears buzzed, and she realized Spense was still speaking. Her head had gone cottony, and her knees threatened to give way. Stiffening them for extra support, she looked back to Spense, squaring her gaze with his.

"I'm not the enemy, Caity."

She was still reeling from the way Thompson had handled Graham. Her nerves were raw, and her mind kept going back to her father no matter how hard she tried to focus on the case at hand. When she'd asked Spense for help with the Falconer case he'd refused. "But you're not my friend either." She hated the bitterness in her words, but she wouldn't pretend, not with Spense.

His body canted away from hers. "You don't think so? You got some high standards there, sweetheart. I carried you to safety in that courthouse. I sat by your bedside every damn day until you got well. I brought you into my home, and quite frankly, I'm ready to take a bullet for you right now should one come flying through that window. How does that song go?"

"I'd catch a grenade for you." She filled in, but her throat was so tight she could hardly speak. Spense had done more for her than any person besides her family ever had, and yet . . . the one thing she needed from him was the one thing he'd refused to give her.

"But that's not enough to prove I care, is it?"

She looked up through a blur of moisture in her eyes. He reached out and tilted her chin so she couldn't look away.

"I know what you want from me, Caity. And I'm going to give it to you. I just hope to God we both survive it."

Her head, already light, started to spin. She pressed her fist to her chest, trying to catch her breath, but her lungs refused to expand. Spense grabbed her by the hand to steady her. Then he walked her to the table where he'd placed the box. She reached out, ran her fingers over the cardboard, and a burst of electricity shot through her, jolting her heart into overdrive.

"You know what's in there, right?" Spense said, his voice steady and easy.

Her world was coming back into focus. "The Falconer files," she whispered.

"Watching Thompson in action today was enlightening. I guess I was seeing him through your eyes. And then . . . I took a good look in the mirror and made a decision. Whatever I can do to help you find the truth—about your father, about what happened to Gail Falconer—I will. And in return, I'm asking you to put your trust in me. Because if you can't do that, this partnership we've got going won't work. The case against your father is strong, but I'm going to be there for you no matter what we find. You said before it wasn't about you giving me another chance. You said it was about me taking one. Well, this is me, taking that chance."

She took a step toward him, and he remained still, didn't move toward her or back away. He just waited, letting her come to him. Then she reached out, touched her hand to his shoulder. Her head dipped to his chest, and he finally moved, tugging her hard against him.

"It's okay, Caity, you don't always have to be so tough." He whispered the words into her hair. His heart thudded against her ear, and she burrowed into him, grateful, wanting to let it all go.

She *needed* relief . . . she *needed* to lose control . . . but the tears simply refused to fall.

Wednesday, September 18
Rutherford Towers
Phoenix, Arizona

AROUND HALF PAST three in the morning, a single sobbing scream awakened Spense. His body played out its role automatically, from sheer muscle memory. If he'd thought about leaping from the bed, grabbing his pistol, clearing the hall and rushing into Caity's room, the memory had already fled. All he knew was that Caity screamed, and he burst through the door with his Glock to find her on the floor of her closet, rocking back and forth, eyes wide open, but maybe not really awake. Hugging her knees, she kept rocking, her shoulders heaving with tearless sobs. Moonlight streamed in from the window, varnishing her alabaster face. Her skin seemed frozen onto her features, like a painted mask. In the dark, her dry blue eyes looked huge and nearly black. *Jesus.* He'd never seen anyone *not* cry with such vengeance.

Lowering his pistol, he crawled into the closet beside her. "Bad dream?" He was the master of understatement.

She stopped rocking, but stared straight ahead, as if he weren't there, and that didn't work for him. He *was* there, and he wanted her to know it. Cautiously, he let his hand fall into her lap. Through her nightshirt, he could feel the heat and moisture of her damp skin, and his body responded automatically. He was an asshole, but at least he recognized it and moved his hand from her thigh to a safer location—her cheek.

Just as he'd thought, her skin was bone dry. "Bad dream?" he repeated.

Seeming to come back to herself, she turned to him. "Yes."

Well, okay. That was progress. Her eyes were wired red, her thick brown hair was a hell of a tangled mess; she had dark circles under her eyes, and he still felt a catch in his chest at how beautiful she was. Minutes passed in silence, then finally she said, "It's an awful dream. Sometimes, I don't have it for weeks, and I think it's left me for good, but it always comes back."

"Sounds like posttraumatic stress. You've been shot at, and—"

"It's not that. I started having the dream a long time before I got shot. I've had it ever since . . . well, I've had it a long time."

"Since your father?"

"Yes. Since I watched my father die."

He wanted to grab her and hold on to her and kiss her and make all her pain disappear. But he restrained himself. "So in this dream, what happens?"

"Oh, trust me, it's just your usual fare. Nothing extraordinary whatsoever. There's a long black tunnel. It's pitch-black inside. I'm running down the tunnel, chasing my father. And all I can hear is my heart echoing louder than our footsteps."

He swallowed hard, dreading what might come next, but *needing* to know. "You chase your father."

"I want to be with him."

Spense leaned in, barely breathing now, but managing to say what he needed to say. "Caity, I think maybe you should talk to someone about the dreams."

"I am. I'm talking to you." She looked at him, and for the first time, he saw trust in her eyes, and that made him determined to deserve it. While his hand stroked her back, she continued, "I don't mean I want to die, Spense. Not at all. I could never throw away the life I've been given. But when I was a girl, I used to wish I could be with my father in prison, so he wouldn't be lonely. So *I* wouldn't be lonely."

And suddenly he understood. The closet was like a cell. That's why she was in here. He reached an arm around her, and she leaned into his touch. Lips parted, she gazed up at him.

This was a dance he knew very well, the softening of the eyes, the lowering of defenses that signaled a woman would welcome his touch.

You can have me if you like.

He would like.

But Caity had put her trust in him, and he craved that more than he craved her body, or the feeling of sinking inside her, the sensation of her pulsing around him. This wasn't the time . . . She was purring up against him now. He closed his eyes and steeled his resolve. If he claimed her for his own tonight, when the light of day brought her back to herself, he might lose her forever. But a stolen kiss . . .

He inched closer, and she tilted her face to him. The softness of her lips thrilled him. Her mouth tasted sweet, like fruity Chapstick, and he licked her lips open. His tongue thrust inside—a promise of what could be between them. With her wrapped tightly in his arms, they kissed until he felt the shuddering in her body subside. Then he whispered in her ear, "Okay if I stay?"

In answer, she nestled her head against his chest. He leaned back against the wall, and together they drifted off to sleep.

Chapter Twenty-Three

Wednesday, September 18
Rutherford Towers
Phoenix, Arizona

THE FALCONER FILES. Caitlin couldn't believe that the evidence files from her father's case were sitting on the breakfast table in front of her. She didn't know what markers Spense had called in to get them, and she didn't care if it was against policy to remove them from the evidence room—from the horror stories she'd heard about old files going missing, they were probably safer in her care than in police custody anyway. The only thing that mattered now was that at long last, fifteen years after her father had been executed, she was going to see with her own eyes the evidence that had convicted him.

A rather jubilant whistling came closer and closer, then Spense wandered into the kitchen and shot her a goofy grin. "Hey, doll," he said, as if they were an old married couple, and this was just another ordinary day. He rattled around at the refrigerator and eventually produced a frosty mug filled with her favorite breakfast drink—her favorite anytime drink really—an Arnold Palmer. "I can whip up some scrambled tofu if you like, doll."

Considering he'd gotten her the evidence files, slept sitting up in her closet after her night-terror, *and* proven himself to be a really good kisser, she decided not to complain about the *doll*. Whatever name Spense chose to call her, she didn't mind. Even when they'd been on opposite sides, she'd secretly liked that he was the only one bold enough to call her *Caity*. Something made her let out a dreamy sigh. Maybe it was the sparkle in his eye when he looked at her, or maybe it was the warmth in his smile. Or maybe it was the way her heart expanded at the sound of his voice—perhaps the feeling of tenderness that sometimes swamped her out of the blue, just because she'd caught a glimpse of his profile. "No thanks. I think I'll stick with this. I don't have much of an appetite." She was too jittery to think of food, and if anything was going to tempt her, it wouldn't be Spense's cooking. She favored him with her own goofy grin, took the mug he offered, and sipped it, resolving to think about last night later. There was no denying that had been a doozy of a kiss. But today, the Falconer files were uppermost in her mind.

"You and me, Caity. We all good now?"

"Yeah. We're good." The mug wobbled in her hand, and she set it down and steadied her hands by wrapping her arms around her waist. "Can I tell you something?"

"Of course."

She shivered, then faked a laugh. "That was semirhetorical."

"Then you should've used the signal." He tugged madly at his ear.

"Right. I'll try to remember. Anyway, here goes. I'm feeling a little nervous about opening this box. Not because I think I'll find out my father killed Gail Falconer. In my heart, I know he didn't. But I don't look forward to reliving all those terrible memories. I'm afraid looking at evidence, reading the witness statements, will bring the trial back to life for me. And that was a terrible time. I don't want to go back there."

"Then don't open the box. No one's forcing you. From what you've told me, your mother doesn't want to relive the past either. She's not pressing anyone to reopen the case."

"But she wants my father's name cleared. I'm sure of it. It's only that she doesn't want me to live in the past. That's the reason she doesn't approve of my digging around and hiring private investigators. She's protecting me from my own obsession—that's how she puts it."

"Have you ever considered the possibility your mother might be right? No matter what you find inside those files, Caity, even if you managed to somehow get your father's conviction overturned, it won't bring him back to you."

That's where Spense had it wrong. She wanted her pure, untainted memories of her father back. And the only way to exorcise that tiny yet malignant seed of doubt was to see the evidence with her own eyes. "I have to do this, Spense." Then, heart pounding in her chest, she opened the box and pulled out the first file. In big red letters it read:

Falconer, Gail
Case Closed.

SPENSE HOPED TO hell he hadn't done the wrong thing getting Caity those files. But after last night, there was no going back. He finally understood that no matter how much he wanted to protect her from the truth, sooner or later she'd have to face it. At least now, he could be there with her when she did. And there was something more, too—Caity was so certain of her father's innocence. Family members often deluded themselves, but she was a smart woman. And whether by nature or nurture, she had incredible empathy for others. It was hard to believe she'd been sired and raised by a sadistic monster. He'd read the trial transcripts, but now he wondered if he'd missed some detail that might suggest her father's innocence.

Caity let out a sharp gasp and covered her mouth, then dropped the crime-scene photo of Gail Falconer's brutalized body.

"Is this the first time you've seen this?"

She nodded, and her hand fell to her lap. She stuck up her chin. "The judge excluded me from the trial on a few select days. This must've been presented on one of those days."

"I'm sorry. You okay to go on?"

"Of course." She was already shuffling through a batch of police reports. "Spense, did you know they found Gail's DNA in the trunk of my father's car?"

He did. That was one of the strongest pieces of evidence against him. Coupled with Thomas Cassidy's confession—coerced or not—and the fact he was on campus at the time, along with a wild story about receiving an anonymous phone call that his wife's car had broken down at the university, meant prosecutors had had a slam-dunk case.

"Don't you think it's odd they never found his DNA at the scene, though? I mean, she'd been tortured and raped, and her engagement ring was pried from her finger. How is it possible for the killer to have left no DNA?"

"It's possible, Caity. If the killer was careful enough." He scratched his head. "But you're right. It doesn't add up. If the killer was organized enough to get rid of all trace at the scene, why would he leave blood evidence in the trunk of his car?"

Her face had flushed bright red. "Because *my father* wasn't the killer."

Suddenly, Spense got to his feet. He had a wild hair of his own, but it wasn't about the Falconer case. It was about Sally Cartwright. "I'm going to ask that Gretchen advise the task force to take another look at the DNA in the Sally Cartwright case. I mean, if Kramer was smart enough to leave no trace evidence, why was he stupid enough to get caught with the temporal-bone trophy in his possession? They need to look again."

"You think it's too late to do that in my father's case?"

It killed him to dash her hopes, but he wasn't going to lie to her. "I'm not saying it's impossible, but it'd be much harder with a case that old. I'm not sure DNA is the right place to start with the Falconer murder."

Chapter Twenty-Four

Thursday, September 19
Federal Bureau of Investigation Field Office
Phoenix, Arizona

CAITLIN FOUND SHE was becoming an expert at compartmentaliza-
tion. Difficult as it was to shift her focus away from her father's case
and onto Ferragamo, she had no choice. Until they found the Man
in the Maze, no one was safe. *She* wasn't safe. Warily, she watched
Thompson pace the circumference of the same fifth-floor conference
room where they'd met with Herrera on other occasions.

"Cool. Never been invited to FBI headquarters before," Thompson said as he walked to the window.

"Don't," Gretchen Herrera said, just in time to stop Thompson
from raising the blinds. "And welcome. Why don't you have a seat,
so we can get started? I understand there's been a break in the Ferragamo case."

Thompson swaggered to the table and dropped into a swivel
chair. "That's right. In spite of all the criticism I received from

certain parties . . ." He looked pointedly at Caitlin. "It seems that thanks to my wheedling an invitation into one Mr. Silas Graham's apartment, important evidence has been obtained from his computer—which is now in our custody—thanks to my good old-fashioned and much maligned police work."

Of course, Caitlin thought, it would have been nice to have both the computer *and* a living suspect in custody. But she said nothing, simply folded her hands on the table and smiled politely, ignoring Thompson's barb.

"Stop showboating and get down to it." Baskin sent Thompson a warning look. "Do you want to read the e-mails or—"

"Maybe just pass them around if you will," Gretchen interrupted. "I think we'd like to see the details, and looking at the hard copies would facilitate our ability to see something others might've missed. You did make copies for everyone, right?"

"Of course." Baskin gestured for Thompson to pass the e-mails around.

Thompson's face fell, and Caitlin suspected he'd been looking forward to a theatrical reading of the two e-mails that'd been found on Graham's computer in a file marked *Labyrinth*. Both the computer and the file had been password-protected, but Graham was logged in to his desktop at the time of his death, giving the Phoenix PD cyber specialists a head start. It'd taken them less than forty-eight hours to hack into *Labyrinth*. Up until now, this whole cyber kill club had been mere speculation on her and Spense's part, and had reportedly caused a good deal of cynicism among the local authorities when Spense shared their theories while loading information into ViCAP—especially with Baskin and Thompson. But Caitlin had a feeling the Man in the Maze and his cyber kill club were about to become a great deal more in everyone's mind than a final *fuck you* from Judd Kramer.

Spense leaned over and whispered something in Gretchen's ear, and she nodded her agreement. Caitlin guessed it was about the DNA in the Cartwright case. Then Gretchen passed the papers around. Like a good hostess waiting for her dinner guests to take their first bites, she didn't look at her own e-mail until they all had a copy in hand. But screw manners, Caitlin couldn't wait anymore. She started reading hers right away:

From: Man in the Maze <395z204@253.0.101.212>
To: Labyrinth <list.27040302@253.0.101.212>
Subject: URGENT
Date: July 10

Greeting students. Thank you for your marvelous postings. As always, I've gotten much pleasure from them. This week's pick goes to Doom for his photographs of the redheaded girl. I find her delightful.

Doom, you've made a fine selection, and your skill in obtaining such intimate shots is impressive. The hidden camera in her bedroom has revealed the girl's true nature. A whore like that will enjoy her punishment, so do not hesitate to take what is yours. And once you've finished with her, don't forget to share your spoils with the group. It pleases us to see you succeed. If you show us the labyrinth, you will, of course become a lieutenant, and therefore will be authorized to recruit new members.

Now then, there is one other matter we must address: the urgent subject of this message. I delayed only because I did not want to forget my praise for Doom. It has come to my attention that one of our lieutenants, Zeus, is in police custody. You may have seen his story on the news and understood by the labyrinth found in his possession, that he is one of us, although the dim-witted authorities do not understand its meaning and refer to his trophy merely as a piece of bone.

It appears he succeeded in his mission—which was clearly outlined here on this forum—but before he could share with the group, he was arrested.

This situation has created anxiety in me, not on my own account, but for your sakes, dear pupils. Let me make you this promise, I will keep close watch on the matter. I would not wish harm to come to one of our own unless it was the only way to protect the group. I may call on you for help if that sad day comes.

One final word, please exercise great caution in your communications. Be sure to use safe transmission guidelines, as outlined in the Labyrinth rules. In particular, you must use only authorized browsers. Feel free to post as usual, as long as you take proper precautions. I will keep you apprised of further developments.

CAITLIN FELT A rush of excitement. This was it. The killer's motivation was suddenly crystal clear. She tapped her finger on the e-mail so hard, she nearly poked a whole through the paper. "Look at this date! July 10."

Thompson began scrolling through his BlackBerry, presumably looking for the date's significance.

"That's the same week Judd Kramer was booked for the murder of Sally Cartwright. You still think the Man in the Maze is some BS Kramer made up?" Caitlin crushed the e-mail in her hand, then opened it and smoothed it out again.

Baskin's face went white. "I don't think anyone can doubt the existence of a Man in the Maze or his connection to the Ferragamo case at this point. The e-mails get even better." He waved at his associate. "Thompson, send around the second e-mail. That one's dated less than a week after Kramer's grand-jury indictment."

Thompson fired a paper across the table toward Caitlin, and she grabbed it, and read:

From: Man in the Maze <395204@253.0.101.212>
To: Labyrinth <list.27040302@253.0.101.212>
Subject: Desperate Times
Date: July 23

Greetings students, and thank you for all your wonderful posts that have brought me great pleasure. Although it is my habit to choose a best pick from among your offerings, today I must forgo the honor. We have pressing matters before us. Our glorious Zeus has been brought before a grand jury, and there is to be a trial.

The situation is most desperate, as Zeus has a clever attorney, and I fear this counselor will urge him to save his own life in exchange for ours. In truth, I am absolutely certain this will be the final outcome as I know our once-loyal Zeus is now selfishly clinging to his own life. To further complicate the matter, I am told he has spent many hours in discourse with a psychiatrist. To the weak, a psychiatrist's couch seems as compelling as a confessional. If our Zeus confides in his psychiatrist, then even without a prosecutorial deal, our group is in grave danger.

I only hope it is not too late. Who knows what Zeus has

revealed of the group to these outsiders. My heart is heavy, but I must call on you for help. Doom, I have chosen you, since I know you have military skills. Doom, please make note of what I tell you next. This is quite important. Do NOT attempt to contact me on the loop. Do NOT reply to this e-mail. I will send instructions, which you may save elsewhere. Let me repeat—do NOT contact me via the loop.

To all of you. Do NOT reply to this e-mail. Let us never discuss it again unless I give the signal. I hold our unfortunate Zeus dear to my heart, but I hold all of you dearer. Those who may know too much must be eliminated for the greater good.

With much sadness and great thanks,

MIM.

THOMPSON PUSHED BACK from the table and spun in his chair. "I accept your apology, Dr. Cassidy. As you can see, I've solved the case in one fell swoop. And all I had to do was take a crap in Silas Graham's john."

She held her tongue, not wanting to answer rudely, but it took all her will to keep silent. Across the way, Spense's nostrils were flaring. Not good. Caitlin tugged on her ear.

Leave it alone, Spense.

Baskin did some facial acrobatics, then clutched the e-mails in his hands so hard they shook. "The case isn't quite solved, now is it, buddy?"

"Sure it is. We got the guy cold. Even found the Ferragamos in Graham's closet. And right in the e-mails, it explains the whole reason he went after Kramer and the rest of them."

Gretchen impaled him with her stare. "Please take note, Detective Thompson, that one of the *rest of them* is seated at this table."

"Detective." Spense's voice could've frozen mercury. "You may have found the trigger man, but you haven't found the man behind the curtain. Until we find the Man in the Maze, this case is far from solved." He turned to Baskin. "Maybe you should have your boy take notes and I'll explain it to him point by point."

Baskin circled two fingers in the air, and Thompson, muttering something beneath his breath, pulled out a pen and pad.

"Ready?" Spense asked, his voice taut and precise.

"Fire away." Thompson kept his eyes on his paper like a schoolboy who'd been reprimanded by the teacher.

"Judd Kramer appears to have been a member of an online kill club known as Labyrinth. Labyrinth is controlled by an individual who goes by the handle: the Man in the Maze. Silas Graham, also a Labyrinth member, aka Doom, was sent by the Man in the Maze to silence Kramer, aka Zeus, before he could trade information about the kill club to save his own skin. Graham was also apparently ordered to take out Harvey Baumgartner and Dr. Cassidy out of concern that Kramer had given them information that could lead back to Labyrinth. Did you get all that?"

Thompson's complexion darkened. "I got it, yes. So I guess we've got to start all over again and find the Man in the Maze."

"I guess we do." Spense raised his voice to be heard over the beeping of Baskin's BlackBerry.

"Motherfucker." Baskin shot to his feet. "We got another DB on campus."

Chapter Twenty-Five

Thursday, September 19
Tempe University
Tempe, Arizona

ANOTHER DB ON campus. Another coed tortured, raped, and killed. The advance report had come in that the MO was different than those used on Sally Cartwright and Darlene Dillinger. But the *signature* was the same. Adjacent to the ear, a section of temporal bone had been removed.

Caitlin looked straight ahead, scanning the horizon as they approached the east-campus parking lot. But from the corner of her eye, she caught the stony look on Spense's face, the determined set of his jaw. "Spense?"

When he didn't respond, she realized he must be gathering his concentration, pulling in his focus. She'd almost forgotten how hard he had to work to tune out the extraneous noise in the world. She raised her voice slightly, just enough to be sure he heard her. "Spense?"

"You think this is the work of Man in the Maze . . . I mean here we go again. Different MO, same signature."

"It could be him, or it could be anyone in the club." His golden eyes darkened until his pupils all but eclipsed the iris.

Her gut clenched at the realization they had no idea how extensive this *Labyrinth* was. But Spense had said it was likely new, given the fact there was nothing in ViCAP. No nationwide grab for the bony labyrinths of college coeds—at least none that had been entered into the system. Once the signature was broadcast via the media, though, more reports might come in. But she could hope for the best, that the club was in its nascent form, with few members, or at least only a few who were true killers.

Spense eased up on the accelerator, and the look he sent her told her he was about to order her to stay in the car. Preemptively, she leapt out the passenger door, just as he finished applying the brake, but before the Rodeo had come to a complete stop. The car screeched to a halt, and Spense bolted out of the car, coming up behind her before she could get a yard ahead of him. He had a good foot in height on her, and there was no way she could outrun him, even if her flank hadn't been burning like a son of a bitch.

"You don't have to do this, Caity." His hand was on her shoulder.

She turned to face him. "Yes, Spense. I do."

"You got nothing to prove here. They already know you're tough—Baskin, Herrera, Thompson. And even if they don't, *I* know you're tough, so there's no sense in putting yourself through another crime scene just to make a point."

"I'm not trying to make any point, Spense. This isn't about *me*. I could give a flying fuck what Baskin and Thompson think of me. I need to see this with my own eyes. Maybe I'll catch something another would miss. I mean you have to admit, I'm the one who connected the temporal bone to the Man in the Maze."

"Photographs are one thing. Dead bodies are another, and if this is the work of a sexual sadist, it's not going to be something you'll soon forget."

"I may be a psychiatrist, but I'm still a doctor. You think I've never seen a dead body before? Never dissected a cadaver or attended an autopsy . . . been on duty in the ER when a gunshot wound came in? Not to mention I was at Graham's crime scene less than forty-eight hours ago. I've seen it all, Spense. I'll be fine." She wasn't going for bravado so much as believability, but Spense didn't seem to buy it anyway.

He put his arms around her, caging her in. "You haven't seen it all, Caity. You haven't seen anything like this up close and in person, and you don't have to . . . not now, not ever. Just leave this part to me."

She pushed her arms up and used her elbows to break out of the cage. "No." Sidestepping, she kept trekking up the grassy hill. It was obvious where the body had been dumped because she could see a team of uniforms up ahead. And Gretchen. Gretchen turned, and when she caught sight of them, she hurried down the embankment.

"What the hell, Spense? Why is *she* here?"

"I can't leave her to fend for herself with a psychopath gunning for her."

"I meant you should've left her in the car! There are plenty of uniforms around."

"You and I both know the killer might be around, too, watching the show."

"We can send Thompson back to the car with her. He can protect her until—"

"I'm right here, Agent Herrera." She deliberately didn't use Gretchen's first name. Today she was all business. "So please don't talk about me as if I'm not. I jumped out of the car before Spense could order me to stay put, but frankly, if he had, it wouldn't have made a difference. You may have forgotten, but I'm a civilian, and I don't take orders from the FBI."

Herrera's eyes narrowed. "At a crime scene, you sure as hell do, *Doctor* Cassidy. And you may be an independent consultant but you do report back to the BAU."

Caitlin pressed her fingers to the bridge of her nose. Her legs were shaking from the uphill climb—she was still a bit weak. Her breath was short, and her heart was just about to jump out of her chest, but she didn't care. She had to see this evil with her own eyes. She had to know, once and for all, what kind of a monster . . . "You're absolutely right. I'm out of line. This is your call, not mine. It's true this is your scene, so if you order me to leave, I will. But I'd like to remind you, I'm the one who was shot, not you. I'm the one who watched Kramer die, not you. I'm the one who connected the Man in the Maze to the bony labyrinths taken as souvenirs. I've been in on this case from the start, and I want to see it through to the end. I'm not a child who needs to be spared the ugliness of it all. I'm a professional, and I can handle an *in vivo* crime scene no matter how violent, no matter how perverse it may be."

Spense shrugged a *what-can-we-do* at Herrera. Gretchen hitched her chin toward the top of the embankment. "Oh, it's perverse all right. But if this is what you think you need to do, you've earned the right. I have to warn you, however, that once you see something like this, Catlin, you can never *unsee* it."

"Then I'll add that to the list." There were plenty of things she wished she could unsee. Whatever fate had befallen this poor girl, Caitlin intended to see it with her own eyes.

She pulled in a deep breath and immediately started to cough. The wind had changed course, carrying a strong smell of blood and excrement to her. Spense pulled a handkerchief from his pocket, and she wasn't too proud to accept it. When she finally crested the hill, she couldn't see the body. Crime-scene tape stretched between the trees, and most of the team stood behind it, barking into their radios or scribbling in their notepads.

Someone handed her a pair of booties, and in a macabre way it seemed humorous, but maybe that was just her defenses kicking in. She thought of all the times she'd watched a female television detective trudge all over a crime scene in Louboutins. Fortunately, these booties would fit easily over her New Balance runners. They all pulled on gloves. It wasn't too different from scrubbing in for the OR. Then the CSIs stopped snapping photos and moved to the side, and that's when Caitlin saw her.

A young woman, probably nineteen or twenty. Long red hair fanned out around her, framing what was left of a face that looked to have been smashed repeatedly with something sharp and heavy. Likely that bloody rock lying at her side. Her nude body was caked with dirt and mud, but Caitlin could see the gashes crisscrossing her breasts and stomach. Her throat gaped open, and coagulated blood pooled around her shoulders like a scarf. Her legs, bent at the knees, had been parted and staked with tent spikes. Her genitals hung open, and from the appearance of her wounds, Caitlin surmised she'd been raped with a knife.

Judging from the carefully tied feet, the stakes that had been driven into the hard ground, the sheer number of wounds on the body, the killer had spent a great deal of time with his victim. And she could only guess at how much additional energy had been spent carving up the victim's skull. She tilted her head, studying the scene, and her vision began to blur, her knees felt rubbery, then Spense was at her side, gripping her elbow.

She covered her mouth with her hand.

The brain was such an odd, protective organ, and denial was its first line of defense.

It had taken her all this time to see. The signature was new, but the MO was exactly the same. Not the same as Sally Cartwright or Darlene Dillinger.

The same as Gail Falconer.

Her eyes closed, and her legs buckled, but Spense held her up. She uncovered her mouth and dragged her palm over her face.

Open your eyes, Caity. What do you see?

The whirring of a camera sounded, and a CSI moved in, stooping low for a close shot of the abdomen. Caitlin steadied herself and stepped up to the body. What was he shooting? She squatted beside him and saw sunlight flashing from the umbilicus. At first she thought the girl must have a belly ring, but she was wrong. At least it wasn't a piercing. It was an actual ring, stuffed in the umbilical recess.

She looked to Spense, unsure if she could touch the evidence.

"Okay if I take a look at that ring before you bag and tag?" He asked a uniform, reminding Caitlin this crime scene "belonged" to the Tempe Police Department.

The uniform nodded. "I think we've got all we need. Help yourself."

Spense crouched next to the girl and carefully retrieved the ring. He muttered something unintelligible, something angry, under his breath. He brought Caitlin the ring, holding it out to her in his palm. "You want to look at the inscription, or should I?" His voice was strangled and hoarse, like he was barely keeping a lid on it.

The ring was a pink sapphire encircled by diamonds. As she held it, her heartbeat stopped, she could feel its absence, the emptiness in her chest. She took the delicate ring between her thumb and index fingers and twirled it until she could see the letters etched inside. Then slowly, her heart resumed its rhythm. Spense fixed her with his gaze, and she nodded at him. "The inscription reads *GF*."

Gail Falconer.

The world tilted, and when she opened her eyes, Spense and Baskin had her under the arms, one man on each side. The look on Herrera's face was some weird combination of worried and pissed. "I fainted?" Lord, she hoped she hadn't fallen and disturbed the scene. Straightening, she took inventory. No dirt on her hands or clothes. Herrera was holding an evidence bag, presumably containing the ring that was no longer in Caitlin's hand.

"Didn't hit the dirt, so I can't give you credit for a full faint," Baskin said, in smooth-it-over tone.

"Take her down to the car, will you, Detective?" Herrera asked, but it was clear it wasn't really a request. She fixed Spense with a glare, one that said she wanted to speak with him alone.

"It'd be my pleasure to escort Dr. Cassidy to a more . . . comfortable . . . spot."

Pressure built in her head, and her hands were trembling as she shoved away from Baskin and Spense. Guilt washed over her. She was drawing the attention away from the girl and from the killer, all the important things, and onto herself. But it wasn't the gore that had gotten to her, if that's what Herrera thought. It was the ring, and all the implications of finding it here today. That ring appeared to be Gail Falconer's engagement ring. The one she hadn't taken off her finger since the night Randy Cantrell had given it to her. The one that had been removed from her body the night she was murdered.

The killer's trophy.

Whoever had taken the ring off Gail that night, whoever had *murdered* Gail, must've left it on this poor girl today as some sort of sick message. And it certainly couldn't have been Caitlin's father. Thomas Cassidy did not murder Gail Falconer, and this ring was hard evidence that might clear his name. Yes, she'd been overcome with the realization. Yes, she'd fainted. If Herrera thought less of her for that, then fuck her. Her chin jerked up, her eyes stung with dry pressure. "Let's go, Detective."

Herrera grimaced at her, and she felt a pang of regret for her harsh thoughts. Gretchen was only doing her job. As she started down the hill with Baskin hovering beside her, Spense took a step forward, but she shot him a look she knew he'd understand: *I'm okay. Stay here and find out everything you can.*

By the time they made it to the parking lot, her legs felt strong and steady again, and her heart was not only beating, it pounded with energy. Adrenaline gushed through her system, pumping up her muscles, heating her skin, heightening her senses. A few yards from the car, the radio on Baskin's shoulder crackled. A distorted male voice ordered, *The chief wants you back here now.*

Caitlin stopped and turned to him, "Thanks, Detective, I owe you one. Now get back up there and solve this case."

Their gazes searched the area. Nothing but open space between her and the Rodeo. Uniforms within shouting distance on all sides. "I can take you the rest of the way. Let the chief wait," Baskin said.

Reaching out, she squeezed his shoulder. "No way. I'm fine, and I don't want to be known as the weak link in the task force. If you don't get back now, they may never let me show my face at a scene again. I'm pretty sure I can walk ten yards on my own. You saw me truck down that hill, didn't you?"

"Sure did." A look of admiration filled his eyes, which made no sense to her. She'd fainted and created a distraction at a time when all attention should be focused on the crime. Still, a flush of warmth and appreciation toward Baskin made her smile as she watched him sprint back the way they'd come.

She took her time getting to the car. Now that no one was watching, she took it easy, gave herself the chance to catch her breath. The pounding in her head had increased to the point of pain, and she guessed her blood pressure must be through the roof. Which was good, because it meant she wasn't going to faint again. Her every thought was on her father as she slipped into the car in the shotgun seat, his stoic face as they'd taken him from her family that night.

Mind coming down to the station? We've got a few questions for you, Mr. Cassidy.

How could he have known what was coming next? The intimidation, the lies, the threats, all designed to force a confession from him.

Her throated spasmed until she could hardly swallow. She leaned across the front seat, to hit the door locks and felt the hairs tingling on the back of her neck. Reflexively, she pushed her hands out, just as a thick muscular arm closed around her neck in a chokehold. A scream built in her chest and pushed and pushed its way up, but only a gurgle came out of her mouth. She caught a glimpse of a dark sleeve. *A uniform.* A gloved hand holding a serrated blade lowered before her eyes, and she knew he intended to slash her throat.

No!

In her head, she screamed, kicking with all her might and jabbing her elbow backward into some soft part of the man's body. He grunted. Then his arm slipped just enough for her to draw a gasping breath before he clamped down again. She'd hurt him.

Good!

A buzzing in her ears drowned out all sound, and a dark veil fell across her vision. Still she kept flailing and kicking, her body growing fiercer as her mind fell into one circling thought.

It's him.

Suddenly, a jolt of pure rage hit her. She slammed her head and elbow back at the same moment, hearing the harsh grunt of her attacker in her ear. She kicked one leg up, managing to somehow get her foot onto the steering wheel. Then she concentrated on that foot, willing it to move. Willing it to press hard until at last she heard it—the blare of the car horn.

The pressure on her neck let up, and she felt the knife draw across the flesh of her arm. She watched blood bubble up from her skin as the car door opened, and the uniform disappeared into the surrounding woods.

It's him.

Chapter Twenty-Six

"I WANT TO be here," Caitlin said. She'd spent the night of the attack under observation in the hospital, but other than a few scrapes and bruises, she'd come out of her battle with someone she firmly believed to be the Man in the Maze unharmed—at least physically. Then she'd spent the weekend confined to the apartment, with Spense dogging her every move. He'd even taken away her cell and replaced it with a burner phone, instructing her not to give the number out to anyone—not even her own mother. She understood his concern, but she wasn't going to lock herself away forever. And now, more than ever, she wanted to be in on every aspect of the case.

"Her name is Annie Bayberry, and she was only nineteen years old." Detective Baskin scraped a chair beside Spense and Caitlin in the precinct viewing room. "A sociology major at Tempe University. Oldest of three children. Apple of her daddy's eye. Also played intramural basketball. Excelled at most everything she did. This girl had family and friends who loved her." To Caitlin, the sheen of moisture coating Baskin's eyes was an unexpected indicator of real empathy.

Starting with the latest victim, she mentally recited the names of the girls—the ones who'd been sexually tortured and whose nude bodies had been salaciously posed for maximum shock effect.

Annie Bayberry, Darlene Dillinger, Sally Cartwright . . . Gail Falconer.

"Did they find any trace this time?" she asked. So far, with the exception of a single bloody shoeprint at the courthouse, the police hadn't been able to find any physical evidence at the scenes that linked the alleged perpetrators to the crimes. All the killers were either highly intelligent, or they'd been trained by someone who was—like the Man in the Maze.

"You saw for yourself, Dr. Cassidy, our guys did their job at the scene. They left no stone unturned in their search for forensic evidence, but so far, we got nothing. Not from the victim, not from the car, not from you," Baskin answered.

She'd been so hopeful they'd find evidence in the car or on her body. But he must've been wearing the same booties and protective gear as the other uniforms. He could've blended in perfectly, despite being dressed to *leave no trace*. And obviously, he'd blended well enough to slip in and out of sight unnoticed. The police had combed the area, but since he was disguised as a LEO at a crime scene swarming with men from several branches of service, who knew if he'd been among those conducting the search?

"Your UNSUB is one cold, calculating asshole, but he's bound to have slipped up somewhere along the line."

Spense nodded his agreement. "He's named himself after a legend, but the truth is, he's only human."

"He's screwed up before, and he'll screw up again. In my book, leaving a pink sapphire engagement ring on Annie's body wasn't the brightest move. Guess he's trying to claim credit for Gail Falconer." Baskin stated the obvious as though it hadn't occurred to Spense and her.

So many things about the Annie Bayberry crime scene didn't make sense. The MO had been carefully matched to the Falconer case, but the signature was the same as that used in the Dillinger and Cartwright cases. Of course, that could be explained by the fact that removing the petrous portion of the temporal bone was the *group* signature for Labyrinth. "But why now, I wonder. It seems strange that after all these years, Gail Falconer's killer would suddenly step forward to take credit. Something must've happened to cause him to act so boldly," Caitlin said.

"Agreed. Divorce and job loss are the most common events that trigger serial killers to come out of a dormant state, but it could be almost any life change. When we find this guy, I'll bet we learn he's suffered a recent loss," Spense added.

"In any event, we've got confirmation from the Falconer family that the ring appears to be the one Gail was wearing the night of her murder. The one presumed taken for a trophy." Baskin eyed Caitlin. "But you need to understand that's only a soft confirmation, it's not *proof* it's the same ring."

She'd already considered the possibility that the Man in the Maze was simply copycatting Gail's murder. "It's true he could be toying with me. Maybe he found a ring like Gail's and had it engraved with her initials, then replicated the Falconer MO just to push my buttons." She shuddered. "But that's a long way to go just to mess with my head, and I don't know why he'd go to the trouble."

"You've escaped his wrath how many times? There's the court-house, then the cyanide pill, and now the attack at the crime scene. He must be getting . . . enraged at you by now. It wouldn't surprise me a bit if he's getting his rocks off watching you squirm."

She saw Spense rising on his haunches and touched his knee to signal that she didn't need help. "Or he might not be toying with me at all. It seems more likely to me that the man who murdered Gail Falconer is still active—and he's hooked into the club—into Labyrinth. Maybe Gail Falconer's murderer has evolved into the Man in the Maze. Maybe he was prowling the crime scene and saw an opportunity for another kill and took it. These sadists are opportunistic. They rehearse their crimes in their heads so often that when they see a target they like, they're prepared to act."

"We're considering the possibility that this is in fact the same UNSUB who killed Falconer. That's why we've invited Gail Fal-coner's fiancé—I guess I should say former fiancé—to come down and take a look at the ring. He's the one who gave it to her, so it's a good excuse to bring him in and see what shakes loose."

"He alibied out at the time, though." Spense sounded doubtful.

"Not just airtight either—vacuum-sealed. The fiancé was away for the weekend with his Army Reserve unit. And just FYI, Dr. Cassidy, the chief will probably have my ass for putting Randy Cantrell under the microscope for you." He leaned in closer. "But I thought it was worth talking to him anyway, and not just because you got such a sweet smile. You see, Randy Cantrell is actually Randy Cantrell, PhD."

"PhD?" She didn't see the significance, other than the fact that he was well educated and likely intelligent.

"History professor. And just see if you can guess his specialty." Her hands gripped her knees. "Native American culture."

"Bingo." Baskin's eyes searched her face with seeming concern. "But his alibi for Falconer is unshakable, so it might be best not to get your hopes up. Thompson's warming him up in the interrogation room now, then I'm going to swoop in and see what I can pound out of him. You never know where a break in a case might come from."

"Would it be all right if I did the honors? I'd like to handle the interview myself if at all possible. *If* he's the same man who attacked me, maybe I'll know him. I'd want you in the room, of course, it's just that this is . . ."

"Personal. I feel you, Dr. Cassidy, but maybe it's best, precisely *because* of your personal connection, you sit this one out. And you've already stated, you saw nothing but a uniformed arm and a gloved hand." Baskin powered on the computer in front of them and rose to leave.

Climbing to her feet, she said, "I can always grab him on his way out of the precinct. I can corner him on the street if need be, but I'd prefer to question him here, on camera. And wouldn't you rather be present and make your own observations instead of hearing about the results from me after the fact?"

"What you're saying is you're going to question him whether I like it or not." Baskin rubbed the back of his neck. "Stubborn little filly, aren't you? I have to be honest. I'm afraid you might spook him."

"I know how to conduct an interview, Detective. And I'm not bragging, just letting you know I've been well trained." She tilted her head and threw in the kitchen sink. "Besides which, I've learned so much from watching you and your men at work."

She offered him a genuine smile and said it without a twinge of conscience. Her statement might've been aimed at greasing the wheels, but it was also true she'd soaked up a great deal of police procedure by watching the task force in action.

He pressed his lips together, then nodded. "Let Cantrell know who you are up front, and if he agrees to talk to you, knowing you're Thomas Cassidy's daughter, then I guess it's okay by me. Sound fair?"

"Sounds perfect." Baskin certainly didn't have to allow her in that interview room. He'd just agreed to do her a big favor—one that might land him in hot water with his chief, and she was grateful. "Thank you . . . *Riley*."

His face flushed, and the corners of his mouth lifted in a smile. "You're welcome, *Caitlin*."

BASKIN ENTERED THE interrogation room ahead of Caitlin, then gave Detective Thompson the *there's-the-door* thumb. On his way out, Thompson brushed against her, his bare forearm, sweeping slowly across first one breast then the other.

"Pardon me." His gaze ran up and down her body. His tone spoke volumes, like he wanted her to know this had been no accident, but he could get away with it easily.

Her stomach twisted in disgust. "Fuck you, Thompson," she said, barely resisting the urge to coldcock him as she slipped past him into the interrogation room. Shutting the door behind her, she took the one remaining chair in the room, positioning herself next to Baskin and directly across from Cantrell. The man bore little resemblance to the Randy Cantrell she remembered. During her father's trial, every day without fail, Gail's fiancé had glared at her from across the courtroom aisle. Back then, his skin had been tanned and his body toned. His hair had been highlighted blond, and his eyes had oozed hatred. Today, his hair had returned to what she assumed was a natural, medium brown, and his physique had softened into that of a near forty-year-old who'd fallen out of love with the gym a long time ago. She doubted he could be the powerful man who'd attacked her at the crime scene, but she couldn't be sure.

She offered him her hand. "Mr. Cantrell, I'm Caitlin Cassidy."

"I know who you are." His eyes scanned her from head to toe, but not in the creepy way Thompson's had—Cantrell's gaze seemed more curious than anything.

Surprising that he'd recognized her. She wouldn't have recognized *him* after all this time. And Baskin couldn't have told him to expect her because he'd only walked into the interrogation room a moment before Caitlin.

"You're Thomas Cassidy's daughter," Cantrell said. "You look older than I expected. Weren't you like eight or something during the trial?"

The trial. That's how she thought of it, too. "I was fourteen. I might have looked younger because of my pigtails." She sucked in her breath, half expecting him to blow poison darts at her.

"Right. I remember now how it pissed Gail's dad off—the way that lawyer paraded you in front of the media every day." He'd kept his tone even. No poison darts . . . yet.

And he was right about one thing. Baumgartner had paraded her in front of the media for the purpose of gaining the jury's sympathy. But sympathy was the last thing anyone had shown Thomas Cassidy's child. The verbal taunts aimed her way during the trial had cut her so deeply, she still felt their sting today—mostly because they'd targeted her father—the man she loved above anyone else in the world. To hear him called a pervert, a monster, the devil's helper, had been more than a fourteen-year-old daddy's girl could take. But the trial, the sentencing, and later the appeals seemed to go on forever, and by the time she was eighteen, she'd already developed her hardened shell. She knocked a fist on her chest now, tapping her armor securely in place.

"I saw on the news you got shot. I just wanna tell you I know you didn't deserve that, and I'm glad you're okay."

From the corner of her eye, she could see Baskin's posture relax, as if he were pleased by Cantrell's acceptance of her presence here today.

"Thank you." Her eyes locked with Cantrell's, and they both leaned in, as if drawn together by a magnetic force—two scarred survivors of the same terrible tragedy, on different paths in life. Yet those paths had crossed in a way that had changed them both forever. "You seem okay, too. I'm glad of that."

A long sigh escaped his lips. "I have my moments, but I've moved on. I teach at the university now, and at least until today, I'd gotten to the point I could even walk by that hill where they found Gail and not think about the way she died. I try to remember the way she lived instead. I have a wife, and beautiful little daughter . . . we named her Rosalind Gail."

Caitlin's breath hitched in her chest. His words rang so true, they all but convinced her of his innocence. Because that was how she, too, had survived—by not thinking about how her father had died but rather about how he'd lived. For a moment she couldn't speak. Searching Cantrell's face, she looked for the hatred she remembered but found the years had seemingly erased it. In his eyes she saw only sorrow and maybe resignation.

Cantrell's alibi's not just airtight. It's vacuum-sealed.

She cut her eyes to Baskin. "Has he seen the ring?"

Cantrell's knees jittered under the table, making a soft banging sound. "I'd like to get it back—can I get the ring back, please?"

"Not at this point. It's evidence in *two* murder investigations now—if we reopen Gail's case that is." Baskin pulled up a set of photographs. "I can't let you handle it right now either, but I've got some real good close-up shots for you to look at, including a few magnified ones of the inscription. Take a look at these if you don't mind."

Cantrell grabbed the photos and studied them only a moment before returning them to Baskin. He looked directly at Caitlin. "That's the engagement ring I gave Gail. That's what you wanted to know isn't it, Dr. Cassidy?"

Mutely, she nodded, struggling to compose herself. "Are you absolutely certain this is the same ring you gave Gail? How can you tell it apart from any other pink sapphire?"

"Because of her initials."

"Sure. But she's not the only woman in the world whose initials are GF. And someone who wanted to convince us it was hers could easily have had it inscribed. It was reported in the news that a pink sapphire ring with the initials GF was taken as a trophy. This is a round cut, which is the most common. So unless there's some other distinguishing feature, I'm afraid we can't be certain it's the same ring."

"It's not just the initials. It has that same fancy script—I paid extra for all those curlicues. Nobody ever said anything about the fancy script in the media—I didn't even mention it to the police, so no one would know how to copy it. The ring is Gail's."

"If that's true . . ." She pressed her hands to her sides, hesitating, choosing her words carefully. If Cantrell was not a killer, she didn't want to cause him more pain, but the truth is the truth, and closure isn't worth a damn if it's based on a lie. "If the ring is genuine, that means Gail's killer may still be at large."

His gaze seemed to freeze on his left hand, and Caitlin noticed a tan line where his wedding ring had been. Maybe there was trouble at home. "If the ring is genuine," he said, "that means your father was innocent. I understand why you're so keen to know if I'm certain. I don't know if just having the fancy script would hold up as proof in court, but for your own peace of mind, let me say I'm *absolutely certain* the ring is Gail's." The lines around his mouth deepened, and he swung his gaze to Baskin. "I've identified the ring, which is why you said you called me down here. If that's all, Detective, I'd like to get back to my family."

"Just a couple of more questions if you don't mind." Caitlin held up a finger.

Resentment replaced the polite expression on Cantrell's face, like a switch had flipped. "I do mind, but somehow I don't think that's going to stop you."

"You may be right about that. Please state your name and occupation for the record," Caitlin took the reins before Baskin could.

"Randall Francis Cantrell. I'm a professor of sociology at Tempe University."

Baskin frowned and scribbled a note. "Sociology? Not history?"

"Sociology. Look it up if you want." His jaw clenched. "You asked me to come down here and identify a ring. Then, without preparing me, you bring in Dr. Cassidy. The cherry on top is I don't even get to see or hold Gail's ring. And now—now you start in on some tangential line of questioning about what I do for a living. If I didn't know better, I'd think you're looking at me as person of interest in Gail's murder again." He spoke through clamped teeth. "How many times do I have to tell you I was on Army Reserve duty that weekend?"

"As many times as it takes. You teach sociology. Do you have any subspecialty or areas of interest?" Caitlin asked, keeping things polite but not letting him get away with dodging her questions.

"My specialty is indigenous Southwestern culture. Is there a point to this line of questioning?"

"Any special interest in Native American art?"

"I collect it. Didn't know that was a crime." His voice rose an octave. "My great-grandfather was Native American, and I grew up on his stories. Am I free to go or not?" Cantrell's eyes seemed to have switched back into that old, angry mode again.

Caitlin studied his face, uneasy about this change in demeanor. Was Randy Cantrell merely a man devoted to his ancestral roots, or was he a cold-blooded psychopath who called himself the Man in the Maze?

"Mr. Cantrell," Caitlin leaned in and caught his gaze, holding it until he hid from her by pressing his hands to his face. "Mr. Cantrell, did you kill Gail Falconer?"

Chapter Twenty-Seven

WHILE CAITY INTERVIEWED Randy Cantrell, Spense watched her on the computer from the precinct viewing room. Her posture was rigid, and her attention intensely focused on the man who'd once been engaged to Gail Falconer. The odd thing to Spense was that when Cantrell declared his certainty that the ring found on Annie Bayberry's corpse belonged to Falconer, Caity's body language evidenced no relief. If that ring was the real deal, it almost certainly meant her father had been innocent, yet her facial expression remained stuck in neutral.

Spense could only imagine what it must be like to be in her position. Suppose they uncovered solid proof her father was innocent of Gail Falconer's murder. How would knowing for certain her father had been executed for a crime he didn't commit do Caity any good? There was no positive outcome in a situation like this. It was a lose-lose for everyone involved. Either her father was guilty, which would destroy her, or a horrible injustice had been done to him.

He closed his eyes, and a tender wave of admiration swept

through him. Caity wasn't just focused on her own family and her own problems. To him, it seemed she had her fists up, ready to defend any underdog against the whole damn world. He pulled in a deep breath and set his jaw. There was one thing he could do for her: help solve the mystery of Gail Falconer's murder. It might have seemed an open-and-shut case before, but the placement of Gail's ring on another woman's corpse had changed all that.

Wishing he could turn back the clock, wishing he could put things right for her, he gathered his thoughts and looked for a means to achieve some measure of good out of this situation. It crushed him to realize that in this country he loved so much, in this place where the law was meant to protect everyone, the courts often failed to either punish the guilty or acquit the innocent. He hadn't taken a head-on look at that truth until he'd started spending time with Caity. Whether or not Caity was right about her father, whether or not Thomas Cassidy had murdered Gail Falconer, it didn't change the cold, hard truth that the system sometimes went badly awry—in both directions.

He was as determined now as Caity was to get to the truth, and he prayed to God that once they found it, the system wouldn't let her down again. If only she could see Gail Falconer's killer held accountable for his crime, maybe that would finally bring her some measure of peace. He opened his eyes. The time had come to set things right. The time had come to show Caity that the system, imperfect though it might be, could still work for her. He wanted justice for both Thomas Cassidy and Gail Falconer, and he vowed he wouldn't give up until he got it.

In the midst of his thoughts, the door pushed open, and Caity entered the viewing room, the look on her face entirely unreadable to him. Considering he was a profiler by trade, that was saying something. She'd always kept her cards close to her chest, but he'd hoped by now he'd have made inroads into her trust issues. "You like Cantrell or not?" He spoke quietly, not wanting to show his hand and influence her assessment.

"What about you?" she fired back.

"Ladies first."

"All right. No, I don't like him for Falconer or Annie Bayberry either. I didn't see the man who attacked me, but I still think I'd *know* him if we were breathing the same air in a tiny room. But maybe I'm fooling myself with that idea." She aimed a pensive look his way. "If Cantrell isn't the Man in the Maze, it's a really creepy coincidence that he teaches at the university, collects Native American art, and specializes in Southwestern American culture. If not for those things, I'd say *no way* he did it."

"This is Arizona, Caity. Plenty of people collect southwestern art, especially when they have a distant Native American bloodline like Cantrell. And let's not forget his alibi is damn good."

"His alibi's not the only reason I'd rule him out . . . if not for the whole sociology-professor thing. I'd rule him out because I can actually *feel* his love for Gail Falconer. Even when he speaks of his wife and family, it isn't with the same reverence as when he speaks of her. He loved her, Spence. He wasn't faking that."

"Love is a terrible motive for murder, but it's a common one. So even if he did genuinely love Gail Falconer, that doesn't rule him out as a suspect."

"Maybe not for a crime of passion. But for a crime like *this*?"

She had a point. Most serial killers went outside their close-knit circle. But a first kill might be the exception. A first kill might result from an argument with a loved one, a wrong word that triggered painful memories or feelings of inadequacy. A first kill was a whole different animal than subsequent ones, and he had a gut feeling Gail Falconer had been *someone's* first kill, even if not Cantrell's.

Worry lines formed around Caity's eyes. "I wish things were falling into place for me, but they're not. Maybe Baskin was right. Maybe I am too close to this case. Usually, I can size a man up in a snap. I may spend hours in clinical interviews before I make a final decision, but my gut generally tells me in the first hour if an individual is capable of maliciously taking a human life. I'm not getting that vibe from Cantrell at all. Quite the opposite, in fact, but it's hard to dismiss him as a suspect altogether. He was Gail Falconer's lover. And we know from the evidence files, they'd been arguing over an alleged affair on her part. The thing about airtight alibis is they don't always hold up over time. At the very least, I'd like to double-check with his commanding officer in the Reserves."

"Agreed." He'd have to do some tracking down of said commander first. He didn't even know if the officer in question was still alive, but he kept that worry to himself.

Her shoulders lowered, and she proffered a small smile. "Thanks, Spense."

"For what?"

"For having my back. For trusting me. For not pointing out that I'm stepping out of bounds with my role as case consultant."

"I got no room to reprimand anyone for stepping out of bounds." He respected the system, and he respected the rules, but sometimes you had to look at the big picture, the greater good.

"Terrific. Then you won't mind making another stop on the way home."

"I'll take you anywhere you want to go, Caity," he said, "Only don't keep me in suspense. What do you have in mind?"

"I'd like to stop by the Baumgartner place on our way home."

Her pronouncement did little to relieve the suspense, but he waited, allowing her to take her time telling him her reasons.

"Ever since Jenny stopped by your apartment that day, something's been bothering me."

His interest was really piqued now. Surely she wasn't jealous of Jenny. He drew his shoulders back, wanting to set the record straight. "Caity, I know it's nothing you'd ever ask me about, but just so you know, there's nothing between Jenny and me."

Her smile tightened, almost imperceptibly. "Jenny is a beautiful, intelligent woman, Spense. I wouldn't blame you for taking an interest, and she's obviously into you."

"All true." His chest puffed a bit. No point denying what was plain as the freckle on his cheek. "But I'm not into her. I'm into *you*." That shouldn't surprise her, but he wanted to be clear. Sometimes, you have to state the obvious.

Her face flushed hot pink, and her eyes lowered, but she sent him a *no-worries* smile. "Spense, I appreciate the sentiment. I'm flattered, and I can't deny I'm interested, too. I'm sure you picked up on that after the other night, but I can't think about you and me right now. I'm stuck someplace where there's just no time for relationships and romance. I used to dream of those things when I was young, but that's all in the past. I'm not knocking the construct, but I simply don't have room in my life for love."

He could practically feel the breeze from the door slamming in his face. "Okay, first off you've got to have one crazy heart-mind disconnect to call love a *construct*. Humor me a minute and admit love is real, not just a hypothetical."

"I'm not saying I don't believe in love, only that I'm not *sure* I do."

"So I've fallen for a love agnostic. Terrific." Whatever feelings he'd been suppressing before came rushing up to the surface now. He wanted this woman, *badly*, and in every way a man can want a woman. When he closed his eyes at night, he imagined the soft lilt of her voice whispering in his ear, the silkiness of her bare skin against his, her body melting beneath his touch, ready and open for him. He couldn't get her off his mind, whether it was night or day, whether she was a couple of feet or a couple of rooms away. "If you don't have space in your life for love, Caity, maybe you should make some."

"You think I don't want to be in love? To have someone at my side I can share life's ups and down with? You think I don't want the kind of relationships other people have? There's *nothing* I want more than to have a normal life. But my life hasn't been normal since the day my father was arrested for a murder he didn't commit, and truth be told, I highly doubt my life will *ever* be normal again. I'm not being cynical here. I'm just being honest. I don't know if I *can* fall in love." She blew out a breath. "Don't give me the puppy-dog eyes, Spense. If I ever do fall in love, I'm sure it will be with someone wonderful . . . like you."

He almost flinched at the puppy-dog remark, but no matter how tempting she was, he wasn't going to show her his wolf. That little speech she'd just made told him his instincts had been spot-on. Caity was terrified of her own feelings, and if he pushed her now, he'd be drilling a hole in his own dinghy. He needed to take things slowly. "Okay, I'll accept that for the time being. But I'd like you to make me a promise. When we wrap this case up, when we find the Man in the Maze, and the danger's passed, promise you'll come away with me. Someplace where the *construct* of love is in the air. I'll whisk you away to Tahiti to drink mai tais or whatever fruity little drink you prefer."

"I like whiskey, Spense. I'll save the drinks with the little um-
brellas for you."

"Good thing I'm secure in my masculinity." As the implication of her words sank in, a wide grin stretched his cheeks. "That
sounded a lot like a yes."

"It's more like an *I'll think about it*. But I do promise to take the
idea under consideration."

That was a step in the right direction. "I guess that'll do for
now, but doll, I can be very persistent when I want something,
and if I come on too strong now and then, it's only because I can't
always stop my thoughts from spilling out of my mouth. Just look
at it as part of my charm." He put a hand up to stop her protest,
then changed the subject before she had time to reconsider her
promise. "Now, then, why are you suddenly so keen on going back
to the Baumgartner place? You've already paid your respects to
the family, and if I'm being honest, Louisa and Junior give me the
creeps."

"Before you went into your little speech about Jenny, and then
segued into the whole love as a hypothetical construct thing—"

"That wasn't me, that was you."

"Right. Anyway before the whole me-and-you thing, I was
going to say something's been bothering me ever since Jenny
stopped by. And it's not her flirtation with you. Who wouldn't
want to flirt with you?"

Her eyes suddenly had a certain glow, and he thought he liked
his chances with Caity, a lot. He just had to be patient. "As usual,
you make a good point." Then with effort, he dragged his attention back to the case. Something about that visit from Jenny had
been bugging him, too, but the deaths of Silas Graham and Annie
Bayberry had been a higher priority, so he hadn't processed it yet.

He wondered if Caity had tuned in to the same issues he had. Wouldn't be the first time they'd wound up on the same page as far as this crazy case was concerned.

"Did you notice anything about the staff at the Baumgartner's home? I'm referring to Elizabeth and the other girl who brought us tea the day we visited."

Yep. He and Caity were on the same page, all right. "You mean did I notice they were both knockouts? Of course I noticed. They were also a lot younger than what I'd expect. As a rule, people with money hire more experienced waitstaff." Caity opened her mouth to comment, but he plowed on. "Let me beat you to the punch and say I find it interesting Jenny called Baumgartner a creeper . . ."

"And then we go to his house and find he had two stunning and very young girls in his employ, and his wife doesn't seem to mind in the least or notice anything is amiss. Which is weird. *Shouldn't* a woman mind these things?"

"Remember Jenny said she tried to warn Louisa, but the woman had a blind spot where her husband was concerned. I'd like to clarify the nature of Baumgartner's relationship with those girls on his staff. I wonder if they're live-ins. That would've given him more access if he really was a *creeper.*"

"There's something else, too. I've been going over and over that day in the courthouse, trying to remember any detail that might help us identify the shooter, and I keep seeing this image Harvey doodled while we talked. It looked like the design on the cup Jenny gave me." Her face drained of color. "Spense—it looked like a *maze.* I hate to even think of such a thing, but I'm beginning to wonder if Baumgartner might've been involved with Labyrinth somehow." Her voice dropped to a near whisper as she said aloud what he'd been thinking.

Harvey Baumgartner was connected to both the Falconer case and the Ferragamo case, and while Caity had been in with Cantrell and Baskin, Spense had done a little Googling. Turns out Randy Cantrell wasn't the only one who taught classes at Tempe University. Harvey Baumgartner was an adjunct professor of law. He hesitated, wondering if he should share a hypothesis that might hurt Caity, but then thought back to their agreement. He'd promised not to hide things from her anymore. "It occurs to me Harvey might've been a member slash advisor slash legal counselor." He watched her face, wondering how she'd react to that suggestion. If that were the case, it didn't look good for Caity's father. If Baumgartner was a sexual sadist, who'd defended other sexual sadists in court, and he'd defended Thomas Cassidy . . .

Chapter Twenty-Eight

Monday, September 23
Paradise Valley
Arizona

ON THE RIDE over to Paradise Valley, Caitlin's stomach did its best to curl up into a fetal position. She wished she could pull the covers over her head and hide from the big, bad bogeyman, and the helpless feeling only multiplied when the minimansion belonging to the Baumgartners came into view. Spense's words had made her more fearful than even the attempts on her life had.

Baumgartner might've been a member slash advisor slash legal counselor for Labyrinth.

She rubbed her temples and shook off the useless, self-destructive reaction to Spense's suggestion. On some level, the idea made sense, and it wasn't far off from what she herself had been thinking—that Harvey might be part of the club. She just hadn't taken it so far as to hypothesize her father's old friend could've been the kill club's attorney in residence.

But if Baumgartner did in fact have a secret life, one he'd kept hidden from his wife and son, it was logical to draw the conclusion he might have been involved in such a club as Labyrinth. And if he was involved with the club, it would be natural for him to assist other members with their legal difficulties. But what was currently chewing through the lining of her stomach like a rabid squirrel was what Spense had *refrained* from saying: that Harvey Baumgartner had defended her father, so maybe her father had been a member of the club.

She forced herself to draw in a deep, calming breath.

No way.

There was absolutely no way *her father* would have been or could have been a member of Labyrinth. According to the cybercrime team, every indication pointed to the club's being a recent development, in its nascent stages.

No way.

The Bureau was certain Labyrinth had not been in existence at the time of Gail Falconer's murder, and *she* was certain her father wouldn't have been part of such a group even if it, or one like it, had been around. Her father was a good man. Her father was neither a misogynist nor a murderer. Her father was the man who gave her piggyback rides and sang her lullabies on rainy nights and picked her mother wildflowers just because.

She heaved a relieved sigh. They had arrived. And she had her certainty back. She wouldn't allow these crippling doubts to infiltrate her psyche and weaken her resolve. There was far too much at stake to hide her eyes like a frightened child at a scary movie— though lately she felt as though she had the starring role in one. There was nothing she wasn't willing to see. No truth she didn't wish to examine.

Because the truth was the *only* thing that could bring her peace.

She opened her door and stepped out of the car. This time, there was no Louisa Baumgartner in the drive to greet them. They had deliberately avoided calling ahead because they were hoping to catch Elizabeth and the other girl alone. Caity didn't even know her name. But there was something about both girls that haunted her. Perhaps it was because their long red hair reminded her of Gail Falconer and Annie Bayberry. Yes. That was it exactly.

These girls were the killer's type.

Elizabeth answered the door.

"I'm sorry, but Mrs. Baumgartner and Mr. Baumgartner Junior aren't home. If you'd like to leave a card, I'll let them know you were here." Like Caitlin remembered, Elizabeth's words were stilted and formal, almost as though she were reading from a script.

"May we come in? I'd like to leave a note, but I don't have a pen or paper," Caitlin lied.

Alarm flashed across Elizabeth's face, or maybe she imagined it, because Elizabeth opened the door and motioned for them to come inside.

"When do you expect them back?" Spense asked. He and Caitlin had not discussed strategy, but one seemed to have evolved anyway. They did have a sort of shorthand between them—one that went beyond tugging an earlobe. It seemed their unspoken plan at the moment was to *indirectly* question the two women. If the girls believed Spense and Caitlin were interested in talking to the Baumgartners and didn't realize the true focus was on them, they'd be more at ease and more likely to offer up unguarded responses.

Caitlin accepted a pen and paper from Elizabeth. "Those cookies we had the other day were to die for, Elizabeth. Did you bake them yourself?"

"Oh no." She kept her eyes downcast just as she'd done the other day. "That was Deejay."

"Deejay. That's a pretty name. Is she around? I might want her to write down that recipe for me if it's not too much of a bother."

"Of course not ma'am. I'll get her." *Ma'am?* Again, so formal with the address. No teenager she knew talked like that, even while on her best behavior.

Elizabeth soon returned with Deejay in tow. Spense turned, and mouthing a *whoa* at her, caught Caitlin's eye. The first time they'd met Deejay and Elizabeth, Annie Bayberry had not yet become a Labyrinth victim. But now the resemblance between Deejay, and to a lesser extent Elizabeth, and Annie Bayberry all but knocked the wind out of Caitlin.

She lowered herself into a chair in the entry hall. "I need some water." She really did. "Deejay, could you give me that sugar-cookie recipe?"

A credenza stood against the wall, and Deejay pulled out a card from one of its drawers and began scribbling out the recipe, while Elizabeth disappeared, then returned with a glass of water.

"How long have you worked for the Baumgartners, Deejay?"

"Oh we've both been here a few years, already. Haven't we Lizzie?" Deejay looked to Elizabeth, as if asking for guidance in her response.

Caitlin gulped the water Elizabeth had brought. Neither girl looked to be any more than seventeen or eighteen, so that meant they'd been working for the Baumgartner family during most of their high-school years. Was it part-time work? Or were the girls dropouts? "Well, I'm sure Mrs. Baumgartner is incredibly grateful for your help at a time like this. Is this a full-time job?"

"Yes. But I'm not sure Mrs. B will want to keep us now that . . ." Elizabeth's voice trailed off a second. "Now that her husband's gone."

"Oh? Why not? This is such a big house, she must have use for you."

"That's right . . ." Elizabeth shrugged and looked away. "I don't know why I said that except, he's the one who hired us, and now it's just her."

Deejay sighed. "And Junior. Don't forget about Junior."

To Caitlin, Louisa Baumgartner didn't seem at all the type to fend for herself. Even with her husband gone, she'd certainly keep a small staff of some sort. But perhaps Louisa was more uncomfortable than she'd let on about having these young girls in her home. Spense arched an eyebrow and gave her the head-tilt. She interpreted that as his wanting her to try to draw a reaction from the girls.

"Mr. Baumgartner hired you. That seems odd that the man of the house would choose the staff, doesn't it? But then again, I heard a rumor Mr. Baumgartner was *very* hands-on. Was he *hands-on* with you girls?"

Elizabeth and Deejay exchanged a wide-eyed glance. This time there was no mistaking the alarm on their faces.

"No." Elizabeth's eyes were watery. "Mr. Baumgartner was a perfect gentleman. He took us in from the goodness of his heart. I got kicked out of my house at fourteen. Deejay ran away from hers. Mr. Baumgartner took us in and gave us a fresh start."

Her stomach knotted. Harvey Baumgartner had taken two

homeless fourteen-year-old girls in and turned them into servants. "And he never bothered you?"

Elizabeth bit her lower lip and sent Deejay what appeared to be a warning look.

"It's okay. I promise I won't repeat anything you tell me to Mrs. B," Caitlin said.

More silence.

"I won't say anything to Harvey Junior, either." Caitlin stood and reached out her hand. "If you need help, this is your chance. All you have to do is ask."

Elizabeth's back stiffened, and she jerked her chin up, then took Deejay's hand. "Mrs. Baumgartner won't like it that you're here while she's away. You should come back later, when she's at home. You have a pen and paper if you want to leave that message."

Caitlin scribbled her name and cell number and Spense's name and cell on the paper, then laid it in Elizabeth's outstretched palm. She looked from one girl to the other. "You have our information if you want to talk . . . about anything at all."

"This house really is something. Are your rooms as nice as the rest of the place?" Spense rattled his keys as they turned to go.

Finally, Deejay's face brightened. "Oh yes, my room is decorated for a princess. Mrs. Baumgartner made sure of that."

Caity almost gasped. Not only did Louisa not object to her husband bringing home beautiful girls, she'd hired a decorator to make their rooms so nice they'd never want to leave.

"Sounds like a very generous family." Spense opened the door, then turned back one last time. "Don't hesitate to call on us if you need to."

Elizabeth all but shoved Caitlin out the door after Spense.

"Please go now. We'll be sure Mrs. Baumgartner gets your message."

Back in the car, as Caitlin snapped her lap belt in place, she noticed her hands shaking. Her entire body, in fact, was vibrating with rage. "Harvey Baumgartner took those girls in for his own nefarious purposes. I feel it in my bones. We need to get back in there and search the house. Can you get a warrant?"

"What would we be searching for, Caity? It's not a crime to employ beautiful girls."

"He wasn't just employing them, and you know it. We have to get back in that house and look for something, anything that could tie him to the kill club."

"And then what?" His look said *take it easy*.

How could Spense be so calm when he had to have seen what had gone on in that house just as clearly as she had? But maybe that was the point. What *had* gone on—past tense. Harvey Baumgartner was keeping company with the worms now, where he couldn't harm those girls or anyone else ever again. "I don't know."

"Exactly. What you're talking about is a trawling expedition, putting out a net and hauling in whatever you happen to trap in it. I can't get a warrant just because you're in the mood for a fish fry. Besides, the easiest way to get back in the house is the same way Thompson got into Silas Graham's house. When you don't have a warrant, an invitation will do just fine."

Chapter Twenty-Nine

Monday, September 23

From: Man in the Maze <395204@253.0.101.212>
To: Labyrinth <list.27040302@253.0.101.212>
Subject: Emergency Meeting

Attention all lieutenants. Those of you who have collected a labyrinth and have earned the rank of lieutenant, you have also earned the right to help steer our group and determine her fate in this time of crisis. I'm loath to tell you, but we are all in grave danger. Our very survival is at stake. It may no longer be safe to communicate via this loop, and therefore this will be the last message you receive from me on this forum.

As for the rest of you, those who have not yet achieved your rank, do not worry. With the help of our brave lieutenants, we will find a way to carry on. You must have faith in yourselves and in the group. However, because the authorities might be monitoring our messages (I hope this is not the case, but I can no longer be certain), I implore you all to cease any file sharing. Your images, your fantasies, your stories must be kept private from here on out.

I'm afraid I have no choice but to invoke the emergency protocol. To wit, I am calling an urgent in-person summit of all lieutenants. Attendance is mandatory, or you will be stripped of your rank. Although I am sorry for the short notice, twenty-four hours should give you time to travel. We will meet at the appointed time and place.

For everyone:

All computers, cell phones, and other devices that may contain evidence of our group should be sanitized immediately.

As of now, this site is no longer operational. At the summit, we will make a plan for moving forward. As a reminder, horror cannot be contained. Although it has no home, it does not wander the earth but rather exists in our heart of hearts. I'll be waiting for you at the journey's end. I know you will find your way. Until then, be well.

MIM

Chapter Thirty

Monday, September 23
Scottsdale Highlands Apartments
Scottsdale, Arizona

DIZZY LEONARD STARED at her computer through a blur of moisture. The words seemed to elevate from the page and float to her on a sea of tears. As she read the tweets, they felt as real as a hand clutching her by the throat and choking the breath out of her. Maybe it was the new medicine they gave her at the hospital, or maybe the words really had come to life.

Don't cry, Dizzy. Don't let them win.

She swiped her eyes with the back of her hand and reread the Twitter stream:

LilaB @QueenBee
He likes a different girl #DumbDizzy @DizzyGal

TrudyCypher @TrudyPie
I heard she got kicked out of the party. Bye-bye @DizzyGal
#DumbDizzy

KakiAndrews @KakiWaki
OMG. Does she think he'd go with a loon? #DumbDizzy
@DizzyGal

LilaB @QueenBee
She took pills but she didn't die #DumbDizzy
@DizzyGal

KakiAndrews @KakiWaki
Take more pills @DizzyGal #DumbDizzy #WhyDon'tYouDie?

LilaB @QueenBee
Take more pills @DizzyGal #WhyDon'tYouDie?

TrudyCypher @TrudyPie
Take more pills @DizzyGal #WhyDon'tYouDie?

Why don't I die?
I want to die.

"Dizzy!" Mom was coming. With her heart pounding in her chest, she clicked her browser closed. If Mom saw the tweets, she'd go to the principal again, and things would get worse.

Worse?

How could things get worse? The whole school already wanted

her to die. The whole school knew she couldn't even do one thing right. All those pills she took, and nothing had happened except Mom took her to the hospital and they put a tube in her stomach and pumped charcoal into her. Then they gave her different pills they said would make her feel better. They didn't even keep her overnight. They said it was a cry for help—but why hadn't they answered it? Mom got a card for a psychiatrist, but the psychiatrist didn't have any appointments until next month, and the new pills didn't help at all. The new pills made her feel strange and say things she didn't mean to Mom. Nothing was *ever* going to get better.

Why don't you die?

Mom poked her head in her room. She didn't even knock. She said Dizzy had lost her privacy rights when she tried to off herself. Now Mom just walked in whenever she pleased, and there was nothing Dizzy could do about it. "Everything okay in here, Dizzy gal?"

"Sure, Mom. Everything's perfect. Abso-fucking-lutely perfect."

"Dizzy! There's no need for language." Mom sounded more tired than angry. Dizzy was wearing her out. She worked all day and came home to a troubled teen. Dizzy overheard Mom's friend say that on the phone. Mom said, no, it wasn't that bad, but Dizzy knew it was all true.

She spun in her chair and faced her mother. "You're right, Mom. I'm sorry." In a way, she really was. She was sorry to hurt Mom, but Mom would get over it. She folded her arms across her chest, determined. Next time she'd get it right. Mom would get over it. In the end, Mom would be better off without her.

Mom tilted her head. "Dizzy, have you been crying again?"

Geez, great detective work. "No, Mom."

Mom crossed the room and stood before her, then she bent and kissed her on the cheek. Mom smelled like tequila. Dizzy had driven her to drinking at night again. "You know you can tell me anything. If something's wrong, I want to help you. I'm going to call that psychiatrist again tomorrow and *make* him give us a sooner appointment. I love you, Dizzy."

"I love you, too, Mom." She really did, even if she drank too much tequila, Dizzy didn't care. Mom always did her best.

Dizzy waited until Mom left the room. Mom left the door partway open, like she always did these days. But once Dizzy heard footfalls on the stairs, she knew it was safe. She opened her browser.

Fuck Twitter.

She had somewhere better to go. She had friends in a secret group. She loved knowing a secret. Even if no one had answered her message, she felt like a part of things already. The deep web was dark and dangerous and the safest place for a girl like Dizzy to hide. The kids at school would never follow her there. They didn't even know how. But Dizzy was smart enough to figure it out. All those hours online had paid off. Dizzy could do just about anything online. And the men in Labyrinth wanted something that she could give them. Labyrinth was one of those fantasy games with photoshopped pictures and made-up horror stories. Her hand trembled on the mouse when a little voice whispered in her head.

Those pictures look real.

They had to be fake, though, right?

She'd told them she would be their whore. It was only a game— but even if it wasn't, she didn't care. If someone wanted to kill her, they would only be doing what she hadn't been able to do for herself.

#WhyDon'tYouDie? @DizzyGal

Nothing felt real anymore. Life was a game.

She listened for noises downstairs to be sure it was still safe. Then she logged on.

When she found the message, she shoved her math book onto the floor. It landed with a loud thud, and she hoped Mom wouldn't come up to check on her again.

No. No. No.

This couldn't be. The e-mail said no more messages could be sent on the loop, and no one had answered her e-mail yet. No one had told her how to become a real member of the group. With her mouse, she highlighted the text:

> As of now, this loop is no longer operational. At the summit, we will make a plan for moving forward. As a reminder, horror cannot be contained. Although it has no home, it does not wander the earth but rather exists in our heart of hearts. I'll be waiting for you at the journey's end. I know you will find your way. Until then, be well.
>
> MIM

SHE HAD TO find the summit. She didn't have the emergency instructions, but she did have the clue: *Horror cannot be contained. Although it has no home, it does not wander the earth but rather exists in our heart of hearts.*

All she had to do was find the summit.

They would all be waiting for her there.

Chapter Thirty-One

Tuesday, September 24
Paradise Valley, Arizona

SPENSE HAD BEEN right. An invitation had been much simpler to obtain than a warrant would've been. Louisa Baumgartner must've been anxious to know the reason for their earlier visit because she'd invited them to return to the house the very next morning. Of course, the situation wasn't ideal since they couldn't access Baumgartner's computer or formally search the house, but it was a start. Elizabeth answered the door and escorted Caitlin and Spense into the living room. Before the girl could announce them, however, Louisa raised one finger high in the air. "That will be all, Elizabeth. I don't require refreshments today, and I'll ring you if I need you."

"Thanks for speaking with us." Spense got straight to it. "I'd hate to have to do this down at the station."

Harvey Junior was seated in an armchair facing his mother. He smiled warmly despite Spense's terse words. "Welcome back.

Mother and I are anxious to be of service. Anything we can do to catch this bastard."

Louisa looked taken aback. "As I've said, I'm not only happy to cooperate, I'm *eager* to be of help. So I cannot imagine why you would suggest we come down to the precinct simply to answer a few additional questions."

"Well, it was more than kind of you to invite us here to your lovely home instead. And I do apologize for the crude suggestion that we interview you down at the precinct. Now that I think about it, I can see how mortifying that would be for the family. I'd never want the press to draw the wrong conclusion. Conducting the remainder of the interview in your home was a much better idea. Now then, since we're all present and accounted for, I just have a few more things I need to clear up." It must've cost Spense dearly to pull out that obsequious tone of voice for Louisa Baumgartner.

"Is it about the death threats Harvey received?" Louisa asked, her shoulders dipping into a more relaxed position.

"No. It's about Harvey himself." Spense softened his words with a smile.

"I'm afraid I don't understand. Harvey was the victim of a terrible crime. I don't know why no one seems interested in tracking down those death threats."

Caitlin couldn't stop herself from speaking. How could this woman be so blind? "Mrs. Baumgartner, are you aware that the two live-in girls in your employ, Deejay and Elizabeth, are underage?"

Confusion filled her eyes. "I don't know what you mean by underage. Both girls are seventeen, and I've completed all the proper paperwork. Even now, they only put in a few hours' work a day. They're paid good wages and have health benefits. I pay social security, too. I can assure you this is all perfectly legal."

"Are Elizabeth and Deejay in school?"

"It's hardly *our* fault the girls dropped out. I don't know what more we could've done. We've put a roof over their heads and provided for their every need. Why, I'd love for them to get their GEDs if they were so inclined. But frankly, neither one seems all that bright or motivated to go on with her schooling."

"So that's a no. They're not in school. Do they have friends? Do they get out and socialize with their peers?" Caitlin tried but failed to imitate Spense's respectful tone.

"Everything proper for a domestic employee has been handled. My husband saw to that."

"I bet he did." Spense said. The gloves had just come off.

Caitlin shot him a smile. Good cop bad cop switcheroo time. Keeps folks on their toes. "Don't be rude, Agent Spenser." She reached out and patted Louisa's hand, and the woman jerked away like Caitlin had coated her palm with flesh-eating bacteria. "*Naturally*, Harvey would have seen to all the legalities, Louisa." She smiled sweetly. "I believe Special Agent Spenser means the girls are below the age to consent to sexual acts."

Louisa's face went as white as her best china. "Sexual acts?"

On a deeply sympathetic sigh, Caitlin said, "I'm sorry to be the one to tell you, but Agent Spenser and I have reason to believe your husband may have been abusing Elizabeth and Deejay."

Mrs. Baumgartner's back straightened. Her expression turned from disbelief to outrage. "*My* husband abused these girls? He absolutely did not. He *doted* on them. He lavished them with . . . with . . ." She stopped, and her eyes flitted nervously about the room.

"He lavished them with affection?"

"That's not what I meant, and you know it. You're putting words in my mouth."

Junior bolted to his feet, and Caitlin worried they were about to get tossed out. She ignored him and kept her attention on Louisa. "What did you mean then?"

"I only meant to say Harvey did what he could for the less fortunate of this world, and that includes not only those girls out there in the kitchen, but *your father,* too. Because of *you,* my *dear* Caitlin, and your family, *I* had to endure all manner of social humiliation. Because of *you,* I was almost kicked out of the Woman's Club. During your father's trial, someone started a petition to exclude me." Her nose went up. "Fortunately, my influence and spotless reputation were enough to prevent such an injustice."

Junior took a seat next to his mother and handed her a hanky. She sniffled into it and blinked away more tears than Caitlin had yet seen her shed.

Such an injustice.

She wanted to grab Louisa by the shoulders and shake her until her teeth rattled loudly enough to wake up her brain. The woman seemed to be walking through life in complete ignorance of the plight of others. Taking an interest in her neighbors only so long as it didn't interfere with her privileged life. Caitlin's father was dead. Executed for a crime he didn't commit, and this woman saw her membership troubles at the Woman's Club as the only injustice worth shedding a tear over. "I'm so terribly sorry for any pain you may have suffered on my account. Really, I simply cannot express how badly I feel about that."

"Well"—Louisa gathered herself and made the effort to send Caitlin a warm look, as if suddenly realizing her façade had slipped—"naturally, *your* family suffered far more than mine. You must think me terribly small to worry over such matters as a ladies' club when your father was fighting for his life." She smiled a sycophantic smile. "I never did believe Thomas Cassidy killed that poor girl. What was her name again?"

"Gail Falconer," Junior supplied.

"That's the only reason I was able to endure that awful, awful trial." Even when Louisa was trying to take the high road, she couldn't quite conceal her own selfish unhappiness over her temporary loss in social standing.

"Back to the girls." Spense played up his *bad cop* role. "Did you know your husband was sleeping with them?"

Louisa put her hand to her throat. "Have they made that claim?"

"No." Caitlin put in quickly. She would never get comfortable with certain tactics, like lying about the facts of a case as a means to an end.

"Then please don't say such things in front of Junior. How dare you accuse my husband, this boy's *father,* of misusing those poor girls. If they haven't said so, it's because it isn't true. For your information, my husband . . ." She sniffled into the tissues and turned to her son. "I'm sorry, Junior, could you leave us a moment."

He put his arm around her shoulder. "It's not necessary, Mother, we're all adults, and you can speak freely in front of me."

Louisa nodded, then looked down at her nails. "My husband and I had a very happy marriage. He was quite satisfied . . . in every way. I made sure of that." Defiantly, she met Spense's eyes. "There was simply no need for him to go outside the marriage . . . for anything."

"What if he wanted something kinky?" Spense challenged.

Louisa tossed back her long, platinum blond hair and thrust her overblown breasts forward. "Then I gave him something kinky. I was a good wife to him, and he was a good husband to me."

Throughout this rather dicey discussion, Junior never took his arm from around his mother's shoulder.

"So then your husband did have some kinky fantasies." Spense was definitely going to get them kicked out, Caitlin thought.

But no one objected to the question. She was amazed at the polite behavior from all parties present. Apparently, this was a home where one kept one's anger in check . . . She could relate.

"Everyone has kinky fantasies, Agent Spenser. If you don't believe me, just take a look at the bestseller lists. And please, stop trying to make my husband out to be something he wasn't. He was a good husband. A *great* one even."

"And a really good provider, right?"

Junior's arm came back to his side, and he leaned forward. "Look here. I'd hoped you had some information for us, but now I see you have nothing new. If you're looking to paint a picture of my father as an unsavory character and trying to say he was killed because of his bad behavior, you're on the wrong track. My father may have defended the corrupt and the perverse"—here he threw a pointed look at Caitlin—"but he himself was an honorable man. In fact, why don't you come with me? I'd like to show you some of his awards."

This was going even better than Caitlin had hoped. Junior was actually going to take them into his father's office. Not that such a thing was entirely unexpected. She'd besmirched the good Baumgartner name, and that was intolerable to Louisa and Junior. Naturally, they'd want to counteract the accusations by showing off Harvey's trophies and reasserting his standing in the community, and by extension, their own. They were either too stupid to realize or too arrogant to care that she and Spense had come here precisely to get a look around Harvey's personal space.

They all got to their feet, and Junior beckoned for them to follow him down a long corridor, past a number of rooms and a guest bath, until finally they arrived at Baumgartner's office: a masculine room with a massive rolltop desk, expensive leather chairs, and multiple diplomas on the wall. Pretty typical at first glance. Then she noticed that the room was windowless and saw that the door had a dead bolt on the inside. Seemed very odd anyone would want to work in a room without windows—and why the need to lock the world out?

Junior pointed out a plaque on the wall—actually a group of plaques. "Take a look at these, and you'll see how beloved, respected, and honorable my father truly was."

To Harvey Baumgartner, JD for services to the Boys and Girls Club

To Harvey Baumgartner, JD, in recognition of twenty years faithful service to the First United Methodist Church

To Harvey Baumgartner, Better Business Association's Humanitarian of the Year

To Harvey Baumgartner, American Bar Association Pro Bono Publico Award

The awards were indeed impressive. Baumgartner apparently collected them the way Louisa did social accolades. In this family, appearance was everything, and like his wife's Botox, the plaques served to erase Baumgartner's imperfections to outside observers. Spense inclined his head toward one of the smaller awards and arched an eyebrow at Caitlin. She stepped in closer and read: *To Harvey and Louisa Baumgartner in recognition of their generous support of the Southwest Museum of Art.*

Creepy, but hardly proof of wrongdoing since the museum was a very popular cause in Phoenix high society. Still, Harvey's role as a benefactor created something of a foundation for a case they'd been building against him from thin air. The weird atmosphere in the room made Caitlin uncomfortable, and she folded her arms across her chest, shielding herself from what felt like an invisible current of evil undulating through the air and wrapping her like a mummy. Had Baumgartner used this room for unsavory purposes? She couldn't shake the feeling that something terrible had happened here.

In an effort to snap herself out of it, she picked up a photo off the desk, one of Harvey and his son as a teen. Like Harvey, Junior wore an expensive gray suit. The two stood stiffly, side by side, with perfect smiles. Beside that photo was another of Junior accepting some type of award at school, again his father stood in perfect, rigid posture at his son's side. Caitlin glanced up at Spense and frowned. She couldn't help noting the contrast between these pictures and the ones she'd seen of Spense and his father.

There was no warmth in this house. All that mattered here was external validation. The entire family seemed focused on achieving perfection. She imagined how hard Junior would've had to work to get his father's affection and wondered if such a thing were even possible. At least her father had loved her unconditionally. At least the only thing she'd had to do to win his approval was be his daughter. So, yes, no matter how short a time she'd had him, no matter how horrible his death had been, between Junior and her, she counted herself the more fortunate child.

Glancing around the room again, her gaze went to a doorway leading off the study. "Where does this go?" she asked innocently, striding to the door and turning the knob. But the door was locked, and she could see by the look on Louisa's face that she'd pushed her luck trying to enter another room without permission.

"Oh, that's a guest bedroom. But Harvey sometimes slept there after working late into the night. He didn't like to disturb my rest. He was so thoughtful that way." Louisa sighed.

Then Junior anticipated Caitlin's next question. "With no one using it anymore, we closed it up."

"Convenient to have it adjoin his office," she replied matter-of-factly. There was an awkward moment of silence. To ease the tension building in her body, Caitlin prowled the study, pretending to admire the décor. When she arrived at the bookcase, there was no further need for pretense. The shelves were filled with tempting treasure. Everything from the classics to the latest thrillers—even a romance or two. Beyond the fiction, which had been alphabetized by author and sorted by genre, were Harvey's law books. She inhaled the luxurious scent of leather-bound books and ran her fingers across the sumptuous spines, tilting each book forward ever so slightly as if it were her very own. Her eyes fluttered closed in enjoyment, then popped open.

What the deuce?

She'd been reveling in the feel of the books, tilting them forward one by one, when she'd come to a book that wasn't right. At least the weight of it was wrong—a thick tome titled *Modern Criminal Procedure,* yet it was featherlight in her hand. A thrill of discovery raced down her spine.

A false book.

Like the kind used to hide valuables. There was something inside this book, and it wasn't dry discourse. Her stomach tilted, and she pressed her palm to her abdomen.

"Are you all right, dear?" It was Louisa's *I-care-so-much* tone—as false as that book.

"Oh, yes. I guess I ate something that disagreed with me." She swallowed hard, truly feeling nauseous from both excitement and apprehension.

"You look pale, darling. Maybe you should go home and get some rest." Louisa slipped her arm through Caitlin's.

Louisa's touch sent a slight shiver across her shoulders. "Good idea." Then she walked arm in arm with her hostess from the room, with Spense and Junior following in silence. They made it all the way to the front door before Caitlin grabbed her stomach again. This time with added flare. "Oh, boy. I-I'm sorry, but I need to use the powder room."

Louisa's face twisted in annoyance, then quickly altered, and a concerned frown appeared. "Elizabeth will escort you." She pressed a call button on the wall.

Caitlin shook her head. "Thanks, but I know the way." Sending a sheepish glance over her shoulder, she said, "I'll be right back," then bit her lip. Wasn't that just what an actress said in a B-movie just before she did something stupid? Something that usually led to her demise?

Too bad.

Whatever was in that book, Caitlin wanted it. She rushed down the ridiculously long hall, past one room, then another, past the powder room and *at last* slipped inside Harvey's study. As she eased the door shut, her shoulders jumped at the sound of footsteps in the corridor. The footsteps passed, and a door slammed a few rooms down. Her breath released in a *whoosh*.

Probably the housekeeper.

Wasting no time, Caitlin scanned the bookshelf and grabbed the copy of *Modern Criminal Procedure*. Her palm left a sweaty print on the leather binding as she opened it and let out a small gasp. Sure enough, there was a false compartment, and in that compartment lay a key.

An old-fashioned skeleton key. The key to a rolltop desk!

Caitlin rushed to open the rolltop. As it creaked open, she cast a glance behind her, but there was no one to hear. She pulled in a

steadying breath and set to work. The inside of the desk was as organized as the bookshelf, with bank statements sorted by month, a
checkbook, and some letters to clients. Caitlin rifled through them
all, looking for something, *anything* that would stand out, but there
was no time to read documents. She'd been expecting . . . what?
Incriminating photographs, a smoking gun? And all she'd found
were papers and . . . and . . . now her hands began to tremble as they
closed over the object winking at her from a cubbyhole.

Another key.

This one with a red ribbon tied through it. She closed the desktop and hurried across the room to the locked door. The sound of
the key turning was magnified in her ears, like someone held a
microphone to the latch. She imagined the sound being broadcast
down the hall and over loudspeakers as she turned the knob and
opened the door to the *guest room.*

She stepped inside, and her head snapped back as if a gale-force
wind had hit her in the face. Her pulse sloshed in her ears, and
her skin went cold, her palms clammy. Reaching out, she put one
hand on the wall to steady herself and willed her knees not to give
way.

In the center of the room stood a crisply made bed, a nightstand
on either side, and a chest of drawers . . . nothing out of the ordinary
there. One wall of the room was entirely mirrored, a feature not at all
in keeping with the elegant yet understated décor of the remainder
of the house. But that wasn't what made her heart bang against her
ribs and her breath freeze into a solid block of ice in her lungs. In one
corner, a display case was loaded with pottery, all emblazoned with
the Man in the Maze motif. As for the east wall of the room—once
again, there was no window to the outside world. No art hung on that
wall because the wall itself was a work of art. A mural to be exact. A

life-size unicursal labyrinth, and posing in the center, arms out-stretched, was a hulking male figure. Reeling from the realization of what was in front of her, she took a step backward.

She had entered his lair.

The evidence before her eyes made her bones vibrate with certainty. Evil painted the air with its sickly-sweet smell. To keep from crying out, she covered her mouth. Harvey Baumgartner had been her father's friend. He'd taken him under his wing and defended him when no one else would. Her father's attorney. Her father's old friend.

Harvey Baumgartner was the Man in the Maze.

She heard the creak of a door behind her and the hairs on the back of her neck sent a warning, but her feet had rooted themselves to the floor. She didn't hear the footsteps on the soft carpet until he was already behind her. She sensed his presence a split second before his hand covered her mouth, and a familiar voice whispered in her ear:

"What the hell do you think you're doing, Caity?"

SPENSE GOT CAITY to the car as quickly as possible. Neither one said a word for a minute or two after they drove off, then Spense jammed his hand into the horn and swerved into an empty parking lot. "I'll ask you again. What the hell were you doing snooping around where you weren't invited?"

"I-I found a book with a false compartment, and I—"

"You what? You decided to act on your own without consulting me. You decided to search a *locked* room. You decided to do something that could've made any potential evidence we found inadmissible in court. You decided to violate the Baumgartners' Fourth Amendment rights. *You* did that, not me."

"I'm so sorry. I didn't mean to break the law or violate their rights. It's just I knew there was something in that book, and when I found the key, I only had a split second to decide what to do."

The horrified look on her face instantly softened his heart.

"And I made the wrong choice. I feel awful, and the worst part is, if I had the chance all over again, I don't know what I'd do. I'd like to think I'd make the right call, but . . . I just had to know what was in that room. There are lives at stake, Spense."

He reached out and took her hand. He didn't know whether to throttle her or comfort her. "I know that, Caity. Which is why we need to be careful." His cheeks stretched into a grin. "That's a hell of a thing, me telling you to mind the rules."

"You must think I'm an awful hypocrite."

"I think you're human, sweetheart. We all are. But in the future, don't go off the reservation without me backing you up. And don't worry about that mural's not being admissible in court. A good prosecutor can get around that—I've seen them do it a thousand times. Besides, it's all circumstantial."

"The mural's not enough to get a warrant to search the rest of the residence, or the computers?"

"I don't think so. But we'll have to let the rest of the gang in on what you found—and *how* you found it—and get their take."

Her hand squeezed his. "I've learned my lesson, I promise. And . . . I just want to say for the record . . . I know I'm not perfect."

"Who asked you to be?" He started the car up but didn't let go of her hand until he pulled into the field-office parking lot, and only then with great difficulty.

Chapter Thirty-Two

Tuesday, September 24
Phoenix Police Department
Mountainside Precinct

DETECTIVE RILEY BASKIN paced the precinct lunchroom with a PB and J gripped in his hand, purple jam dripping down his bulky wrist and matting the golden hairs on his forearm. Caitlin and Spense had interrupted his lunch, and he seemed none too happy about the matter. "I'm sorry, but I just don't buy it. How can Harvey Baumgartner be the Man in the Maze? It just doesn't make sense."

At first, it'd seemed illogical to Spense, too, but after giving it due consideration, he'd changed his mind. Also, seeing that gargantuan mural of a labyrinth on Baumgartner's wall had made a big impression and gone a long way toward convincing him. "It's the only thing that does make sense. He fits the profile Caity constructed at the museum to a T. And by the way we've already confirmed he and his wife, Louisa, made large donations to the museum—he's even got a plaque on his wall praising his generosity. Harvey Baumgartner was highly intelligent, and as it turns out, he was also an adjunct professor of law at Tempe University. We believe the Man in the Maze is a teacher, and given the fact two coeds have now been found with their temporal bones removed, we believe his preferred hunting ground was the university."

"He may fit your profile in that respect, but so does Randy Cantrell. In fact, if we go with your theory, that the Man in the Maze killed Gail Falconer, too, Cantrell moves to the head of the line. He was her fiancé. He teaches at Tempe. He collects Native American art . . . and here's a new piece of information you might like: Annie Bayberry was in Cantrell's sociology classes."

"Which makes him the perfect guy to take the fall for her murder. Maybe that's one of the reasons she was chosen. Randy Cantrell has an alibi for the night Gail Falconer was killed. One of your own men from the task force tracked his old Reserves commander down in Yuma yesterday. Cantrell could *not* have killed Gail Falconer. So he's not the guy who planted her missing ring on Annie Bayberry's corpse. Harvey Baumgartner, on the other hand, was never even looked at for Falconer, so we don't know his whereabouts on the night of her murder."

"But we sure as hell do know his whereabouts on the night of Annie Bayberry's murder—Green Valley Cemetery." Baskin dragged a hand through his hair, then scowled when he realized he'd just gelled himself with grape jam. "So hold your horses, if you don't mind. It seems you're saying that Baumgartner's not only the Man in the Maze, but also that he killed Gail Falconer. That would put him in possession of her ring. But a dead man didn't plant that ring on poor Annie Bayberry. Like I said before, this just doesn't add up."

Caitlin tapped Spense on the shoulder, signaling she'd like to cut in. "Let's just take this one step at a time, Riley." Spense shook his head as Caity turned on the charm. She was good. He'd give her that much. "If we can just start with looking at Baumgartner as the Man in the Maze, the leader of Labyrinth, I'm good with that. We can always discuss the Falconer case and Annie Bayberry and how all that fits in later. But for now, let's look at the facts. First, Baumgartner fits the profile of the Man in the Maze. Second, he's got a giant unicursal Labyrinth painted on the wall of a windowless guest room that locks from the outside. Third, I'm certain he's abused two young women in his employ. Isn't that enough to get a warrant to search his computer?"

"Not without a sworn statement from the girls, and they've already said he never touched them."

She blew out a hard breath. "Yes, but as I told you when we first arrived, one of them slipped me a note as I was leaving the house today. She wants a meeting, and I think she *might* be willing to give a statement if I can just make her feel safe enough. The original denial isn't surprising, considering Elizabeth and Deejay are still in that house and still dependent on the Baumgartners for their livelihood. I'm sure if we can just help them see they have other options—"

Baskin screwed up his face. "Options? No disrespect, Caitlin, but if those girls had been abused in any way, if Baumgartner had so much as given them a friendly pat on the behind, they'd have been shouting it from the rooftops by now. They could sue Baumgartner's estate, and as long as they backed each other up, they'd have a good shot at winning, or at the very least at settling for a sizeable jackpot. So the fact they said it ain't so, to me, means it ain't so."

"I understand your doubts. But if I *can* get Elizabeth or Deejay to talk . . ."

"Then we *might* have enough for a warrant for the computer," Baskin said, stroking his chin. "But that brings me back to square one. Harvey Baumgartner as the Man in the Maze just does not make sense."

He tossed his ruined sandwich into the trash, opened the door, and motioned for them to follow him out of the break room and over to his desk. Rifling through stacks of papers he located the one he sought and handed it to her. "Remember this e-mail we recovered from Silas Graham's computer?" With his pointer finger he indicated the relevant text.

The situation is most desperate as Zeus has a clever attorney, and I fear this counselor will urge him to save his own life in exchange for ours.

Baskin shook his head. "We've established that *Zeus* was Judd Kramer's online handle. Baumgartner therefore is the counselor who supposedly urged him to make a deal, thus putting Labyrinth as a group in danger. Therefore . . ." He looked up. "Stay with me here. Therefore, when the Man in the Maze sent this e-mail to Graham, ordering him to eliminate Zeus *and his counselor,* he's ordering Baumgartner's assassination." Baskin held up one finger. "So now then, which one of you wants to explain to me why, if Harvey Baumgartner was in fact the Man in the Maze, he would order a hit on *himself.*"

"Clearly, he didn't." Spense said, his expression unfazed, then checked his watch. "And I'd be happy to explain myself, but we need to pick this up later. It's complicated, and right now, Caity and I have a meeting with Elizabeth Johnson. We need her cooperation and, I don't want to be late for our appointment."

Chapter Thirty-Three

Tuesday, September 24
Papa's Restaurant
Paradise Valley, Arizona

ELIZABETH JOHNSON LOOKED like a redheaded angel with the sunlight from the diner window spotlighting her flowing hair and creamy complexion. Huddled into a booth across from Caitlin and Spense, the girl's expression was demure to the point of submission, and Caitlin was grateful she'd somehow found the courage to slip her that note as they were leaving the Baumgartner mansion. "Thanks for meeting us, Elizabeth. Agent Spenser and I are here to listen to whatever you have to tell us. We only want to help."

Casting her glance down at the glass of lemonade she spun between her hands, Elizabeth nodded. The muscles around her mouth tightened, and she blinked rapidly, then shaded her eyes from the sun. When she took her hand away, her eyes were wide, their color a deep midnight blue. A hiccup preceded her words. "I don't want to go to jail."

Caitlin and Spense exchanged a glance. Caitlin's first inclination was to promise Elizabeth that wouldn't happen, but until she heard what the girl had to say, it was a promise she couldn't make. And how could she expect the girl to trust her if she offered up something she couldn't deliver? Elizabeth would see through that, then she'd never feel safe enough to speak freely to her again. "I don't want you to go to jail either. But if you think it's best to have this conversation with an attorney present, Agent Spenser can arrange that. Believe me when I tell you, I don't want any harm to come to you."

A tear slipped down Elizabeth's cheek. "I don't want a lawyer. I just want this to be over." She hiccuped again and took a sip of lemonade.

"You want what to be over, sweetie?" Caitlin braced herself, knowing Elizabeth's story wouldn't be easy for her tell or for them to hear.

"I ran away from home when I was fourteen. My mom's boyfriends . . ." Abruptly, she stopped and took a sip of lemonade. "When my mom was away, they'd do things to me. So I ran. Only I had no place to go. I was sleeping in boxes and hiding out in people's garages until I found some other kids on the street who showed me what to do. How to make it on my own. You know, turning tricks and stuff."

From the corner of her eye, Caitlin saw Spense's jaw tighten, and a flush crawl up his neck. But he kept quiet and said nothing. They both waited for Elizabeth to settle in with her story.

"Anyway, it was pretty rough down there on Van Buren Street. I got beat up a couple times, and I don't even know how many times someone put something in my drink and I'd wake up and have no idea what happened to me. What the hell did they have to do that for when I was willing to do it for just a little bit of cash? Just enough to get me a place to sleep for the night. That's all I asked for." She stopped, picked up a napkin, started shredding it. "That was the absolute worst part. Not knowing what they'd done to me. I thought no matter how bad it was, I wanted to *know*. Not remembering made me feel like a ghost. Like I didn't exist, you know?"

"I'm so sorry, Elizabeth. No one should have to endure what you have. Whatever you've done, it's because you were *surviving*, and you have every right to survive. I promise we're going to help you, no matter what."

She shook her head. "I don't think so. I did something really bad."

Caitlin reached her hand across the table to Elizabeth, but the girl didn't take it. Caitlin's throat clogged with emotion, seeing how hard it was for Elizabeth to trust anyone enough to let them show her the smallest bit of compassion.

"*I'm* the one who brought Deejay home for him."

"Do you mean for Mr. Baumgartner?" Caitlin asked.

Elizabeth nodded. "Yes. Mr. Baumgartner picked me up off the street a few times, and he treated me real nice. Then one day he said if I came home with him, he'd help me make a better life." Her eyes bounced between Spense and Caitlin as if suddenly realizing she'd been given false promises of help before. From a man no doubt wearing an expensive suit, much like the one Spense had on now.

"We're not like him, Elizabeth." Spense pulled his creds from his wallet. "You see this? I'm with the FBI. This isn't a fake ID. And Dr. Cassidy is a real doctor, a psychiatrist. We don't want anything from you. We're not promising help in exchange for favors. We're just promising help."

Her eyes held mistrust. "You want information. You want me to snitch on my friends."

"Harvey Baumgartner was not your friend, Elizabeth. And even if you think he was, your loyalty won't help him now. Think hard, and I know you'll see you owe him *nothing*." Spense leaned back and spread his arms over the back of the booth.

Elizabeth, looking only at Caitlin, continued. "I'm sorry—it's just I trusted *him,* too, in the beginning. He was so nice to me. He gave me food and clothes, and he bought me so many things. Stuff I never had . . . he even bought me an iPhone. And Mrs. Baumgartner—she hired an interior decorator to help make our rooms, mine and Deejay's, nice. She said our rooms should be fit for princesses. She said we were like the daughters she never had."

That must've been before she'd dressed them in maids' uniforms and set them to work in the kitchen. "Did Mrs. Baumgartner know what was going on?"

A lost look came over her face. "I'm not sure. She never said anything, and she never seemed angry at Mr. Baumgartner, so I thought she couldn't know what he was doing to us in that room by his office. But then sometimes . . . I'd wonder why she didn't ask more questions. Didn't she wonder why the door was locked, and no one could come inside? Didn't she wonder why he wanted us to be in the office with him for hours at a time? Sometimes I thought she *ought* to have known, and it had to be on purpose she didn't see what was going on in her own house."

"Elizabeth . . . what *was* going on in that house?"

"Bad things. Not at first. At first he was nice and gentle with me, a lot gentler than most of the johns from the street. But after a while, he started to hurt me. Pretty bad. It scared me when he would choke me, and sometimes I thought I was going to die. But then he'd let up and let me catch my breath, then do it all over again until he was finished. And it was hard for him to finish. It seemed like he had to hurt me more and more until eventually nothing was enough to get him off, and he'd punch me in the stomach and tell me it was my fault. I wasn't sexy enough."

"Why didn't you leave, Elizabeth?"

"I had nowhere to go. On the streets, I didn't know what they did to me. At least with him, I could remember the awful things he did. And if he killed me, at least I would be awake when it happened. But when I wasn't enough for him anymore, I got so scared he really would kill me that I did something bad."

Caitlin's heart started to beat too fast, and she prayed Elizabeth had not been forced to participate in a murder.

"That's when I helped him find, Deejay. She was my friend from the street. And I lied to her and promised her it would be so great at the big house in the hills. I told her Mr. Baumgartner was a good man, and he only wanted to help us. I lied to Deejay because I thought if he had two of us, we would be enough for him, and he wouldn't need to hurt me so much to get off." Her chin dipped to her chest. "I'm so sorry. I'm so ashamed."

"You were scared, Elizabeth, we understand that. But now it's over. Mr. Baumgartner can't hurt you anymore."

She shook her head, tears streaming down her cheeks. "That's why I'm here. Talking to you. Because it's not over. I've got nowhere to go if I leave, and if I stay, it will *never* stop."

A sickening feeling washed through her. "Someone is still hurting you, right now?"

Elizabeth nodded. She didn't have to say a name. Harvey Baumgartner Junior was a man very like his father. He must've taken up where his old man left off. She knew it, but she waited for Elizabeth to tell her.

"Junior moved into the house after his father died. He said now Mr. Baumgartner is gone, Deejay and me belong to *him*."

Caitlin tried to breathe through her anger, waiting to speak until she could do so in a calm voice. With a soft vibration, Spense's cell rattled on the tabletop. He looked at it, then slapped down a twenty on the table. "No one is going to touch you again, Elizabeth. You have my word. I'm sending someone out to get Deejay, and you can both stay with my mother until we figure a safe place for you. It's not the Ritz, but no one will lay a hand on you, and it's a damn sight better than some social-services placement. We'll drop you on the way." He swept his gaze to Caitlin. "Herrera wants us at headquarters ASAP. There's been a break in the Sally Cartwright case."

Chapter Thirty-Four

Tuesday, September 24
Federal Bureau of Investigation Field Office
Phoenix, Arizona

As THEY RODE the elevator to the fifth-floor conference room for the second time that day, Spense turned to Caitlin with a puzzled expression.

"What?" she asked. Everything was happening so fast, she wasn't sure how to interpret the question in his eyes.

He shrugged. "I've been waiting for you to say something about me leaving the girls with my mom. I've been preparing my arguments this whole time. I thought you'd say it was a conflict of interest."

"I have no problem with it. These girls are emancipated minors—they don't have to go with protective services if they don't want to, and I'm sure they'd refuse. They'd be on the streets in a heartbeat if we tried to place them with a foster family or group home. They might even go back to *that house,* and I'm really not willing to risk it."

He nodded grimly. "Neither am I."

The elevator opened, and she followed Spense into the conference room.

Gathered already were Baskin, Herrera, and Thompson. Caitlin sat next to Spense, putting as much distance between herself and Thompson as possible. Herrera's message had been marked urgent.

Thompson had a nervous look on his face, and she wondered if he was worried she might've told Spense about his shenanigans the other day. She hadn't. She could handle Thompson and a lot worse all on her own.

Thompson spoke first. "So what's this big development in the Sally Cartwright case? We've got Kramer cold on it, and the asshole's dead, so I'm not really sure it's worth our time to keep talking about a crime that's been sung a lullaby and put to sleep."

"Judd Kramer was never tried or convicted for Sally Cartwright's murder." Some days she felt like the only person in the world who believed in *innocent until proven guilty,* but looking around at the others seated at the table, Spense, Herrera, even Baskin, today wasn't one of those days. Today she felt surrounded by good people—people with integrity. Her shoulders dropped, and she relaxed back into her chair.

"Would a DNA hit be worth your time, Detective?" Baskin seemed to have lost all patience with Thompson.

"DNA from where? We got no DNA on Cartwright." Thompson leaned back too far in his chair and almost tipped over.

"Turns out we do." Baskin straightened in his seat, and extended his hand toward Spense. "At Agent Spenser's behest, we took a second look, and this time we found something. DNA from Cartwright's otic capsule."

"Jesus H., buddy. Just talk English. What the fuck is an otic capsule?"

"The section of temporal bone that was taken as a trophy," Caitlin supplied.

Baskin continued, "The lab found the perp's blood mixed with the victim's—I wondered how anyone could carve out a piece of skull and leave absolutely no trace evidence. The UNSUB did a hell of a job of cleaning up after himself, but in this case not quite good enough. He probably didn't even realize he'd nicked himself until after he'd left the scene."

Caitlin's gaze jerked to Thompson's bruised, cut-up knuckles. She could still see the swelling from the fist to the cheek he gave Silas Graham.

"You're welcome, gentlemen." Herrera's voice drew Caitlin's attention back on point.

"Now we owe you a thank you? For what?" Thompson asked.

"The Bureau is responsible for getting the DNA in the Cartwright case handled so quickly. You'd be waiting a year at the very least if the Bureau hadn't thrown its weight around on your behalf."

Caitlin knew the DNA backlog could run up to two years. And given the critical implications of such evidence, the delay was infuriating, not just to her but to the cops, the attorneys . . . and yes, the families. She was very grateful indeed. "Thank you, Gretchen."

A series of polite *thank-yous* sounded around the table. All this talk, and they still hadn't gotten to the punch line. Caitlin was growing impatient. "You said you got a DNA hit. That means the blood matched DNA found in the criminal database?"

"Not in this instance. We ran it through the criminal database first, and when we came up empty, I ordered a separate comparison with individuals related to the case—even those remotely connected. The task force collected voluntary swabs from all Sally Cartwright's family and friends. Kramer, Graham, and Baumgartner we already had from the autopsies."

Her hands started to tremble. She'd always hoped DNA might clear her father. Gail Falconer's DNA had been found in his car, but none of his DNA had been found at the scene. Spense thought it was a long shot they could recover a sample from the Falconer case after all this time, and she had to agree. With effort, she refocused on Sally Cartwright. "And your match came from one of those sources."

"Yes and no. The blood mixed with Sally Cartwright's, found on her outer ear, was a *close* but not exact match." Herrera met Caitlin's eyes. "To Harvey Baumgartner."

Thompson wrinkled his forehead. "So what? *Close but not exact.* Is it or isn't Baumgartner's blood? What the hell does that mean, close but not exact?"

"The DNA found at the Cartwright scene is not a match for Harvey Baumgartner, but we believe it would match a close relative. We've sent an officer out to Paradise Valley to request a voluntary sample from Harvey Junior."

"You think he'll give it?" The tension in Caitlin's neck ratcheted up a notch—no, make that two notches.

"I've run it by the DA already. We've got enough for a warrant for whatever we need, including a swab. But I figure why not try the easy way first," Herrera said.

"I like him." Caitlin stretched her neck to ease the tension, then tried to size up the reaction of everyone else to the news Herrera had just delivered. "And if I'm right, I doubt he's going to simply hand over a DNA sample. He has the means and connections to put up a hell of a legal battle. And my guess is he's going to do so. Spense and I just came from a meeting with Elizabeth Johnson." For Thompson's benefit, she added, "A young woman employed as a live-in kitchen maid in the Baumgartner home. She's willing to sign a sworn statement that both Harvey Senior *and* Harvey Junior abused her and another girl in the household."

"Motherfuckers." Baskin spit at the floor, his face turning a dusky, angry red. "Like father like son. Well, if we can't nail the one, at least we got a shot at bagging the other." He turned to Spense. "You fill Agent Herrera in on your theory that Harvey Senior is really the Man in the Maze?"

"I've outlined the basics, but this is a good time to finish up our discussion. You asked me earlier to explain why, if Baumgartner was the Man in the Maze, he'd order a hit on himself."

"And you said he didn't."

"Correct. The e-mail ordering the hit on Kramer, Baumgartner, and Caity was signed *the Man in the Maze,* but if we assume that *is* Harvey Baumgartner, then someone else, someone *impersonating* the Man in the Maze, had to have sent that e-mail."

"You mean like another member of the group. A rival maybe?"

"That's exactly what I mean. Suppose someone didn't like the way things were going down with Kramer and how Harvey was handling it. Maybe he was power-hungry and looking to take control of the group. Kramer's arrest presented the perfect opportunity to do that. All that our would-be leader had to do was pretend to be the Man in the Maze and order the hit for the good of the group. Since the members are likely only known to one another by their handles, Silas Graham probably had no idea he'd assassinated his own fearless leader."

"It's a kill-club coup." Thompson slapped his knee.

"And an ingenious one, too, since the club won't even know it happened. The members will simply assume the new Man in the Maze is their original leader."

Herrera slid forward on her elbows. "I have a few questions for you, Spense. The e-mail ordering the hit was sent while Baumgartner still lived and reined as leader. The sender of that e-mail had to have known Baumgartner's true identity, and he also had to have known Baumgartner would not see the e-mail. How does that work exactly?"

"At the risk of oversimplifying, here's my take. If you look carefully at the early e-mails, the sender is adamant that no one in the group should send a reply. The sender made sure Baumgartner didn't have access to the original message, and that no one referenced it in a reply—it was risky, but I'm guessing our imposter thrives on risk."

Thompson's lower lip pushed out, and a general look of confusion settled over him. He kept silent, letting others do the talking for once.

"But who would know Baumgartner's true identity and be able to pull this off?" Herrera asked.

Baskin passed copies of another e-mail around the table. "Someone close to him. Maybe even that *close but not exact* match."

"Dammit!" Thompson's fist came down on the table. "I shoulda known the way Junior was so overly helpful, trying to insert himself into the investigation and all. This whole time, he was probably just pumping me for information."

Ah. She'd suspected it all along, and now she felt quite certain it was Thompson who'd leaked the bloody shoeprint to the Baumgartners. She didn't bother asking him about it at this point. He'd never admit it anyway.

"At any rate." Baskin cleared his throat dramatically. "The man who ordered the hits has got to be the same person who sent *this*."

He'd saved the best for last. A heavy silence settled over the group as they read an online communication that had been discovered by the cyber task force less than an hour ago.

"Fuck me." Thompson said. "The new Man in the Maze is getting all these assholes together in one place for a killers' summit?"

"Apparently." Baskin pressed his hands to his temples.

"Sometime in the next twenty-four hours?"

"Probably a lot less than that. We think this communication was sent out sometime yesterday."

"Fuck me."

Caitlin sighed. Thompson was starting to get on her nerves. "Can you say anything else, Detective? Something helpful, perhaps?"

"Sure. How about we take this chance to take all these motherfuckers down at once. Operation Labyrinth. This is perfect. They're all huddling up in one location, and all we have to do is go get them."

Baskin shot Thompson a look. "Great suggestion. You got any idea *where* this summit is, Bozo? Because if you do, I'll call out the cavalry."

Spense got to his feet. "Thompson's right."

Detective Thompson tipped back too far in his chair again and said nothing, apparently stunned into silence.

"We have an opportunity, and whether it's a long shot or not, we have to try to figure this thing out. If you were the Man in the Maze, where would you hold the summit?" Spense began working his cube, and Caitlin knew he was gathering his focus.

Herrera shook her head. "You're grasping, Spense. We can't

send our officers off on a goose chase based on a brainstorming session. What we can do is keep eyes on Baumgartner, and if he's the new Man in the Maze, he'll lead us to his flock. Unfortunately, we may not locate him in time."

Caitlin clutched the edge of the table. "What do you mean?"

"I mean we sent men out to get a swab and keep eyes on him, but they haven't located Junior yet. Nobody's home, and he's not at his place of business or known hangouts. So I'm afraid we may miss this chance."

Spense shoved his Rubik's cube back in his pocket. "Sometimes the hardest puzzles are the easiest to solve. You just have to look at them the right way. I'll ask again. If you were the Man in the Maze, where would you hold a summit?"

The sound of squeaking filled the air—Thompson was tipping in that chair again. Caitlin closed her eyes, and tried to imagine the room without him. She heard Spense's question repeating in her head. If you were the Man . . . If you were the Man . . . of course! She jumped to her feet. "In a maze!" Spense was right. It was better to think simply in some situations. "And as the leader of the group, surely he'd expect his minions to come to him, not the other way around."

Laptops flew open, and the race was on to Google the location of every maze in Arizona. Turned out there were eight. Four in Phoenix, and the rest spread throughout the state. The plan was to call in the officers in the vicinity, and the task force would divide and conquer. Spense gave her first pick since she'd been the first to see the obvious. After studying the various sites, she got a hunch. She and Spense were headed to Casa Grande.

Chapter Thirty-Five

Tuesday, September 24
Casa Grande Corn Maze and House of Horrors
Outside Casa Grande, Arizona

THE MUSCLES IN Dizzy's legs ached, and her sweat-dampened T-shirt stuck to her back. The pathways through the maze were narrow and overgrown, and when the wind picked up, whipping the stiff, dried-up corn stalks against her bare arms, it felt like she was running a gauntlet instead of winding her way through a six-acre cornfield. The scent of an approaching storm was in the air, and the sun had set awhile ago. Her flashlight, strapped to her belt, banged against her hip as she walked. Between the scorching temperature and the thick, high stalks trapping the heat inside the maze, she was miserable.

And she was lost.

She'd arrived at the deserted maze around 5:00 P.M., and she'd been traveling down one dead end and turning around only to bump into another ever since. She told herself the center of the maze *had* to be nearby. And she was certain that once she found dead center, she'd find the Man in the Maze. A gust of wind filled her nostrils with debris. Her throat closed up, and she started to cough.

Suck it up, Dizzy.

That was the reason she'd come here, wasn't it?

To find the Man in the Maze.

Only . . . maybe this wasn't the place after all. She'd been so sure.

Horror cannot be contained. Although it has no home, it does not wander the earth but rather exists in our heart of hearts.

That's what the message had said. And this particular maze had an attached house of horrors to attract the crowds at Halloween. Surely, that was what the message meant when it said *horror has no home.* This maze had been closed to the public the past six months, so no one would bother them here. It was the perfect place for a summit. Yes. This had to be it.

The Casa Grande Corn Maze and House of Horrors was a good fifty miles south of Phoenix and another ten miles from the highway and the nearest town of Eloy. She'd taken the bus to Eloy and paid a kid at the Circle-K ten bucks to drop her off, so no one knew she was here. And that was a good thing . . . wasn't it? She touched the cell in her pocket.

No.

She wasn't going to call Mom. She'd come all this way, and she wasn't going to chicken out now. Her wet T-shirt acted like an adhesive for the dust blowing everywhere, and she decided she must look like a creature from the black lagoon by now. Her skin itched, and her feet grew wearier with each step she took. She stumbled over a rock in the path and fell onto her outstretched hands. Now her palms were raw and bleeding and burned like the devil. A little voice started up in her head:

You don't have to do this, Dizzy.

That same stupid voice that had stopped her from taking *all* her pills instead of only a handful of them. If not for that nagging refrain in her head, *you don't have to do this,* she might've succeeded the first time. She shouldn't have listened to the voice then, and she wasn't going to listen to it now. She hadn't come all this way for nothing. Instead, she'd listen to that *other* voice. The one that whispered:

Why don't you die, Dizzy?

She'd be better off, and eventually Mom would be, too. Without a depressed, unlikable teenager weighing her down, she'd probably find a good guy and remarry. Mom was lonely—like Dizzy. At least one of them should get to be happy, and she was sure she never could be. It wasn't fair to drag Mom down, too. Who wanted a woman with a *troubled teen*?

She batted away the corn stalks, and, just as quickly, the wind blew them back in her face. Her throat was starting to itch, and her lips and tongue felt thick. Her allergies were pretty bad this time of year, and there was something in the air that was making her nose run and her lungs burn like fire. Her nose was clogged, and her sense of smell was way off. For a while now, she was sure she'd been smelling and tasting gasoline. But that was impossible. She rubbed her arms, sore now from being attacked by the corn. She should've worn long sleeves. But then she realized it wasn't important. Maybe this was real and not just a role-play club. Maybe she'd be dead soon. She shivered in the heat. What if it wasn't a game? In her heart, she hadn't really believed it, but, suddenly, she wasn't so sure. Suddenly, she wanted to go home.

Don't do it Dizzy.

"Why don't you die?" she said aloud. And that's when the wind answered back.

Her hand went to her heart where it was banging against her ribs. That wasn't the wind, and it wasn't a hallucination or even the tiny voice in her head talking now.

People!

She'd found them. She should run fast toward the voices, but instead her feet soldered themselves to the ground. The wind battered her, and she tipped and swayed, but her legs didn't budge. Her sneakers had turned to lead. She didn't dare breathe in case *they* could hear her like she could hear them. But why not make noise? This was why she'd come!

Wasn't it?

To find the men. To let them enjoy her, then end the misery that was her life. It was just a game anyway, so why be scared? Either way, she'd be welcome here. They were looking for a whore, and here she was. She *belonged* here. So why didn't she move? Call out and tell them she'd come to play?

You don't have to do this Dizzy.

Mom loves you, you know.

Her limbs wouldn't move. Some deep, deep part of her brain refused to go along with the plan. Her ears strained to hear the conversation nearby, and to her surprise she heard not only a man's voice, but a woman's, too. She couldn't quite make out the words at first, but then the voices got louder. The man sounded angry. She didn't like the way he was yelling, and now she could make out a word here and there. The shouting man was making her insides shake.

You don't have to do this, Dizzy. Just turn around and go home.

Now it was the woman's voice, she heard, pleading and desperate: "Please, son, don't do this. I've taken care of everything. I can make it all go away."

Dizzy couldn't understand the man's words, but the sound of his voice was horrible and frightening. He must be a hateful, awful man.

"I'm sorry. Sorry. Sorry. Please try to forgive me. Please try to understand." It was the woman again.

Then she heard a loud moan, and the sound of something thudding against the ground.

You don't have to do this, Dizzy. Turn around before it's too late.

But she didn't turn around. Her feet were still soldered to the ground. She was confused. There wasn't supposed to be a woman here. *She* was supposed to be the only girl. The voices got louder, like they were moving toward her.

"Why did you do it, Mother?"

"Because I *loathed* him."

The woman's voice was as loud now as her son's. Yes. It was a mother and son.

"He was your *husband,* and you gave the order to have him killed. Now you expect me to look the other way and pretend we're a happy family. You want me to stay with you—the woman who killed my father? I *loved* Dad."

The man yowled, and the sound carried on the wind and raised goose bumps on her arms despite the god-awful heat. It was so hot, even at night, this place was like what Mom called *a living hell.* The voices got closer still.

"I'm your mother. What about that? Why doesn't that count for something? Why does everything always have to be about your father? He never paid attention to either one of us, and all you want to do is build him a goddamn shrine. He wasn't a good father to you, and he wasn't a good husband to me."

"And I suppose you were a good wife, you little bitch."

The woman started to sob. "Please believe me, Junior. I tried to be a good wife. Oh how I tried, especially in the beginning, and I always looked the other way about his women. But then, when he brought Deejay home, everything changed. Your father showered that girl with attention like he never gave me. So I gave him an ultimatum. Get rid of the girls he kept at home and stick with the ones he hunted, or I was going to divorce him, and do you know what he said? He said he loved Deejay. He said he loved her, and if I wanted a divorce, he was a lawyer and could make sure I never saw a dime. After all these years, after everything I did for him, everything I endured for the sake of our family, he was going to leave me with nothing and keep his little slut."

"You were the one who threatened to leave. Deejay was just his whore. You were his wife. He gave you everything."

"Like he gave you everything? He forgot all about both of us. You as much as me. I used to be of some value to him, his silent partner. But then, all of a sudden, he didn't need me anymore. And now, the police are coming after you, and that's because of him, too. He's the one who taught you to kill. He's the one who didn't take care of business after you hunted Sally Cartwright. He promised to put it all on Judd Kramer, and yet now the police are looking for you because your father failed you. Why don't you hate your father instead of me? I'm the one who fixed it all. I'm the one who'll make sure they don't find what they need to convict you."

Dizzy could hear their footsteps, coming closer and closer. She pushed the corn stalks apart and peered into the semidarkness.

The man, the one called Junior, looked like Satan himself, his face black and contorted with hate, his hands waving wildly in the air. "You've destroyed everything that's important to me. Dad is dead because of you, and now you want to destroy his legacy, too. You want to end Labyrinth? Well, I won't stand for it."

"I'm trying to get rid of the evidence that could lead back to you. Just like you tried to get rid of Caitlin. And besides, you have no choice. The deed's already done." The woman's blond hair was so bright, it looked white as the moon in the dim light. She threw her head back and cackled like a real witch. Maybe this was all part of the game. Just a show they were putting on. But for whom? No one else seemed to be around. Where were the others? Where were the lieutenants?

"What the hell are you talking about, Mother?" Junior stalked toward the woman.

"They're here—and they're both dead. Your father's precious lieutenants. The only ones strong enough to turn their fantasies into reality. The remaining lieutenants are the only ones who could keep the group going, and I've eliminated them. I Tased them, then I poisoned them. Take a walk back with me, and you'll find their bodies pointing to the center of the maze."

"You *bitch*! Those were *my* lieutenants. With Dad gone, the club's *mine* by rights."

"Your father's dead, and so is *Labyrinth*. I hate this goddamn club."

"You mean you hate Dad." Junior fell to his knees, wailing.

Slowly, the mother approached, "Don't you see this is better? Your little slut of a wife left you, and I no longer have to cater to your father. You and I are both *free* to do as we choose. And we're rich, son. There's life insurance, too. It's yours, baby boy. I'll give it *all* to you."

His sobbing subsided, and he looked up. For a moment, Dizzy thought he'd seen her through the corn stalks, but he turned his face to his mother. "What have you done!"

"I've destroyed the club, that's all," the woman said. "And with it, all the evidence against you. Your father should never have let you kill that Cartwright girl on your own. It was far too risky. You weren't ready, and he didn't do a good enough job setting up Kramer. What if Kramer had gone behind your father's back and made a deal with the DA? What if Kramer told Caitlin the truth about the club? When I asked him to take care of them, your father just said, *don't worry*, he could control Kramer, and he was having fun toying with that Cassidy woman again." She spit on the ground. "Your father was an arrogant fool. *He's* the one who got you into this mess."

"There was no need to kill *Dad*. So don't pretend you did this for *me*. You did it for *you*. I nearly got caught going after Caitlin on campus that day, and all because you tried and failed to get rid of her and left me no choice. Dad would never have let that happen. And they've got my *DNA*—they're calling everyone looking for me, but thanks to you, Dad's not around to save my ass."

"Don't you listen? *I* just saved your ass. They'll never be able to convict you on a tiny little bit of DNA. Just the fact they brought a case against Kramer first is enough to get you reasonable doubt for Cartwright. *As long as we destroy any and all trace of this club*, but you have to promise to stop hunting. I don't care about the women, God knows. They're dirty little whores who deserve what they get. But it's too *dangerous*. I don't want to lose my son to these stupid games."

"I'll never give up the hunt, Mother. Even if I wanted to, I couldn't. Believe it or not I tried, for my wife's sake, but it's in my blood. I'm just like Dad, and there's *nothing* you can do to change that."

"You *can* change. We can travel. Your father left us *so much money*. And you can have it all—only please, don't ruin our lives. You have to stop. I know you can stop."

"But I don't *want* to stop. I *live* for this pleasure, for the power I feel watching the life drain from a woman's eyes. Do *not* expect me to go traipsing the globe with you like your little pet dog." He climbed to his feet and loomed over the woman. "I could kill you now, Mother, and never think twice about it."

"Please, Junior, don't say these things. You know you love me. Please, I can't go on without you."

"Oh, you won't have to go on without me. You won't have to go on at all."

Dizzy covered a scream with her hands and tried to move her frozen feet. Junior had his mother by the throat. Then the woman twisted and something flashed in her hand. Dizzy heard a buzzing noise.

Click click click click click.

Junior stumbled back, and Dizzy heard more of that sickening noise. Her breathing was coming in hard pants now, and she worried they would hear her. The woman stuck the Taser on him again and his body writhed on the ground.

"Please, don't. Just don't." He tried to grab the Taser, and she kicked him in the gut. He rolled onto his back and let out a harsh moan. "I'll stop. I'll go anywhere you want."

"Liar!" She kicked him again. "You said you could kill me now. After all I've done for you? No. No. No. *You're* the one who's dead." She pressed the Taser into his neck, and he screamed an awful, terrible scream. Like nothing Dizzy had ever heard before. "It will only hurt for a minute. You'll be with your father soon." She pulled something from her pocket. It looked like one of those plastic syringes mothers use to give their babies medicine. She stuck the syringe in his mouth, only Dizzy was sure this wasn't medicine.

Junior grabbed his throat, and Dizzy saw foam coming from his mouth. Then he threw his head back, and his eyes rolled up in his head. Dizzy covered her mouth, but it wasn't in time to stop her scream. The woman looked up and turned her head. Then, through the high stalks of corn, she met Dizzy's eyes.

That's when Dizzy knew for sure: She didn't want to die.

She started to run.

THE SUN HAD already set when Spense swung his Rodeo into the Casa Grande Corn Maze parking lot. A cruiser from the Pinal County Sherriff's Office had arrived ahead of them, and two deputies waited outside their vehicle, leaning against it and talking with each other as if this were a church social. The men barely glanced up as he climbed out of his car. Frustrated, he slammed the door to his Rodeo. They needed more men out here, and they needed them now.

Caity came around her side of the car, and they headed over to where the deputies were lounging. The thought had crossed his mind to have her wait in the car, but he'd quickly dismissed it. The last time she'd stayed behind, she'd been viciously attacked despite the ubiquitous presence of Phoenix's Finest. So no way was he going to trust Caity's life to these local boys. Pinal was a sleepy county, and its deputies likely didn't see a lot of action. In fact, there was a real good chance neither one of these men had ever fired his service weapon in the line of duty. This haunted corn maze just might be the designated location for a killers' summit, and he wasn't letting Caity out of his sight.

Looking over his shoulder at her, he asked, "You bring your heat?" He knew about that little Ruger she usually carried, and he hoped she hadn't been lying when she'd claimed she was a decent shot at close range.

She jerked a nod, a grim expression on her face.

Okay, then that made at least two folks out of the four present who seemed to be taking this summit seriously. Of course, no one knew whether this was the actual location for the Labyrinth meeting, or if, at the end of the day, they'd all just be standing around with egg on their faces, waiting for psychopaths who never showed.

Spense pulled his creds and flashed them to the one of the deputies. "I'm Special Agent Spenser, and this is Dr. Caitlin Cassidy. Have you gentlemen seen any unusual activity so far?"

"I'm Bill Plummer. This is Sam Campbell. We just got here. And no, we haven't seen a trace of nobody since we arrived. This place doesn't even open until the week before Halloween, so we're thinking this isn't the right spot."

"You don't think the fact the maze is closed, deserted, and out in the middle of nowhere might make it an ideal spot for criminal activity?" The word had been put out a good forty-five minutes ago to get a team from Pinal County up to the Casa Grande Maze. These boys were all of ten minutes away, and yet they'd just arrived. Another indication the sheriff wasn't taking the matter seriously. "Gentleman, I realize this may seem unusual."

"Unusual? A meeting of an online kill club taking place in a shut-down corn maze—in Pinal County?" Bill Plummer removed his hat. "Killers flying in from across the country to meet up in Casa Grande. Nah. We get that all the time around here. We're a regular kill Club Med." He winked at Campbell. "Get it—a kill *Club Med*?"

As Plummer's chortle bloomed into a hearty laugh, Campbell covered a grin. Tension rolled down Spense's arm, but he controlled the urge to raise either his fist or his voice—barely. In truth, these men didn't know him, didn't know the case, and their skepticism was to be expected. That didn't make it any less foolhardy. "I promise you, gentlemen, this is potentially a very dangerous situation. These men may be armed, and they're ruthless killers."

His laughter spent, Plummer scuffed a bootheel on the unpaved ground, sending up a cloud of hot dust between him and Spense. "Well, like I said before, so far we ain't seen anyone come or go. Not ruthless killers, not nobody."

"But you only just arrived," Caity pointed out more politely than Spense was about to. "Have you taken a look *inside* the maze?"

"Ain't no cars in the parking lot."

"You think they'll just park in the designated visitor spots?" Spense felt his blood pressure rise along with the decibel level of his voice. Rather than spew the epitaph that was on the tip of his tongue, he pulled in a long breath, and as a reward for controlling his temper, got a mouthful of dust. "Did you search the surrounding desert for vehicles?"

"The sheriff instructed us to secure the perimeter of the corn maze, and that's what we're doing. There are two more deputies 'round the other side. If there's anyone inside the maze, they gotta come out one of two ways, and we got both ways covered."

"So that's a no. You haven't looked for vehicles, and you haven't checked out the maze," Caity said in a clipped tone that, again, was far more polite than the one Spense could've managed.

"Yes. That's a no." The deputy stuck a diagram in Spense's face. "Here's the layout if you wanna have a look for yourself."

Spense took a fast glance and memorized the key to the maze. This was a true maze, not a unicursal labyrinth, and that meant there were blind alleys everywhere. "Got it." He handed the map off to Caity to keep. In the unlikely event they got separated, she was going to need it. "We're going in. Uniforms from the Phoenix PD should be here shortly."

"We'll keep securing the perimeter." Bill and Sam resumed their slouches.

As they entered the high corn, Spense took the lead, signaling Caity to keep close behind him. The stalks were a good eight feet tall, making it impossible to see anything except the path directly in front of them and providing plenty of places to hide. Leading with his gun and his eyes, Spense cleared the way the best he could, but it was slow going. Even with the sun down, it felt like they were trudging through an oven. There was still a bit of ambient light, and he wanted to avoid the use of a flashlight if possible. If there was anyone else in this maze, he didn't want to tip them off to their presence. He and Caity had been making their way slowly toward the center of the maze for about twenty minutes, gagging on the scents of dirt and sweat and fertilizer, when he noticed a different, more ominous odor layered among the rest. He halted and narrowed his eyes, filling his lungs with a big breath through his nose.

Caity took a big breath, too, and turned in a circle, then her face drained of color. "Do you smell gasoline?"

Dammit. His jaw clamped down hard, and his heartbeat kicked up. This had to be a setup. He just didn't know for whom. "We're going back. *Now.*"

Caity had an uneasy look on her face, and her posture went stiff, defiant. "I don't want to turn around. If this place has been doused in gasoline, that means it's the right location. That means the Man in the Maze is in here . . . *somewhere*."

The Man in the Maze was the key to everything, including Gail Falconer's murder. Spense's fingers clenched around his flashlight. He ached to find this bastard and make him pay for what he'd done to those women—for what he'd done to *Caity*. Being this close, only to have the motherfucker slip from his grasp, made Spense's throat constrict to the point it was hard to get his words out. "He's here all right—in a six-acre cornfield that's rigged to catch fire. We're turning around, and we're going to haul ass."

Caity's body slumped like the last bit of air had been kicked out of it, but she nodded and trotted back the way they'd come.

DIZZY'S LEGS PUMPED faster and faster until the ache in her muscles simply disappeared. She was pure energy now, her body flying through the maze. The whipping of the wind in her face, the scratching of dirt and debris on her skin, acted like jet fuel. Because, suddenly, faced with the reality of death, she understood just how very much she wanted to live. Fuck those mean girls at school. They weren't going to take away her life. Mom loved her, and she loved Mom, and things were going to get better. Mom was going to find her help. She'd probably already called the doctor. She wasn't going to do this to Mom. She wasn't going to do this to *herself*.

Run, Dizzy! Run!

"Stop!" A thousand pins stabbed her in the back, and her body jolted like she'd been hit by lightning, but she kept on going.

Run Dizzy!

Then the lightning struck again. This time an arm came around her neck, crushing it. The pain shot through her chest, and she fell to the ground, her head striking the hardened dirt, making her vision go blurry.

That woman—that white-haired witch crawled on top of her, a syringe in her hand. But Dizzy knew what to do. She grabbed the witch's arm, chomped onto her wrist, and felt her teeth sink deep. She twisted and tore and tried to bite the witch's arm off.

With a yelp, the witch's hand opened, and the syringe fell to the ground. "You little bitch!" She arched away from Dizzy, and Dizzy managed to get air under her shoulders. Heaving with all her might, she head-butted the witch and rolled, flipping their positions. Now the woman was under Dizzy. Dizzy punched her in the face. Her fist exploded with pain, and blood splattered onto her blouse. She punched her again and again and again, until, finally, the woman stopped shouting, and her eyes closed. Dizzy sprang to her feet and started to run.

Her arms pumped hard like before, but this time, her legs were weak, and she didn't feel right inside. Blood dripped from her forehead and ran into her wet, burning eyes. She couldn't see. She couldn't breathe, but she kept running.

Run, Dizzy! Run!

Too late, she saw the mound of debris and sticks on the path, and she tumbled forward, landing on the ground. At first she didn't know what had broken her fall, she was just grateful she hadn't hit the dirt face-first. Pushing up with her elbows, she rolled off the big lump beneath her, and her mouth gaped in disbelief.

A dead man had broken her fall.

A SCREAM STOPPED Spense and Caity in their tracks. The voice was high-pitched and terrified, like that of a young girl. *Christ,* Spense thought. The adrenaline already flowing through his body surged, sending his heart into overdrive. He didn't want to leave Caity's side, but he had no choice. He couldn't ignore the cry for help, especially knowing the maze had been rigged for fire. Reining in his racing thoughts, he forced out a breath. At least Caity had a map. She should be able to find her way out. Before speaking, he shook his head hard at her, just in case she had any thought of coming with him. "Get the hell out of here. Do not stop for any reason. I'll get the girl."

The look on her face told him she wanted to stay and help him, so he said the only thing he knew that would convince her to keep running. "You're in my way, Caity. I can't help the both of you, so please get out now." He forced himself to turn his back, his chest heaving from the pain of letting her go. When he heard the sound of Caity's footfalls running the opposite way, he flipped on his flashlight and began to run, his feet sure on the dirt path, picking up speed with each beat of his heart. The terror in the girl's cries drove him forward even as the stench of gasoline grew stronger, then, suddenly, his breath stopped. Too late, it hit him—Caity might have the map, but she didn't have the light.

Help!

His pulse pounded in his ears, nearly drowning out the desperate cry, but he had to keep going. By now it was too dark to read the map, and the only thing he could do was trust Caity to find her way on her own. As his legs carried him farther from her and closer to the sound of the voice, he pictured Caity with her fists up, defending her underdogs against the whole wide world. Smiling to himself, he ran harder and faster.

So hard, in fact, he nearly ran straight over the body.

With the beam from his flashlight swinging back and forth across the path like a drunken moon, he skidded to a breathless halt. His free hand went to his Glock, ready to draw if need be. After a rapid assessment of the situation, he decided to keep it holstered . . . for now. Less than a foot in front of him, a disembodied face poked its way out of its hiding place in the corn.

The girl.

Blinking hard, Spense bit back a curse. At his feet, a bald, burly giant lay perfectly still—apparently dead on the ground. He was wearing a hockey mask. A single trickle of blood ran down his white plastic cheek like a tear.

The stalks of corn surrounding the girl's face began to shake, creating a sound not unlike a child's rattle. Spense put out his hand and made his voice low and friendly. "I'm FBI. I won't hurt you."

With the wind rustling through the corn like a movie sound track, the girl stepped out onto the path. "You really FBI?" she asked in a shaky voice that held way too much trust. Her arms were thinner than the tall stalks swaying behind her, and her brown eyes were round, the pupils large with fear. This girl would be easy prey for the likes of the kill club.

"Yeah. You know this guy?" Spense knelt beside the corpse. "You see what happened to him?"

"N-no." She took a step closer. "He was dead when I found him. I-I fell on top of him." Her shoulders shook, and tears began streaming down her cheeks.

Hoping to lighten the mood and ease her fears, Spense grinned a false smile up at her. It was going to be hard enough getting her out of the maze as it was, and if she panicked, she might freeze up and refuse to come with him. Then he'd have to subdue her and carry her out, and in this heat, that would be a monumental task even for him. "That must've been one hell of a surprise." He wouldn't have thought the girl's eyes could get any bigger, but they did. "Take it easy," he said, then out of his peripheral vision he saw it—a flash of movement as the corpse beside him roared to life.

The giant's body jackknifed to a sitting position, and he head-butted Spense, then jumped on him. His massive weight pinned Spense to the ground, crushing his chest, making it impossible to breathe. Spense's flashlight tumbled down the path, leaving them in semidarkness. He tried to reach his pistol, but his arms were trapped behind his back, and his legs were paralyzed beneath the big man. He could do nothing to stop the giant from jerking his service weapon from its holster. As the man pressed the muzzle of Spense's own pistol between his eyes, sweat poured down his forehead. The girl let out an earsplitting scream.

"*One hell of a surprise* at your service, asshole." The giant's voice was strong—and cruel.

The pistol might be in Spense's face, but in the process of getting it there, the giant had shifted so that his full weight was no longer on Spense's chest. At least he could breathe again. At least he could speak again. His opponent outweighed him by a good fifty pounds . . . and sixteen bullets. Obviously, brute force alone was not going to get him out of this mess. As he tried to visualize a way out of this predicament, Spense's eyes fluttered open and closed. Then, just like the solution to the Sunday crossword, it came to him. It was really quite simple. There was only one way out from under this goon—the man was going to have to let him up voluntarily. And while Spense didn't have a fully formed plan to accomplish this, he did have an opening gambit. "Good one, buddy. You sure got me. Now, how 'bout giving a man some air . . . *Lieutenant.*"

Behind the mask, the goon's flinty eyes shifted rapidly over Spense's face. *Good.* Spense could see the confusion he'd caused, and all because he'd uttered a single word. *"Lieutenant,"* he repeated, emphasizing each syllable as much as possible with only half his usual lung volume at his disposal, "You've proven yourself worthy and had some fun in the mix. But if you don't mind, I'm not keen on getting suffocated or shot by one of my own."

The giant shook his head violently. So violently the mask slipped to his chin, exposing a vast expanse of oily red skin, small gray eyes, and thin lips. Air hissed between his teeth. "You're not the other lieutenant."

Spence grimaced as the giant's sour breath hit him in the face. "Not the other lieutenant, you moron. I'm your teacher."

The goon's chin jerked back. "You're not *him*. I heard you tell that whore you're FBI."

"Because she's a stupid whore. Haven't you learned any tricks from me after all this time? How the hell did you get your labyrinth if you don't even know how to fool a little girl? And now you're going to defy *me*, the Man in the Maze?" He felt the weight on top of him shift again and focused on cooling his blood down. The goon had ice churning through his veins, and Spense damn well better act as cold. He had to convince him they were brothers. Two fearless men without the capacity for human empathy—two empty shells that, at best, could be momentarily filled by the thrill of violence.

"If you're the Man in the Maze, prove it." The goon kept the pistol between Spense's eyes but crawled off him.

"Sure." Spense slid his hands from behind his back and held them far out to the sides. "We'll do that little whore together. If that's something that would please you."

The girl started to sob, but she didn't try to run. Spense knew she'd given up. He'd been her last hope, and now she must believe he'd turned on her. His heart wanted to split in his chest at the way he'd betrayed her. He wanted to cry out for her to run and run hard, but the goon would only shoot him, and she'd be next. This was the only way. "You want the first piece, or do I get it?"

"Ah, fuck me. Is it really you? That bitch who Tased me said you were dead."

"Well, as you can see, I'm very much alive." Slowly, he sat up, the gun still pressed to his forehead and moving with him. "Just like you're alive. I could've sworn . . ."

"You thought I was dead." A smile twisted the goon's mouth. "After she Tased me, she tried to squirt some kind of shit in my mouth. Poison I figured. It dripped off the mask, but I just lay there, playing dead, and she went away. I was on my way back out when I heard someone running down the path, so I just laid down again, and here we are."

"Here we are—the Man in the Maze and his lieutenant. Now, are you going to put the gun down, so we can do this chick, or should we go after the bitch who Tased you first?"

Together, he and the giant climbed to their feet, the gun still glued to his forehead. "You're the boss."

As soon as he heard the acquiescent words, Spense went for the gun, not giving the giant so much as a split second to change his mind. The man's guard was down, and his hand was relaxed. Spense pinched the nerves in the man's wrist, simultaneously slamming his knee into his groin. The gun thudded to the ground, and Spense lunged for it. The familiar cold of his trusty Glock molded itself to his hand as he rolled onto his back, just in time to see the giant leap for him. Pistol pointed at the giant's chest, Spense squeezed the trigger hard. Blood exploded into the air like he'd fired on him with paintball ammo. Spense rolled out of the way just before the massive body fell. The giant hit the ground with a *thunk* hard enough to make the earth rumble beneath them.

Ears ringing from the shots, Spense jumped to his feet and strode to the sobbing girl. They were getting out of this hellish maze *now*. He flashed his creds and reached out his hand. "I'm FBI. There's nothing to be afraid of."

CAITLIN HADN'T ARGUED when Spense told her to go on without him. Her eyes burned with unshed tears, and her hands finished in painfully clenched fists, but she hadn't uttered a single word of protest. As hard as it was to leave him behind in this tinderbox of a maze, she knew the truth. He was absolutely right—she'd only be in the way—just one more person whose welfare he'd put ahead of his own. And that would surely cost him time, or worse, it might even cost him his life. So as Spense raced toward the screams, she turned her back and ran the opposite way, barreling down the paths she believed would lead her out of the maze.

At first it was easy. Despite the low light, her memory served her well. On the way in, they'd tread carefully, and she'd made it a point to look for landmarks—broken areas in the corn, a discarded beer bottle, and the like. But after a while, the descending night seemed to blend everything into one homogenous pattern. She was running through a tunnel of darkness—like the one in her dreams—and that old feeling of panic clutched at her throat. Slowing her pace, she tried to control her breathing, tried to focus on finding her way instead of on the pounding of her heart. Then she hit another blind end and noticed that the smell of gasoline had gotten much stronger.

What the deuce?

This was wrong. The smell should be disappearing. She'd been running at least twenty minutes. And that was longer than the time they'd spent walking into the maze. There was no denying it anymore.

She was lost.

She stopped running and noticed the tightness in her legs and the hard spasms in her left flank. Maybe it was better to slow down anyway, before her body shut down and made that decision for her. Doubling over to catch her breath, she pulled the map from her pocket and opened it. The map was old and the markings faded. Straightening, she brought the paper close to her face. No matter how hard she squinted, the old Xeroxed map was too faint to make out. She pulled her cell from her pocket. No bars—she'd expected that, but she could use the flashlight feature to read . . .

Dammit.

Her heart sank as she stared at the phone in her hand. This was the burner phone Spense had given her. There *wasn't* any flashlight app. She folded the map and stuck the useless thing in her pocket, along with the phone.

Just think, Caitlin. Which way did you come from?

Mentally, she shook a finger at herself. It was no use thinking like that. She'd gone too far wrong for retracing her steps to work now. What she needed was a new plan and a point of reference—one that wouldn't disappear in the darkening night or be obscured by the tall stalks of corn. She looked up and saw the stars twinkling overhead. She remembered her father taking her out at night and showing her how to find the North Star by using the pointer stars in the bowl of the big dipper. She found the pointers and drew a line to the North Star. Like Spense always said, sometimes the best solution to a complicated problem is the simplest. Now she had her point of reference, so even if she wound up in the center of the maze, there were two exits and eventually, she'd find her way out. Just keep heading in one direction. That's all you have to do. That, and breathe. She let out a relieved sigh and walked to the next fork in the path. Keeping the North Star ahead of her, she took the left alley.

Another dead end.

Pop. Pop.

Gunfire!

Her heat leapt in her chest, and she whirled around. She had no idea where the shots had come from. Pressure built in her lungs until it felt as if they would explode. Her legs trembled beneath her like they couldn't bear the weight of her body much longer—and this was exactly why Spense had cut her loose. She slammed her fist into her thigh. She refused to let fear cripple her.

Don't think about the gunshots.

Focus on getting out.

There had to be a way. Maybe she should go off trail and fight her way through the tall corn, just bushwhack it. Then she spotted it, a small opening in the maze leading to a trail she'd missed before. A trail that would keep her headed in the right direction. Squeezing between the corn stalks, she followed the path and noticed it was broader and flatter than the others. This must be the road that led to the center. The center wasn't where she wanted to go, but the way out might be clear from there. And at least now, she could keep her bearings. The moon started to rise, illuminating her path, and relief lifted her spirits. She felt almost giddy. Rounding the corner, sure enough she found herself in the center of the maze. Then a thunderclap of dread struck her in the chest.

For there sat Louisa Baumgartner, bloodied and caked in dirt, cradling her son's head in her lap, and he, Junior, looked . . . dead. Louisa seemed to spot Caitlin at the exact moment Caitlin saw her. Both women froze, and time lost all linearity. It sped up, then slowed down and changed course altogether, expanding, giving Caitlin all the time she needed to think—but soon, she knew it would cut her off at the knees.

Better act now.

Her Ruger was holstered at her ankle, concealed by her jeans, but she didn't dare bend to retrieve it. Grateful for the moon, and the fact her eyes had finally accommodated to the low light, she scanned Louisa's hands and the surrounding area checking for weapons . . . and found them.

Louisa held a bright red gun that had to be a flare, and beside her lay an open box containing what looked to be syringes and Tasers. Someone had come prepared.

But for what?

Louisa's platinum hair was coarse and tangled from sweat and wind. Twisting trails of white flesh streaked through the dirt and blood on her face, clear evidence she'd been crying though her eyes were dry enough now. Her expression seemed hard . . . and desperate. The woman to whom appearances were everything now seemed to have nothing left at all.

The thought stopped Caitlin's breath.

There's nothing more dangerous than someone with nothing to lose.

With a shaking hand, Louisa pointed the flare gun at Caitlin. "Don't you dare judge me, Caitlin Cassidy. Don't you *dare*." Her hand lifted, and Caitlin thought again of going for her Ruger. She'd heard of flare guns being used as weapons, and it was possible Louisa meant to shoot her with it, but the worst danger in this gasoline-soaked maze was fire. Louisa's weapon was every bit as deadly as Caitlin's.

Deciding to chance it, she eased down, holding her breath. Slowly, she clasped her pistol and drew it from her ankle holster, then straightened. The gun was so small it was almost entirely hidden in her hand. *Almost.*

Strangely, Louisa smiled. "Go ahead and shoot me. I really don't care anymore. And I'd like to be the one to bring little Miss High-and-Mighty down to the level of the rest of us sinners. You think you're better than me and my boy—you think I don't know that? Even when you were a kid, you acted like you were nicer, or smarter, or I don't know what."

The air was thick with fumes and heat and the smell of blood. Junior was dead, and Louisa was talking nonsense. Could some old resentment harbored against a teenage girl really be upper-most in her mind at a time like this? Caitlin almost laughed but caught herself. That would surely make things worse.

Louisa waved her gun around. "You think you know every-thing, but you don't know *nothing*. You are white trash, young lady. And your father, your father was a stupid, stupid man. What kind of moron confesses to a crime he didn't commit? Your *father* destroyed my family."

Louisa was talking crazy. Even her grammar was devolving. And though Caitlin had always sensed the woman lacked empa-thy, always known Louisa cared most about how any problem im-pacted *her,* the realization that this vile woman blamed Thomas Cassidy for her own problems made Caitlin dizzy.

"If good old trusting Tom hadn't been such an easy mark, Harvey would *never* have killed Gail Falconer and none of the others either." She leered sideways, her voice drunk with bitterness. "Every last one of those girls would be alive if only there hadn't been a first. Harvey wanted to hunt a long time before he ever did. He was always too scared of getting caught until he found your father. And then, suddenly, it was all too easy to get away with murder. All we had to do was pretend to be good Christians and you pitiful Cassidys leapt at the chance to socialize with us."

Caitlin's pulse bounded everywhere, her wrists, her ankles . . . *her trigger finger.* Hate shivered down her spine, then wracked her body with tremors.

So it was true. Harvey Baumgartner murdered Gail Falconer.

And Louisa had known all about it. Caitlin straight-armed her Ruger, aiming it at Louisa's chest. "You *knew.*"

"Of course I knew. I helped Harvey set your father up to take the fall. I helped him put Gail's blood and hair in the trunk of your father's car. And that anonymous phone call, the one your father claimed he got that night, telling him your mother's station wagon had broken down on campus . . ."

"Harvey made that call?" She couldn't breathe. Her chest was so filled with rage, there was no room left for air.

Again, Louisa laughed. "You're as stupid as your old man. *I* made that call. And *I* chose Gail for Harvey's first kill. I was *trying* to be a good little wife, you see, not that it did me any good."

Caitlin's breathing resumed, and her hand went rock steady. Somehow, her rage had changed to calmness—*deadly* calmness. "Why are you telling me all this? I've got a gun pointed at you, and all you've got is that flare."

"A flare in a corn maze ready to ignite? I've got *everything.*" She slipped Junior's head off her lap.

His skin was reddened, and Caitlin realized it must've been

cyanide. Louisa had poisoned her own son. She wouldn't hesitate to make good on her threats. And if she set fire to the maze, who knew how many would die? Had Spense found the girl yet? Had they made it out alive? Louisa really did hold all the power. Caitlin's Ruger was useless as a threat because Louisa *wanted* to die. She was just too weak to do it herself. Apparently, she only had the guts to kill *other* people. The hate that had been building inside Caitlin for fifteen years changed to a whisper in her head:

Go ahead, Caitlin. Help the woman out.

"The only way you are going to leave here alive, my dear, is to shoot me. If you don't, I fire my flare, and the whole place goes up. You'll never find your way out before the flames or the smoke gets to you. So what are you waiting for? Kill me now before I change my mind and shoot you first."

"You think I won't do it." She took a step closer, and Louisa didn't flinch.

"I *want* you to do it. I'm the one with all the power now. I'm the one who pulls the strings and makes the puppets dance." She spit on the ground. "*I'm the Man in the Maze now*, not Harvey. And you *will* shoot me. Because you're just the same as the rest of us. All your pretty words about justice and playing fair. Let's see what you do when you have the chance to get revenge."

"You deserve to die." Her voice sounded eerily steady to her own ears, and her words had the ring of truth.

"Now you understand. You want justice for your father? Then reach out and take it. All you have to do is come down off your high horse and get your hands dirty."

Caitlin's finger squeezed the trigger, ever so slightly. She'd have to pull hard to fire the first round. Just a little more pressure, and the woman who had lied, who had held her mother's hand in church at her father's funeral would be obliterated from the earth. It would be so easy to claim self-defense. No one would question her. Her mouth twitched in anticipation. Louisa was pointing a flare at her chest. *It really would be self-defense.*

Louisa rose to a stand and raised her flare gun. "You can do this, Caitlin. Just show the world, show *yourself,* your true colors."

"I want to know everything, first. You want me to kill you, then you tell me why you set up an innocent girl to be raped and murdered and an innocent man to take the blame."

"It was them or me." She shrugged as if anyone would've done the same. "Harvey hit me. And he choked me to get himself off. He always used a cloth to protect my skin so the marks wouldn't show, and when he punched me, he made sure he got me in the stomach or the back. Once, he decided to punch me in the chest, and my implants burst." She started to laugh, a hysterical laugh. "Cost him thousands to fix these beauties. You better believe that was the last time he got me there. My husband was a sadist, sweetheart, and not the pretty kind like the ones in books who give you a safe word. He was the kind who can't get off until he hears you screaming in agony. So when he decided he wanted to hurt *other* women, I was all for it. Like I said, it was them or me." She jerked the flare gun. "So don't you goddamn judge me, you little piece of trash. I had no choice, and now you don't either. You want justice for your father. Here's your chance. I didn't have any choice, and now you don't either."

Justice for her father.

Someone had to pay for his life, and for Gail Falconer. For *all* those girls. Caitlin's heart beat out a slow and steady rhythm. A countdown to Louisa Baumgartner's death.

One.

Two.

She wagged her pistol at Louisa like Louisa had wagged the flare at her. "On your knees."

Louisa slowly got to her knees, pointing her flare off to the side. "I didn't have a choice, and neither do you."

"You had a choice, Louisa. You could've gone to the police."

"I was too scared . . . and even if I wasn't, I had a baby and no job. Without Harvey, I'd have had nothing."

Her finger felt heavy on the trigger. "You wanted Harvey's money. *That's* why you stayed."

"Sure, honey. I'm a greedy bitch. So just do it already."

Caitlin aimed the Ruger, her heart resuming its countdown.

One.

Two.

She squeezed the trigger, releasing all the tension in her body with one long slow, deliberate pull. Her arm jerked from the recoil of the gun, and a loud boom reverberated through the air as ears of corn exploded, sending dried kernels spewing into the air, and falling around them like confetti. She was a decent shot, and she'd hit the mark she'd intended.

"You chicken-shit little bitch." Louisa's arm jerked up. "Now we're both going to die in a cornfield."

As Caitlin jumped on top of her, she heard the whiz-bang of the flare going off, and Louisa's hysterical cackle. Then other sounds, the crunch of her shoulder hitting the ground, and a sickening tearing coming from inside her. Excruciating pain ripped through her left side, and her vision went gray. Blood leaked onto her shirt where her old wound had torn open. A wave of nausea rolled through her, and she heaved up bile. For a split second, her arms went limp. Louisa seized the chance to flip on top of her and wrench her wrist backward, jerking the gun from her grasp. Somehow, Caitlin managed to get one knee up and kick out hard. Her foot landed on Louisa's hand, sending the Ruger flying into the night. Where was the flare gun?

Louisa growled and closed both hands around Caitlin's throat. She must have dropped the flare when Caitlin jumped on her. Caitlin bucked her body but couldn't get out from under.

"You can't hurt me, sweetheart. I've been through much worse than anything you or that girl can do. But I wonder about your pain tolerance. You seem all done in from just a little scuffle." Louisa's hands were like steel, slowly clamping tighter and tighter around her throat. "How does that feel, dear?"

Like everything was falling away. Like a curtain was closing over her brain. Her arms went numb, and her fingers tingled from the lack of oxygen. She forced herself to wiggle them and felt something cold at the very tips. She closed her eyes, pretending she didn't have any fight left in her and stretched her arm until it felt like a rubber band ready to snap back. She had no idea if the object just beyond her reach was a rock or the flare or . . . her fingers tugged it closer, but Louisa didn't seem to notice. She was too busy strangling her. Using her last ounce of will, Caitlin allowed her body to submit to the choking, all the while slowly inching the object closer. Her hand gripped it hard, and when she was certain of what she had, she raised the object and pressed it into Louisa's side.

Louisa screamed, and her body twitched, her hands released Caitlin's throat. Caitlin Tased her again. And again. Finally, Louisa fell onto her back, and Caitlin grabbed the rope from the box and secured her wrists and ankles.

Louisa moaned and opened her eyes.

"You made your choice, Louisa, and I made mine. You and I are *not* the same."

"We are. You're going to leave me behind, aren't you?"

If only she *could* leave her behind. Caitlin's body was bruised and bleeding, both her legs and arms were watery and weak, but there were thick black clouds of smoke rising in the distance. It wouldn't be long before the fire blazed out of control. It wouldn't be long before it reached them. She could try dragging Louisa out, but that might be even more difficult than carrying her. At least the woman was thin.

She couldn't lift her if she struggled, so she gritted her teeth and Tased her again. Louisa went still, and Caitlin hefted her over her shoulders, then began limping toward her star. She could hear sirens in the night. The police were here somewhere. Probably the fire department, too. All she had to do was keep going until someone found her. A sudden thought clouded her mind. What if no one did? Who could find her in a maze, when she didn't even know where she was herself. Then a light appeared, and near it, another. Not stars but *flashlights,* on either side of her, dancing in the night.

"Caity!"

She heard his voice and cried out with all her might. "Over here, Spense, we're over here!"

And then he was beside her. Asking no questions, he grabbed Louisa and dumped her over his own shoulder. "Haul ass."

"I hate to disappoint you," Caitlin huffed to Louisa's limp form, as she hustled after Spense and the Uniform who appeared from behind him. "But you are not going to die in a cornfield. You're going to die in prison, after standing trial for conspiracy to murder Gail Falconer."

Chapter Thirty-Six

Tuesday, October 1
Superior Court Building
Phoenix, Arizona

CAITLIN GLANCED AROUND the first-floor conference room in the Superior Court Building. Nothing about the cream-colored walls, unadorned save for a photograph of the governor, sturdy table and chairs, and fluorescent lighting hinted of the drama that had taken place here a month ago. Spense motioned for her to take a seat, and she pictured Harvey Baumgartner sitting across from her, speaking to her like an old friend. A shiver ran across the backs of her knees. "No thanks, I think I'll stand if you don't mind."

He arched a disapproving brow. During her struggle with Louisa, her wound had dehisced, requiring surgical repair and a transfusion. But that was a week ago. She'd been out of the hospital two days already and now considered herself good as new ... or at least capable of standing for more than a few minutes at a time. He narrowed his eyes at her, and she returned the glare.

That made him grin. "Okay, okay. Stand if you want." He crossed to her and took her hand. "Sorry to bring you back here."

The DA wanted to meet with them, and given her packed schedule, this had been the most convenient spot for her. Caitlin's fingers entwined with Spense's, and she gave him a full-on smile. "It's no problem." In fact, if anything, returning to this room might be good for her. She didn't want to give an ordinary room the power to make her feel frightened or small. She didn't want to give any person or place that kind of power. Closing her eyes, she drew in a fortifying breath, then slowly released it.

"Spense . . ." He tugged on her hand, pulling her closer, and she could feel the heat wafting from his body. If she wanted to lay her head on his chest, feel his heart beat against her ear, all she had to do was take one more step. "Do you think Elizabeth and Deejay will stay long with your mother?"

"Mom's got them both enrolled in school again. They're up to their eyeballs in homework and cookies, and I think the plan is for them to stay awhile."

Caitlin nodded. With Spense's mom, Elizabeth and Deejay would get the kind of motherly affection they'd never had before, and she felt better knowing someone was around to reach those high boxes. The girls' needing a place to stay might turn out to be the best thing that could've happened to all of them.

"Is that what you're thinking about? I figured you'd have your mind on Louisa."

Lately, just the sound of his voice made warmth spread out from her solar plexus. What she'd really been thinking about was taking that last step. The one that would put Spense in her world for real. It'd just been easier to ask about the girls instead. "Dizzy's doing really well, too," she offered, though she knew Spense had seen her yesterday—and just about every day since he'd carried her out of that burning cornfield. Caitlin had found Dizzy a spot in an intensive, outpatient, counseling program, one where her mother could participate, too, and the initial report from her therapist was encouraging.

"Caity, why are we making small talk?" His gaze swept over her in the most unnerving way.

Apparently, Spense wasn't going to let her keep avoiding the issues between them. "I'm sorry. The DA should be here any minute, what else did you want to talk about?"

"Tahiti." He lifted her hand, joined with his, turned it over, and pressed a kiss to her palm. "You promised to consider coming away with me once this was all over. And doll, it's all over."

She swallowed hard, imagining lying beside Spense on the warm sand. Sliding her hands up and down his body while they played in the surf. She looked up at Spense and found he'd been waiting to meet her gaze. His irises deepened to the most intense shade of amber, and he looked at her the way a man does the moment before he enters you. She drew in a sharp breath at the unbidden thought, but it was true. In this moment, Spense concealed nothing from her. And she wanted to conceal nothing from him. She took that last step and laid her head over his heart, felt the beat, so strongly against her ear. "Yes. I'll go to Tahiti with you."

"Thank God." His voice came out in a low growl, and he pressed against her. Titling her chin up, he bent his head to hers. His lips brushed over her eyelids, then her cheeks, and, finally, her mouth. She wrapped her arms about him and tiptoed up, pulling his mouth down hard against hers, opening for him, wanting to taste and touch and feel him inside her.

Just then, she heard the click of heels down the hall and quickly pulled away, smoothing her hair into place as Gretchen Herrera entered the room. "The DA can't make it. But I've got news from her *and* from the BAU."

As usual, Gretchen got straight to the point.

"What from the DA?" Spense asked. Caity had been on edge ever since they got the request for a meeting, and Spense was putting her needs first.

"She's offered a deal to Louisa Baumgartner, and it appears she'll take it."

Gretchen's words dumped over Caitlin like a bucket of ice. There wasn't going to be a trial. Louisa Baumgartner wasn't going to face a jury of her peers. "But she will be held accountable?" Caitlin finally managed.

Gretchen waved a hand in the air. "Of course. The death penalty has been taken out of play, that's all. Louisa knows where the bodies are buried. Literally. According to Louisa, Harvey Baumgartner killed five women, and the DA thinks it's worth it to bring closure to the families of these missing girls to offer Louisa a deal. It's a good trade."

"I'm sorry, Caity, but I have to agree," Spense said in a hushed voice.

Closure for the families. Mutely, Caitlin nodded. Of course it was the right thing to do. "What about Gail Falconer?" she immediately thought not just of herself and her mother but of Randy Cantrell.

"It's in the deal. The DA is recommending your father's conviction be vacated. Louisa will plead guilty to conspiracy in the Falconer case, the murder of her own husband, and Judd Kramer. She's also pleading guilty to the murder of Junior and the man she poisoned in that cornfield." Gretchen leaned forward. "And do you remember that courthouse janitor found dead of a heroin overdose?"

Spense planted his hands on the table. "That was Louisa, too?"

Gretchen shot him a look that conveyed admiration. "Sure was. It was just like you originally suspected. The janitor brought that gun into the courthouse piece by piece and left it hidden for Silas Graham. Louisa targeted that particular worker because he had an expensive habit, and she'd known he wouldn't be able to resist a bribe." She turned back to Caitlin. "I know it's overwhelming, but if you think about it, at least this way she's going away for life. There are a lot of arguments that a clever attorney could make on Louisa's behalf, including painting her as the victim of an abusive husband. And there are some jurors who might secretly think she did the world a favor by getting rid of Labyrinth."

"What about Annie Bayberry? Is Louisa pleading to conspiracy in that case, too?"

"No. She claims Junior murdered Annie entirely on his own. After the courthouse shootings, he replicated the Falconer case and planted Gail's ring on the body as a tribute to his dead father. He wanted to "honor" his father's first kill. Louisa supposedly knew nothing about it until after the fact, then she was furious with her son when she found out what he'd done."

Spense grimaced. "Tell me the deal is life without parole."

Gretchen nodded. "Life without parole. She's never getting out, Caitlin."

Relief welled inside her and something else, too. She felt her eyes brimming with emotion, and she started to blink hard, pushing down the feelings that threatened to break loose. Spense put his hands on her shoulders and turned her body to his. "Don't Caity. You don't have to shut down, this time. You're among friends."

She looked from Spense to Gretchen and back again. The tears fell slowly at first, then began falling furiously down her face, but she didn't try to stop them. She *was* among friends. She stepped close to Spense, and his arms tightened around her.

She wasn't sure how long she'd been crying before Gretchen finally cleared her throat. Caitlin wound down and accepted the tissue Gretchen held out to her. Unapologetically, she blew her nose, then said, "Thanks, I needed that. You said you had news from the BAU?"

Gretchen eyed Spense. "Yes. I heard you put in for leave, but . . ."

"I *need* the leave." He shook his head violently, and Caitlin knew he was thinking of her and their plans.

Knowing they'd have time in the future, she swallowed her disappointment. She wasn't letting go of Special Agent Atticus Spenser anytime soon. "It's okay, Spense, if you're needed back in Virginia—"

"Not Virginia," Gretchen interrupted. "Los Angeles."

"Hollywood?" Interest lit his eyes, and Caitlin could see he had some idea of what Gretchen was about to say.

"The locals sent up a distress signal. They're looking for assistance with the Walk of Fame Killer, and the BAU figured since you're the closest profiler, you might as well have a look." Gretchen's lips quirked into a smile. "It was my idea to have Caitlin assist, too. They're expecting you both by the end of the week. If Caitlin is well enough and willing, I've got contracts for her to sign back at the field office."

Caitlin could see by Spense's expression he was conflicted. He wanted that vacation, and she did, too, but this was big. And they'd be working *together*. Grinning, she tugged her ear. He tugged his back.

Gretchen shook her head. "Geez, people. Get a better code, will you? A two-year-old could crack that. I presume this means you'll do it?"

"We're in," they said at once. Then Spense offered his hand to Caity, and she took it, holding on tight for a partners' shake.

Acknowledgments

Thank you to the real FBI profilers whose lives inspired this series. For forensic, procedural, and other technical advice, I'd like to thank Angela Bell and the FBI Office of Public Affairs, Randi Woods, RN; Nancy Flovin, RNC; Sergeant Alan Goodman, Elizabeth Heiter, the Crime Scene Writer's loop, Lee Lofland and all the instructors at the Writers' Police Academy, especially my ride-along instructor, Deputy Michael Eckard; all my mistakes are my own.

Thank you to my family, Bill, Shannon, Erik, and Sarah. You guys are my everything. Thank you to the women who keep me going, inspire me and help me not only in my writing but in my life, Courtney Milan, Leigh LaValle, and Tessa Dare. Thanks to the many others who share their brilliance and offer support, Brenna Aubrey, Sarah Andre, Diana Belchase, Manda Collins, Lena Diaz (with a special shout out for all her emergency brainstorming help and overall plotting genius), Rachel Grant, Krista Hall, Gwen Hernandez, and Sharon Wray.

Finally thank you to my wonderful agent, Nalini Akolekar, and to my amazing editor, Chelsey Emmelhainz, who manages to keep me on my toes and at the same time be a dream to work with.

Author's Note

There is no Tempe University, Southwest Museum of Art, Good Hope Hospital, or Mountainside police precinct in Phoenix, Arizona. I've taken a writer's liberty with these names. I've also taken care to use IP addresses that are not currently in use. If at some future date these become activated, they have no connection to any events in this work of fiction.

Ready for more suspense?
Don't miss Carey Baldwin's heart-
pounding psychological thriller

CONFESSION

Available now wherever ebooks are sold.

An excerpt from

CONFESSION

Saint Catherine's School for Boys
Near Santa Fe, New Mexico
Ten years ago—Friday, August 15, 11:00 P.M.

I'M NOT AFRAID of going to hell. Not one damn bit.

We're deep in the woods, miles from the boys' dormitory, and my thighs are burning because I walked all this way with Sister Bernadette on my back. Now I've got her laid out on the soggy ground underneath a hulking ponderosa pine. A bright rim of moonlight encircles her face. Black robes flow around her, engulfing her small body and blending with the night. Her face, floating on top of all that darkness, reminds me of a ghost head in a haunted house—but she's not dead.

Not yet.

My cheek stings where Sister scratched me. I wipe the spot with my sleeve and sniff the air soaked with rotting moss, sickly-sweet pinesap, and fresh piss. I pissed myself when I clubbed her on the head with that croquet mallet. Ironic, since my pissing problem is why I picked Sister Bernadette in the first place. She ought to have left that alone.

I hear a gurgling noise.

Good.

Sister Bernadette is starting to come around.

This is what I've been waiting for.

With her rosary wound tightly around my forearm, the grooves of the carved sandalwood beads cutting deep into the flesh of my wrist, I squat on rubber legs, shove my hands under her armpits, and drag her into a sitting position against the fat tree trunk. Her head slumps forward, but I yank her by the hair until her face tilts up, and her cloudy eyes open to meet mine. Her lips are moving. Syllables form within the bubbles coming out of her mouth. I press my stinging cheek against her cold, sticky one.

Like a lover, she whispers in my ear, "God is merciful."

The nuns have got one fucked-up idea of mercy.

"Repent." She's gasping. "Heaven ..."

"I'm too far gone for heaven."

The God I know is just and fierce and is never going to let a creep like me through the pearly gates because I say a few Hail Marys. "God metes out justice, and that's how I know *I* will not be going to heaven."

To prove my point, I draw back, pull out my pocketknife, and press the silver blade against her throat. Tonight, I am more than a shadow. A shadow can't feel the weight of the knife in his palm. A shadow can't shiver in anticipation. A shadow is not to be feared, but I am not a shadow. Not in this moment.

She moves her lips some more, but this time, no sound comes out. I can see in her eyes what she wants to say to me. *Don't do it. You'll go to hell.*

I twist the knife so that the tip bites into the sweet hollow of her throat. "I'm not afraid of going to hell."

It's the idea of *purgatory* that makes my teeth hurt and my stomach cramp and my shit go to water. I mean, what if my heart isn't black enough to guarantee me a passage straight to hell? What if God slams down his gavel, and says, *Son, you're a sinner, but I have to take your family situation into account. That's a mitigating circumstance.*

A single drop of blood drips off my blade like a tear.

"What if God sends me to purgatory?" My words taste like puke on my tongue. "I'd rather dangle over a fiery pit for eternity than spend a single day of the afterlife in a place like this one."

I watch a spider crawl across her face.

My thoughts crawl around my brain like that spider.

You could make a pretty good case, I think, that St. Catherine's School for Boys is earth's version of purgatory. I mean, it's a place where you don't exist. A place where no one curses you, but no one loves you, either. Sure, back home, your father hits you and calls you a bastard, but you *are* a bastard, so it's okay he calls you one. Behind me, I hear the sound of rustling leaves and cast a glance over my shoulder.

Do it! You want to get into hell, don't you?

I turn back to Sister and flick the spider off her cheek.

The spider disappears, but I'm still here.

At St. Catherine's, no one notices you enough to knock you around. Every day is the same as the one that came before it, and the one that's coming after. At St. Catherine's, you wait and wait for your turn to leave, only guess what, you dumb-ass bastard, your turn is *never* going to come, because you, my friend, are in purgatory, and you can't get out until you repent.

Sister Bernadette lets out another gurgle.

I spit right in her face.

I won't repent, and I can't bear to spend eternity in purgatory, which is I why I came up with a plan. A plan that'll rocket me straight past purgatory, directly to hell.

Sister Bernadette is the first page of my blueprint. I have the book to guide me the rest of the way. For her sake, not mine, I make the sign of the cross.

She's not moving, but her eyes are open, and I hear her breathing. I want her to know she is going to die. "You are going to help me get into hell. In return, I will help you get into heaven."

I shake my arm and loosen the rosary. The strand slithers down my wrist. One bead after another drops into my open palm, electrifying my skin at the point of contact. My blood zings through me, like a high-voltage current. I am not a shadow.

A branch snaps, making my hands shake with the need to hurry.

What are you waiting for, my friend?

Is Sister Bernadette afraid?

She has to be. Hungry for her fear, I squeeze my thighs together, then I push my face close and look deep in her eyes.

"The blood of the lamb will wash away your sins." She gasps, and her eyes roll back. "Repent."

My heart slams shut.

I begin the prayers.

About the Author

CAREY BALDWIN IS a mild-mannered doctor by day and an award-winning author of edgy suspense by night. She holds two doctoral degrees, one in medicine and one in psychology. She loves reading and writing stories that keep you off balance and on the edge of your seat. Carey lives in the southwestern United States with her amazing family. In her spare time she enjoys hiking and chasing wildflowers. Carey loves to hear from readers so please visit her at www.CareyBaldwin.com, on Facebook https://www.facebook.com/CareyBaldwinAuthor, or Twitter https://twitter.com/CareyBaldwin.

Visit www.AuthorTracker.com for exclusive information on your favorite HarperCollins authors.